I0712249

MARK OF THE INDICATIVE

KARLENE STAVES

VARIIA PRESS

Copyright © 2024 by Karlene Staves

All rights reserved.

No part of this publication may be reproduced, distributed, or transmitted in any form or by any means, including photocopying, recording, or other electronic or mechanical methods, without the prior written permission of the publisher, except as permitted by U.S. copyright law. For permission requests, contact Karlene Staves.

The story, all names, characters, and incidents portrayed in this production are fictitious. No identification with actual persons (living or deceased), places, buildings, and products is intended or should be inferred.

Cover Art by Ashley Holland

First edition 2024

DEDICATION

For Vaughan, Marion, and Delia
whose imaginations helped me
believe in magic again.

CONTENTS

Content & Trigger Warnings

- On page murder of children

- Depictions of War

- Blood

- Violence using fantasy magic & weapons

- Near drowning

- On page murder of parent

Pronunciation Guide

Raelia - *Ray-lee-uh*

Rokoa - *Row-ko-uh*

Vysha - *V-eye-sh-uh*

Nazario - *Nuh-zah-ree-oh*

Tanijak - *Tan-ee-sh-ack*

Yaila - *Yay-Luh*

Caeda - *Kay-duh*

Eloi - *Ee-l-oi*

Dhovina - *Doe-veen-uh*

Dirythia - *Dur-ri-th-ee-uh*

Taevidian - *Tay-vid-ee-un*

Paodra - *Pay-oh-druh*

Ouma - *Oh-muh*

Veleshein Tiago - *V-el-e-sheen T-ah-go*

Caias - *Kai-us*

Galys - *G-al-us*

Luella - *Loo-el-uh*

Vairek City - *Vay-rec City*

Calyx - *C-al-ix*

Truliach - *Troo-lee-ah-k*

Prologue

The setting sun reflected brightly off the ocean as Vysha was led out onto the sandy shore by royal guards. The rich shades of red and orange filled the dimming sky, making the horizon look as if it had been set ablaze. The waves crashed loudly against each other as she looked up at the castle, not even a mile down the coast – its beauty and grandeur at odds with the grief and hatred stirring within her. She vaguely wondered if King Nikolai was watching the atrocities being carried out in his name.

The guards stopped their forward procession as the man they'd been following came to a halt ahead of them. Cedric Lowther, a short, pudgy, balding man, turned to face her, as those following congregated around them. His beady blue eyes met Vysha's dark brown ones, which were wide with fear, as a malicious smirk spread across his features.

"Mama!" a little voice shouted, making Vysha turn and search for its source. "Mama!"

She finally spotted her blonde-haired boy, trying to escape the arms of his guard. She pulled against the men holding her. She hadn't given them any resistance before then, so the two were taken by surprise and she slipped out of their grip easily. She quickly ran to Adric, taking him into her arms. The guard holding him didn't hesitate to hand the little boy over to his mother, something that Cedric did not miss.

As he started yelling at the man for his compassion, Vysha held the small boy tightly to her chest, his little arms wrapped around her neck, and hugged her back just as fiercely.

"Mama!" the boy cried, tears leaving streaks in the dirt on his chubby cheeks. "Mama! I scared!" He buried his face in the crook of her neck, fearful sobs shaking his tiny frame.

"Shhh..." the woman soothed, while tears poured down her cheeks, "Mama's here, Adric, I'm here."

The next moment, her eyes spotted movement. The guard, having been thoroughly threatened into cooperation, reached for the child once more. Vysha held him tighter, stepping back from the guard, determined no one would ever take him from her. "I beg you," she sobbed, eyes connecting with his. "Please. Don't."

The man before her looked regretful, but didn't stop in his pursuit. She took another step back, gripping her crying son like a vice. She felt adrenaline coursing through her veins as she tried to put more distance between them.

She let out a scream of surprise and panic when she felt hands grab her – the two guards she escaped only a few moments before caught her up from behind. "NO!" she bellowed. "YOU WILL NOT TAKE HIM FROM ME!" Adric's cries for his mother became increasingly panicked, as more hands appeared to try and pull the mother and son apart.

Vysha held on as tight as she could, but the strength of the now seven men wrenching her arms open finally won. The howl of fury and grief she emitted as they pulled her shrieking son from her body seemed to shake the very earth. She pulled and fought against those restraining her, crying out as she watched her three year old, her baby, her Adric, trying to escape his captor. The toddler's fearful screams echoed through the night air as the large man holding him walked to the small pyre, and started to tightly tie his small body to the stake in the center.

"Please!" she screamed, hysterically. "He's only a baby! You can't do this!" Her shouts went ignored by guards, and onlookers alike, but she continued, "Take my life! I'll give you anything! Please just don't do this!"

Her legs kicked at the men restraining her, her arms pulled at their vice like grips. As she watched Cedric, his face aglow with malice, light the pyre beneath her son, her efforts became more, and more frantic. She pulled, and kicked, and fought, using every bit of strength she possessed. Her eyes never left her son, as the flames licked higher and closer to the small boy. Adric's agonized howl's ripped through the night air as the flames connected with his amber skin – every one of his screams seemed like a thousand knives in Vysha's heart.

She continued to fight, shrieking and sobbing, pulling and kicking, anything she could do to get to her boy, but as the pyre burned brighter, she realized his tiny form had gone completely still. The only screams left on the night air were her own.

The light from the flames burned her eyes, as anguish filled her, and her screams turned to tormented sobs. Her legs gave out underneath her, and she dangled from the arms of her captors. Her shoulders were twisted awkwardly, but she couldn't feel the pain it should have caused. The grief she felt was unbearable. She felt hollow, and hopeless, and profoundly alone.

Images flashed in Vysha's mind. First her husband, Wymond, the crack of his neck when he hit the end of the hangman's noose, his body dangling eerily after his death. The next, her beautiful twelve year old daughter, Asmi, fighting to breathe, as the noose slowly choked the life from her. How her eyes bulged when she recognized her mother running toward her, how her raven hair was blowing in the wind as the light left her eyes. Last, the agony on her beautiful boy's face, as the fire crawled up him until he was completely engulfed by the flames. They played on repeat in her mind, as her eyes stared blankly at the place her son had been.

Seeing all of the fight had gone out of her, the men dropped Vysha to the ground. She crumpled in a heap, eyes glued to the flames, fully intending to never move again. Every part of her body ached, but she felt nothing but devastation at the loss of those she loved the most in this world.

"Now, now," Cedric couldn't seem to keep his vile amusement contained, "What a display," he smirked, almost joyfully, as he sauntered towards her, each step crunching in the wet sand. The citizens that followed them out looked on with bated breath, giving him a wide berth.

The once vibrant woman laid where she'd dropped in the sand, a broken heap. Her face was turned towards the still burning flames, eyes staring blankly at the bright blaze, tears still streaming. Her long, ink colored hair was spread all around, like a black flame surrounding her. She was so lost in her pain that his words didn't register in her mind. She could see nothing except a replay of that evening's events, until his boot stepped in front of her face.

Cedric crouched down. "Sit up," he said quietly, the threat clear in his tone. "You worthless witch, sit up!" he demanded. He wrapped his fingers in her hair tightly, pulling her to face him. He reeked of filth and sweat. The scent overwhelmed her, and she felt rage awaken underneath her pain.

She shifted her weight, sitting on her knees, fingers digging into the sand so aggressively the grains pierced the skin under her nails. As her eyes connected with his, she felt a pure and utter hatred course through her. It was unlike anything she had ever felt before. It was so strong that her very body seemed to vibrate with the force of it.

'*He is enjoying every minute of this*,' Vysha thought to herself when she saw the sadistic joy in his eyes.

The thought made her sick to her stomach, "You'll pay for this," she said in a hushed tone only he could hear.

He barked out a laugh, his eyes taunting, "Is that so? And what, pray tell, are you going to do?"

She felt a quick pain shoot through her skin, directly behind her left ear, directly where his hand wound tightly into her hair. A flicker of fear crossed his features as a deep red light began to glow from Vysha's skin. He quickly let go of her.

Vysha, fingers still digging into the sand, felt a pulsation coming from somewhere deep in the earth. A heartbeat. Then something snapped within her. It was as if there had been a chain wrapped around her heart, and suddenly, the links shattered. Her grief stricken expression shifted, and she smirked viciously at the pathetic man, as he took a step back.

Cedric took another hesitant step in retreat, his eyes never leaving her, as Vysha slowly rose to her feet. The energy she felt in the sand seemed to be vibrating all throughout her body. The glowing light that had given Cedric pause was gleaming so brightly now, it looked as if her hair was starting to burn.

"What are you doing y-you filthy wench? I order you to s-stop!" He took another step in retreat, and watched in horror as her eyes turned black, and her pupils shone a bright, vibrant red. The same shade of red glistening from her skin. "R-restrain her!" the terrified man screamed at the guards that had been holding her. "Grab her, you idiots!"

The men hesitated, but two of the five stepped forward with determined expressions. "I wouldn't..." Vysha's voice was threatening, but calm. When the men didn't stop their pursuit, the woman stretched her arms out from either side of her body. Her palms facing directly at both men, as she yelled a string of words none of the onlookers or guards understood, and a beam of red light shot from each hand.

When the luminous beams struck the face of each man, they let out a tormented scream. Their hands covered their faces, thick red streams of blood poured from every orifice, as one, then the other, dropped to their knees. Vysha grinned as their screams dwindled, their bodies lowered into the sand. Seconds later, they were dead.

For a moment in time, the scene seemed frozen. The onlookers, the guards, even Cedric, looked on in paralyzing fear. The only sounds anyone could hear were the ocean waves crashing onto the shore, and the crackling of the fire.

"I did warn them," Vysha said, bringing people back to their senses. Everyone in the vicinity ran. Fearful shouts rose into the night. The statuesque woman laughed before throwing her head back, her eyes towards the stars, as the same red light radiated even brighter. The beams hit every person still in the vicinity. One after the other, their pained cries were quickly followed by the thuds of their bodies hitting the ground.

As the light dissipated, Vysha looked back to where the bodies lay, smirking, when she saw the last man standing. Cedric was barely ten feet from her, tripping over every corpse in his path. She reached her hand towards the disgusting man, palm outward, her voice a caress. "Stop."

Cedric's body froze, though not of his own volition. He clumsily fell to his knees, some sort of invisible bonds having wrapped around his ankles, and wrists. The color drained from his face, as he watched

Vysha step slowly closer — her palm facing him, "P-please. Vysha p-please," the portly man begged, "Please d-don't kill me..."

"Kill you?" Vysha asked, seeming confused, "I'm not going to kill you..." her voice trailed off, and Cedric let out a sigh of relief, before she continued, "at least not before I make you suffer." A malicious expression spread across her features, as she dove for him. Her fingers grasped his throat tightly, as she pinned him to the sand.

"You'll be begging me to kill you soon enough."

The sun had finally set. The stars shone in the sky on what should have been a beautiful summer night. The young Prince stood next to his father, as they listened to the man's agonized screams.

"How did she do it father? She didn't even touch them."

The King looked at his son, his brow furrowed, "The devil has touched her, child," King Nikolai replied. "He has bestowed on her a curse. A curse that no creature on this earth should possess." He looked down the coastline, watching the red woman pin the screeching man to the ground, their forms illuminated by the still burning pyre. "And after tonight, no one ever will again."

CHAPTER I

The sun lowered in the sky over the Kingdom of Dirythia that late winter's evening. Temperatures dropped quickly as people scurried to their homes, bundling themselves against the chilly breeze blowing through the small village of Frayis. On the far south side of town a horse trotted through a pasture. Its rider pulled against the reins as they approached the barn and she hurried to dismount.

Raelia set down her bow and quiver before she reached underneath to undo her horse's saddle. The tall, elegant colt rubbed his head against the seventeen year old's shoulder affectionately.

"Prickle!" she laughed. "You have to let me get this off you! I can't be late for Papa and Caias's going away dinner!" She gave him a quick scratch on the forehead before reaching under him once more. "I still can't believe Caias gets to go to the tribal lands before me... He's so lucky! And he doesn't even *want* to go! But think of all the history and legends he'll get to learn!" she continued, as if the horse could understand every word. "I hope he asks about the Red Lady! I read that she came from the Tanijak tribe too!"

She fell quiet for a moment as she pulled off Prickle's saddle. "They'll be gone for so long... eight weeks seems like an eternity!"

"Whatever are you going to do with yourself if I'm not around to pester you for a full eight weeks?!"

Raelia jumped at the sound of her elder brother's voice and turned to see his tall frame stalking in her direction. "How long have you been standing there?!" she demanded as she tried to calm her now racing heart.

"Long enough to know Prickle thinks you've lost it!" His blue eyes danced with amusement. "You do know he's a horse, don't you? He doesn't know nor care about the legends... Just like me!"

Scoffing, Raelia rolled her eyes as she turned back to the task at hand. "It's part of Papa's heritage, which means it's part of our heritage! I don't get how you don't understand that!"

"And that's why you're Papa's favorite," he chuckled, as he grabbed Prickle's reins.

"I am not," she protested, but a smug smirk crossed her features. She knew it was true, even if their father would never admit it out loud.

"Sure you're not," her brother returned with a knowing look, before sighing. "You know, it's not that I don't want to go. I just don't get the point of this coming-of-age ritual. I'd much rather stay here and-"

"And make sure Cyra Plyts doesn't get married off?" Raelia laughed at the dumbfounded look on Caias's face. She pulled the reins from his hand and led the speckled horse into the stable, closing the door behind him. "You know, maybe if you took interest in more than just her, you might see more value in the whole excursion."

Caias reddened, but snickered and grabbed a handful of hay. He threw it at her, hitting the back of her head. "Well, maybe if the excursion was as amazing as the lovely Ms. Plyts, I would take more interest!"

"Hey!" Raelia protested, shaking her head in hopes of ridding it of hay. "You're ridiculous. You know that?"

"But you wouldn't have me any other way," her brother returned with a cheeky grin.

They walked up the stone path to the front of the house, laughing most the way, before Raelia paused. She looked to her brother who watched her quizzically.

"Will you ask about her?" she asked. "About the Red Lady, I mean."

"It's nothing but a fairytale, Rae. Why would I ask about a fairytale?" Caias rolled his eyes, and started moving along the path once more.

"But it's *not* a fairytale!" Raelia insisted, hurrying to follow him. "And Ouma would know so much more than any book could tell us! They have books about her! Papa told me!"

Caias looked skeptical, but nodded his head as he opened up the front door. "Fine. I'll ask Ouma."

"Really?!" she nearly shouted as she walked inside. "Make sure to write down everything she says! I want to know it all!"

He looked at her, appalled. "You want me to take notes?! No way! I don't even do that for Mama!" He shook his head, and his expression shifted as he looked his sister over. Her long auburn hair was tangled and practically standing on end. The hay Caias threw held onto her waves for dear life, and now stuck out at odd angles all over her head. Her wet riding clothes were muddy, and she had little smudges of dirt on her nose and cheeks.

He smirked as he pulled a piece of straw from her wind ravaged hair. "You might want to go get cleaned up before-"

"Oh good! You found..." Yaila's dark blue eyes widened as she stepped around the corner and saw the state of her daughter. Her short, round frame seemed to deflate as she wiped a hand down her face in exasperation. "Oh, Goddess help me!"

"Too late," Caias chuckled under his breath as he ran a hand through his short blonde hair. He moved past his sister, kissed their mother on her round cheek, and disappeared into the other room.

Raelia resisted the urge to roll her eyes at Yaila's exasperated expression. "I'll go clean up."

"Supper will be on the table in ten minutes, so make it quick!" Yaila shook her head, as Raelia turned on her heel and hurried up the stairs.

Once in her room, she began dragging a brush through the tangled mess her hair had become, cursing her brother's name with every piece of hay she pulled out. It took some doing, but eventually she tamed it with a simple plait, resting it on her shoulder.

When she turned to choose something to wear, a glimpse of royal blue caught her attention. An empire waisted, satin dress sat laid out on her bed. Her eyes lit with excitement as the door opened behind her. She turned to see her mother peeking in with a smile.

"Do you like it?" Yaila asked.

"Like it?! Mama, it's gorgeous!" Raelia smiled brightly. "But I don't understand...?"

"I thought, since Papa and Caias won't be here for your birthday next week," her mother grinned, looking much younger than her forty years, "it was only appropriate we celebrate tonight, as a family," she answered, fiddling with the bottom of her daughter's braid. "Now hurry! Go get washed up and out of those filthy clothes!" she laughed. "I'll meet you downstairs."

Raelia hurried to clean herself up and dress into her new gown. The contrast of the rich blue against her amber skin was stunning, and when she looked at herself in the mirror, Raelia struggled to believe it was really her in the reflection.

Laughter and cheerful conversation echoed up as she made her way downstairs. It felt odd to be so dressed up for a meal in her own home, but she couldn't suppress the happiness bubbling within her as she made her way into the dining room.

All three of her siblings sat across the table from where she walked in. Her younger sister's black hair and amber brown skin stood out sitting between her two pale, blonde brothers. Caias and Blaze were nearly identical to their mother and each other. The only difference that stood out being their size and slightly different eye color. Caeda, like Raelia, resembled their father more closely. Caeda had his brown eyes, Raelia his auburn-red hair, and they both shared his amber skin tone.

Her parents sat at opposite ends of the table, waiting patiently as everyone chatted amongst themselves. Her father's golden brown eyes crinkled when he smiled at her walking in.

"There she is!" he proclaimed, standing from his seat. She smiled up at him as the others in the room shouted a chorus of, "Happy Birthday!"

Surprise flitted through her as a blonde blur raced to hug her. Her best friend, Luella, squeezed her tightly before pulling back. "You were right Mrs. Kesby, it's beautiful!" she exclaimed as her blue eyes slid over the new dress.

"It really suits you," Yaila smiled proudly at her daughter. "Now, time to sit down."

Raelia nodded, a small giggle escaping her as she sat down next to her father, swiftly kissing him on the cheek before settling in her chair. Eloi gave her a smile in return before standing and lifting his glass.

"To my first lovely daughter," he said, brushing a tuft of auburn hair from his eyes as he turned to look at Raelia, "may your eighteenth year be the best so far. Happy birthday, Glimmer," Eloi smiled as he sat back down. "Now let's eat!"

There was a collective chuckle around the table and everyone started to fill their plates with the delectable dishes laid before them. Potatoes and curried beef. Steamed broccoli and herbed rice. Every dish tantalized her senses. The food was delicious, and the joy around the table, infectious. Even knowing her father and older brother were headed off in the morning, she couldn't help but feel happy.

After everyone ate their fill, Yaila stood and started clearing the table. "Caeda, Blaze, bring your plates," she said, grabbing hers, and Caias's cleared plates. "It's your night for clean-up."

"But Mama..." the little girl whined, her velvety black curls bouncing, as she stood and stomped her foot. "I don't wanna!"

The boy next to her rolled his eyes, as he rose and grabbed his own plate, "Are you ever going to learn that whining is only going to make it worse?" The twelve-year-old nudged his sister with his elbow. "Come on."

Caeda pouted, but followed her brother into the kitchen, stomping the whole way. Yaila watched, suppressing a chuckle until the pair were out of earshot. She looked at Eloi, also grinning. "That little girl is going to be the reason we go gray," she said to him. He nodded his agreement as she made her way to follow her two younger children.

Luella let out a giggle as Yaila disappeared behind the kitchen door. "That kid is gonna be more of a handful than even you are, Rae!"

Eloi laughed, his golden brown eyes twinkling. Caias joined in, nodding along.

"Hey!" Raelia laughed. "I wasn't as bad as Caeda!"

"No," Caias agreed, "you were worse!"

Raelia shot her brother an indignant glare, but before she could respond, Yaila appeared once more, collecting the last of the empty plates from the table. "Luella, dear, you better get going on home. You know how worried your mother gets."

"Mama," Raelia said, looking out the window at the dark sky, "don't you think it's too late for her to walk by herself? It's pretty dark..."

Yaila followed her daughter's gaze to the window, and nodded. "You're right."

She looked at Eloi, who smiled a knowing grin at his wife. "Caias?" he said, turning to look at his eldest son. "Would you mind walking the young lady home?"

"Oh could you?" Lue asked, turning to look dreamily at Caias. "I'd feel so much better to not go alone."

Raelia didn't miss the sparkle in her friend's blue eyes, amazed at how obvious it seemed. She knew Luella harbored a fondness for her elder brother, and had for quite some time. Caias never showed an interest in Lue, however, and Raelia doubted he even recognized the affection in her gaze, but she knew her parents did, and they did little to discourage the possible pairing.

Caias chuckled and agreed. They all stood to leave and Yaila gave a quick hug to the short girl. "Be safe. We'll see you soon."

After a quick hug, and promises to see each other the next day, Raelia watched Luella and Caias make their way out into the night. Standing in the doorway for a few moments, she watched as the pair walked down the road. The moonlight reflected off Luella's long blonde hair like starlight, momentarily mesmerizing Raelia. She felt a pang in her heart at the thought of Caias finally recognizing the girl's affections and confusion at the unexpected emotion pulled her from the trance.

A shiver ran up her spine as the wind blew against her amber skin causing the tendrils of hair framing her face to blow across her vision. She felt goose pimples raise on her arms. Shaking her head to clear it, Raelia quickly stepped inside, closing the door. She started down the long hallway to the right of the stairs. She knocked lightly before letting herself into the door at the end.

The soft light had a golden hue and illuminated the modest room. Shelves lined the walls, and books filled every available space. A small couch, and a plush, comfortable chair sat in front of the fireplace. The warm fire crackled happily, and Eloi stood at the small desk in the corner. He flashed a smile at her before returning his attention to a travel bag sitting on top of the desks surface.

Raelia plopped herself into the comfy chair and picked up the book on the side table. This was her favorite room in the Kesby home, commonly referring to it as her happy place. She spent countless hours reading through the books, or watching her father work. She never felt as comfortable or as content anywhere else in the world. She pulled her feet under herself, snuggling into the pillowy back as her eyes scanned the pages.

"Glimmer?"

She looked up, surprised at how close he sounded, and realized he now sat across from her on the small couch. He gestured for her to sit next to him.

As she sat down, he pulled a small box out of his breast pocket. The bow on top had been squashed and wrinkled, but her eyes lit with curiosity all the same.

"Turning 18 is a big milestone for our people. The Tanijak Tribe believes it is the year a person starts the journey of discovering their magic," Eloi's eyes flickered to his daughter's ear, behind which her tribal birthmark hid, "which, in turn, allows them to discover their truest self."

Raelia's hand moved to the hair behind her ear, pulling it forward, worried it hadn't been hiding the small Dandelion Mark she'd been born with. Shock and confusion colored her features as her eyes connected to her father's. They never discussed her Mark. They never discussed the magic it indicated she was born with. She altogether preferred to pretend it didn't exist.

Her birthmark, and all others like it, had been illegal in the Kingdom of Dirythia for nearly five hundred years. Every child born within the Kingdom's borders was presented to the Council of Perception by the time they were two months old. Most parents needn't worry about what the council might find, most Marks children were born with were normal, run of the mill birthmarks. However, Raelia's was different, and as far as she knew, every other child born with an Indicative Mark had been put to death at their council review, or had been smuggled out of the country by their family before their review even happened. She'd just been lucky, her mother told her. The woman that reviewed Raelia shortly after birth didn't pay close enough attention, and as she'd been born with long, thick auburn curls it was easily overlooked. Easily hidden.

Her fingers tugged roughly through her plaited hair, undoing it so it fell around her. She continued pulling at it until her father gently grabbed her hand, drawing it back down. He squeezed it reassuringly.

"Dialev Diyalay," Eloi said in his native tongue.

'Calm, child,' Raelia recognized before replying, *"Eleil."* Okay.

She took a deep breath, calming her nerves before she spoke softly, "I thought 20 was the important year," she remarked. "It's why you and Caias have to go tomorrow, right? So you make it in time for his 20th birthday?"

"Well, for a non-Mark Bearer, yes," Eloi answered. "He will go through the coming of age ritual, as all of the tribe do at 20."

"But..."

"But, there is nothing to awaken before then. Not for him," Eloi interrupted, "because he does not have the gift you do."

"Ah," was all Raelia could respond. She didn't like being reminded of her 'gift', or of the Indicative Mark that provided it. It made her feel different. It made her feel dirty.

Eloi and his eldest daughter saw eye to eye on nearly everything. They agreed on politics, travel, books, they even liked the same foods! But this topic, Raelia knew, was different. The conversation they'd had the last time they'd discussed her Mark stirred in her memory as her father's voice echoed in her mind, *"For the life of me Raelia, I don't understand! How can someone so curious about the world have no curiosity for the gift she was born with?"* It hadn't been the first time he'd expressed such sentiments, but it still stung.

"Do I have to do something?" she questioned, tersely. "What makes being 18 so special?"

"Your gift awakens," her father answered. "There's nothing for you to do. There's no ceremony as there will be on your 20th birthday, but it's important nonetheless."

"But what does that mean?" she pushed, still confused.

"It means different things for different people, and," he sighed, "as I don't have the gift, I'm not exactly sure all it entails." He placed the small disheveled box into her hand. "But I do know this is the traditional gift for Mark Bearers on their eighteenth birthday, and Ouma would not approve if I didn't keep the tradition alive. In fact she helped me procure it. She said it will protect you from the shadows. Of course, she didn't explain what she meant by that."

A knowing chuckle escaped her — her grandmother always enjoyed seeming mysterious.

Raelia's eyes lit up as she undid the crinkled ribbon and opened the box. Inside a small silver ring sat on a puff of cotton. It was shiny, though had a few scuffs. Most likely a polished hand-me-down, Raelia realized as she picked it up. As she rolled it around in her fingers, she caught sight of a small engraving on the outside — an open circle, with waves around the outside edge, inside of which swirled a leafy vine. The Tanijak tribe's mark.

Her father took it from her, and held it up to the light, tilting it just slightly, so Raelia could see the inside of the silver ring.

"Aye peu aevotu ver lepasc leio tyziat ver ulmr alyezmi," Eloi read softly, "Do not doubt in darkness..."

"What you believed in the light," Raelia finished with a smile, as he handed it back to her.

It was a saying she knew well. One of her father's favorites, and one he relayed to her often when she woke up from a bad dream in the middle of the night, or when she doubted herself or her capabilities.

She slid the ring onto her left middle finger, before hugging her father tightly. *"Mimiple leio, Didi,"* she said quietly. "It's beautiful."

"You're welcome, daughter."

CHAPTER 2

I t was early when Raelia woke the next morning. Beams of moonlight streaked through the gap in her curtains, and all she wanted to do was go back to sleep. She forced herself out of bed, shivering against the cold as she quickly found her dressing gown, pulled it tightly around herself and hurried downstairs.

She found her parents in the kitchen. Her father's tall, lanky form hunched over the small, round table in the middle of the room, while her mother bustled around packing food into a large picnic basket on the counter.

"Good morning, Glimmer!" Eloi smiled, much too cheerful for the early hour.

"Morn-," she replied through a yawn, "-ing."

Yaila placed a plate of food before her with a smile as she sat down across from her daughter. "I didn't expect you to get up this early."

"I couldn't not say goodbye!"

Her mother laughed at the indignance in her eyes as the door opened once more and Caias walked in. His cheeks and nose were red from the cold and his sandy blonde hair stuck up on end as he announced, "Marah is hitched up." He plopped down in a chair, stealing a sausage off of his sister's plate. "Everything is loaded into the cart. We can take off any time you're ready."

Eloi stood, nodding. "I'll meet you outside in ten minutes," he said before disappearing out the kitchen door.

Their mother stood as well, and once again began bustling around the kitchen packing things into the basket. A nervous energy hovered around her, and Raelia could practically see the waves of anxiety rolling off of her.

"Mama? Can I help?"

"I can get this," Yaila answered, patting her daughter on the cheek. "You need to go get dressed. You can't be seen outside in your dressing gown! What would the neighbors say?"

Raelia resisted the urge to inform her mother she didn't care a single bit what the neighbors had to say, especially considering they'd all be sleeping anyway. She thought better of it, however, nodding and quickly making her way back upstairs to her room to dress for the day.

❦

Dawn approached and the sky began to lighten with beams of red, purple and orange shooting through the night. The distant mountain range appeared only as shadows against the painted sky.

Raelia stepped outside into the crisp winter air, small clouds appearing with every breath she took. She walked down the stone path leading to the cobbled road, where a beautiful white mare stood, attached to a small cart. Eloi stood behind it, lifting two small travel bags into the back before tucking the cover around them.

Caias looked to be on the verge of suffocation from their mother's tight goodbye hug, and Raelia smirked as she walked up. "Mama, if you smother him, he'll never become a man!"

Yaila pulled back, and Caias shot his sister with a comical look of indignance mixed with gratitude, before turning back to their mother.

"You've packed everything you'll need?" she fussed. "Enough warm clothes?"

Raelia felt a tap on her shoulder. She turned to find her father there, arms open. She leapt into them, squeezing him tightly. There were tiny pricks of emotion behind her eyes, as she embraced her father, but she held the tears back. She would miss him. He was her best friend and confidant. He always seemed to be the only one who ever truly understood her. Eight weeks seemed like a dreadfully long time for him to be gone.

"I'll miss you, Papa," she said quietly.

"And I, you," he replied. "I love you, Glimmer." Eloi pulled back, looking into his daughter's jade-green eyes. "Take care of your mother, okay? Make sure Caeda doesn't give her too much trouble."

Raelia laughed. "Now that's an impossible task!"

"Nothing is impossible for you, Raelia," he said, his voice serious. "You are more powerful than you know."

Before she could respond, her mother's fingers gripped his shoulder from behind. Eloi turned to smile lovingly at his wife, letting go of Raelia completely. They embraced for a long moment before sharing a gentle kiss, prompting their daughter to turn away.

"I hate when they do that," Caias remarked with a laugh. "Mama's 'proper etiquette' goes right out the window when it comes to Papa."

Raelia snorted, nodding her agreement.

Caias wrapped his arms around his sister. "Make sure Cyra Plyts doesn't start on with anyone while I'm gone," he teased.

She hugged him tightly and laughed. "Oh, I'm going to encourage it! I'll get her married off in no time without you around to interfere!"

He pulled back, a look of feigned hurt and shock crossing his features, before he smiled and hugged her one more time.

"I'll miss you, sis."

"I'll miss you too."

After a few more farewells and hugs made their way around the group, the two men climbed atop the small cart. Then Caias grabbed the reins and Eloi waved one more goodbye as the wagon started slowly moving down the narrow path.

⁂

The rest of the morning went as normally as any other. Raelia made breakfast for her younger siblings while their mother got ready for work. Once she left, Raelia helped Caeda and Blaze with schoolwork Yaila set for them. Then they played upstairs as she did her own.

By midday, they'd all studied and completed their household chores, and Raelia found herself in the kitchen packing a large picnic basket. Sooner than expected, she was interrupted by a loud knock on the front door.

"Hi, Lue!" Raelia smiled brightly at her friend and stepped aside to let her in. "I've just got to finish packing the basket and then we can go!"

"Great!"

"Mama will be late today though," Raelia sighed dejectedly and started making her way down the hall towards the kitchen. "So Caeda and Blaze will have to come with us..."

"That's fine!" Luella responded, ever the optimist. "They'll have enough to do and leave us alone, I'm sure."

Raelia chuckled, shaking her head, "You have met them, right?"

The sun was high in the sky by the time the group pulled themselves atop their horses and trotted toward the dense forest backing up to the edge of the Kesby's pasture. As they entered the canopy of the wood, leaves rustled in the breeze, and birds sang a sweet melody in the distance. Beams of sunlight peeked through the branches of huge oak and fir and pine trees, casting a soft green glow to light the dirt path they followed.

A few minutes later they broke through the trees and into a bright clearing alongside the river. Caeda grinned from ear to ear, as she took in the brilliantly colored wildflowers starting to bloom throughout the open space, and Raelia could tell she'd be wearing a flower crown by the time they headed home.

The moment their feet touched the ground, both children ran towards the river bank. Luella handed Raelia the picnic basket before hopping down off her horse and they both grabbed onto the horses leads and headed further in.

"Don't go into the water!" Raelia shouted at her siblings. "It's too cold!"

Both children nodded at her before disappearing behind the river bank. She released the horse's reins, and laid out a large picnic blanket a few paces further into the clearing.

The warm sun felt good after the long winter. Luella and Raelia enjoyed talking about the preparations being done around the village for the upcoming equinox festival, which happened to land on Raelia's 18th birthday. Caeda and Blaze stood by the water's edge playing in the sand, and competing to see who could throw a rock the farthest across the swift river.

When lunch time arrived, Raelia handed out food to her siblings and then Luella before fixing a plate for herself. Blaze and Caeda both dug in without a word, forgetting all manners. Luella cleared her throat. The look on her face so appalled at the lack of proper etiquette that Raelia had to hold back a laugh.

"Excuse me you two," Luella rebuked in a shrill voice, "I know for a fact that your mother-"

Suddenly, a loud howl of pain interrupted the scolding. All four looked up from their meal, peering across the river into the dense bush across the way. Raelia set down her plate and stood up, squinting her eyes to try and see through the dim shadows. The distressed yowls continued to echo through the clearing.

By the time Raelia started to walk over the bank to the sandy stretch along the rushing water, the other three stood as well. She followed the pained cries up the river's edge. As the sound became louder, the image on the other side of the water became clearer.

"Oh, the poor thing!" she gasped.

Across the river, a few feet behind the sandy bank, a tiny fox pup looked to be tangled in some sort of vines. It's matted fur had clumps of a reddish-brown substance. It wriggled against the plant, howling in pain with every movement.

The other three caught up with Raelia, and Caeda started whimpering about her concern for the small animal. Blaze looked at the pup with distrust, as if he expected the tiny thing to attack them at any moment. Luella's blue eyes, however, watched her friend closely, seeming to anticipate her next moves.

Raelia didn't seem to hear them as she looked first downstream, then up for a way to cross to the other side. Walking through the water would be like taking an ice bath this time of year, and though the sun was out, it wasn't quite warm enough to help her overcome that kind of cold. Plus, with all the extra water coming down the mountain now that the snow caps were beginning to melt, the current was too strong for her to make it across without being swept away.

A little way upstream she spotted a fallen tree. The roots were pulled from the ground and sticking up in the air a few yards back from the river's edge. Its long, mossy trunk had fallen across the riverbed. A few branches were sticking from it at random angles, though it looked as if most had broken off either by the fall or by the winter weather. Either way, to Raelia, it looked as good a place as any to try and get across. She pulled up her skirts and moved quickly towards the makeshift bridge.

"Rae!" Luella bellowed after her. "Don't you dare! You could fall in!"

Blaze shook his head at the blonde girl. "You've known her most your life, and you think she's not going to at least try?"

He smirked at her when she stopped to glare at him.

Raelia continued up the rocky beach, ignoring the other three completely. She made it to the fallen timber and looked closely at the path it created. The surface was wet, though it didn't appear the water splashed more than halfway up the side. Where she stood was narrow, just barely wide enough for her to stand atop it. However, it widened around the middle of the river, and by the time the wood crossed over the bank on the other side it was at least three feet across.

As she climbed atop, she noticed how slick the patches of moss were and made a mental note to avoid them. Raelia bounced slightly, trying to gauge if the wood was solid enough to cross, her braid flounced around on her shoulder with the movement. It seemed to be sturdy, and didn't twist one way or the other, so with one hand holding up her skirts, she started the slow journey across.

"Be careful!" Luella cautioned, as she approached. The worry in her voice was distinct, but Raelia didn't look back to reassure her. Her eyes focused on the slick surface beneath her feet, making sure to bypass the moss patches that were sure to send her tumbling down into the swift current below.

Reaching out her free hand, Raelia gripped a branch that stuck straight up from the log and was very nearly the same height as her. Gripping it tightly, she turned to look back at the bank where her friend stood. Caeda and Blaze followed Luella up the beach and stood waiting. Neither of her siblings looked concerned for her well being, they only seemed excited at the adventure that had been thrust upon them.

"I'll be fine, Lue!" she reassured, "Look! I'm halfway across already!"

The rest of the trek went smoothly, though it felt like it took longer than it actually did. When she reached the other side, she hopped down and threw her hands in the air above her head.

"Ta-Da!" she shouted at her companions across the way.

Caeda and Blaze clapped as if their sister had put on a marvelous performance for them. Luella, however, sighed in relief before crossing her arms in front of herself.

"Don't get ahead of yourself!" she scolded. "You still have to make it back!"

Raelia laughed as she started heading back downstream. "Quit worrying! If I made it across once, I can do it again!"

The beach on this side of the river was more narrow, so Raelia stepped slowly, watching to make sure she didn't step into the water. Even with that, however, it didn't take her long to find the small pup.

"Hey little one," she said softly.

She knelt slowly, not wanting to startle the poor thing. It watched her closely with two different colored eyes. One a cold, ice blue, the other a soft yellow with a slitted pupil – more like a cat's than should have been possible. She struggled to see the color of it's dark fur with as matted and muddy as it was. However, as she got closer she recognized the brownish-red substance squished into the hairs as clay from the riverbed a bit further downstream.

Raelia held her hand out letting the small canine sniff. It gave her a small lick as if to say it understood why she was there. Taking that as permission, she gave it a scritch behind the ear.

"There now," she said softly, "let's see if we can get you out of these prickly vines."

She pushed around the shrubbery and realized that it wasn't only the bush it was encircled by. There was a fine silver wire wrapped around its middle and a couple of its paws. Raelia realized it must have cut into the fox's flesh when she noticed fresh blood in a couple of the large mats.

Thorns from the bush pricked her hand as she used her fingernails to cut into the vine and tear bits of it apart. It was strong, and difficult to separate cleanly. When she'd think it was ready to split, it would pull apart in stringy chunks. As she continued to work at the fox's binding Caeda, Blaze, and Luella made their way back downstream on the other side.

"Is she alright?" Caeda bellowed across the water. "Can you get her out?"

Raelia looked up from her work, and over at her younger sister. The little girl stood directly next to the river's edge – the expression on her face tight with concern.

"I think she'll be okay!" Raelia hollered before turning back to the task at hand.

It didn't take long before she'd completely cleared the pup of shrubbery and Raelia pulled it into her lap. It was light, and very thin. She could feel the fox's ribs underneath its knotted fur. It sat perfectly still as she looked closely at the wire around its body. She didn't want to hurt the poor thing, and was relieved to see the cuts in it's skin were shallow and few.

She slowly unwound the thin line from around the pup's body. In a couple of places the wire lay underneath clumps of matted fur, so Raelia gently tugged and pulled at the knots to free it. Then she gradually untangled the wire from the fox's legs one by one. It was slow, tedious work, but after a bit she'd freed the small creature. She smiled brightly, sighing in relief and gave the fox a couple of scratches behind its ear before setting it down on the ground and standing up. She brushed off her skirt, stretched, then gave a thumbs up towards the others across the river.

"Stay away from the sticker bushes. You're less likely to get tangled that way," she chuckled down at the pup, starting back upstream toward the fallen tree. She only took a few steps before she realized she had a shadow. Turning to see the fox following closely behind her.

She looked at him curiously, and crouched down. "You can't come with me. Go find your Mama." She gave the pup a scritch under its chin then continued her way towards the makeshift bridge. When she reached it, she looked back to find the fox still at her feet. It easily jumped onto the log and started its way across.

Raelia shook her head, laughing. "You're smarter than you look, but no one likes a show off!"

She watched for a moment as the small creature made it easily to the other side of the river. Letting out a huff as she stepped onto the fallen tree, she began her trek back.

It was smooth sailing, just like it had been the first time around, and this time Luella was too distracted by the fox pup to be worrying over her friend. Raelia had no fear on her second go. She reached the halfway point rather quickly, stepping around the middle branch that stretched upward. Abruptly, the heel of her boot caught a patch of slick moss on the back side of the bough, and she was only able to catch herself by grabbing onto it.

The wood was thick, and sturdy, but the sudden addition of her weight caused it to splinter. It broke across the middle, taking away what little balance Raelia regained, and sent her plunging into the raging waters below. She barely had time to let out a shriek before hitting the icy river and being pulled underneath.

She fought to resurface as the current carried her downstream, but the water threw her this way and that as if she were nothing more than a rag doll. Her body smashed roughly against rock after rock, as she kicked and paddled as hard as she could. Finally, she broke the surface. She breathed the fresh air greedily into her aching lungs, only to be pulled under once more.

The rough current threw her in every direction, and a moment later she was thrown so viciously against a boulder that it knocked out what little air she had left in her lungs. She tried with all of her might to grab onto the rocks and logs under the water, but the lack of light, and swiftness with which she was being flung made it nearly impossible to get a good enough grip on anything.

Her lungs burned for oxygen, and fear overwhelmed her thoughts.

Suddenly, something grabbed her leg, stopping its forward movement and whipping her body in a forward circular motion. Her eyes burst open again just as she felt her skull collide with a large boulder. She heard a sickening crack before everything went dark.

CHAPTER 3

"Come on!" A deep, unfamiliar voice insisted above her. "Raelia you have to wake up!"

Her muscles ached, and something kept pushing down roughly on her chest. Her back met resistance. With every downward motion, small, sharp pin pricks poked her through the wet cloth of her dress.

Suddenly, she felt as if she were choking. Water came spitting out of her as she coughed. A pair of large hands turned her on her side, and more liquid spilled from her nose and mouth. She continued coughing and choking until there was nothing left, and she tasted bile on her tongue.

Her throat and chest burned as if fire lined them, and every breath sent shooting pains through her rib cage. Every muscle in her body tensed as she shivered uncontrollably against the cold. She heard a strangled cry, and then the crunching of rocks as someone quickly made their way closer.

"There you go," the unfamiliar voice soothed. "Get it all up."

A hand slowly rubbed up and down her sore back, as a pair of small knees fell to the ground in front of her.

"Raelia!" Caeda sobbed, throwing herself on her sister. "We were so scared!"

A hiss of pain escaped her lips. Caeda's weight felt like a ton of bricks being thrown on her weakened and aching body. She slowly moved her hand up to the girl's back, setting it there heavily. It was all she could manage.

"Caeda, love," she heard Luella's soft voice, distorted with emotion, "give her a second."

Raelia felt the child's weight being pulled off of her, and her arm dropped back down to her side limply. She looked up thankfully, only to see Luella and Blaze looking down at her with varying degrees of concern. Blaze's arms crossed over his chest, his hazel eyes a storm of emotion, and rimmed red. Lue's eyes were puffy, and her cheeks tear stained. She stood behind Caeda, who hiccuped through her tears, holding her shoulders to keep the girl from jumping onto Raelia once more.

Slowly and painfully, Raelia pushed herself into a sitting position which gave her a full view of the clearing they were in. It was vaguely familiar, but different to the one they'd be picnicking in. This one was a fraction the size and seemed to be much less grassy field, and much more rocky beach.

She started when she turned toward the unfamiliar voice and realized there was a young man on the opposite side of her. He smiled kindly, his teeth bright and perfectly straight. His dirty blonde hair was longer than most boys Raelia knew and fell nearly to his shoulders in thick waves.

"How are you feeling?" He asked in a gravelly tone, seeming genuine in his concern.

"I-" she croaked. Her voice was raspy and her throat raw, making it difficult to get any sound out. She tried clearing it, but that was even more painful.

"It's fine," the stranger reassured. "Don't speak if it hurts. Just nod or shake your head, okay?"

As she nodded slowly in reply, realizing then her head was pounding. The sound of pumping blood throbbed in her ears like the rushing river close to where she lay.

"Are you in pain?"

She nodded once more, even slower this time.

"How far away is your village?" the stranger asked, turning his eyes to Luella. "She needs to have that head wound looked at by a healer."

Raelia moved her fingers slowly to the back of her head, only faintly aware her friend responded. She winced in pain as her fingers slid across a deep cut, and wasn't surprised to see blood on her fingertips when she pulled them back into view.

"Not far," Luella was saying. "Her mother is the village healer, but I don't know how we'll get her back. She can't ride like this!"

Her friend's voice rose in pitch with every word. The worry was so obvious, Raelia wanted to reassure her friend she was okay. Her muscles resisted as she rolled to her hands and knees, painfully getting to her feet.

The stranger stood with her, placing a gentle hand on her elbow to help her balance. "I think it would be better if you stayed seated. You've lost a fair bit of blood with that wound."

"I'll be fi-" Raelia's words cut off when she stood to her full height. She swayed on the spot as the clearing spun violently. She was thankful he was there as she fell into him, not being able to hold her own weight.

He caught her, and easily swept her into his arms. "I think it's best if I ride back with her." He looked toward the forest behind them, and Raelia saw a beautiful spotted horse against the green backdrop.

"No," she managed to wheeze. "Caeda... She can't... Ride..."

Luella stepped forward. "She can ride with me."

The stranger nodded, and started toward his horse. "I'll get her up, and then meet you in the other clearing."

"Okay..." Luella sounded hesitant. "Do you need any help?"

"I think we'll be okay," he replied.

Luella nodded and the three of them turned and started back up-stream.

When they stood beside the mare, the young man clicked his tongue twice and the horse kneeled down on her front legs.

Raelia's eyes widened, surprised. "How...?" she started to ask, letting the question sit in the air, as it hurt too much to finish.

"A lot of practice," the man said with an amused grin, as he swiftly set her onto the horse's saddle.

He clicked his tongue twice more, and the horse stood back to its full height. The sudden shift in elevation brought on another dizzy spell, made worse when the man heaved himself onto the horse's back behind her. The shift of the saddle felt like a wave crashing into the side of her head, pushing her to one side and knocking her off center. If it wasn't for his arms wrapping around her on either side she was certain she would have tumbled to the earth below.

Once the stranger settled in, his hands placed in front of her to hold the reins, they started towards a narrow path that wound into the trees toward the other clearing.

By the time Raelia and her rescuer broke through the trees, the picnic had been packed and Luella was just pulling herself up behind Caeda. Blaze's eyes turned to see Raelia, watching her closely, as if he could see every bit of pain she felt. She gave him a small smile, trying to placate his scrutinizing eyes. His expression turned protective as his gaze turned to the man behind Raelia, and she had to hide a smirk. Blaze always did his best to act as if he didn't care about anyone or anything, but that protective look in his eyes proved otherwise, and it made Raelia happy to see his true kindness.

A few minutes later, with everyone situated, they headed back into the cover of the trees. Leading the charge, Luella and Caeda guided the group as a gust of wind blew, causing Raelia to tense and shiver against the cold of her soaked clothes. She could feel the young man's body against her back, and noticed a shiver run through him only a moment later.

Raelia turned her head to look at him from the corner of her eye, only to find his eyes watching her. He smiled shyly, as if embarrassed to be caught, before looking ahead once more.

She cleared her throat painfully, before rasping, "I... never asked your name...?"

"Well, you were a bit incapacitated," he chuckled. The corner of his mouth quirked up before he spoke again. "You don't recognize me?"

This took Raelia by complete surprise, and she forced her eyes to focus on his face, searching his features for some sort of familiarity. It was painful work with the way her head throbbed, but his soft brown eyes seemed amused, as he watched her scrutinize his face.

"Should I?" Raelia questioned. She watched his eyes closely, confused to see what appeared as disappointment in them.

"I, uh, well... I guess not," he said through a forced chuckle. "Al...um-ister," he stumbled out.

"Al-*um*-ister?" she retorted, putting extra emphasis on the 'um.'

"I'm Alister."

"Are you sure?" Raelia inquired with a wary smirk.

He laughed, but didn't make eye contact when he replied, "I'm sure."

"And is there a reason you thought I should know you? Do you know me?"

Again, disappointment flashed across his features. "You just seemed familiar is all," he said in a sad tone. "I'm obviously mistaken, though."

"Then why-"

"Here we are!" Luella called from ahead, interrupting Raelia's question. She looked toward her friend. "Are you doing okay?"

Raelia turned back to nod at her friend. The change in focus made her head spin again and she had to grip the saddle to keep herself steady. She closed her eyes and took a deep breath. Alister wrapped his arm around her waist holding her tightly.

"We're almost there," he said softly in her ear. "Don't faint on me now."

He urged the horse beneath them to speed up. Raelia felt the wind pick up against her face, and involuntarily leaned back onto his chest. His arm tightened, and she couldn't help but feel thankful for his strong grip holding her in place.

They moved quickly and when Raelia opened her eyes once more, they'd stopped just outside the stable. She looked behind them, noticing the others were catching up, before she looked back at Alister. She jolted with the realization that he was watching her, concern evident when he asked, "Are you okay?"

"I'll be okay," she replied through chattering teeth. "I just need to lay flat and get warm again."

Alister clicked his tongue as they reached the pasture gate, and the horse lowered herself to her knees once more. Raelia felt her toes brush the ground for only a moment before he stood and swept her into his arms, cradling her as if she were only a child. The quick movement caused the world to spin even faster than before, and suddenly the world went black.

"Raelia," a soft voice called out.

Her mother's voice, she vaguely realized.

"Rae, can you open your eyes?" Yaila asked softly. She ran a cold hand down Raelia's cheek, and then placed it on her forehead. "You have to wake up, sweetheart."

Raelia groaned and squeezed her eyes closed. Her lungs still felt like fire burned inside of them, and her head throbbed, though, thankfully, the room had stopped spinning. She ached all over and her muscles protested as she shifted her weight to turn toward where her mother sat beside her.

She opened her eyes slowly, blinking against the light – her vision blurry from sleep. Though, she found her mother's round face peering down at her, and after a few blinks it cleared enough to make out her soft features.

"There she is." Yaila sighed in relief.

When Raelia looked beyond her mother's relieved face, she saw Caeda's tiny face peeking over their mother's shoulder, her eyes puffy, and still rimmed in tears.

Yaila's voice became all business when she spoke again, "Okay, you need to sit up, so I can properly look at that head wound."

With help, Raelia did as she was told. Yaila looked at the wound for a few moments and then dabbed it with a clean, wet cloth.

"Where's Alister?" Raelia asked quietly, wincing with pain at the pressure her mother was putting on the back of her head.

"Alister?" Yaila asked.

"The man who pulled her out of the river," Luella clarified as she walked into the room and sat at the end of Raelia's bed. "He had to leave, but," she added, stretching out the 'but' in a telling tone, "he said he'll stop by in a few days to check on you."

Raelia winced again, and closed her eyes, mentally shaking her head at her boy-crazy best friend.

"Luella, dear, could you hold this until I get back?" Yaila asked, indicating the cloth she held to Raelia's wound.

"Of course!" Luella agreed before moving and taking it from the elder woman.

"Caeda, come with me," Yaila instructed as she made her way to the door.

"But Mama!" Caeda protested, quickly changing her tune when she noticed the stern look on their mother's face.

When the door closed behind them, Raelia closed her eyes, hoping Luella would realize she was too tired for the boy talk she knew her friend wanted to rush into. She was surprised, however, when she heard a sniffle come from her friend. She opened her eyes to see tears welling in Luella's eyes.

"You could have died," she said, her blue eyes locking on Raelia's. "When I heard your scream and watched you go under..." she held back a sob as she continued, "If Alister hadn't been there... You would have died!"

A tear rolled down Luella's round cheeks, and she looked down as if ashamed of her emotion. Raelia lifted her hand and gently wiped it away with her knuckle.

"I'm sorry," she said softly, letting her hand fall back to her lap. "You were right. I shouldn't have done it," Raelia sighed heavily, eyes staring at the tear still on her knuckle. "I just couldn't... I couldn't watch an innocent creature suffer." She reached for her friend's free hand, lacing their fingers together and squeezing gently. "I'm sorry," she said again.

Luella looked back at Raelia, seeming to struggle holding back a sob.

"I know..." she sighed quietly, "But I can't lose you. You're my best friend."

Raelia lifted her eyes to look into her best friend's. "And you're mine."

"I love you, Rae."

Raelia felt her heart flutter at the words, and her stomach knotted with nerves when she returned, "I love you too, Lue."

They both jumped when the door opened once more and Yaila waltzed back into the room.

"Okay now," she said, walking over and taking the now bloody rag from Luella's hand, "Let's get this wound stitched up."

"I-uh-I should probably get home before it gets dark," Luella started, her eyes darted to the window where the sun began its descent behind the mountains in the distance. "Mother will worry if I'm not home soon."

"And she'll be wondering about Raelia's condition, as well. I was with her when Caeda and Blaze turned up to tell me what happened."

"Oh! I didn't realize," Luella replied, seeming flustered. "I should have left earlier!"

"I told her you'd be along before dark," Yaila said as she pushed Raelia's head down to get a better look at what she was working on, "so it is definitely a good time to get home. Tell her I'll be over tomorrow afternoon."

Luella nodded and gave one last concerned look at her best friend before heading out the door, leaving the two of them alone.

For a few moments, they were quiet as Yaila threaded the needle and started to stitch together the wound in her daughter's head. Raelia winced in pain every time the needle pierced her skin, but kept quiet while her mother worked.

"Do you want to explain yourself?" Yaila finally asked in a harsh tone. "You're lucky you're not dead!"

"There was a fox pup, and he was-"

"Oh I know all about the fox pup!" Yaila interrupted, pulling a bit rougher than she was a moment before. "What I want to know is why you can't behave properly for once in your life!"

Raelia closed her eyes, trying to keep calm. Her head still ached and she knew getting into a fight with her mother would only make it hurt worse. Besides, she'd been stupid, and her mother had every right to be angry at her.

"I'm sorry, Mama," she said quietly.

"You should be sorry!" came her response as she pulled the thread roughly through Raelia's scalp. "If that man hadn't been there, Caeda and Blaze would have had to live with the guilt of watching their sister die and not being able to do anything to stop it!"

Raelia stayed quiet. She knew her mother needed to get out the anger she felt. The pit of guilt in her stomach grew larger as Yaila continued.

"I'd have had to write to your father and tell him you were dead!" she nearly shouted. Her lip quivered, betraying her anger. "They'd have to come home and feel the guilt about not being here to save you!"

Her mother's voice shook, and she felt Yaila's hands move from the wound and into her lap. Raelia lifted her head enough to see the tears welling in her mother's eyes.

"You're needed in this world, Raelia Aster. You are needed and so, so loved," Yaila said, her eyes finding her daughters. "You are needed in this world more than you could ever realize."

"I'm sorry, Mama," she repeated. "I won't do it again."

Yaila sniffled, and fidgeted with her apron, before moving her hands back to Raelia's wound. "You better not."

CHAPTER 4

"Rae?" Blaze whispered through the door. "Rae, are you awake?"

Raelia groaned. She was so tired and very nearly asleep, but she sat up in her bed and looked at the door. "Come on in."

Her brother tiptoed through the door, as if he wasn't supposed to be there, and his strawberry blonde hair looked windblown, as though he'd been outside for quite some time. When she looked up, she was surprised to see him carrying something bulky under his shirt, and she gave him a sly grin.

"What are you sneaking up to my room that you don't want Mama to see?" she chuckled.

He returned her sly smirk and pulled out a ball of black fluff. It took Raelia a minute to realize he held the fox pup from earlier.

"Wha-?" she started.

"I found her outside when we got home with Mama," Blaze explained. "She was sitting on the rock out front. It seemed like she was staring at your window."

"She's much better looking than earlier," Raelia noted as Blaze handed the small creature to her.

"I washed her up and brushed her," Blaze said as a proud smile spread across his features. "I even fed her!"

It took a lot for Raelia not to chuckle at how adorable her normally surly brother was acting, but she managed and smiled up at him. "You did all that? That's great!"

She looked back at the creature sitting in her lap, watching her as if it expected something. She reached out and scratched behind its ear, before running her hand down its back. The fox's fur was black as night, except a strip that ran down its spine and on its muzzle. The fur in both places, while mostly black, had tips of white, giving the patches a peppered look. His two front paws were white as well, though speckled with black dots, much like her horse, Prickle. She marveled at the markings. They were so distinct, and yet, somehow, subtle. When she went to pet it again, the fox nuzzled into her hand, licking her softly as it continued to watch her with its two colored eyes.

"I think she likes you," Blaze smiled, as he sat on the edge of Raelia's bed and gave the pup a scritch behind the ear.

"And I think," Raelia said, picking up one of the fox's hind legs and peering under, "she's a he."

They both laughed. The fox moved to Raelia's side, spinning around a few times. Then he scratched and sniffed at her blanket before laying down — curling into a small puffy ball.

"Thank you, Blaze," Raelia said softly to her younger brother.

His eyes shifted to hers, and she could see a war of emotion happening behind them. He said nothing, but after a moment of silence, flung himself at her, wrapping his arms around her tightly.

The movement surprised her, but, ignoring the painful ache in her muscles, she wrapped her arms around him in return. Placing one hand on the back of his head, she pressed a kiss to his temple.

"I'm sorry for worrying you," she said quietly.

She couldn't see his face, but heard a small sniffle escape him before he replied, "Love you, RaeRae."

The words took her by surprise, and she tightened her hold on him. "I love you too, Blazie."

With that he pulled away, a look of disgust covering his features. "Don't call me that! I'm not a baby anymore!"

Raelia forced down a laugh, but couldn't keep the smile off her face. "Of course you're not!"

Blaze gave her a withering look, which made Raelia's laughter impossible to contain. He rolled his eyes as she giggled and headed towards the bedroom door.

"Wait!" Raelia called, trying to get her laughter under control. "I really mean it. I'm sorry."

He grinned at her once more, letting her know she was forgiven before he walked out, closing the door behind him.

Raelia looked at the sleeping fox as she wiggled down into the blankets. She smiled as he stretched and yawned before shifting himself into a more comfortable position.

"You caused so much trouble today."

✦━━━━ ━━━━✦

The next few days were frustrating for Raelia. Her mother insisted she stay in bed, certain the wound on the back of her head came with a concussion. She tried to argue against being bedridden, but the stern look Yaila shot at her stifled her protests quickly.

Raelia slept quite a bit on the first day, though in the few hours she was awake, she felt like she was going stir crazy. She was thankful when Blaze and Caeda turned up with the fox in the little girl's arms.

"Have you decided on a name for him yet?" Caeda asked, placing the pup on the bed next to Raelia. "I have some ideas if you haven't!"

She couldn't help but laugh at her little sister's boldness.

"Well, let's hear them!" Raelia said with a smile.

Her sister smiled brightly in return and plopped herself at the foot of the bed. "Let's start with the most obvious! River!"

Blaze scoffed, rolling his hazel eyes as he sat in the chair next to the window. "River? That doesn't suit him at all! Just because-"

"It does too!" Caeda cut in. "We found him right next to a river! Of course it suits him!"

Sensing this conversation would quickly turn into a war, Raelia stepped in. "It does seem a bit obvious. What are your other ideas?"

Caeda groaned, slumping her shoulders as if she was suddenly carrying the heaviest weight upon them. "Fiiiiiiiiiiine... What about Pepper?"

A look of disgust flashed across Blaze's face. "Why can't it be something that isn't so obvious? He deserves a strong name!"

Raelia agreed with her brother, but she held back her chuckle so she didn't hurt Caeda's feelings. "Pepper is cute, but... what if we did both?"

"What do you mean?" her sister asked.

An idea was forming. She hoped it would appease them both and avoid any further bickering. "What if we named him something in Taevik?" Her sibling's looked intrigued, so she continued. "Say we name him River, but use the Taevik word for it?"

"What's the Taevik word for River?" Caeda asked.

"Zayric," Blaze answered before Raelia could.

"Zayric?" Caeda seemed to mull that over. "I like it! I vote to name him Zayric!"

Raelia turned to look at their brother, who nodded his agreement.

"It's decided then," she said, turning to look at the fox pup and scratching behind his ear. "Welcome to the family, Zayric."

The following day, the restlessness returned so Raelia convinced Blaze to bring her a few books from their father's study. A few hours after he'd delivered them, she found herself curled up on her bed, devouring the words like a starving man would devour a meal. She lost herself in the worlds they painted.

She read about the legends of her Kingdom.

She read about the mythical creatures that used to walk freely before being conquered by the Kings of the past.

She read about the Drykuan's and Zarhaish.

She read about their immortal races and how King Nikolai had wiped them out with one go to protect the citizens from their 'demonic presence'.

She'd always been intrigued by the legends of the immortal races, and caught herself, more than once, entranced by the few pictures her father's books offered of the beings. Most believed the stories told of the mythical creatures were tall tales, meant to scare young children into staying out of the forests. However, to Raelia, the delicate sketches and paintings within the books gave them life. She felt connected to them somehow, and had read every piece of literature her father owned that spoke about them. She'd long since worn out the patience of her family and friends with the information she found about the immortal races, and now just made notes about them for herself.

On the third day after the incident, she sat, still in her room, curled up in the middle of her bed, captivated by one such picture. It was of a Drykuan woman. The delicate painting showed her rich ochre skin shining in rays of sunlight coming through the branches of the mossy forest surrounding her. The beautiful brown had a slight sheen of silver to it, appearing almost luminescent, until it touched the tip of her pointed ears where the ochre tone faded into a brilliant opaque silver. The woman's silver eyes were piercing, as if they could see into the soul of anyone who crossed paths with her. Her inky black hair was long, and even though only painted, seemed to be moving with the breeze that Raelia could hear blowing through the leafy tree outside her bedroom window.

Mesmerized as she was, Raelia didn't hear her door click open, and jumped at the sound of someone clearing their throat behind her. Her hand jumped to her heart as she turned around.

"Alister!"

He smiled kindly at her. "I'm sorry. I didn't mean to startle you," he said in his deep, soothing tone.

Raelia smiled in return, and closed her book as she shifted to face him, "It's alright! Please, join me!" she gestured to the chair next to her window, "It's nice to have company that isn't my mother or siblings!" she laughed lightly.

He reached his hand towards her, holding out a bouquet of wildflowers. She took them graciously and inhaled deeply at the aroma they gave off.

"Thank you!" she exclaimed as Alister took a seat. "That's so thoughtful!"

She set the flowers down on the bed next to herself before turning her eyes to look at him with a grin.

"You seem to be in much better spirits than when I saw you last. How are you feeling?" he asked.

"I'm actually feeling much better!" she smiled, and then sighed, rolling her eyes "Though, I'd be much happier if Mama would let me out of bed and back into the real world!"

"Most people would be happy to take a few days to recoup after what you went through," he laughed lightly, before his eyes moved to the book next to her. "What are you reading?

Raelia handed the heavy, leather-bound book to him.

"Fabled Beings and Their Downfall?" Alister read, quirking up a questioning eyebrow.

"It's fascinating, I promise," Raelia replied, cheeks burning as she sighed, "I know it's bizarre..."

"No that's-"

Before he could finish his response, Caeda burst in through her bedroom door with a small fluff ball in her arms. Her eyes went wide when she saw Alister sitting in the corner chair.

"I didn't know you had a boy in here!" she practically shouted. "Mama's gonna be mad!"

Raelia's amber skin flushed an even deeper red, and it took a lot of strength to not yell at her sister for bursting in. Before she could figure out what to say, however, Alister spoke up.

"Your mother is the one who let me up, actually," he smiled. "I wanted to check on how you all were doing. What's that you have there?" he asked, eyes watching the wiggling fluff in Caeda's arms.

As if he knew someone asked about him, Zayric lifted his head and looked at Alister with apprehensive eyes. He went still for only a moment before he quickly wriggled out of Caeda's arms and hurried into Raelia's lap, glaring at Alister once settled.

"Well hello there," Alister said, reaching out to pet the fluffy fox. Zayric growled at his approaching hand, and backed up into Raelia's stomach.

"Okay. No touching. Got it," Alister chuckled, pulling his hand away. His eyes found Raelia's once more with a smirk, "Myths and legends, I can understand. A fox as a pet? Now that's a bit more bizarre."

Raelia looked down at her fluffy friend and ran a hand over his head as she spoke. "I can think of weirder things," she laughed.

Alister laughed along while Caeda moved to sit next to her sister on the bed. The three talked for a while, before being joined by Blaze, and eventually Luella. Raelia was surprised at how comfortable she felt around Alister. It was as if she'd known him for years. As if she could tell him anything, and she couldn't put her finger on why.

A few hours after his arrival, Alister stood to leave. Caeda jumped at him, hugging him around the middle. "You'll come back soon, right Al?"

Alister looked to Raelia who shot him a 'you got yourself into this, buddy,' look before he peered down at the top of the girl's head. "Absolutely I will! I've got to make sure you're taking care of your sister!" He smirked at Raelia before continuing, "Night and day. Maybe you should sleep in here until she's recouped?"

Luella pursed her lips, clearly trying to contain her laughter. Raelia's jaw dropped open as if gasping for breath, while her eyes looked at Alister with betrayal, "I don't think that will be-"

"That's a GREAT idea!" Caeda exclaimed, interrupting Raelia's attempt at refusal. "I'm going to go get my blanket!" And without another word, the small child went running from the room — only her footsteps heard thumping down the hallway.

As soon as she was out of earshot, Luella burst into a fit of giggles. Blaze just shook his head with a smirk. "You're never going to get away with that," he said to Alister, holding back a chuckle of his own. "I'd leave now before she comes to her senses and knocks you out."

Alister laughed and turned to Raelia, who was still staring at him in disbelief. "It was really nice to visit. I know there's a festival in a few days in the village," he paused, seeming suddenly unsure of himself. "I've heard it's quite the spectacle to behold... Would - uh -would you be willing to show me around the festival one day?"

Raelia's betrayed expression shifted quickly into a kind smile, "I'd be happy to," she answered. "It's the least I can do for the man who saved my life."

"Great! I can't make it for the first day, so I'll plan on seeing you for the second," he said with a bright smile, before he turned to bid farewell to Luella, and Blaze.

A few moments later, he was gone, and Raelia stood to stretch her limbs. She froze mid stretch when she noticed everyone's eyes on her.

"What?" she asked, confused. "Do I have something on my face?" She pressed her fingers to her cheeks and then her nose, waiting for an answer.

"He asked you to accompany him to the festival!" Luella announced, emphasizing each word as if Raelia was the dumbest person she'd ever laid eyes upon.

"I... uh... I know that..." Raelia replied. "And?"

"Oh come on Rae!" Blaze burst out before covering his face with his hands and shaking his head.

Luella laughed loudly. "Isn't it obvious?"

Raelia stared at her best friend for a moment, her stomach churning with embarrassment. "I... Clearly it's not... What are you both on about?"

"You are the smartest person I know! How in all of Dirythia can you be *this* dense?!" Luella shook her head, still giggling. She took a breath, calming her laughter before continuing. "Alister wasn't asking you a favor! He was asking to escort you around the festival! He wants to *court* you!"

"Wh-wh-what?!" Raelia spluttered, feeling her face grow warm. "You can't be... He didn't... Nuh-uh!"

The following morning, Raelia was exhausted, though when her mother announced she was finally allowed to leave her room, she perked up. She had never before been so excited to walk down the stairs and into the cozy kitchen for breakfast. After eating, Yaila put her to work as she would any other day, and she was so happy to be out of her room, she couldn't bring herself to mind.

The Equinox festival started the next day, and it was one of the largest events in this part of Dirythia. The residents of Frayis and other nearby villages did a fair amount of trading and selling of their wares — the Kesby family was no exception.

Raelia spent the day packing crates with medical salves and elixirs, a ton of dried herbs from Yaila's garden and soaps that Caeda helped her make a few weeks ago. When the crates were packed, she loaded them into the cart they would ride to the village in, and then spent some time with Prickle and Onyx. She'd missed her horses in the few days she'd been locked in her room and if Prickle's prancing around his stable was any indication, they'd missed her too.

All in all, it had been a good first day back in the real world and by the time she laid down that night, she had only excited thoughts about what the festival would bring the following day.

CHAPTER 5

The sky swirled above Raelia's face as she twirled herself around. Her tiny legs tangled with one another as she kept trying to spin. She fell to the ground, laughing as the world continued to spin around her. Her father sat near her, laughing joyously at his daughter's happiness.

"Raelia!" she heard her mother shout. "Raelia! You must come here!"

Eloi picked up his cherub cheeked daughter, and the world swirled around them until they were standing in the kitchen with a panicked looking Yaila. A small blonde boy sat at the table eating a platter of fruit, his cheeks covered in blueberry juice.

"She saw it!" her mother was saying. "I think she believed me when I told her it was a scratch from her playing with Caias, but..."

"It will be okay," Eloi replied in a soothing voice.

"How will it be okay?!" Yaila asked in a hushed whisper. "If that thing is discovered, it's not only Raelia who will be put to death!"

Eloi looked at his daughter, whose face was a storm of emotion as she watched her mother's fear and panic. Raelia's chubby little hand moved to the Mark that her mother referred to, and her eyes welled up with tears.

"I'm sorry, Mama," the little girl said sadly. "I didn't mean to have it..."

Eloi looked at his wife. "We just have to be more careful."

Yaila sighed and looked at her daughter as a few tears escaped her eyes, hurrying their way down her cheeks. "I just wish there was some way to get rid of it," her eyes shifted to Eloi. "Isn't there some way to get rid of it?"

"It's a part of who she is," he answered.

"I won't let anyone see again, Mama. I promise."

Tiny Raelia sobbed as the world began to swirl around her again.

When it stopped, the scene around them changed.

Her hair was braided to one side—styled so as to keep her Mark hidden. She stood a fair distance from a group of children playing together, and she wanted so badly to play with them. Her elder brother Caias jumped around with the others, and she thought how unfair it was that she was the only one in her family cursed with this wretched Mark.

She saw a young girl with long blonde hair, and a beautiful, frilly blue dress approach the group from the opposite side of the clearing. The girl watched the group for a breath and then shifted her eyes to Raelia, smiling sweetly.

She smiled back, and again the world twirled.

She was back in the kitchen now. She watched as her mother and father talked in hushed voices at the table. They hadn't seen her yet, and Raelia couldn't bring herself to interrupt. There had been another close call today, and her mother was in a panic once more about Raelia's Mark being discovered.

"I don't know how to keep doing this!" Yaila fretted.

"We can go to Taevidia if it's too much here, my love," Eloi soothed. "She would be safe there. We all would be."

"I can't leave my mother," was the only reply she gave before Eloi spotted his daughter in the doorway.

"Glimmer!" he exclaimed. "You should be in bed!" He stood and walked to her, swiftly lifting her into his arms and heading for the stairs.

The next moment she was laying in bed looking up at her father as he tucked the blanket around her.

"Papa?"

"Hmm?"

"Does Mama hate me?"

Eloi stopped what he was doing and sat down on the edge of her bed before looking into her eyes. "Mama could never hate you. She loves you very much. Don't ever doubt that. Remember what we say? Do not doubt in darkness what you believed in the light."

Raelia nodded. The sincerity in his voice and the promise in his eyes showed he spoke the truth, though it did nothing to stymie her frustration.

"Maybe I should go to Taevidia and live with Ouma? Then my stupid Mark won't get anyone hurt..."

"You belong with us, my child. You always will."

"I hate my Mark!" she nearly screamed.

"Don't hate your Mark, child," Eloi said, sadness coloring his tone. "Your Mark is a part of who you are. It's a part of who we are. It is a gift you were chosen to receive." He sighed and brushed a strand of red hair off his daughter's face. "My Glimmer, your Mark is one of power and of responsibility. You are more powerful than you know. Don't reject something that makes you who you are."

She felt a tear slide from her eye and into her hair as she held her arms up to hug her father. He wrapped his arms around her, pulling her up and squeezing her tightly.

"I love you, Papa,"

"And I you, my child."

The colors of the world twirled once more and when it stopped the scenery changed very little. She was still in her room, only her father was gone and a girl sat next to her, laughing melodically. The same blonde-haired girl from the field where the children were playing. Luella, she realized, as she laughed along.

"And then I told him he didn't know what he was talking about, and do you know what he did?" Luella tried to stifle her laughter, failing miserably.

"What did he do?" Raelia asked, still giggling.

"He actually said he was going to tell his mother on me!"

They both burst into even more giggles.

Without thinking, Raelia tossed her braid behind her shoulder. "I wish I could say I can't believe it, but-"

She realized suddenly that Luella stopped laughing and was looking at what appeared to be her ear with scrutinizing eyes.

"What is that?" she asked, her eyes going wide as if she knew exactly what it was.

Raelia jumped to her feet, immediately pulling her braid back into place, covering the Mark she knew Luella had seen.

"N-nothing!" she stumbled, "It's n-nothing!"

Raelia felt tears well in her eyes and her hands began to tremble as her mind raced over what would happen if Luella continued to push. She'd be killed. Her family would be killed. Her heart raced and felt as if it was trying to jump out of her chest.

"Rae," Luella said in a reassuring tone, "it's obviously something."

She stepped forward, arm extended, as if about to sweep her hair out of the way. Raelia stepped back.

"I-I-I can't tell you."

"But we're best friends!" Luella protested. "We have been since we were seven! That's a whole four years, Rae! If you can't tell me, who can you tell?!"

"I'm not supposed to have it. It could get my family in trouble!"

Luella again stepped forward. Her eyes were concerned, but the kindness she saw there made Raelia stay where she was this time.

She swept Raelia's auburn braid out of the way and a small smile appeared on her face.

"I always knew you were magic."

"I'm not magic. I'm deformed," Raelia replied, sorrow touching her features as she continued. "You can go now, you don't have to stay."

"Rae," Luella said softly, "you're my best friend. You will always be my best friend. All that Mark does is make you even more amazing than I already knew you were." She grabbed Raelia's hand, squeezing it tightly, looking directly in her eyes. "I'm not going anywhere."

Again the world swirled, and the scenery changed. She stood in the village square. Loud music rang out from a small platform where a group of musicians played for the crowd. Raelia and Luella laughed and twirled together, Caeda clapped, as they all danced to the music.

Luella pulled Caeda's hand and swung the young girl around, just as Raelia felt a tap on her shoulder.

When she turned, a tall man with long silver hair was holding a hand out to her. He wore a white mask that was overlaid with a delicate black lace. Attached on each side was a satin ribbon that wrapped over his ears and tied behind his luscious silver locks. A long emerald green cloak hung from his large frame, dusting the ground beneath him.

She smiled, excitedly grabbed his offered hand, and swung outward from him. He pulled her back, and she felt his hand snake around her waist, pulling her close.

In an instant, the world changed. She remained in the village square, wrapped in the masked strangers arms, but there were no other people, and flames grew around them. The music stopped, and the only sounds she could hear were distant, agonized screams.

She tried to push away from the man, but he held her tightly in place.

"Let me go!" Raelia pleaded, dread filling her at the thought of where her family was. "Please, I have to find them!"

He watched her with bright silver eyes, but didn't respond and didn't release her.

Her panic grew as the flames reared up even higher and the village disappeared from view. "Please," she sobbed, pushing hard against his chest, desperate to get away. "I have to save them!"

He watched her panic for a moment in silence.

"You will not be able to save them." His voice was deep. The hint of an unfamiliar, lilting accent rounding out his tone. "You will not be able to stop it."

She sobbed, feeling her legs give out from under her, only staying upright because of his arms still wrapped around her waist.

"There is nothing you can do, but I will come for you."

She looked at him, bewilderment coloring her anguish.

"Stay alive."

Raelia sat bolt upright, her body sweating as she looked around, only to realize she was in her bed. Zayric looked up from his cozy spot beside her pillow and cocked his head to one side.

"It was only a dream," Raelia said softly to herself.

Her heart pounded in her chest, adrenaline coursing through her as she laid her head back down. She took a few deep breaths, trying to calm the erratic pounding, and turned her head to face Zayric. He stretched over, licking her cheek softly. She scratched behind his ear before burrowing into her blankets and squeezing her eyes shut against the faint light coming through her window. She turned over once, twice, three times, but as the sun continued to rise, sleep became a distant memory.

She stretched and threw her blankets back. "I guess I may as well get up," she said to Zayric.

She got ready for the day slowly, still sifting through the broken memories of her dream. It seemed so real, and it left her with such an unsettled feeling she couldn't think about much else.

Her stomach clenched in knots as she ran through the images. Most of what she saw, she knew to be memories from her childhood, but her village going up in flames? Who was the masked man? Why did he burn down her village? Her mind raced with questions, distracting her and making the process of dressing for the day much longer than it should have been.

When she'd finally finished, she headed downstairs, letting Zayric out the front door on her way toward the kitchen. She nearly fell back at the loud chorus of "Happy Birthday!" shouted at her as she walked through the door into the cozy space. Caeda, Blaze, and Yaila all stood waiting for her with nearly identical grins on their faces.

Her younger sister was the first to come over, giving her a tight hug, followed by Blaze and then her mother.

"Happy birthday, RaeRae," Yaila said softly, cupping her cheek, and kissing her forehead. "Officially, you are grown, but you will always be my baby."

Raelia smiled. "Thanks, Mama."

Yaila patted her cheek before turning around and stepping over to the stove. "Your birthday breakfast is all ready!" she exclaimed, gesturing for Raelia to sit down at the small table in the center of the room. "I made all your favorites!"

Raelia's face lit up as she looked at the pile of pancakes on the counter next to where her mother stood. "Oh goody! I'm starving!"

Yaila dished everyone up a heaping plate of all of Raelia's favorite breakfast foods, and all three of her children made quick work with what was put in front of them.

By the time they finished, Yaila had only eaten half of what she'd given herself. She laughed, and told them to go get themselves ready for the festival. Raelia watched as her brother and sister took off running, laughing at them pushing each other through the doorway.

"Thank you for breakfast, Mama," she said as she turned to look at Yaila sitting across from her.

"You're so very welcome, my child," she replied, smiling lovingly at her eldest daughter. "You're officially 18 now, and I can't believe how quickly it's gone. Soon enough I won't get to make you breakfast on your birthday's, so I'll hold on to these for as long as you live under my roof."

Raelia stood, kissed her mother on the cheek before she headed back upstairs to bathe and change into something more presentable than her dressing gown. She didn't have to think about what to wear. Her new ocean blue, empire waisted gown seemed the perfect dress for the occasion.

After twisting the top of her hair into a beautiful braided crown, low around her head, she pinned the sides to keep her Indicative Mark covered. She let the rest of her red-auburn hair hang in loose tendrils, her waves curling just slightly as they hung down to her waist.

When she looked over herself in the mirror she was surprised to feel a tight sadness in her chest.

'*I'm 18 today,*' she thought, spinning the ring her father had given her around her finger a few times before looking down at her hand. '*I wish you were here, Papa.*'

"I miss you," she said to the empty room.

"Wooooow," Caeda gasped, from the doorway, startling her sister. "You look like a Princess!"

Raelia smiled at her, and gestured to the frilly green dress she wore. "As do you, Princess Caeda."

The pair headed downstairs and soon they and Yaila were squished into the seat of the cart hooked up to Onyx. Blaze pulled himself into Prickle's saddle and once he was settled, they began their journey into town. It was only a short trip into the village, but in their excitement it seemed to take ages.

The Kesby family had been selling during the Equinox festival for Raelia's entire life, so setting up their family booth was a quick process with both her and her mother working together. Soon after they were ready for business, Luella turned up, smiling brightly.

Yaila took the opportunity to walk the horses to the corral and sight see for a bit with Caeda and Blaze, leaving the two girls to handle the booth.

"Happy birthday, Rae!" Luella said, holding out a small package for her friend.

Raelia smiled. "Aw! Lue! Thank you so much!"

She tore open the delicate paper and was excited to find a beautiful silver hairpin with a crescent moon and a few star-shaped gems surrounding it. Raelia gasped, "Lue! It's beautiful! But," she hesitated, chewing at her bottom lip, "this is too much! I can't accept something so expensive!"

Luella rolled her bright blue eyes. "Of course you can! It's from Mother and Father too." She took the pin from her friend and walked behind her to tuck the pin into the braided crown in Raelia's hair. "We all decided that you deserved something really special for your eighteenth birthday. It's a milestone, after all!"

Raelia touched her fingertips to the cold silver in her hair, and her eyes connected with her best friend's. "Thank you, Lue," she said softly. "I love it!"

She hugged her friend tightly and felt a fluttering sensation in her stomach as she pulled away. She didn't understand it, but before she could explore it further, a festival goer came up and started inquiring about Yaila's medical salve.

A couple hours passed before her mother returned with Caeda and Blaze in tow. Caeda looked about to burst with excitement when she saw her sister, and it took a lot to not laugh at her excited expression.

"RaeRae!" she burst out as she got closer to the booth. "RaeRae, we have something for you!"

When Blaze caught up to his younger sister, he grinned as he handed over a present beautifully wrapped in a deep blue cloth with a silver string tied in a bow on the top.

"Sorry we couldn't give it to you this morning," Blaze said with a smile.

"We bought it ourselves! Special just for you, RaeRae!" Caeda said, beaming from ear to ear.

Raelia took the rectangle from her brother, opening it gently. In its center was a small, leather-bound journal engraved with a dandelion on the front. Normally, Raelia hated dandelions. They only reminded her of the Indicative Mark that kept her apart from other people. However, this? The work was stunning, and she felt a surge of emotions as she wrapped her arms around both of them, pulling them in for a hug.

"Thank you so much, you two!" she said happily. "I love it! I can't wait to write all my new notes in it!" She exclaimed as she pulled back to look at them once more. She hugged the small book to her chest, and put it in the pouch she wore at her hip, "I'll keep it with me, so I always have a place to write them down!"

She hugged them both once more before turning to Yaila, who had started talking to a customer. She turned and shooed them all off, and Raelia knew that was her cue to start exploring.

Blaze stayed behind as she, Caeda, and Lue made their way to where the food stalls were, using their pocket money to buy a few tasty treats. After that, they stopped by the corral to see Prickle and Onyx, before they headed to the village square where the music playing echoed in the air.

They danced together and laughed, each taking turns to twirl Caeda around and then each other. The music was quick paced and jovial, which brought out quite a few people to dance in front of the small platform where the musicians played. Raelia watched as Luella pulled Caeda and twirled her once more, just as she felt a light tap at her shoulder. She had such a strong sense of déjà vu her stomach tensed, terrified the masked stranger from her dream would be standing there. She let out a sigh of relief when she realized it was a boy she knew from the village.

"Eja!" she said with a smile of recognition.

The boy held his hand out, asking if she would care to dance. Any other day, Raelia would have turned him down, but her spirits were high, and she didn't have a care in the world. She took his hand, smiling as he swung her around the dance floor.

They danced for a few songs before Raelia, still smiling, needed something to drink. She excused herself, looking for Luella and Caeda, only to realize that neither of them seemed to be on the dance floor any longer.

Her brows knit together with confusion, *'Where could they be?'*

Deciding she would find them after she quenched her thirst, she turned, heading back toward the food carts, only making it a few steps before a solitary, terrified scream ripped through the air.

CHAPTER 6

Raelia's heart raced as she, and the others near her, looked around for the source of the scream. A few more echoed through the afternoon sky, and more and more joined in. Raelia looked around, frantic to find where the screaming was coming from.

The musicians stopped playing in the middle of their melody as the screams became harder to ignore. At the far end of the road, Raelia could see bright orange flames growing in bales of hay. A flaming arrow flew only a few feet from her, hitting the stomach of the young man she'd just been dancing with.

"Eja!" she shouted as he fell to the ground.

His kind brown eyes connected with hers. They were wide with confusion and pain as she knelt down beside him. Her hands fluttered over his wound, trying to find some way to help, as the surrounding people started to shriek and run for cover. Eja let out a solitary whimper of pain, before his body stopped moving. The flames grew within him, and his eyes became unseeing.

When she realized he was gone, it only took a moment for Raelia to get to her feet and race for the shelter of the alleyway between two of the buildings. While she ran, her eyes caught glimpses of large men in leather armor running the festival attendees through with their swords. Every attacker was huge, tall and muscular, all seeming to have the same alabaster hue and dark hair. She watched as body after body fell. In her mind, she screamed at herself to just get to the alleyway.

'You can't save them,' the masked man said in her dream. She knew the 'them' he referred to were her family, and the terror of what would happen to the people she loved drove her feet to keep moving, even when fear made her want to hide.

When she came through the alley on the other side, she darted around a few stalls, doing her best to avoid attention as she crossed the street. It slowed her down, and that thought terrified her, but the thought of being run through with one of the large swords the attackers were carrying scared her more.

"Raelia!" she heard a familiar voice shout from behind. She turned, looking behind her and found Violet Rominst, Luella's mother. She watched as the woman she'd known most of her life was grabbed by the hair from behind. One of the large leather clad men dragged her toward him.

Mrs. Rominst screamed, just as Raelia turned and ran at her attacker. Her shoulder rammed into the man's gut, knocking him off balance, and he let go of the blonde hair in his grasp.

"Luella! Where's Luella?!" Mrs. Rominist screamed, grabbing Raelia by both shoulders.

The attacker steadied himself behind where Violet stood, and Raelia's eyes went wide as he stepped towards them once more.

"Run!" she screamed. "RUN!"

Gathering her point, the woman turned around, screaming when she saw the sword coming down. Raelia only had a second to react, shoving her down to the ground. The sword missed its intended target, but did not miss Raelia. The sharp blade dragged along her forearm, blood erupting from the wound coating the silver metal.

She hissed in pain, twisting just in time to avoid the sword piercing through her stomach. She watched Mrs. Rominst scrambled back to her feet, and without a word, the woman ran away into the dark alley Raelia had only just come out of.

Without thinking, Raelia twisted once more, now behind the attacker, and dove under a horse cart behind him. She crawled quickly to the other side of the cart, standing just in time to see the village baker run at the attacker with a sword of his own.

It was the distraction she needed, and she wouldn't ignore it.

Raelia ran the rest of the way across the street and ducked into the next alleyway, bursting out the other side with a speed she didn't know she was capable of.

Finally reaching the road where her family's stall stood, she hurried as fast as she could toward it. A familiar voice crying a desperate plea reached her ears. Her mother's voice. As she skirted around one last stall, she could see one of the leather clad attackers approaching the stall where her mother stood, shielding Caeda and Blaze behind her.

She was still so far from them, and fear exploded within her. She lifted her skirt and urged her legs to move even quicker.

The man stepped closer to her frightened, desperate mother.

'Faster.'

Yaila's arms spread wide, making sure her children were safe.

'Faster.'

The man raised his sword.

'Faster.'

Raelia was so close, and yet she watched as the man swung his sword down in a swift, fluid movement.

The world seemed to freeze as Raelia watched her mother's head part from her body. Her loving, intelligent, joyful mother. Yaila's body fell to the ground, and Raelia nearly tripped over her own feet as she came to an immediate halt, trying to process what she had just seen. Her blood ran cold, body trembling as she watched her mother's head fly into the air and come back down to the earth with a sickening thud.

A shrill scream of terror ripped from Caeda's chest, and in the next breath, Raelia began running once more. She watched Blaze push their little sister behind him, and both children stepped back. Once again, she saw the man lift his sword.

"NOOOO!" Raelia screamed, distracting the man long enough for her siblings to duck under the table next to them. Caeda in front of Blaze, they crawled as quickly as they could. Caeda made it under the cart next to the stall, but before Blaze could clear the table, the man heard their shuffling. Turning back, he quickly grabbed her brother's ankle, and dragged him out from under the table. Again he raised his sword.

"Please," Blaze sobbed, tears streaming down his cheeks. "Please don't hurt me!"

As her brother begged for his life, Raelia jumped as high as she could. Missing the sword held above his head, she wrapped her arms around the man's neck and her legs around his waist. She hooked her ankles together as she shoved the tips of her fingers into his eyes.

The beast let out a holler of pain as Raelia shouted at her brother to run. Blaze quickly followed the path Caeda had taken, and both kids watched on in terror as the man dropped his sword and flailed around with their sister on his back.

The man was large, over six feet tall. He swung this way and that, trying with all his might to fling Raelia off of him, but she only held tighter. He pulled one of her hands off his eye, but she quickly wriggled free from his grasp and gripped tightly onto the tunic sticking out from the top of his leather armor.

After a lot of effort, he finally managed to entwine his fingers into the auburn crown braided atop her head, ripping it forward. She let out an agonized shriek, but, miraculously, held her place on his back. He continued fighting to get her off, twisting, turning, and flailing forward and back.

On his next forward flail, she managed to grasp onto a large jar of salve from the table before them. When he flung back into a standing position, Raelia lifted it high, and brought it down onto the top of his head. She heard a nauseating crack, the force of the impact shattering the glass. She felt a few shards embed themselves into her skin, but her efforts weren't in vain as the man slumped to the ground.

She scampered up and ran to her siblings. She whisked Caeda into her arms, blood dripped down the girl's back from Raelia's open wound, and grabbed Blaze's hand as she turned to head back the way she'd come.

"We have to get out of here!" She shouted to the children over the sounds of the fray. "We'll get to the horses and get home!"

The horse corral was between home and where they stood. It was risky to try for the horses first, but being a little over a mile from their home, she knew it was highly unlikely they'd make it all the way there without them. Caeda sobbed on her shoulder, and she could feel Blaze tripping over his feet as they ran, but she didn't slow down. She couldn't.

"We're almost there!" She shouted when the alley came into view, "We just have to get to-"

Her words cut off as she watched a large, beefy man step out of the alley she had been running for. He wore the same brown leather armor as the man she'd knocked out, and looked nearly identical. Eerily so. She skidded to a halt as the man's eyes landed on the three of them.

Everything around her seemed to slow down as Raelia took a step back, then another. Her heartbeat thudded in her ears, and she turned around to run back the way they had come.

She dragged Blaze behind her, as they ran back up the street, flying past where their mother's body lay. She darted behind a cart, doing her best to avoid the surrounding melee while she tried to figure out where to head next. Her mind was a mess. Caeda's loud sobs in her ear, the sounds of fires blazing, and blades striking against each other made it hard for her to focus.

"He's-He's still coming," Blaze's voice was small and tight with terror.

Raelia turned, looking behind them. He was right. The man who spotted them at the end of the alley still headed toward them. His feet fell heavily, and his pace quickened when he saw her spot him.

Without hesitation, she grabbed Blaze's hand, and they were off once more, dashing across the street.

They made it only a few steps before a whooshing sound caught her attention. She stopped, paralyzed as an arrow flew towards them. She watched, frozen as it buried itself in her brother's chest. Caeda shrieked, reaching out for him. His tear-stained face looked up, into her jade green eyes.

"Rae...lia..." Blaze's voice was only a whisper as his beautiful hazel eyes rolled back into his head and he crumpled to his sister's feet.

She let out a gasp of horror as Caeda screamed their brother's name. The world around her seemed to freeze and quiet all at once.

"Blaze?" Raelia whimpered. Tears filled her eyes as she looked down at her brother. "Blaze?" She reached down, shaking him as tears flooded down her cheeks. The stillness of his body scared her more than anything else had so far. She couldn't help but to look away from his crumpled form.

When she looked over her shoulder, Raelia saw the man from the alley getting closer, a wicked smile taking over his features as he picked up the pace. It took everything in her to let go of her brother's hand.

She wiped her face furiously. "I'm sorry," she whispered, choking down a sob as she forced her legs back into action. She ran at top speed towards another alley. Caeda continued to scream, a deep, guttural screech that bounced off the buildings, stretching her arms out for her brother. A scream that reverberated through Raelia's entire body.

"Go back RaeRae! We can't leave him!" she hollered, kicking against her sister's hold. "He needs us! Blaze needs us!"

Raelia felt tears threatening to spill down her cheeks again as she looked for the next place to run. She knew if she let her emotions take over, they'd never make it out of here alive, so she shoved them back, and kept running.

When she found the alley she was looking for, Raelia quickly darted down it, making it swiftly out the other end. The village square was one more road over, and the horse corral one more past that, so she took a right, then shot into the open road and headed towards another alley.

She ducked behind stalls and carts, doing her best to stay out of sight as she watched swords swinging and arrows flying. Bodies littered the streets. People she'd known her whole life lay motionless on the ground, as fires grew in multiple shops and carts, up and down the road. The stench of death overwhelmed her senses.

'Stay alive,' the dream man had said. His voice repeating the words in her mind as she continued to force herself through the fray. 'Stay alive.'

Finally, she made it to the village square and halted for a moment at the edge of the building, peeking around the corner as the sounds of battle got louder. There were so many people running, screaming, fighting around the open space. Everywhere she looked, there was bloodshed.

She hid behind a couple of carts and made it across into the next narrow alleyway. She almost sighed with relief as she stepped to the edge of it and was able to see the horse corral only a couple of buildings down and across from where they stood.

When she peeked out, she realized there weren't as many people on this road, but she wasn't sure if that should be a relief or not. With fewer people, they would be easier to spot.

She looked at her sister, still sobbing on her shoulder. The sounds of which echoed loudly between the buildings. She backed up against the wall and took a few deep breaths — her lungs burning with every one.

The voice of the masked stranger from her dream bounced around her head like a ball, *'Stay alive.'*

Raelia pulled her sister back just enough to see her tear-streaked face, "Caeda," she whispered to the sobbing child, "Caeda you have to stop crying. We have to get to the horses so we can get out of here, but if you're crying, someone will hear you. We'll be easier to find."

Caeda's chubby cheeks were dirty and streaked with tears. She sniffled, but nodded and, with effort, was able to get control of her loud, vocal sobs. Tears continued to run down her cheeks, but they were quieter now as Raelia poked her head back out of the alley once more.

She looked toward the horse corral, hesitating for only a moment as her mind screamed that this was their only chance to make it out of here alive. She didn't look around as she darted out, making a beeline for the corral. Her legs ached and her wounded arm burned furiously, but she forced herself to keep moving. She ran as quickly as she could, keeping her eyes focused on the gate of the corral.

"We're almost-,"

Raelia let out a small shriek as the tip of her boot caught on a rock and sent her and Caeda plummeting to the ground. Using the momentum of her fall, she twisted, landing hard on her back and Caeda landing on top of her, knocking the air from Raelia's lungs.

She looked at her sister briefly before trying to sit up, but in that split second of time, she caught sight of a tall figure walking up behind the little girl. She recognized him immediately. The wound on his head and blood running down his face only confirmed he was the same man who murdered their mother.

How had he found them? Why had she not seen him before leaving the sanctuary of the alley? Her mind raced as the color drained from her face, and she pulled Caeda tightly to herself, trying to get up and away from this beast of a man. He took a large step forward and grinned at her. His face was lit up with an evil glow as he loomed over them.

He stretched his arm out, entwining his fingers into Caeda's curls, and pulled her back from Raelia's chest. The strength of both girls holding each other with all of their might wasn't enough to stop their assailant from dragging Caeda out of Raelia's arms, while terrified screams ripped from them both.

As he yanked her back, the sword pierced through the flesh of her back, blood shooting from the wound as the blade came through her tiny chest. Caeda's eyes stayed on her sister's, but the little girl didn't speak as blood dribbled out of her mouth and the light left her eyes.

Raelia sobbed out her sister's name. It happened so fast. All of it had happened so fast, and her head seemed to spin with fear at witnessing the brutal deaths of those she loved most in this world.

The man pulled his blade from her tiny torso, throwing her body to the side. She landed only a few feet from where Raelia lay on the ground, her soft brown eyes still wide open and now staring blankly in Raelia's direction.

"You're a pretty little thing," the man growled at Raelia with an appraising look, grasping onto her cheeks with his filthy, sweaty hand. He squeezed her jaw, pursing her lips painfully before tossing her head to one side. "Got a mean streak 'bout ya, though."

Raelia looked up at the monster who had butchered first her mother, and now her sister. Despair filled her, and she seemed to deflate, all the adrenaline that had kept her moving, vanishing in a blink of light. For only a moment, Raelia let herself feel the pain of her loss, before she lay back down, arms spread wide, and gave up.

Her fight was gone.

She had lost the people she loved.

She had failed them.

The masked man was right. She couldn't save them. She never stood a chance. They were gone from this world, and now she would follow them into the shadows.

She turned her head towards her sister and was just able to grab onto her little hand. It was still warm as Raelia's jade green eyes found Caeda's brown, unseeing ones.

"I'm sorry," she whispered to her, even though she knew she could hear her no longer. "I love you, Sissy."

Out of the corner of her eye, she saw movement as the man raised his blade into the air directly above her chest.

She wouldn't fight.

She couldn't anymore.

She closed her eyes and imagined her family, whole and alive, smiling back at her in the darkness.

'I'm sorry, Papa. I'm sorry Caias. I tried to save them,' she thought, *'I'm so sorry I wasn't strong enough.'*

A tear escaped the corner of her eye, falling to the dirt below as she took a deep, calming breath and waited for death to take her on the anniversary of her birth.

CHAPTER 7

The sounds of battle around her became quieter. The screams and melee morphed into nothing as the sound of her beating heart throbbed in her ears.

Thump.

'Will dying hurt?'

Thump.

'Will I even know I'm dead?'

Thump.

'Or will my conscience just cease to exist?'

Thump.

Raelia waited, the short moments feeling like an eternity as she expected the strike of the sword above her.

Suddenly, she felt a steady drip of thick, warm liquid hitting her face and chest. She wiped her fingers across the droplets and opened her eyes, all the sounds and smells of the ongoing battle overwhelming her senses as they returned. She held her fingers in front of her face, and had to choke back a scream as she realized what it was.

She looked past her fingers and saw the man's form still hovering above her, dripping blood from an open wound where the tip of a sword protruded downward through his chest. He still held his weapon above his head.

When Raelia heard him gargle his last breaths, she quickly pulled herself out of his shadow. A second later, the large sword thumped to the ground directly where she had been laying. She watched the sword pierced through her attacker's body jerk to the left, causing him to slide off and thump to the ground with a sickening thud.

She looked up at the newcomer who saved her life. Sitting upon a tall, dark brown mare, the man was nothing but a shadow as the sun sat directly behind him. He turned and swung his leg over the horse, stepping to the ground in front of her.

When he faced her, Raelia gasped, immediately recognizing him. He wore a mask, a solid white surface which was overlaid with a delicately patterned black lace. The mask sat on pale skin that seemed to shimmer with an iridescent silver sheen, covering from the point of his nose to just over where his eyebrows would be and from one ear to the other, being held on by a thick black satin band that tied behind his head. A few strands of his long silver hair hung framing his face, the rest tied underneath the hood of an emerald green cloak, the edges of which were embroidered with a pattern of silver leafy vines wrapping around themselves. He was tall, 6'1" or so, and it took everything in Raelia not to get up and run from him at first sight.

The man from her nightmare.

He held his hand down to her, offering to help her stand, but she couldn't bring herself to touch him. She stood up on her own, on wobbling legs, and forced herself to look away from the one who saved her, her eyes finding Caeda's tiny, broken body. She choked down a sob and leaned down to pick up her sister.

Against her will, tears streamed from her eyes as she pulled Caeda close, cradling her in her arms. She looked around them. Activity on the street had dwindled, and only a few people remained at the far opposite end of the road. She turned toward the corral where Prickle and Onyx and a few other horses stood, and purposefully walked the last few steps towards the enclosure.

Behind her, the man called out, but she ignored him. Something had snapped within her, and she couldn't think of anything but getting home. Even knowing she was gone from this world, Raelia had an overwhelming urge to get her sister back to their family home. It felt as if it would change the day's events and everything could go back to normal the second she walked through the door.

The corral gate had been opened, and many of the horses were gone. Whether their owners took them to ride away or they ran off in fear of the surrounding commotion, Raelia didn't know. She found Prickle and Onyx, both looking distressed. They seemed relieved when they saw her coming toward them, though that could have just been a trick of her mind sensing her own relief at the sight of the familiar horses.

The man hurried to follow Raelia, leaving his own horse in the road. He moved more quickly than should have been possible, and suddenly was stepping into her path, stopping her in her tracks. She paused for only a moment before she attempted to move around him.

His voice was deep with the slightest lilting accent when he asked, "Are you Raelia?"

That brought her to a halt. How did he know her name?

Her eyes found his and saw the same bright silver eyes she'd seen in her dream. It didn't make sense. How did he know her name? Who was he? What was he? Her mind raced with possibilities, but she couldn't bring herself to speak. She slowly nodded, still cradling her sister's body in her arms.

"You have to come with me," the man's tone was urgent. "I was sent here for you."

It took her a moment to find her voice, but even when she did, she didn't know what to ask first. "What do you... How... Who are..." she tried to put her confused thoughts into words and failed miserably. She closed her eyes, breathing deeply before she spoke again, "What do you mean you were sent for me? Who sent you?"

"There's not enough time to explain," he replied. "We have to get out of the village before they find you."

"Before who finds me?" she asked, bewildered. "I can't just go riding off into the unknown with someone I've never even-"

Before she could finish her sentence, there was a shout from behind them. They both turned to see one of the village attackers running toward them, drawing his sword as he closed in. Panic filling her, she hugged on to Caeda as tightly as she could, as the stranger moved to stand in front of her, drawing his own sword.

"Get on your horse," the masked man insisted. "I'll take care of him, but you have to come with me! I can protect you!"

She gave him a curt nod, not thinking about what she was agreeing to. Her only thought was getting out of here, and she knew she couldn't fight her way out on her own. She quickly laid Caeda's lifeless body over Onyx's back and then heaved herself up, swinging her leg over the giant horse and settling into his saddle. She shifted Caeda's body, cradling her with one arm, before she reached over to grab Prickles rein's. She couldn't imagine leaving him. Not after all she'd already lost that day.

By the time she turned back to the masked stranger, he'd already taken down their attacker, and started for his horse. Raelia tapped her heels into Onyx, and urged him to move forward, but before they made it out of the enclosure, she looked up to see two more men in the same leather armor running toward the masked man.

"Watch out!" she shouted to him, just in time.

He was taken by surprise, and before he could pull his blade from the scabbard at his waist, the two men attacked. They didn't seem to have their swords, lost in battle Raelia assumed, but they were massive, just as the other attackers she'd seen had been.

The masked stranger's arms were grabbed from behind, as the second beast of a man came toward him from the front. He pulled a dagger from his waist, as a malicious smirk took over his expression.

Her rescuer pushed his back against the man holding him, using him to hold his weight as he kicked his legs into the chest of the man holding the dagger, causing him to fly back and to the ground. Raelia heard a hiss of pain come from the masked man as the dagger sliced along his calf. It didn't slow him down, however, and while one man was picking himself up, he forcibly pulled the other over his back and threw him to the ground. The attacker thudded heavily onto the dirt road as the masked man drew his sword from his hip, and drove it down into the other man's chest.

Raelia was about to yell for her new ally to watch out, as the man with the dagger had gotten up and was nearly to him, but then, something strange happened.

Before the masked man could turn around, a blur of what appeared to be black smoke engulfed the head of the man with the dagger.

The metal blade clattered to the ground, as the man screamed in agony. His hands moved to his face, grasping over and over for something he couldn't hold. When the masked stranger turned he took a startled step back, looking on in shock at the dark blur. When the screaming finally stopped the man fell heavily to the ground, eyes open but unseeing. His skin had withered, like a rotting apple sitting in the sun, and what little hair he had, had gone white.

The blur of smoke stretched out long and thin, as if it were riding the air and moved toward where Raelia sat watching the second fallen man in confusion.

"NO!" the masked stranger shouted. "Raelia get out of there!"

Before she could react the smoke reached her. Turning a pure white, like a tiny cloud, it coiled around her hand, winding up her arm. She expected pain, as the man's screams had been filled with it, but there was none. Instead she felt a warm, soft sensation along the skin it touched, and a second later, it floated onto Onyx's back. The shapeless white vapor slowly became more opaque and took form. In the blink of an eye, the smoke had disappeared, and Zayric sat where it had been.

Raelia gasped out the fox's name as the masked man approached, looking almost terrified and ready to kill the creature before him. She grabbed his hand before he was able to grab Zayric.

"No!" she shouted. "You can't hurt him!"

He looked up at her with confusion. "Do you know what that *is*?" he demanded. "It is not a creature that should be allowed to live! He will kill you the second your back is turned!"

Raelia looked at the small creature behind her. She thought Zayric was only a fox, but what she had seen him do proved that theory wrong. She didn't know what he was or what he just did, but she knew he would never hurt her.

"He won't," she replied confidently.

The masked man looked at her like she was crazy, but before he could retort, Raelia spoke up once again, "We need to get out of here before anyone else comes this way. We can argue about this later."

The man looked from Zayric to her, and then, seeming to decide she was right, gave a quick nod, and moved swiftly back to his horse, hoisting himself up with ease. Raelia followed on Onyx, pulling Prickle along with them as they quickened their pace to a gallop and turned down a dark alley heading south toward the village square. She was worried as speed increased that Zayric would be unseated from behind her, but when she looked back, he was curled up in a ball sleeping as if he wasn't able to feel the movement at all.

When they raced out into the square, Raelia was shocked to see the chaos and destruction of the village she called home. The bodies of people she had known all her life littered the road, businesses and carts burned brightly and the screams still echoing in the afternoon air had become even louder here.

"We have to be quick!" her escort shouted over the noise.

They darted across the square and down a side road. There seemed to be even more bodies and chaos here, and Raelia felt completely overwhelmed at the brutality that she was witnessing everywhere she looked. The screams were loud, and seemed to be coming from every direction, but one shriek struck a chord in Raelia's heart. It was a voice she recognized. She looked to the left, and dread filled her as she recognized her best friend, covered in blood and tightly clutching the body of her father.

"Stop!" Raelia shouted, not waiting for a response before she turned and urged Onyx to where Luella sat.

"No! Please!" Luella screamed, as she saw the massive beast approach, clearly not recognizing it or who rode him.

"Lue!" Raelia shouted over her friend's terrified screams. 'Lue! It's me!"

It took a moment for Luella to focus on Raelia's voice, and then her face. When she realized who sat upon the massive horse in front of her, her screams died, though her sobs did not.

"My mother... She... And now Father... They... Yaila... She can help them..."

Raelia's heart broke at the sound of her mother's name, and then again at the sight of her friend so confused and unable to even form a cohesive thought. She choked down a sob, refusing to let the threatening tears fall from her eyes.

"Lue, we have to go," she told her friend, her voice betraying the fear she felt. "You have to-"

"We have to go!" the masked man interrupted as he rode up, eyes darting all around as he watched for any approaching threats. "If she won't come, we need to leave her!"

Fury blazed in Raelia's eyes at what he was suggesting, she looked at him directly. "I will not leave the people I love behind!" she shouted at him. Her eyes looked down at Caeda's tiny face, the upper part of her body still cradled in Raelia's arm, and then looked back at Luella.

"Lue," she said in an urgent tone. "Lue, please, you have to get up." She held her hand down toward her friend. "Please."

Luella stared blankly at her offered hand, as if she couldn't see it at all and only knew its approximate location. Zayric then stood and stretched on the back of Onyx, as if waking from a peaceful nap, before jumping down, landing in front of the blonde girl. He gently nuzzled into her arm as if trying to get her attention. It worked. Luella's puffy eyes looked at him, and recognition flickered in her expression. Her arms released the corpse she was holding, laying him down gently before running a hand down Zayric's back.

When she looked back up at Raelia, she was still crying, though the choking sobs dwindled, as Luella nodded to her best friend, who handed over Prickle's reins. She quickly kissed her father once on the forehead, and then climbed atop the speckled colt.

A second later, Zayric was once again sitting behind Raelia and the three horses were galloping out of the burning village. They rode hard and fast, quickly making it to the forest's edge, only a quarter mile from Raelia's home. She looked longingly at it in the distance before the trees blocked her view.

"Wait!" she yelled to the masked stranger. "Please!"

The man slowed his horse, and let out a deep groan of frustration before turning to look at her.

"What?!" he hissed through gritted teeth.

"I want to go home," was all she could say. The words sounded childish even to her own ears, but she kept eye contact with him all the same.

"We're running for our lives and you want to 'go home'?!" he asked incredulously. "We don't have time for that!"

"We're not far from it," Raelia urged, "and the fighting hasn't made it this direction yet! Besides, won't we need some sort of supplies if we're in for a long journey? It won't take long!"

He stared at her for a moment, his eyes looking at her quizzically, like he couldn't believe what he was looking at. It was silent for a moment while he continued to look at her. Then his eyes shifted to look at Caeda's body still cradled in her arms. That seemed to break his resolve as he sighed.

"Okay, we'll go," he agreed, "but we must stay in the forest canopy so we aren't spotted. We also must be quick about it, I want to get as far as we can from here before nightfall."

Raelia smiled at him kindly, "Thank you."

He nodded, and she turned her eyes to Luella, who still hadn't said a word since climbing into Prickle's saddle. Her face was pale, and her eyes were glazed over. Tears still streamed silently down her cheeks, but she seemed to be breathing steadier than she had been before.

"Lue," she said softly. "Lue, we need to get to my house and get you cleaned up, okay?"

The blonde girl stared blankly, but nodded.

Raelia looked back to the masked man, and jerked her head in the direction of her home. "It's this way."

CHAPTER 8

It didn't take them long to follow the forest's edge to the Kesby's pasture, and sooner than expected, they were climbing off their horses behind the stables. Zayric jumped quickly to the ground, but didn't go far, plopping himself onto a fence post as he watched Raelia intently. She still clung desperately to Caeda's tiny body, which had already begun to cool. She awkwardly climbed down, nearly falling with the effort of holding onto her sister, and was surprised when she turned around to the masked man reaching for her.

"I'll bury the child while you gather the provisions we need," he offered, his voice solemn.

Raelia's gaze was piercing when she looked into those silver eyes. Logically, she knew that Caeda was gone, and had been for at least an hour, maybe more, but her emotions couldn't handle that fact. She'd been shoving them down from the moment she had watched her mother's body fall, and this offer from a stranger to bury her beloved younger sister seemed to uncork the bottle they were held in.

A sob rose in Raelia's chest, and tears poured down her cheeks, blurring her vision as she hugged the tiny figure that she cradled against her. Her knees wobbled and her entire body trembled with the weight of her grief. The man stepped forward and attempted to lift Caeda's body from Raelia's arms. The girl hugged her sister tighter, and refused to relinquish her.

She stood there sobbing, hugging onto Caeda's body with all her might, as her mind raced with the impossible turn her birthday had taken. Images flashed in her mind of the morning she had with her Mother and younger siblings. The laughs they shared around the breakfast table, Caeda's goofy grin as she tried to smile around her pancake stuffed mouth, Blaze rolling his eyes at his younger sister's antics, but having to hold back the laughter that danced in his loving hazel eyes. How had everything gone so wrong so quickly? Her head was a torrent of questions and memories, and they overwhelmed her. She felt her knees start to give way, only staying upright due to the man's strong arms catching her fall.

"Raelia, you must be strong now. There is much to do," he said in a much softer voice than she imagined possible from this stern looking man. "The first thing is to get yourself cleaned up. I will take care of your sister."

Being given a task seemed to distract Raelia. Her sobs quieted as she straightened her spine and nodded to him. She knew he was right, but when he reached once more for Caeda's body, she took a step back. "In the stable," she said in a hushed tone. "Grab one of the riding blankets, and a shovel."

Then, without another word, she walked briskly toward the gate leading out of the pasture. There'd been no reason to close it before they left the house that morning, and she was grateful she didn't have to stop to open it. She could sense Luella following her, and a moment later felt the man join in her wake as she made her way to the edge of her mother's garden.

Her eyes turned to her companions, locking on the silver eyes behind the mask, "Can you lay it out?" she asked in a quivering voice.

He looked at her quizzically for a moment before realizing she meant the riding blanket he carried. He quickly laid it out, and Raelia gently laid Caeda's body on top of it.

She knelt down next to her sister, feeling her eyes well up as she wiped the velvety black curls off of her face. She gently pressed her lips to Caeda's forehead. "I'm so sorry I couldn't save you." She felt another sob rising up in her chest, threatening to make her crumble into her grief once more. She took a deep breath and swallowed it down before whispering, "I love you, Sissy."

She stood up, silent as she wiped her wet cheeks with the back of her hand. She looked at Luella, who hadn't spoken since she climbed atop Prickle in the village square, and now stared unblinking down at Caeda's lifeless body. Raelia sighed before turning her eyes back to the masked stranger. "Please don't bury her until I come back."

Stepping into the house felt like going back in time. Standing in the back doorway, looking into the kitchen, it felt as if her mother or younger siblings could come in at any moment. Raelia shook her head at the thought, and shoved down the sob threatening to rise again in her chest.

Her grip on Luella's hand tightened as she pulled her friend through the kitchen, down past the living room, and up the stairs to her bedroom. The only sound Luella made were soft footsteps padding behind Raelia as they moved, and when her hand was released just inside Raelia's room, even those stopped.

She looked up at Luella, whose eyes were open, but blank, as if she couldn't see anything outside of the window she stared through. Raelia looked the girl over, and then looked down at herself. She stifled a sob as she looked at the gown she wore. Her mother had been so happy to give it to her, only a week before. It had been so beautiful. Now it was covered in blood and caked with dirt, the skirt had torn at the seams revealing more of her leg than she ever had before, and the hem was ragged, practically shredded up to her knees.

It was completely destroyed.

Her heart ached when she looked back at Luella. The beautiful girl was filthy. Her blonde hair was matted and stained with blood. The same blood that mixed with mud and soaked her dress. She was so quiet, which is something Raelia could safely say she had never been before. Her once bubbly, outgoing friend seemed a broken shell of herself.

"Lue?" the girl's glossed over blue eyes turned to look at her. "Lue, we need to get you cleaned up, okay?"

She nodded, but said nothing, but Raelia took that as the okay to help her clean up. She gently grasped onto her friend's hand, and pulled her down the hall to the washroom.

Luella's eyes followed Raelia's movements as she slowly cleaned the blood and grime off of her skin and hair. It didn't take as long as she'd expected, and she was surprised to notice it seemed to help wake her friend up from her shock.

When the blood and mud was gone from her friend's skin and hair, Raelia began cleaning herself. A hiss of pain escaped her lips as the rag scraped over the wound in her arm. It was long and jagged. She knew it needed stitches, but also knew they didn't have time for that, so she quickly cleaned and dressed it.

After they were both mostly cleaned up, she slowly turned Lue's back to her, and unbuttoned the now ruined dress she wore.

"I'm going to get this off of you and then I'll get you something to wear."

"Okay," Luella replied, surprising her friend. She hadn't spoken since the village square, and it was a relief for Raelia to hear her voice, even if it was smaller and weaker than normal. After stripping her down to her undergarments, Raelia handed Luella a dressing gown, and sent her into her room before heading downstairs to her mother and father's room. Luella was so much smaller than her, so none of her clothes would fit her friend, but Yaila was about the same size. She stood outside of the door for a few moments. Her hand trembled as she reached out to grasp the knob. Tears threatened to fall, but she shoved them back, refusing to let her emotions win her over once more.

"I only need to go in quickly and grab some clothes," Raelia said quietly to herself. "Just in and out. No need to linger."

After her pep talk, she took a deep breath, and twisted the knob. When the door opened, she was struck in the face with the smell of her parents. The smell of her mother. The mixture of rose and chamomile got stronger as she moved closer to Yaila's dressing table, and it took every ounce of strength she had to keep her tears at bay.

When she opened the cedar chest where her mother's clothes were kept, she quickly pulled out Yaila's riding clothes, and held them up, gauging the size. Figuring it was the best she could offer her friend, she closed the lid of the chest, and hurried out of the room, holding her breath until she had closed the door behind her.

She found Luella sitting on her bed, wrapped in her dressing gown, staring out the window in silence. Raelia cleared her throat as she came through the door, bringing her friend from her reverie.

Her eyes looked more alive than they had before, so she felt she must be on the right track. She handed her mother's riding clothes to Luella. "I think these should fit." Her voice was rough with emotion when she handed them to her. "Do you need help dressing?"

Luella stood and took the clothes from her with a grateful expression. "I think I'll be able to handle dressing on my own."

"Okay, well I'm going to-,"

"What happened?" Luella asked, her voice so quiet it took Raelia a moment to process what the words had been.

"I... I don't know..."

"Who is the man outside? Where is he taking us?"

She thought her friend wasn't aware of anything since they left the village, but clearly she had been paying some attention.

"I don't know that either."

Luella looked appalled at Raelia's admission, "You don't know where he's taking us? Rae! We can't just go riding off into the forest with some strange man we don't know!"

Raelia chewed her bottom lip. She knew her friend's logic was sound, but she also didn't see another option. Her father and brother were halfway to the tribal lands now, and it wasn't a trip she could take on her own. Her eyes flickered to the window, where she could see black smoke rising over their village, screams still echoing in the air. Who knows what would happen if they stayed here? Would the men attacking look to the homes on the outskirts once they'd finished with the main village? Would they leave when they were finished? She wished she knew the answers, but she wasn't willing to risk her or Lue's life.

When she spoke again, her voice was small, tired, and pained. "I don't know what else to do... He was sent here specifically for me. He saved me more than once during all of that, and..." Her voice trailed off, her mind processing her emotions for a moment before speaking again, "He feels safe... I know that sounds crazy, but... There's something about him that makes me feel safe."

Luella stared at her as if she had never seen her before. "Let me get this straight. You, Raelia, someone who is afraid of almost every person you come in contact with, feels safe with a bizarre looking, masked stranger that wants to take you away from everything you've ever known?!"

"Everything I've ever known has already been taken away from me!" Raelia shouted. A look of shock and hurt flashed across Luella's face, and she instantly regretted her words. She hadn't been the only one to lose loved ones today, and at least she had her father and Caias to think about. Luella had no one left. Her mother and father were all she had.

"I'm sorry, Lue," Raelia said softly, "I didn't mean to yell. I just don't... don't..."

Luella sighed, and reached for Raelia's hand. "You don't need to be sorry," she said softly.

"Something tells me it's important I go with him. I can't explain it..." Raelia added, biting her lip. "But I won't go without you. If you want to stay here, we'll stay here."

"No. I think we should go," Luella said, plainly. "We can't stay here like sitting ducks."

"Thank you."

Luella gave her friend's hand a quick squeeze before heading out and down the hallway to get dressed.

While she was gone, Raelia began stripping herself down. She set her ruined satchel on the bed before dressing in her riding clothes. She pulled out the beautiful hair pin Luella gave her earlier in the day, setting it down before she brushed out her hair and tied it into her normal, simple braid.

When she sat on the bed to put on her boots, her eyes lingered on the small pouch, now covered in blood. With trembling hands, she opened it, pulling out the dandelion journal Caeda and Blaze had been so proud to give her. She was surprised to see it wasn't damaged at all. The satchel was a complete loss, so she assumed everything inside would be too. A small smile spread across her lips as she hugged the book to her chest. Luella returned moments later and before they made their way downstairs, Raelia tucked the journal and her hairpin into an older satchel she owned before tying it around her waist.

They made their way downstairs, and into the kitchen. She grabbed one of the family's picnic baskets, filling it with easy to grab food that would keep their bellies full as they traveled. She didn't know how long they'd be on the road, but at least they wouldn't go hungry. Both girls bustled around preparing as if they were going to be traveling for a month, and, who knew? Maybe they would be.

Once everything had been packed and they were about to head back outside, Raelia handed her friend the picnic basket and blankets and told her she'd meet her outside. Luella looked at her quizzically, but didn't comment, just took the items and headed out the door. When she was alone, Raelia hurried back upstairs. Instead of heading to the left, towards her room, she turned right.

Standing outside of the two doors leading to her younger siblings' rooms, she placed her hand on the knob of Caeda's door and turned. The door swung open easily, but Raelia struggled to leave the hallway. Stepping into the room felt like a burden she didn't know how to bear. She shook her hands out, taking a deep breath as she did so, and bounced on the balls of her feet.

'You can do this,' she thought to herself. 'You have to do this. Do it for Caeda.'

Thinking of her feisty and beautiful little sister was the key. She stepped into the small room, and in three strides had made it to Caeda's bed. It was covered in frilly pink and yellow pillows, the comforter in the same colors had embroidered flowers all over its surface. Gently, she picked up one edge of the blanket, and pulled it off of the bed, folding it in her arms. She turned then, looking for the item that had brought her here in the first place.

Raelia glanced over the room, finally spotting the ceramic doll in the corner. It had once been her mother's, and Caeda loved it so dearly that Yaila had given it to her youngest child only with the promise she'd take care of it, which the young girl always had. It was pristine, and if she didn't know the backstory of the doll, Raelia never would have guessed that it was as old as it was. The soft pink dress and bonnet the doll wore were outlined in white lacy trim that was scratchy against her skin. She hugged the doll to her chest tightly, feeling the prick of emotion behind her eyes, before turning and heading back out into the hallway.

Once back outside, Raelia stood next to the deep grave the masked man dug for her sister. She set down the comforter and the doll before she lowered herself into the hole. Luella's eyes were wide, as she watched her friend, and had she not still been holding the picnic basket, Raelia was sure she would have stopped her.

"Can you hand her to me?" Raelia asked the man.

He gave her a quick nod, before running his arms under the blanket the child was on and lifting it and her up and then handing her down. Raelia had to hold back a sob when she felt the weight of her sister in her arms. She laid down the blanket and Caeda's body gently onto the soft dirt below, before turning back to the man.

"Now those?" she pointed to the comforter and doll.

He made quick work of handing them down, and once in her hands, Raelia looked at her sister. She set the doll on her side, cradled in her lifeless arm, and then gave her one more kiss goodbye, before spreading the thick comforter over her, and crawling out of the hole.

"You should ready the horses," the stranger said.

Raelia's eyes stared down at the flowery blanket, the form underneath barely even noticeable. At his words, she nodded, but couldn't seem to move. How did she say goodbye to her little sister? An image of Caeda smiling flashed in her mind and she felt tears well in her eyes.

"Goodbye, Sissy. I miss you already..." she whispered to her sister's unmoving form.

"Rae," Luella's voice chimed in with a gentle tone. "Rae, we need to go to the stable."

Her friend's voice pulled her from the trance, and her eyes found Luella's blue orbs. She nodded and then looked at the masked man.

"Please be careful with her."

He nodded, and the girls made their way back to the pasture.

Onyx and Prickle stood lazily in their stall, eating their leftover grain and hay from that morning. The horse the man rode was sharing in their food and made no notice of the girls returning. The speckled colt perked up and walked to them, rubbing his forehead on Raelia's shoulder affectionately. She leaned into Prickle's touch, and gave him a grateful pat on his side with her opposite hand.

After the girls readied the horses, adding on saddlebags to each, and filling them with items they packed, Zayric appeared. He expertly jumped from the ground to the table that sat on the wall, and from there onto Onyx's back once more. He watched them closely with his dual colored eyes, cocking his head when Raelia smiled at him.

Luella turned to her friend. "Do you know his name? The man, I mean."

"It's Rokoa," came an answer from the door.

Luella and Raelia both jumped at the unexpected voice, turning to see the masked stranger in the entranceway. It hadn't been long since they had come into the stable, and it didn't seem possible he was done yet.

At her questioning look, he said, "It has been done."

"Rokoa?" Raelia said, feeling the strange word on her tongue. "Where are-"

A howl of laughter rang through the air, followed by a horrified scream. Luella's eyes widened in terror as Rokoa poked his head out and around the corner of the stable.

He returned quickly, his face tense. "They're not far. We must go!"

It only took a moment for all three of them to pull themselves into the saddles of each horse. Raelia on Onyx, Luella on Prickle, and Rokoa on his own, the three shot out quickly from the stable, and across the pasture. Only seconds later they were in the safe haven of the forest canopy.

Raelia turned to peer back, but even though she could still hear the loud, deep laughter, she couldn't see the men it came from.

"Raelia!" Rokoa called in a hushed voice. "We need not worry about them. Let's go!"

She looked at her frightened friend, who nodded, before turning back to him and nodding as well. That was all the encouragement he needed before ushering his horse into a heavy gallop, Raelia and Luella keeping pace behind him.

CHAPTER 9

They rode through the forest quickly. It wasn't until they came out on the other side that Rokoa slowed his steed. They continued to ride north and as the sun started to set behind the hills, Raelia worried he intended for them to ride through the night. Her body ached, her eyes were heavy, and her stomach gurgled with hunger. She looked over at Luella and saw that she looked about ready to fall asleep riding — that's when she decided it was enough.

"Rokoa? Shouldn't we stop soon?" Raelia hollered to him as a shiver ran up her spine. They'd ridden much further north than she thought they would, and the weather was much colder here than it was back home.

"There's a village about ten minutes up the road," he called back to her. "We'll stop for the night."

The next ten minutes seemed like the longest of her life, and she almost whooped with excitement when she saw the lights of the village up ahead. The first building they came across was the inn, and when they stopped, a young man approached them.

"Mr. Rokoa, sir," the boy nodded respectfully. "Can I take your horses?"

A smile appeared on his stern face, making him appear much kinder and gentler, as Rokoa swung his leg down to the ground. "Yes. Thank you, Rylik."

Handing over the reins, he looked to the girls, both climbing down from their own horses.

"Rylik, this is Miss Raelia and Miss Luella. Please see to it their horses are as well taken care of as mine."

The boy grinned and nodded, as he reached out for Prickle and Onyx's reins. Zayric, who hadn't moved all day, proceeded to jump from Onyx's back, he stretched and rubbed against Raelia's leg, much like a cat, giving her a quick lick of affection as she reached down to pet him, before running off into the forest.

"Not one for a crowd, is he?" Rokoa asked with a smirk.

Raelia smiled. "No, he's not. We're quite a bit alike in that way."

Soon after seeing off their horses, the three travelers sat in a back booth of the Inn's pub, waiting for a meal.

"Are you ever going to take off that mask?" Luella asked their escort. "We know your name now. Is there a reason we can't see your face?"

"Lue!" Raelia scolded.

"What?!" the blonde retorted. "I think it's a fair question! I'd like to see the face of my travel companion!"

"I think I preferred you not speaking," Rokoa replied in a reflective tone, sounding as if he was unaware she could hear him.

Before Luella could respond, the barmaid brought over their bowls of beef stew. It didn't look appetizing, but Rokoa dug in as if it was his favorite meal. Both girls poked around at the muddy brown slop put before them, but only Raelia had the nerve to taste it.

Once the spoonful was in her mouth, she realized why their masked companion was devouring his own; the stew was delicious! It didn't look like anything special, but the thick broth was flavorful, the meat tender, and the seasonings were complementary to each other. Raelia's eyes brightened and she had to resist the urge to lift the entire bowl to her lips. When she realized Raelia was enjoying the brown sludge,

Luella gave in, and soon the only sounds at the small round table were chewing and slurping.

Rokoa finished first then stood and disappeared around the corner. The girls barely noticed his absence, as entranced with their meal as they were. He returned quickly, though, holding up a key.

"They only have one room."

Luella nearly spit her last bit of stew out. "You're joking?! We can't share a room with you!"

"Well, you could always sleep in the barn."

"Why don't *you* sleep in the barn?! It'd be the gentlemanly thing to do!"

"And when exactly did I claim to be a gentleman?"

"Lue," Raelia butt in, before her friend started yelling. "We'll figure it out. It's not a big deal. Not for only one night."

"We're *ladies*, Rae! It's improper for us to room with a strange man!"

"I'm no stranger than any other man, *Princess*," Rokoa smirked as he sat back down. "Besides, I'm not exactly a man."

Luella's pale cheeks flared red. With embarrassment or anger, Raelia wasn't sure. One thing was certain: she needed to deescalate the situation before it got worse.

"Care to elaborate on that?" she asked. "If you're not a-,"

"I'll explain once we're out of earshot of others."

That was all he said on the matter.

Both girls finished their meal and stood, following him out of the crowded pub.

The room was small, but comfortable. Against one wall, underneath a window overlooking the village square was a double bed with a blue and green plaid comforter. The pillowcases were mismatched, but Raelia was so excited at the thought of sleeping, she couldn't bring herself to care. Next to one of the side tables stood a door, slightly ajar, which she assumed was a washroom. On the opposite wall, a small sofa behind a coffee table hosted a candelabra with many arms, but only one candle.

"It's not much," Rokoa said, pulling Raelia from her surveillance, "but there's a small washroom and enough space for all of us to sleep."

A snort of disgust emitted from Luella, but before she could follow it up with something argumentative, Raelia cut in.

"Thank you," she said, grabbing onto Luella's hand and walking to the washroom, pushing her friend inside.

"You can't be okay with this?" Luella demanded. "I know you're not as fussed with propriety as I am, but *this*?!"

Raelia sighed as she turned the tap on, letting the cool water warm up over her fingertips. "We don't have a choice, Lue." She splashed the lukewarm water over her face, and grabbed the towel hanging over the sink, dabbing the water away before continuing, "Besides, it's only for one night, and I am too tired to argue about it or anything else.

"Fine," Luella said, nodding before reaching for the water, "I just... just..."

Tears welled in Lue's eyes, and Raelia set the towel down on the countertop before wrapping her friend in her arms, holding her tightly.

"Shh," she soothed just as the first sob broke free.

Luella's face burrowed into Raelia's chest, sobs shaking her round frame. She could feel her shirt soaking through with her friend's tears, but she wouldn't push her away. The loss they endured that day was overwhelming, and the grief they both felt wasn't going to disappear just because they were in a new place.

After a few moments, Luella pulled back, sniffling and wiping her cheeks. She reached for the warm water still running from the tap, and turned to wash her face.

They didn't speak again, nor did they cry. Both cleaned themselves up as best they could before heading back into the cozy room, where Rokoa sat removing his bracers. A Mark on his left hand caught Raelia's attention. It reminded her of an Indicative Mark. Strong black lines seemed to outline a flower, but on closer inspection, the head of the flower wasn't a flower at all. It was a flame, curling up and in on itself. Three dots ran up his middle finger and down from the base of the stem as well. It was beautiful. He had also removed his cloak, exposing his long silver hair that shimmered in the soft lantern light.

"You wanted to know why I wear this mask."

It was a statement, not a question, but both girls nodded in response, taking a seat on the bed across from him.

"Your kind has believed mine to be extinct for five hundred years." He reached back and slowly untied the satin ribbon holding the mask to his face.

Raelia didn't know how, but she knew before he removed it what would lie underneath. His strange silver eyes had confused her, but the silver sheen to his skin should have been a dead give away. With the mask removed and his silver tipped, elongated, pointy ears now visible, she didn't know how she hadn't seen it before.

"You're a Drykuan."

Luella nearly burst out laughing. "Don't be ridiculous, Rae!"

"I am," Rokoa replied as his eyes connected with Raelia's.

That snuffed out Luella's laughter quickly. Her eyes went wide with fear, and she grabbed onto her friend's hand. "Did you know this whole time?! Why didn't you say anything?!"

"If I wanted to hurt you, I'd have already done it, Princess," Rokoa smirked, rolling his eyes, before looking back at Raelia. "That is a good question, though. How long have you known? Most mortals-"

"I've never believed in the tales that your race is extinct. There has always been too much evidence to the contrary. I don't believe the Zarhaish are extinct either."

"You are correct," he informed her. "Most of your mortal tales get the endings wrong. Take for instance... the Red Lady."

Luella rolled her eyes, but before she could mock Rokoa's words, Raelia chimed in, "I have heard tales she is still living, but I have always been skeptical. She was a mortal woman, after all. How could she be alive five hundred years later?"

"That is a question you'll have to ask her."

"Wait... What?!" Raelia gawked at him. "What do you mean ask her?! Is that... is that who...?"

"The Red Lady sent me to collect you, yes," Rokoa confirmed. "She has been watching over you your entire life, and when she heard about the attack on the village, she sent me to keep you safe."

This new information baffled her. "When you say she's been watching over me...?"

"The council woman who let you live only did so because the Red Lady paid her. She's had people monitoring you and your family ever since your council exam."

This new information explained so much. It never made sense the way her mother told the story. Raelia definitely had thicker and longer hair than most infants from what she'd been told, but the way people talk about the council — the thoroughness of their evaluations — it never sat right for Raelia that they just happened to miss her Mark.

Her mind raced with questions, but there was only one she could get out, "why me?"

"It's not just you. Every council throughout the Kingdom has someone watching for Mark Bearers. It is important for the magic to survive. It is important that the wielders of the magic survive. Vysha has her spies all over the Kingdom."

"Vysha?" Luella cut in.

"The Red Lady's name is Vysha," Rokoa responded, his eyes never leaving Raelia. "Never let her hear you call her the Red Lady. She hates it."

Soon after their conversation, the three settled in for the night. Raelia tossed and turned for hours. When she did finally fall asleep, her mind repeated images of the day's events. The nightmares tore her from slumber, then she'd be tossing and turning once more.

By the time sunlight peeked through the small window, she had decided it wasn't worth the effort to try sleeping any longer. She got up and made her way into the small washroom to clean herself up.

When she walked back into the small room, Rokoa sat awake with a cup of tea in his hand. He gave her a groggy smile, lifting a second cup out to her.

Raelia smiled and stepped across the small space, taking the mug from him gratefully as she sat next to him on the small sofa.

"Thank you."

"You're welcome," he answered. "You didn't sleep well."

It wasn't a question, but a statement, and Raelia felt her cheeks flush.

"I'm sorry. Did I keep you up?"

"Not at all," he replied. "Don't worry yourself over my sleep. I assure you, I slept fine."

She smiled at him before lifting the steaming mug to her lips, the smell of chamomile, a scent that would forever remind her of her mother, overtaking her senses.

Rokoa cleared his throat. "I'm sorry. For your losses, I mean. It is never easy to lose one's family."

The unexpected mention of her family brought on a flood of emotions. It took her a second to compose herself enough to speak, but when she did, her voice was calmer than she felt.

"I never thanked you for saving my life."

"There are no thanks necessary," he replied.

"Isn't there? You saved me. You saved my best friend. Neither of us would be here if it wasn't for you."

A flicker of emotion flashed across his features. Sadness? Guilt, maybe? It was gone before Raelia could identify it and before she could question him, he spoke once more.

"You are different than I expected."

"I am?" she asked, surprised by the change of subject.

"You are stronger than I thought you'd be," he explained, "and kinder."

"I... Um... Thank you?" Raelia was taken back by his words, confused as to what made him think that she wouldn't be kind or strong in the first place.

Rokoa laughed lightly and nodded. "It is a compliment, I assure you."

"If you say so," Raelia replied with a small smirk.

He grinned back at her, amused, as they both took another sip of their tea.

Once Luella woke, and they had all eaten a quick meal in the pub, the three of them walked to the stables. All three horses were saddled and waiting. Rylik smiled brightly as they came in.

"Mr. Rokoa, sir, the horses have all been fed and tended just as you asked."

A smile spread across Rokoa's normally stoic features as he bent down to the young boy's level and handed him a small coin bag, looking ready to burst. "Thank you, Rylik. I will be forever grateful for the care you take of my dear Rosette."

The boy's eyes were wide, as he grasped onto the bag of coins, and his mouth gawked. Rokoa chuckled slightly, bringing him out of his daze. He quickly put the coin bag in an inside jacket pocket and looked up with a grin.

"The fox you rode in with was in a right state last night. He was trying to get into the Pub, but Mr. Headler wasn't having it," Rylik said to Rokoa, as he pointed upward, "I made him a space to sleep in the loft with me though! Didn't want him to freeze outside!"

As if he'd heard the young boy, Zayric popped his head into view from up above, and hopped his way down to their level. When he hit the ground, he walked right up to Raelia, and put his front paws on her knee, begging to be picked up. She obliged him and gave him a cuddle while Rokoa finished with Rylik.

Once everything was squared away, and they had loaded back into their saddles, they were off again.

Riding at a more manageable pace this time around, Raelia enjoyed watching the sights around them as they traveled through the countryside. The long ride became monotonous and tiring quickly, however, and she felt relief when they finally came to Gourdist, the largest northern village in Dirythia.

"We'll stop here for the night," Rokoa told them as they turned the horses toward the stable. "We'll need to get provisions before we head out tomorrow morning. There isn't another village to stop in before we hit Paodra tomorrow evening."

Both girls nodded their understanding, and soon they were climbing down from their horses, and once again handing over their reins to a young stable boy. This one didn't seem to know Rokoa, but was kind enough to all of them.

It seemed being kept from Raelia the night before had traumatized Zayric, and when they went into the pub that hosted the upstairs inn, he pawed at her to pick him up.

She obliged him, and snuggled him close when she lifted him to her chest. Rokoa's eyes widened when he saw the fox in her arms, as if surprised at the affection they showed each other.

He turned his body to face hers, stopping her forward progress. "You cannot bring him in. They will not allow it."

"But-"

"The owner is a very superstitious person. If he even sees the beast, he will turn us away!"

Raelia's heart fell. It was so cold outside, and she didn't want to send Zayric out on his own for the night. As if he understood the exchange between the two of them, Zayric lifted his head, licked Raelia's cheek gently., and then his entire body became a white smoke disappearing on the wind.

Luella's eyes widened in shock, and Raelia remembered that her friend had not seen Zayric's power. She still thought he was an everyday fox pup.

"Wha-" she began, her mouth hanging open on the word.

"I'll explain when we get into the room," Raelia answered, realizing she didn't know how to answer the question Luella asked, her eyes shifted to Rokoa.

"Or rather I will," he said with an amused smirk.

After they ate a meal in the pub, and Rokoa spoke to the innkeep, they headed upstairs for the night. Luella entered the room first, and let out a small shriek of surprise.

Rokoa burst past her, preparing to draw his sword, when he noticed Zayric sitting where Luella's eyes focused. A smirk appeared on his face, as Raelia peered around his broad shoulders.

"Zayric!" she exclaimed, just as surprised as her friend. She rushed across the small space and scooped the fox up in her arms. "What are you doing in here?!"

Zayric yawned, and stretched up to put a paw on Raelia's chin.

Rokoa chuckled. "I didn't know that a kyloxis bonded with mortals."

"A what?" Luella asked. "What in the world is a kyloxis?"

"It's a mythical beast," Raelia said, recognizing the name from a book she read years prior. "I thought they were dogs. Not foxes."

Her eyes were curious as she looked at the content pup in her arms.

"They can take the form of any canine, including foxes."

"Oh," she responded, feeling stupid for not having a more eloquent response.

"What did you mean by saying he's bonded to her?"

"They normally shy away from all beings. Even immortals. However, there have been a few stories I've heard through the years," Rokoa explained, reaching a gentle hand out to scratch Zayric behind the ear. "Some have bonded with immortal beings. Usually ones they feel safe with, or that they sense have a strong power or need for them."

"Well, I think we know why Zayric chose you," Luella laughed, as the fox rolled onto his back in Raelia's arms, exposing his belly to them all.

A smirk appeared on Rokoa's face, before he turned and started out the door.

"Wait! Where are you going?" Luella asked, confused.

"Tonight, I'm sleeping in a bed," he smirked. "I'm in the room across the hall, if you need me, *Princess.*"

Luella's face scrunched with irritation as he shut the door behind himself.

⁓

When Raelia and Luella met Rokoa downstairs early the following morning, he held out thick, warm jackets for each of them to put on, explaining it would only get colder as the day continued. They took them gratefully, and it wasn't long before they were loaded up and riding out once more.

Today the ride felt longer than the two previous days. Maybe because Raelia was so tired, or maybe because there wasn't a stop to break up the time spent on the horses. Either way, she couldn't help but sigh in relief when Rokoa told them they were only an hour outside of the Paodra Forest.

As the end of the hour ticked closer, Luella spotted a large, dense forest a couple miles ahead, which, when asked, Rokoa confirmed to be their destination. Watching the trees get larger on the horizon felt like counting down the minutes on a clock before an anticipated event. Everything seemed to be moving slower than it should. It was maddening.

As they approached the first few large evergreen trees, Rokoa pulled his mare to a halt, turning to look at his riding companions.

"We need to go on foot from here."

He swung his leg down, and started into the forest. The girls followed suit, looking at him in confusion when their feet hit the ground.

Zayric sat on Onyx's back and watched curiously as Raelia grabbed onto Onyx's reins and headed further into the trees, following Rokoa deeper into the thick canopy of trees.

They didn't make it far before all three horses became jittery. They pulled back on their reins, stopping their progression and refusing to move any further into the dense trees. Onyx's eyes were alert, and fearful, which surprised Raelia. She'd never seen him seem scared before. Prickle spooked easily, but Onyx never had.

"Okay," Rokoa sighed, "this is far enough. We'll go ahead alone from here."

"WHAT?!" Raelia shrieked. "I'm not leaving our horses behind! They won't be safe!"

"You misunderstand me," Rokoa soothed.

Before she could question him further, the Drykuan stretched his arm from his body, palm outward, and waved it in a half circle above his head. The next second, a soft whooshing sound met her ears, and all three horses and Zayric disappeared into thin air. Both girls gawked at the places their horses had been before looking back at Rokoa.

"Nevermind your questions," he said before they could speak. "They are safe, and waiting for us inside."

"Inside?" Raelia questioned.

Rokoa only smirked and waved for them to follow him.

They walked for a few more minutes before their guide stopped once more. This time in front of a small, perfectly round clearing. It seemed almost unnatural in its perfectly circular shape. Raelia wanted to ask about it, but before she could form the words, he stepped into the open space.

Chapter 10

Two large trees stood in the center of the clearing. Both of them entwined with the other. Branches, roots, and trunks wrapped together as a snake wraps around its prey. The only thing making it clear there were two separate trees and not one large was a gap between the trunks.

As Raelia followed Rokoa into the circular space, she noticed the sounds of the forest became muffled the closer they stepped to the moss-covered trees. Standing only a few feet from the small opening between them, silence overtook her senses. Not only did the sounds of the forest creatures disappear, even their own movements were silent. Their feet stepped onto dry leaves, and pine needles, and yet no crunching or rustling came from their footsteps.

Raelia looked to Rokoa, who didn't seem phased in the slightest. She tried to ask what had happened, but when she opened her mouth, nothing came out. Her lips moved over the words. She could feel her throat and vocal chords tensing with speech, but there was no sound. She looked at Luella and realized she looked equally confused.

When she turned back to Rokoa, he was watching her with an amused expression. He smirked and held up a finger, asking for her to wait a minute. She gave him a terse nod, and he turned toward the small open crevice between the two mossy trunks.

He moved his hand slowly, palm outward toward it, and Raelia let out a silent gasp of shock. Before he could touch it, his hand disappeared from the end of his arm. The further in he reached, the more of his arm disappeared. Just when his elbow vanished, and Raelia worried she needed to step up to pull him free, he began pulling his arm back out.

Sliver by sliver, his arm became visible again, and when his hand fully reappeared, he held tightly onto a circle of what appeared to be an ivy vine. He pulled it back, leaning into the movement, when there was a sudden click. It wasn't audible. It made no sound, but Raelia felt it deep in her chest, like a popping joint.

She looked to Luella who, she was surprised to see, watched her, fear clear in every line on her face. Raelia reached out to grasp her friend's hand and squeezed it reassuringly, before turning back to see Rokoa opening the crevice.

Her jaw dropped as the Drykuan appeared to fold the wood of each tree as easily as one would fold the pages of a book to mark their place. One side, then the other, until there was an opening wide enough for him to step into.

He looked up at her and let out a silent laugh at her expression before putting one foot into the open hole and stepping down. It only took a few small movements before he completely disappeared, and Raelia was left to gawk at the place he had been. She jumped when Rokoa's arm poked out to wave her in. It was an eerie sight, even knowing the arm belonged to him. Seeing it float and move on its own, free of a body, was enough to give anyone the creeps.

Her eyes shifted to Luella, whose face was horror stricken. Even though there was no sound, Raelia could imagine her friend was letting out a terrified scream. She squeezed her hand once more, drawing

Lue's attention, and the girl shook her head as Raelia attempted to pull her closer to where Rokoa disappeared.

Releasing the girl's hand, Raelia put a hand on each of her shoulders and stared directly into Luella's terrified blue eyes.

"We'll be okay, but we have to follow." She spoke the words, but no sound came out, and she watched for a sign that Luella understood what she was trying to convey. Thankfully, she swallowed deeply, before nodding to show Raelia her readiness to step into the unknown.

Grabbing her friend's hand once more, she took a step closer to the opened crevice. She stepped one foot in at a time, surprised to feel a step underneath her. The second foot followed, stepping next to the first. When she looked down, she realized she could no longer see her feet, which felt strange by itself, but knowing she also had to figure out how to get her whole body into this crevice without seeing how, was a whole other level of weirdness.

Slowly and carefully, she scooted her foot forward a few inches and felt the edge of a stair. She dragged the bottom of her foot on it as she pressed downward a bit more, and realized there was another stair after the second. Raelia repeated the movement a few more times and when she looked again, from her chest down had completely vanished.

As the invisible barrier approached her neck, she looked back at Luella, who was following her down, the horrified look on her face was almost comical. Her jaw hung open, and her eyes were wide, but she continued to follow after her friend. Raelia bent her knees momentarily, her eyes dipping under where the barrier met her neck, and was shocked to see an entirely different scene. Rokoa stood smiling at her, and sound reverberated in her ears once more.

She looked at her feet, realizing they were only a few stairs up from the bottom, and she took them quickly, being careful not to pull Luella down by their connected hands in her excitement. Her hand stretched barely above the barrier, still wrapped with her friend's, her rich amber skin a stark contrast to Luella's pale white. When she looked up, she understood why Rokoa looked so amused — from below there didn't seem to be a barrier at all. It seemed only open air. She couldn't tell where the barrier was on Luella at all, and looking up at her friend's terrified face at what appeared to be only a staircase, made Raelia smile as well.

She looked at Rokoa from the corner of her eye. "Can she hear me now that she's so close?"

"Could you hear anything when you got close?"

She shook her head, and a crooked grin appeared on her face. "I guess that was a stupid question."

Luella's face lit up with relief when she was able to see them once more, and her audible sigh let her know her ears were working properly again.

"What was that?" she asked, looking at Rokoa. "Why couldn't I hear anything? And what is with that invisible hole?"

While Luella threw her exasperated questions at the man, Raelia's eyes roamed over their surroundings. They were in some sort of tunnel. The only source of light came from two sconces on either side of the staircase. Soft green flames shot through with streaks of gold, danced happily within each, and the delicate light they emitted seemed brighter than should be possible. The dirt path beneath their feet was a deep, rich brown similar to the soil her mother used in her garden bed. It led into a long path behind Rokoa, though past the lights edge there was only inky darkness. The walls and ceiling were rounded together, and covered in a thick, dark green moss that had an ethereal glow in the delicate light. She ran her fingers over it gently, and pushed her hand into the pillow-like cushion it created.

"-it's the magic surrounding this place," Rokoa was saying as he watched Raelia take in their surroundings. "If you hadn't been with me, you would have turned and gone from this place before you could search any further."

"What do you mean?" Raelia asked, intrigued.

"Didn't you feel it?" Luella asked. "The pull to turn around?"

Raelia shook head as Rokoa reached up, and swept his hand into the soft dancing flame. He pulled it out to reveal a bit of the green flame in his palm, before turning to walk toward the darkness.

"It's how mortals are kept out of the forest," he explained. "It's an ancient magic that's been in place for longer than most of us have been alive. When a mortal enters the *triseyule*, or the 'silent place,' as a lot of Mark Bearers call it, something within the person tells them to leave. Most don't make it even a step into the silence barrier before racing back the way they came."

The girls followed him quietly, listening to his explanation, as the flame illuminated further down the slightly inclined path. Raelia dragged her fingers along the mossy surface of the walls as they walked, and it made her heart feel lighter than it had since before everything went so very wrong only two days ago. It reminded her of riding into the forest with a book, and laying on the moss covered ground to read. She used to lay there for hours turning page after page.

"Are you enjoying yourself? Have you never seen moss before?" Rokoa asked. His tone sounded critical, but when his eyes connected with hers, amusement glimmered in them. "I've never seen someone so enchanted with the tunnel walls."

Raelia pulled her hand away sheepishly, and looked down. "It's just very beautiful, is all."

He smirked and turned back to continue on the path they were following, as Luella squeezed Raelia's other hand reassuringly. She squeezed back, and they continued in silence.

A few minutes later, a light appeared at the end of the darkness, and Raelia felt a flutter of nerves in her stomach. It seemed so far away, but it only took a few moments to reach, and when they did, she realized it was the same light as before. Soft green flames shot through with streaks of gold in identical sconces on the mossy wall.

When he was close enough to touch the flames, Rokoa upended his hand over one of them and let the smaller flame he'd been carrying dump into the sconce. Both flames merged, as if never having been separated. Both girls watched on in wonder, as Rokoa stepped up a small set of stairs leading to a wooden door.

Stepping into the sunlight seemed blinding after the dimness of the tunnel, and both girls squinted against it as they came through the doorway. As her eyes adjusted, Raelia saw the compound that Rokoa explained on their journey, but there was so much more than what he said, and she smiled at how beautiful it was.

The lush, tall pine trees were massive, the trunk of each seemed to be the size of her family's home, and between every two of them were small cabins, all roughly the same size. Most of them seemed to have a second level set up a little way up the tree from the main cabins. Spiraling, wooden staircases that wound around the outside of each tree connected the two levels of the homes. The wood they were made from matched the bark so closely the stairs seemed to grow from the trees rather than built against them, as she assumed they would have to be.

In the base of some of the enormous pine trees were ornately carved doors seeming to lead directly into the trees themselves. No cabins or staircases were built into them, so it made Raelia curious to see people walking in and out of them.

"Those doors lead to the underground market," Rokoa's deep voice said, interrupting her thoughts. He pointed to the right of the doors Raelia had been looking at and added, "and those doors lead into an underground community made up mostly of Mark Bearers. That's likely where you'll stay while you're here."

Her eyes shifted to the door he indicated, and she nodded, before she heard Luella's voice behind her. "And what about those, er, cottages? Are the levels up high separate homes, or connected by the stairs?"

"The ones between the trees usually house the city guards when they are on duty. The houses above are mostly homes of the Zarhaish," he answered, turning to look at her. "It is hard to see through the branches, but most of these trees have three to four homes built upon them. The ruling family designates who gets to live where." Rokoa walked across the main square they stepped into, before continuing, "Most of my people live below the earth, not in the trees."

Only a few small groups of people strolled through the square. Their voices were quiet as they spoke amongst themselves, but Raelia noticed many eyes watching them as they followed behind the tall, silvery Drykuan. The hushed tones in which the other people spoke made Raelia feel as if she was on display. It made her skin crawl, and even knowing she was in a place that was safe for her, she pulled her braid over her shoulder to make sure her Mark remained hidden from view. They turned left just past one of the cottage's and relief flooded through her when they moved out of view of the onlookers.

"Is there a reason we're being watched so closely?" Luella asked as they approached one of the ornately carved doors. Apparently, Raelia wasn't the only one that noticed the others' attention.

"Most know that Vysha sent me to get someone of importance," Rokoa answered as he pulled open one of the large doors leading into the earth. "They don't know which one of you I was sent for, nor do they know why, but it is a rare day when the Red Lady sends for someone, so they are intrigued at what it could mean."

"And what does it mean?" Luella pushed.

"You're about to find out, Princess," Rokoa answered.

As they entered into the tree, Raelia was stunned at the grandeur of the entry hall. The walls were made of the wood of the tree they'd entered, elegantly carved from the floor, up the walls and across the ceiling with twisting vines and leaves. Raelia realized after a moment the pattern used was the same that embroidered Rokoa's cloak. The stairs they walked down were also made of the tree's wood, and were sanded and polished into a perfectly smooth surface.

Much like the tunnel they'd entered into the village through, the walls and ceiling rounded together making an exquisite hallway. The honey color of the wood brought out the beautiful lines and knots of its grain. Fixtures holding the same beautiful green flames were mounted every few feet along both sides of the walls.

The stairs down seemed nearly endless, but eventually they reached the last step, and Rokoa led them into a long hallway where a number of decoratively carved doors lined the walls. They passed all of them, and turned left at the end of the path. Dimmer than the others, the new hallway had only a few sconces to light their way, and no doors except for at the very end where an enormous set of double doors stood, glimmering in the soft green light.

Made from the same polished wood as the floor and walls, the pattern carved into it was different. Instead of leaves and vines, flowers of all different kinds were whittled deep in the surface. The largest of the designs, spread across both doors, was massive in comparison to the others. Starting from the bottom left corner, two dandelions were twisted around each other, the head of each releasing their seeds that seemed to blow in a curved line upward to the right top corner of the door. A small gasp escaped Raelia's lips when she realized that the large carving perfectly matched her Indicative Mark.

Rokoa didn't miss her shock, and smirked at her surprised expression. "Look familiar?"

A nod was her only response. As they came close enough to the door, her fingers gently ran over the surface of one of the dandelion seeds, following onto a much smaller carving of a poppy flower, then a hydrangea, and after that a lupine flower. As she looked, it seemed every flower she'd ever seen or studied was represented by a carving in this door.

"It's beautiful," she said, eyes still gliding from blossom to blossom.

"They represent the Marks found under each of the six natural elements," Rokoa informed her. "Every one of those is the design of a different Indicative Mark. Each Mark holds its own power."

Raelia spent most of her life avoiding even thinking of her Mark. She'd never had even an ounce of curiosity about what her Mark meant or gave her, but seeing it like this, seeing the shape of her Mark carved into the beautiful wood, clearly the centerpiece of all the other smaller flowers, intrigued her.

"I thought there were only four elements," Luella chimed in as she looked at the door.

"Mortals don't account for things they do not understand," he said, plainly.

"Fire. Water. Earth. Air. There's more than those?" Lue asked.

"There are," Rokoa answered. "Humans, or at least, Dirythian's always leave out Light and Shadow. Fire, water, earth, air, light and shadow. Those are the six elements."

Luella scrunched her face. Raelia recognized her friend's irritation, and before Lue could argue with the Drykuan's insulting attitude, she asked, "So each flower belongs to an element?"

"Not exactly," he replied. "Every flower represents a distinct gift. Each gift falls under a specific element."

"If each flower has its own gift, why does it matter what element it falls under? How do you know which gift falls under which element?" Raelia's mind raced with this new information, and was surprised to feel genuine curiosity. Much to her father's chagrin, she'd avoided learning anything about Indicative Marks or their powers her entire life. Wanting to know more about it seemed foreign to her. "Are all the powers element-based? For instance, would someone with a water flower control water?"

"Not exactly," Rokoa answered, his eyes curious as he watched her continue to look at the door, entranced by every flower.

After it seemed he wasn't going to say more, Raelia turned her eyes to his. "Care to elaborate?"

"Not really," he returned with a chuckle, placing his hand on the door. "Wait here."

In a swift movement, he pushed the door open, stepped through and closed it once more, leaving Raelia and Luella alone in the dim hallway.

Luella cleared her throat, drawing her friend's attention. "Rae?"

"Hmm?"

"I don't like this," she said. "It feels like we've walked into a wolves den... I want to leave."

"I can't leave until I know why she sent for me," Raelia replied.

"She's the Red Lady, Rae! You know what the stories say about her even better than I do!" Luella continued, "She's violent! She massacred 200 people in a matter of minutes! Anything she wants can't be good!"

"Lue, I-,"

"So, you're the new dandelion, huh?" a bold voice interrupted from behind them.

Both girls turned, blinking into the dim light of the hallway to see a tall figure taking a deep inhale, as though smelling the air, as they glared at them. The person was thin, but clearly strong. It was apparent not only in the way they stood, but also by the sculpted outline of their exposed arms and stomach muscles. They wore a tight top that stopped just below the bust, and had no sleeves, leaving their shoulders and arms bare. Their form fitting pants were torn in a few places on both legs, and their boots looked similar to the heavy ones Raelia had seen soldiers wear, though they buttoned up to the knees.

In the hollow of their neck a Mark caught Raelia's attention. Similar to the one on Rokoa's hand, it had strong black lines and looked like two flames swirling together and apart. These flames didn't have a stem as Rokoa's had, however, there were leaves and three dots around the outside edge of one of them.

It took a minute to process the person before them, and out of the corner of her eye, she noticed Luella's jaw hanging open in shock. Raelia had always been far from what anyone in Dirythia would call 'proper', but even she was shocked at the scantily dressed person before them. Luella on the other hand was proper to a fault, and Raelia didn't think she would be recovering from the scandal of them anytime soon. If the stranger's body didn't curve in the chest the way a woman's did, between the way they dressed, and their shortly shorn hair, she would have assumed the person who'd spoken was a man. As it was, she wasn't sure how to refer to them. Were they a she or a he?

The newcomer smirked, as they scrutinized the pair, eventually connecting their golden eyes with Luella's blue. "What's the matter, blondie? Never seen a stomach before?"

Raelia glared at the newcomer, but before she could defend her friend the door behind them opened, and Rokoa stepped out. His eyes were dark as he looked at the person before them, but he bowed respectfully before speaking. "Dhovina."

The smirk remained on Dhovina's face as they walked past all three of them, nodding in return at Rokoa, and into the room beyond. He closed the double doors again before speaking in a hushed tone, "Did they say anything to you?"

He seemed concerned, almost fearful, which surprised Raelia. He didn't seem to be someone who would fear anything or anyone. That this person invoked such an emotion from him made her nervous.

"Nothing of importance," Luella chimed. "Just a snide comment. Is it normal for women to dress like that here? She's wearing pants for gods' sake!"

"Pants are worn by all here, not just men," Rokoa replied. "That being said though, Dhovina is not a woman. They are a *Fludrian*."

"A... what?" Luella asked at the same time Raelia said, "Oh!"

A proud smile flickered across his features when he realized she knew the word. He nodded to her, indicating Raelia should explain to her friend.

"*Fludrian* is a Taevik term for someone who is neither male nor female," she told Luella. "Sometimes they're called 'In-Betweens,' too. While their bodies align with one sex or the other, their spirit doesn't."

Luella looked at her as if she had grown an ear in the middle of her forehead. "How is that even possible?"

"It is something that's a natural part of the world. Not only for your kind, but for immortal kinds as well," Rokoa answered. "Even the world's animals do not always align one way or another. Honestly, it seems the only creatures in the world who don't understand it are Dirythians."

Luella flushed at the obvious jab, causing Raelia's anger to flare. This wasn't the first time Rokoa made such comments, and they always seemed to point at her friend. She opened her mouth to respond, but once again, was interrupted.

"Vysha is ready to meet you."

Chapter II

Raelia's mouth closed, and her throat went dry. When she tried to swallow, she found there was a lump in the way. She didn't fully understand why she was so nervous. She had read every story she could ever find about the Red Lady, fascinated by the histories about her, and had wanted to know everything she could about her. Now presented with the opportunity to not only learn about her, but meet her face to face, she was scared out of her wits.

"You needn't worry, Raelia," Rokoa reassured her. "She has been waiting to meet you for eighteen years."

"I'm not sure that helps in the way you think it does," she said with an awkward chuckle.

She felt Luella's fingers entwine with hers, and squeeze gently. "You aren't alone, Rae."

She looked at her friend, whose bright blue eyes were focused on Raelia's green. Something in those cerulean orbs filled her with the strength she needed in the moment, and she nodded once to Luella before turning to the man in front of her.

Without another word, Rokoa turned and pushed open the double doors, this time leaving them open as the three walked through.

The room before them was magnificent. Beautiful blue fabric draped from ceiling to floor, complimenting the green mossy walls.

The wooden floor beneath them was smooth under their feet, and she could tell it had been polished recently, its shine giving it away.

Ahead of them, a massive throne on a dais, the seat made of the same beautiful wood as the floor, only it wasn't as smooth. Intricately carved into the wood were the same flowers she'd seen marking the door. The large entwined dandelions, the same as her Mark, made the entire back of the seat, where a statuesque middle aged woman sat before them.

Her long, jet black hair fell in silky waves to her waist, and her dark brown eyes washed over both of the girls, before pinning on Luella.

"I sent you for Raelia," the woman said, her tone rich and commanding. "Why have you brought along a spare?"

Raelia felt anger rise in her as Rokoa quickly knelt, bowing his head over his knee.

"Forgive me, Vysha," he replied. "Raelia did not want-,"

"I wouldn't leave my friend behind," she interrupted, stepping forward, next to Rokoa's kneeling form. "Rokoa is not to blame."

Vysha's eyes pierced Raelia like a knife through the heart. Nerves grew within her, but she held her composure, staring back at the woman with a strength she didn't feel.

Suddenly a person entered Raelia's line of focus, leaning in to whisper something to Vysha.

Dhovina.

When Raelia widened her scope of view, she noticed three people standing next to the throne on which Vysha sat. On one side, Dhovina, still whispering in Vysha's ear. On the other, a petite but curvy Drykuan woman with long black hair knelt at the feet of what looked to be a normal woman, one not unlike herself.

"Beings that do not possess magic are not permitted in the confines of Paodra, and that one," Dhovina, pointing to Luella, explained in a harsh, angry tone, "stinks of mundane, human blood. She does not possess any magic qualities." Her eyes shifted to Rokoa. "*He* knows that."

Stepping forward once more, Raelia's eyes connected with Dhovina's, body tensing with frustration, anger flaring once more. "As I said before, it is not Rokoa's fault. Either Luella came with us or I didn't come at all."

Vysha reached up to put a hand on her companion's pale, golden arm. "It's alright, Dhovina. Raelia has a strength of will that most have never seen. I have no doubt Rokoa would have failed in his mission to get her here had he not allowed for the human to accompany them."

Her body relaxed, grateful Vysha clearly understood the situation. Dhovina, however, scoffed.

"He knowingly brought a—"

"It is none of your concern." Vysha didn't raise her voice, but her tone was unmistakable. The discussion was over.

The golden sheen glistening from Dhovina's pale skin grew bright. The rage in their eyes flashed at Raelia, before the Zarhaish stormed down the steps, right past the three of them, leaving out the door in which they'd come through.

"Now, Raelia," Vysha started, ignoring Dhovina's tantrum completely. She stood, stepping down the stairs to where the three of them stood. Once close enough, she took both Raelia's hands in her own, grasping them tightly. "I am so happy to finally meet you, though I am so sorry for the circumstances."

Raelia didn't know what to say. She couldn't understand why, of all people, the Red Lady wanted to meet her, and the reminder of what she'd lost, the reason for her standing there in the first place, caused her breath to hitch in her throat.

Vysha smiled, continuing as if she couldn't see the pain in Raelia's eyes. "I'm sure you have many questions, and I have much to tell you. Where would you like to start?"

Before she could respond, Vysha gestured to the far wall where a large table surrounded by eight chairs stood. The woman walked over and pulled out the chair at the head of it.

"Let's sit, shall we?" Vysha's smile was kind and welcoming. She turned to Luella and Rokoa, and then the two women still next to the throne, gesturing for all of them to sit as well.

"Now, Raelia," Vysha started, once everyone was seated, "I assume you have plenty of questions that Rokoa hasn't answered yet?"

She cleared her throat, trying to give herself more time to think. So many questions ran through her mind. She wanted to know about the magic and the other Mark Bearers. She wanted to know how Vysha had been alive for over five hundred years. She wanted to know...

"Rokoa mentioned you sent him for me when you found out Frayis was going to be attacked," Raelia's voice was quiet, but curiosity rang through. "How did you know the attack was going to happen?"

Raelia thought Vysha's eyes were the darkest color she'd ever seen, but somehow they darkened even more at her question. She watched as the elder woman pursed her lips, deciding how to word a response.

"I have a number of spies throughout the Kingdom. Most of them on various Perception Councils to save our kind. To save the magic," Vysha explained. "They keep me informed of babes born with Indicative Marks."

"Yes," Raelia nodded, "he mentioned that."

"Williana, the Council member who discovered you... Well, she went missing recently," Vysha continued. "About a week ago I got word that Royal Guards had taken her captive. That is also when I learned she had betrayed your secret."

Raelia's eyes widened in confusion. "My secret?"

"The secret of your existence," Vysha replied. "Under their torturous interrogation, she revealed your identity to the King. She told him about your Indicative Mark."

"I... I don't understand..."

"My dear," Vysha said, stretching her arm out to take Raelia's hand, "they attacked the village in search of *you*. In the eyes of the King, the villagers have been harboring you." The woman sighed heavily. "He made an example out of them."

Raelia's breath caught in her throat as her heart hammered against her chest. Her mind raced with images from the attack. Watching her mother's body fall, then Blaze's, then Caeda's. She watched them and others fall over and over again in her mind.

'It's my fault,' her mind screamed. *'It's all my fault!'*

"Be-because of m-me?" was all Raelia could stammer out.

"The descendants of King Nikolai are as greedy and bloodthirsty as Nikolai himself. They are terrified someone with our power will rise to take the Kingdom from them," Vysha explained. "I'm told when King Calyx learned of you, he went into a rage unlike any other. He ordered the execution of every man, woman, and child in the village of Frayis."

Raelia didn't have words. Her mouth hung open in disbelief. Her blood went cold, the guilt spreading through her was physically painful — as if all over her body icy blades stabbed her repeatedly. It took everything in her to look back at Vysha when she continued.

"It's my fault," she said, sorrow coloring her tone. "I should have sent for you the minute I heard Williana had gone missing. I should have sent for you years ago, really. Only," she sighed, "you seemed so happy there with your family."

Swallowing down a sob, Raelia found her voice. "Were there any others that were found out? Did Williana give any other names, I mean?"

"Yours was the only name to give."

"How is that possible? Are there so few Mark Bearers?"

"Not overall, but those left with their families? Yes, there are very few in Dirythia still living in their family's care," Vysha explained. "Williana explained your Mark was well hidden, so there wasn't concern you would be discovered. At least not for a long while after your council review."

"And if that hadn't been the case? What would have happened then?" Raelia asked.

"For babes that make it through their Council reviews, whose Marks aren't as easily concealed, we approach the parents, and offer safe haven for their child here in Paodra." Vysha smiled, softly. "Quite a few of our residents here came to us as infants. For those that can't bear to be separated from their child, we offer them safe passage into the tribal lands where they can live unafraid of the vengeful monarchs."

"How many Mark Bearers live here?"

"A little under 200," a soft, delicate voice answered.

Raelia had nearly forgotten the two women sat across from them, and her eyes found the rich jade green eyes of the one who answered. Eyes the same shade as her own.

"I'm so sorry. Where have my manners gone?" Vysha said, as she gestured to the two women on her right. "This is Ekry," she said, indicating the Drykuan woman whose cold eyes glowered at Raelia, before gesturing to the woman who'd spoken. "And this is Jamina."

"It's nice to meet you," Raelia and Luella both said, nodding their heads.

"Jamina is also a Mark Bearer."

Raelia had never met another Mark Bearer before, and at Vysha's announcement, her eyes went wide. Jamina smiled back brightly, as she ran a hand through her rich brown hair and tossed it to one side, revealing a flower outline along the left side of her neck. It was larger than Raelia's Mark, and very prominent with her hair moved out of the way.

"Is that an oleander flower?" Raelia inquired, fascinated.

"Yes!" Vysha replied, pride clear in her tone. "Jamina is our only Oleander here in Paodra. How did you know that?"

She tore her eyes from the tattoo-like Mark on Jamina's neck and looked at Vysha, her cheeks warming, "My mother. She's a-," Raelia cleared her throat, and looked down to hide the pain she felt at the mention of her mother, "she *was* a healer. She taught me about a lot of different plants. Especially the ones to stay away from."

"Well, what a pleasant surprise!" Vysha responded, clapping her hands together.

"What-What power does the Oleander provide?" Raelia asked, eyes looking to Jamina for the answer, but again Vysha spoke.

"Jamina has a useful ability. She is able to help me find other Mark Bearers in need of help."

Confusion colored Raelia's features as she turned to look at Vysha once more.

"I can track people," Jamina explained. Raelia's eyes looked back to the dark-haired woman before her, as she continued. "If I know the person's name, I can see them in my mind and scent them."

"Scent them?" Luella asked, clearly intrigued.

Jamina's friendly smile vanished, her eyes darkening when she looked at Lue, who nearly cringed away from the withering look she received.

"What does that mean?" Raelia chimed in.

"I know what they smell like," the girl replied, smile returning as she looked back at Raelia. "It's hard to explain, but if I know their name, the image in my mind comes along with a scent. I'm able to track their scent to find them."

"You can track the scent of someone you've never even met?!" Raelia's shock got the better of her as she gawked at Jamina.

The brunette smirked and nodded. "I can find anyone with only their name. Of course," she added, "the scent becomes stronger the better I know someone, so it's easier to find people I have already met."

"Wow," was all Raelia could reply. A smile touched her lips as she looked closely at the Oleander Indicative Mark and her mind raced with questions she wanted to ask.

Vysha cleared her throat, pulling her from her thoughts. "There are a lot of amazing talents here, and yours is no exception."

That made her falter. "I-I don't have any talent, though. I mean, I have a Mark, but I've experienced no powers."

"As a Dandelion, your powers will appear when you need them," Vysha told her. "The dandelion isn't held down by one element, as most Indicative Marks are. It can touch on gifts from all the elements, and manifests in a unique way for every one of its bearers." Vysha reached out and squeezed Raelia's hand gently before pulling it back. "The dandelion is meant to watch over the others. That's why it's not tied to any specific element. Your power will show itself, you have my word. And, if you're willing, we'd love to train you here. You'll learn to call your gift forward and wield it. It's not always something that comes naturally, but it's important you know how."

Raelia tugged at her braid, making sure it was still in its proper place covering her Mark. The idea of other people having powers was fascinating to her, but the idea of having powers herself was a different thing entirely. A terrifying thing. Her eyes raked over Jamina's exposed

Mark once more. It was beautiful, and the gift it provided sounded so interesting, but she wasn't sure she wanted to know what kind of power she might possess.

"What's wrong, my dear?" Vysha's concern was clear in her tone, and her eyes looked at Raelia with worry. "Don't you want to know how to wield your power?"

Raelia took a deep breath, and twirled the ring on her finger around, trying to calm her nerves. Touching the ring made her think of her father and his voice rang through her mind, speaking in his native tongue, *'Dialev Diyalay.'* 'Calm child.' It soothed her, and when she spoke once more, it was with a confidence she didn't feel.

"I think this is just a lot to take in right now. Sleep hasn't been kind to me on our journey, and-,"

"Oh! My sweet *Aldaehima*! Say no more," Vysha exclaimed, flashing her a warm smile, "you must be exhausted! And here I am chittering on!"

'Aldaehima.' Raelia was surprised to hear the elder woman use the Taevik term. She knew it meant 'Dandelion,' and that others had already been referring to her as such, but she wasn't sure how she felt being referred to it in the Taevik tongue. Something about it didn't sit right with her, but she let it go for the time being, too tired to fight it.

Vysha turned to Rokoa.

"Will you please show our guests to their room, Rokoa? I think it's time for them to get some proper sleep." She turned back to Raelia then. "Tomorrow we can continue our conversation, and you can meet more of us."

Vysha looked to Luella then, her eyes losing a little of their vibrancy. "You will have to be careful here, most of us have not been treated kindly by the Magicless community, and we aren't used to being around those who do not share our gifts."

Luella nodded her understanding.

A few minutes later, after a few farewells and 'nice to meet you's', Rokoa led them back down the long hallway and up the stairs into the fresh air. He took them across the main square and to the wide double doors he'd pointed out when they arrived. Luella walked closer to Raelia's side than she normally would. When she looked at her friend out of the corner of her eye, Lue was chewing the inside of her lip nervously.

When they approached the double doors, Raelia noticed the wood was carved beautifully, as all the other doors were. Instead of flowers, though, this one was decorated with leaves and vines, even a pinecone here and there. The call to nature in this place made her feel more comfortable than she'd expected.

They went through the doors, and once again followed Rokoa down a long staircase. This one, however, led them into a large room. It had the same beautifully polished wood floors and mossy walls, but seemed to be more for people to relax and socialize.

In the center of the room were a sporadic placement of tables, all of which seemed to have some sort of games or books on their top. Large, overflowing bookshelves lined two of the massive walls, and when she saw them, Raelia had to restrain herself from running over to peruse the titles. There were easily five times the amount of books here than in her father's study.

There were large plush sofas, the likes of which Raelia had never seen before, with massive pillows for the seat and backs of them. The mossy green couches were grouped sporadically around the edges of the room and they seemed to get good use, as there were groups of people on almost all of them.

Raelia noticed quite a few people in the room had zeroed in on their appearance following their progression across the large space. It made her skin crawl. She felt like she was on display, and she really hoped that the 'newness' of their arrival would wear off soon. She hated being stared at.

"This way," Rokoa said, cutting into her thoughts.

She looked back at him as he took a swift right down a long hallway. They only walked past a few doors before he reached for a knob on the left.

Rokoa stepped in and held the door open for them to follow. "Vysha sent someone to prepare this room for you both. Tomorrow, we can talk about other arrangements, if this doesn't suit." He looked at Luella, as if he expected her to complain about sharing living quarters with her friend, but, caught up in her thoughts, Raelia wasn't sure she'd even heard what he said.

"Where are the beds?" Raelia asked, confused when she walked into a cozy sitting room. The couches were smaller in size, but the same style as the ones in the big room they had just walked through, and there was a small coffee table in front of them. Behind one sofa was a tiny circular table with four chairs around it, much like the one that sat in her family's kitchen back home. Her heart ached at the reminder.

"Around the corner, you'll find a room for each of you, as well as a washroom," he explained. "You should both eat and get to sleep. It's been a long journey, and I'm certain you're tired."

Rokoa waved his hand, as he'd done in the forest earlier, and heaping plates of food appeared on the small table. Raelia's mouth watered at the inviting aroma, her stomach groaning with hunger she hadn't realized was there before the food appeared.

"I'll stop by in the morning to show you around further," Rokoa said, stepping out of the room.

"Wait!" Raelia called. "Where did you send our horses? And Zayric?"

He smirked at her, eyes twinkling with amusement. "The horses are being tended to in the stable. Zayric, on the other hand, well, let's just say you'll know which room is yours." Rokoa chuckled, as he said, "Goodnight," and shut the door behind himself.

Raelia let out a sigh of relief. She didn't know what she'd been expecting, but she was happy to know Zayric waited for her, and Prickle and Onyx were being tended to.

She turned to Luella then, who had come only far enough into the room to sit rigidly on the edge of one sofa. Her eyes were distant, and she was still chewing at her bottom lip, nervously.

"Lue?" Raelia said, walking over to her friend. "Lue, what's wrong?"

"Nothing," Lue's voice was small, unsure. "Let's eat."

She stood up, and Raelia watched as she sat at the table and started to pick at the food before her. She followed, sitting at the second plate, and just as before, her mouth started watering.

The roast chicken and potatoes smelled amazing, and she was surprised to see steamed beets on the table with a few other vegetable dishes. They were her favorite, and she couldn't grab them fast enough.

Knowing Luella didn't like them, and hoping to pull her from whatever this stupor was, she wiggled a piece in front of her friend.

"Lue! Look! It's your favorite!"

The girl just rolled her eyes and took a bite of her chicken, not saying a word. Raelia followed suit and fell quiet as they ate.

The food was delicious, and before she knew it, she was dishing up a second plate.

"Rae? We need to talk," Lue said.

"Going to tell me what's going on?" she asked, a concerned look crossing her features as she popped a bite of potato in her mouth.

"I think we need to leave."

"What?!" Raelia nearly choked, not expecting the complete turn in conversation. "Why would we leave? Eventually, I mean, yes, but we just got here and we have nowhere else to go!"

"I don't trust Vysha," Luella said, simply.

That pulled her up short. "But... *why*? What reason has she given you to distrust her?"

"There's not one specific thing," she explained, "but something is just... just... *off* with her — with this place."

"You're just tired, Lue. There's nothing wrong with this place," Raelia replied, "and Vysha is kind! She's excited for us to be here!"

"She's excited for *you* to be here. You heard her, I'm not wanted here!" Luella said, her voice rising as anger crept through her. "She practically told me I'm in danger here!"

"Oh Lue, you're being dramatic! She said to be careful – not that you were in danger!"

"She implied it!" Luella said, standing now. "I don't trust her! I don't trust any of these people! I don't want to stay here!"

Raelia stood as well, completely baffled by her normally too trusting friend. "You're imagining something that's not there, Lue! We're safe here!" she tried to reason. "Besides, where would we go if we didn't stay here?"

"We could ride to the tribal lands," Luella argued. "Your father, and Caias, that's where they are! You have family, Rae, we need to find them!"

Raelia had done her best to push down the thought of where her brother and father were. Even though they were her only family left, she was a coward. She couldn't face the pain they would feel when they found out the rest of their family was gone. That *she* was all they had left. That *she* had failed to protect her mother and younger siblings.

And now, knowing it was her fault they were gone... How could she face the anger they would feel when they found out?

"And how on earth are we going to get to the Tribal lands with no money between us? We couldn't even make it to Frayis again on our own, let alone that far south!"

"They need to know, Rae!" Luella nearly shouted. "You can't let them show up at home and find it empty! They don't deserve that!"

"I know they don't!" she shouted, emotions swirling in her, tears pricking in the corners of her eyes. "But what else am I supposed to do?!"

"Vysha said they help people flee to the tribal lands. Why not ask her to help us get there?"

"I thought you didn't trust her?" Raelia said, rolling her eyes. "If you don't trust her, why would you want to rely on her to get us there? What is this really about?"

"I ALREADY TOLD YOU!" she yelled, turning red in the face. "I don't want to be here! I'm not safe here! And there is a woman who is over five hundred years old that is building an army!"

Raelia scoffed in disbelief. "Building an army?! Why would you say that?!"

"She said she wants you to train with them! Why would you be training if not to fight? If not to learn how to use your magic against people?!"

"She's not building an army! She's protecting people like me who are forced to live in secret! She's making sure we can defend ourselves!"

"Raelia! Don't be so naïve! You know the stories about the Red Lady even better than I do!" Luella rolled her eyes. "I know you aren't used to being around people, but even *you* have to see she's up to something?!"

It was true the legends about Vysha spoke of her malicious and violent ways, but the stories spoke of all Mark Bearers that way – not just the Red Lady. Raelia couldn't imagine the woman they met tonight was as violent as they say.

"Legends aren't kind to any of us! It talks as if all people that possess magic are evil by nature!"

"Maybe they are! You've met no one else with a Mark until tonight! What if they're all just as violent as the stories make out?!"

Raelia felt her heart fall into the pit of her stomach. It would have been kinder for Luella to slap her. She never believed her best friend could believe the very worst of her, but now she wondered if she'd always been waiting for her to be violent.

Luella's face showed an instant remorse for her words, but they had triggered Raelia's anger to reach a tipping point.

"This isn't about Vysha at all, is it?" Her voice was low and seething, becoming a shout as she continued, "For once, precious Luella isn't the center of attention! For once, you have to look on as I am sought after! Something I've watched happen with you for years, but this one time someone wants me, and *not* you, and *you* can't handle it! What?! Don't you like the shoe being on the other foot?"

Raelia didn't give Lue a chance to respond before turning on her heel and marching down the hall, indiscriminately choosing a room and slamming the door closed. Leaning against the door, she slid to the ground as tears began to slip down her cheeks. She jumped at a sudden touch on her leg.

Zayric.

He rested his paw on her and cocked his head, clearly worried. The anger she felt quickly fizzled and turned to hurt and guilt as the pup crawled into her lap, nuzzling her. She scooped him up in her arms, and walked over to the bed, throwing back the blankets. She cocooned herself in them and tried her best to go to sleep.

Chapter 12

The following morning, when Raelia woke, the pit in her stomach that appeared after her fight with Luella last night had grown. It felt like a watermelon sized stone sat there, and she knew it wouldn't go away unless she worked things out with Lue. She couldn't bring herself to wait for her friend to wake, though. She was still angry and plagued by guilt. No matter how much she knew they needed to talk things through, she wasn't ready.

She hurried to dress and braid her hair. In minutes, she was out the door, down the hall, and climbing the stairs to the outside. It surprised her to see the large lounge room so empty, and even more so when she stepped into the morning light to see no one in the main square.

She looked up, noticing the sky above had only begun to lighten, and mentally cursed herself. She'd been in such a hurry to get out before Luella woke she didn't pay attention to the fact it was barely sunrise.

"No wonder no one is up," she grumbled to herself.

A chuckle from behind caused her to jump. She turned around to see a tall, slender person smiling at her as they stood leaning against the large tree she'd come out of. Their dark, rich, sepia skin shined beautifully in the morning light, and Raelia couldn't help but smile back.

"Oh! Hello!"

"Hey," they replied. "You're one of the new arrivals, right?"

They stepped closer, their features becoming more clear and defined. It surprised her to see the person wore makeup around their eyes, and what she had taken for long shorts was actually a short, but loose fitting skirt. She remembered Dhovina from the day before and realized this person must be a *Fludrian*, as well.

"Yes. I came in yesterday afternoon," she answered. "My name is Raelia."

"I'm Nazario," they replied, holding their hand out to her. "Most call me Naz."

She took their hand, shaking it gently. "It's nice to meet you, Naz."

"And you," they said, still smiling kindly at her. "I'm usually the only one up at this time of the morning. Where were you headed in such a hurry?"

"I-uh, well, I have no idea. Just needed some air, I guess," she felt her cheeks warm at her feeble reasoning. "What are you doing up so early?"

They gestured to where they'd been leaning, and Raelia saw an easel with a large canvas on it.

"I like to get up early to draw," Naz told her, a light blush appearing on their cheeks. "It's quieter, so I can focus better."

"What do you draw?" she asked, intrigued. She never had a talent for art, but always admired those that did.

"Portraits mostly." They walked over to the easel, gesturing for Raelia to follow. "I've always found people fascinating. Don't judge me too harshly, please," they requested with an embarrassed chuckle.

She gasped when her eyes saw the portrait in front of her. The blonde hair and blue eyes were drawn exquisitely. The curve of the jaw and the bright smile were features she'd recognize anywhere. Luella.

Raelia gawked at the beautiful portrait. "But that's-,"

"The girl that arrived with you yesterday, yes."

"How did you capture her so well in such a short amount of time? I mean, we haven't even been here for twelve hours yet!"

Naz awkwardly scratched the back of their head, color rising on their cheeks. "I get a little bit carried away when inspiration hits."

The awkward laugh that followed their statement reminded Raelia of herself when someone would call her out for reading through the night.

"Now, that's a sentiment I can understand," she laughed.

"Something about her hair..." they started, "it just... I don't know... the way it danced when the light hit it. Probably sounds stupid..."

"Not at all," she reassured with a kind smile. "I know exactly what you mean!"

They smiled back at her, and for the next while, the pair chatted about the portrait. It didn't take long for Naz to pull out a large satchel holding dozens of rolled up papers. Each one contained a stunning work of art. Some painted, some just sketched, but every one was absolutely beautiful. Raelia had never known anyone so talented before.

As they talked, the world around them seemed to come alive. People emerged from doors in every direction. Some from above, some from the underground homes. A few people waved to Naz as they headed past.

Raelia was fascinated by Nazario, and the more they spoke, the more true that became. Not only were they a talented artist, but Raelia learned they possessed the Mark of the Lupine Flower which gave them the power of illusions. Which she, of course, wanted a demonstration of immediately.

"Oh, come on!" she begged. "You can't just tell me something like that and not show me!"

Naz laughed. "Okay, okay!"

In her next breath, she stood on a rocky beach, the salty sea air enveloping her completely. The water before her, crashed on the shore, and seemed to go on forever, no other land in sight. A soft breeze rustled through her hair, which now hung in loose tendrils down to her waist. Her clothes changed too. Instead of her filthy riding clothes, she now wore a white linen dress fluttering as the wind caressed it.

She stepped forward a few steps and squatted down to dip her fingers in the water. It was cold, icy even, reminding her of the river back home. Her heart ached at the thought. Suddenly the world stretched, throwing her back into reality when it snapped back into place.

The sudden change in scenery, and the jolting feeling she had just experienced, made Raelia's stomach tighten. She felt nauseous and had to close her eyes for a moment to keep the world from spinning.

A couple of deep breaths later, she opened her eyes once more, and looked around her. She was further into the square than she'd been before – still squatted down trying to touch a river that was no longer there. When she turned back, Naz stood in the same position, a look of mild bewilderment on their face.

"What happened?" she asked, as she stood and walked back.

"I'm not sure," Naz told her. "You seemed to pull yourself out of it. I've never seen that happen before."

"I didn't mean to pull myself out! I could have stayed there forever," she said, dreamily, "it was beautiful!"

Raelia felt a hand grip onto her shoulder, and whirl her around.

"Rokoa!" she said, surprised.

"I thought I told you I would come for you this morning."

"Oh! I, well...," To be honest, she'd completely forgotten about it by the time she'd gone to bed the night before. The argument with Luella wiped it from her mind, and this morning she'd raced out so quickly, she didn't have a chance to remember. "I'm sorry! I completely forgot!"

"Where's Luella?" he asked.

"Hey..." Naz's voice interrupted from behind her, their hand gently coming to her shoulder. "Are you okay?"

Something flashed in Rokoa's eyes at their question, but it was gone before Raelia could identify it.

Quickly, she turned her head to look at them. "I'm fine! This one just seems to be living with a stick up his butt."

She smirked and then laughed at the baffled expression on Rokoa's face.

A few hours later, after she and Rokoa retrieved Luella from their room, the three of them had seen most of what Paodra offered. He'd taken them through many of the tunnels and showed them some of the tree-top homes. He showed them where the Mark Bearers trained, not only to use their Indicative abilities, but also how to fight, something that brought a smug smirk to Luella's face.

The training arena was an expansive space. Over the left side was a loft area accessible by two spiral staircases at either end. Attached underneath the overhang were a dozen, evenly spaced black punching bags, where a few people were hitting the firm surfaces.

On one side of the arena there was a sparring ring, on the other, rows and rows of different weaponry. Swords, maces, lances, flails, it seemed every kind of weapon Raelia had ever seen had its place, and there were even more that she hadn't.

"In the loft," Rokoa said, pulling back her attention, "there's a small seating area to oversee the trainees. You can't see it from here, but there are two doors leading to an outdoor archery range, so all the archery supplies are up there as well.

At the thought of using an actual range, a flicker of excitement bloomed in Raelia. She'd always loved archery, but had to hide her efforts to learn, as her mother never approved of her picking up what she deemed a 'men's hobby.' Her eyes lingered on the loft, as she and Luella followed Rokoa to the exit, only turning her eyes back to him, once it was out of sight.

They continued on, following the Drykuan through the twists and turns of many hallways until they came to a stop once again.

"And here is where everyone gets their meals," Rokoa explained, arms extended, gesturing to the large room around them, as if they'd finally reached the highlight of the tour.

Similar to the lounge room down the hall from where the girls slept, this one didn't have any books, but had quite a few more tables and chairs. Plush sofas dotted along the walls, here and there, but instead of a deep, mossy green color, these were a rich red. They reminded Raelia of the cherries her father brought back with him from the palace every year.

Rokoa led them to a small window-like opening in the wall. There was a counter at the base, behind which stood an older Drykuan woman.

"Hello, Brixxi," he greeted the graying brunette with a flirtatious smile. "How goes the life of my beloved?"

Raelia couldn't help but be surprised at the Drykuan's change in demeanor. He was usually so unfriendly and tense, but now he seemed relaxed and charming.

Brixxi giggled like a schoolgirl in response, flopping her hand at him. "Oh stop it! You're young enough to be my grandson!"

"I don't believe that for a second!" he smirked.

The older woman shook her head. "You're incorrigible," she laughed. "Now, what is it you need?"

He smirked and chuckled, gesturing to Luella and Raelia behind him. "I thought you might want to meet the new strays I brought home with me yesterday."

Luella emitted a disgruntled 'hmph' at his remark, but smiled at the woman behind the counter. "How do you do?" she asked with a proper curtsy. "I'm Luella."

"What a beautiful name!" Brixxi smiled, nodding to Lue, before looking at Raelia. "And you must be the new dandelion?"

"I'm Raelia," she replied, reaching her hand out to shake the other woman's.

Brixxi grasped it firmly. "It is an absolute pleasure! You've been the subject of much debate since Vysha sent for you," she chuckled, piercing her with a searching gaze. "It will be fascinating to see how much of what's been said is true."

Raelia felt her cheeks warm. She'd been right then. That's why they'd all been watching her. She wasn't sure how many of them had figured out *she* was the bearer of the Dandelion Mark, but she was sure that's what they were all trying to determine.

As if he could sense Raelia didn't know how to respond, Rokoa cleared his throat. "Brixxi handles kitchens here. I highly recommend you get on her good side now."

Brixxi rolled her eyes at him, as she reached for a folded up piece of parchment from a pile at the edge of the counter. She waved for the girls to step closer, and unfolded the paper in front of her, laying it flat on the wooden counter.

"I don't offer this to most people, but as you're so new, I'm going to give you this to take with you. It's a list of everything we make here in the kitchen. You use it to order the food you'd like."

She slid the parchment closer to Raelia, where she was able to read it easier. The writing was loopy and elegant, and there was a stream of very light, decorative lines along the left side of each column on the list. It seemed like there were foods from every part of the world on it, and her stomach growled at all the tasty sounding dishes. Different steaks, stews, pastas, even cakes all seemed to grab her attention, and she realized how hungry she was.

"These all sound so delicious," Luella said. "Can we get something now, or do we have to wait for a specific time?"

A bright smile spread across Brixxi's features. "You can order anything you want at any time. Someone is here at all hours."

"You haven't asked *how* you order yet," Rokoa interrupted, a sly smirk on his face.

Raelia's eyes knit together, not sure what he meant.

"Don't we just come here and tell you what we want?" Luella asked, clearly as perplexed as Raelia was.

"If that's how it worked, there would be a line around the room all day, every day!" Brixxi chuckled, her olive skin stretching to reveal a pristine smile.

"Well then," Raelia started, "how does it work?"

"The secret is in the list," the elder woman explained. "Look closely, don't you see it?"

Raelia's eyes looked to the parchment once more, focusing closer on the decorative lines along the edges of each group. Next to each dish was a picture of a tiny rose entwined in the curly lines. She hadn't noticed them before, but now she was amazed she'd missed it.

Each rose glowed faintly in a pale, light blue color, and seemed to hover above the page, almost as if it didn't touch it at all.

"The roses?" Raelia asked. "They... Are they... What are they?"

"Well, that's how you let us know what you'd like to eat!" Brixxi told her. "You hold down the ones that are next to the food you'd like for three seconds. Go ahead," she encouraged. "Give it a try!"

Without hesitation, Raelia pressed her finger on the rose that stood next to 'shrimp curry'. It was a funny sensation, tingly, and cold, as she counted to three, then released it.

"Now in just a moment, you'll have your-"

Raelia jumped as a dish of food appeared before her, the smell of the curry engulfing her senses.

It smelled fantastic, and Luella quickly crowded next to Raelia to get a look at the small paper she'd used to place her order.

"Go on, dearie," Brixxi encouraged her with a chuckle. "Give it a go!"

Without hesitation, Luella pressed the rose next to Beef Stew. It appeared the same way Raelia's had, almost instantaneously.

"Why don't you two sit down," Rokoa told them, gesturing to a table near to where they stood. "I have a couple of things to discuss with Brixxi. It won't take long."

The pair nodded, grabbing their meals and special menu, only stopping when Brixxi gestured for them to wait.

She took the paper from Raelia, and pointed to a small rose in the upper left hand corner. "Press this when you're done," she told them with a smile.

She nodded and took the parchment back, following Luella to a table. Neither of them had eaten since last night, so there were no words exchanged before they tucked in.

After a few minutes, Rokoa appeared, sitting across from Raelia with his own plate of brightly colored and unusual food. It smelled just as amazing as her own, but she didn't know what it was. She watched him as he speared a bright pink ball onto his fork and popped it into his mouth.

"Is there something wrong?" Rokoa asked, quirking up an eyebrow at her.

"I just, uh, what *is* that?" she blurted out.

He smirked as he speared another pink ball and held it out for her to inspect. "It's called a *gristoa*," he told them. "A berry that grows here in Paodra."

Raelia's eyes scoured the small fruit. It reminded her of a radish in shape, but the pink was vibrant, iridescent, — as Rokoa twisted the fork in his hand, the pink shifted into a stunning violet.

"It's similar in texture to your potato," Rokoa continued, "except it has a tangy, sweet taste. It makes the *very* best nectar!"

Reaching into his jacket, Rokoa pulled out one of the menus, and laid it flat, touching a finger to it, as he popped the second gristoa into his mouth.

In an instant, two glasses of bright pink liquid appeared in front of him. He slid one to each Luella, and Raelia, giving them an encouraging smile.

Raelia picked up the cup before her, peering into the vibrant liquid. It swirled with thin strands of purple and smelled more floral than she expected.

When she brought the glass to her lips, it was a struggle not to gasp out loud. It *was* delicious! The best she'd ever tasted, and she downed the glass in two deep pulls. She noticed Luella did the same, a grin spreading across her friend's face as she set her cup down.

"What is it called?" Raelia asked, pulling her own parchment out and scouring through the items listed.

"One glass is enough," Rokoa laughed. "Trust me!"

He reached to take her menu, but she slid it out of his reach. "One more glass won't hurt!" she told him. "Oh! Here it is!"

She held down the rose next to *'Gristoa Nectar'* and grinned when her glass appeared. She quickly ordered another for Luella as well, and once again, they both quickly drank the sweet and tangy liquid.

Before she could order a third, Rokoa flicked his wrist, pulling the paper to himself — as if attached to an invisible string.

"Eat," he told her, pointing to the curry in front of her. "We have other things to see, and I'd like you to remember how to get around."

Luella giggled, covering her mouth just before snorting. Both Rokoa's and Raelia's eyes shot to her, widening in surprise, as she tried to control her laughter.

A smirk crossed his features, as he shifted his gaze to Raelia. "Hopefully, you're not such a lightweight."

After they'd finished eating, and Luella finally got her giggles under control, Rokoa continued his tour. When she stood from the table, Raelia understood why he hadn't wanted her to drink more of the nectar. Her legs felt shaky beneath her, and the lights seemed to twinkle in a way they hadn't before, making the colors of the world slowly swirl around her in fascinating beauty.

She was distracted when Rokoa spoke while he guided them about. He took them to visit the stables, allowing Raelia to check up on Onyx and Prickle. If the swirling colors of the world hadn't clued her in to the effects of the nectar, the fascination she had with Prickle's soft muzzle definitely did.

"Aren't you glad you didn't have a third glass?" Rokoa asked with a chuckle. "I would have had to carry you back to your room."

The trio soon started the trip back to the living quarters. It had taken a couple hours for Raelia to feel herself again, and she had to admit, she *was* happy she hadn't had a third glass, though she'd never admit that to him.

They walked down a narrow path, headed toward the main square of Paodra when an angry shout echoed through the air, surprising the three of them. Rokoa darted ahead, turning the corner quickly, Raelia following closely on his heels, and Luella following her.

When the square appeared before them, she noticed two people in the center. A tall man stood shouting at the other, who was curled in a ball at his feet. There were at least a dozen onlookers, not including themselves, but all seemed to be too afraid to get close, standing a far distance away, looking ready to bolt out of sight if need be.

Raelia stepped forward, stopping next to Rokoa as the man standing lifted his arm. It took her a second to realize, as he brought it down, there was a whip in his hand, the cracking reverberated through the square mingling with the screams of the person at the man's feet.

"How *dare* you?!" the man shouted. "You will learn to do as you're told, one way or another!"

"I'm sorry, sir," the person cried. "Please, I'm so sorry!"

The man continued shouting, as Raelia looked to Rokoa next to her, "What's going on?"

Her eyes went wide at the fear etched in every line of the Drykuan's face. She'd never seen him look like that before. The silver sheen of his skin seemed to flicker, as his eyes watched the whip with terror.

"Rokoa?"

He didn't answer.

The man continued his rampage, his whip cracking loudly again, this time ripping open the back of the person's tunic. They screamed in agony.

The pain in their cry reverberated through Raelia's chest, and her feet moved of their own accord.

'How could anyone treat another person like that?!' she thought to herself, storming forward, and ignoring Luella's cry for her to stop. *'Nothing they could do deserves this violence!'*

The man raised the whip again, his voice echoing as he continued to shout.

Another crack.

Another scream.

When she got closer, she noticed the man holding the whip had the golden shimmer of a Zarhaish that seemed to dance upon his pale skin. Much like Rokoa, this man's ears were long and came to a sharp point, but instead of silver, the tips faded into a strong gold color. He also had the same Mark at the base of his neck that she'd seen on Dhovina. The woman on the ground, she realized, had the silver sheen of a Drykuan, though she couldn't make out her features, crouched on the ground the way she was.

The man lifted his whip once more, and Raelia hurried to put herself in front of him.

"STOP!"

Her voice was commanding and strong, but it didn't stop her from wincing when the man's hand started its descent once more.

The whip's thin leather struck her, tearing into the thin linen of her dress, and wrapping around her shoulder in a way that seemed intentional, as the man used it to pull her to him.

"Who *are* you?!" he growled out, the gold shimmer over his olive skin seeming to brighten in intensity with every word. "What do you think you are doing?!"

"What do you think *you* are doing?!" she spat back. "She's on the ground and bleeding! Surely, she's had enough?!"

Before he could answer, the thudding of heavy feet running caught their attention. Both turned to see Rokoa speeding toward them. He grabbed her arm roughly, painfully, and yanked her away, bowing his head.

"Forgive her, Qiralst, sir," he said in a fearful tone. "She is new here. Only arrived yesterday. She has yet to learn her place."

It was silent for a moment, as Qiralst eyed them both. The only sound the muffled sobs of the Drykuan woman behind them.

His voice was deep and gravelly when he spoke to her once more, "You must be Vysha's new pet."

It wasn't a question. It was an accusation.

"You are correct, Rokoa," he agreed. "She hasn't learned her place. That much is obvious."

"Yes, sir. I will take her with me now, so that-"

"You will do no such thing," Qiralst told him. "Let go of her, and return to where you came from."

Rokoa's grip tightened momentarily, before she felt his hand release her, trembling as he did so. He stepped back from where she stood, arm still wrapped in the bullwhip, and kept his head bowed.

She felt a wave of fear course through her as her gaze connected with the large Zarhaish. The corner of his mouth twitched upward, and his eyes grew dark with menace as he yanked the whip from her body. She winced as it slid across the wound on her shoulder, but stayed silent, refusing to give this man the satisfaction of her cries.

"Privina, get up," he ordered his victim, his eyes never leaving Raelia's.

The short round woman did as she was told, keeping her eyes on the ground, as blood dripped from her wounds, "Yes, Master Qiralst. How may I serve you?"

"You are to hold this bearer tightly as I teach her what her place is."

Without another word and before Raelia could even react, the Drykuan woman moved at supernatural speed, grabbing and turning her around so her back was toward Qiralst. Privina held both of her wrists with one hand, crossing them and pinning them down, while her other hand wrapped into her hair. Her fingers gripped tightly against her skull and pulled her head forward painfully.

Raelia cried out, and her heart pounded in her ears as she wrestled to free herself, to no avail.

"Now, *pet*," Qiralst mocked in a slimy tone that made her skin crawl, "why don't we try this again?"

She flinched at the sound of the whip whistling through the air, chilling her to her bones. She closed her eyes, her mind screaming in defiance as she continued trying to wriggle free of Privina's grasp.

'Don't you dare!' her mind shouted while her mouth screamed, "No! Let me go!"

She waited for the pain, wincing in anticipation, but none came. She heard the whistle and then the crack of the whip once more, and again felt nothing. She didn't understand what was happening.

A deep growl of frustration echoed through the square, and twisting her head just a smidge, allowed Raelia to see that it was coming from Qiralst. He was whipping and whipping, but the thin, braided leather never touched her. The whip stopped inches from her body, as if it was hitting an invisible barrier between them.

Throwing his whip to the side, the enormous Zarhaish grabbed onto Privina and threw her away from them, separating the two women. Raelia cried out in pain, as she felt her auburn hair being ripped from her head with the speed and force at which he threw the small Drykuan to the ground.

His grip on Raelia's arm was excruciatingly tight as he lifted her face to his own. Her feet dangled above the ground, as he searched her eyes for answers.

"What was that?! What *are* you?!"

"What she is, is none of your concern!" a regal voice cut through the air from behind the large man. Vysha stood, feet from him, glaring daggers at Qiralst. "She is not yours to touch. *Put. Her. Down*," she ordered.

Raelia wasn't sure what she'd expected, but when her body was lowered, and her feet came in contact with the ground once more, she realized she never believed that Qiralst would listen to Vysha.

Why would such a powerful being let himself be ordered around by a human?

"Now let her go."

His grip loosened, and Raelia could feel the reluctance as his hand released her arm.

Qiralst glared right back at Vysha with a hatred that made Raelia quiver in fear. He stepped to where Privina lay on the ground and yanked her up. She let out a squeak of pain, and then without another word, Qiralst dragged her out of the square in a blur of speed.

"Are you alright, *Aldaehima*?" Vysha asked, as she stepped towards her.

Raelia's eyes still watched the corner where the two had disappeared as she answered, "Uh-Yeah... Yeah, I'm fine."

She turned swiftly to face Vysha when she felt the woman's hand on her uninjured shoulder.

"You're bleeding. Let's get you cleaned up."

She gently pulled her arm, hooking her hand onto Raelia's elbow, and guided her toward Rokoa.

Luella appeared quickly, worry pasted on her face, as she wrapped an arm around her friend's waist, opposite of Vysha.

They were silent as they walked towards their living quarters, and Raelia was surprised when they didn't turn down the hallway toward hers and Luella's room.

"We'll take you to see Nafeezar. He'll get you cleaned up," Vysha told her. "Rokoa, why don't you take Miss Luella to their chambers? I'll see Raelia makes it back soon."

He silently nodded, and grabbed Lue's elbow, pulling her away.

Raelia watched them disappear before being pulled into a sterile medical room.

CHAPTER 13

After her wound was cleaned and tended to, Vysha walked Raelia back to the room she shared with Luella. It seemed much quicker this time around, and she was surprised when they were at their door sooner than expected.

Before she opened it, Raelia looked at Vysha with a sheepish expression. "I'm sorry for causing so much trouble... Thank you for stopping him."

"There is no need to thank me," Vysha replied. "You are here under my protection. Qiralst knows that. He doesn't like it, though," she sighed, seeming to deflate. "You need to steer clear of him. He will not take kindly to what happened today, and I cannot always be there to make sure he doesn't harm you."

Raelia nodded, as the woman continued.

"You are a very powerful being, and there will be people, Zarhaish, Drykuan, and Mark Bearer's alike who will wish harm on you," the woman said. "You must give them no reason to come after you. They will watch for one."

Raelia didn't know what to say to that.

"I will leave you now. Get some rest," Vysha told her. "You'll need it for tomorrow."

Before she could ask what tomorrow held, Vysha disappeared. Not down the hallway, not into her living quarters. She just vanished.

Raelia didn't know how long she stood there, standing and gawking at the place where Vysha had been, but eventually, she came back to her senses and walked into the cozy living quarters.

A blur of blonde hair tackled her before she took two steps through the entrance, nearly knocking Raelia off her feet.

"Lue?" she said softly, returning her friend's embrace. "Lue, what's wrong?"

"Why did you do that?!" Luella demanded, voice muffled against Raelia's shoulder. "What in the world would possess you to go against an enormous mythical being?! I thought he was going to *kill* you!"

"I'm okay, Lue," she assured her. "Really. I'm sorry I worried you."

Luella's blue eyes were puffy and red when she pulled back to look at her. "Are you sure you're okay?"

"I'm sure."

She took a step back, taking a deep breath before smacking her on the arm. "Don't ever do that again!"

Raelia laughed, putting her hands up in surrender. "Okay, okay."

With that, Luella sat on the sofa, looking at her friend expectantly. Raelia moseyed over and plopped next to her on the plush couch with a sigh. She didn't want to fight again, but she knew they needed to talk after everything they'd said to each other the night before.

"I'm sorry," Luella offered. "What I said last night was inexcusable, and I am so sorry for hurting you. You're right. I don't have a solid reason for not trusting Vysha, other than histories that have never been kind to any person who is able to wield magic. And..." she looked down, wringing her hands in her lap before continuing, "I know they can't all be like that, because you're not like that. I wish I could say you were wrong last night, but you weren't. I'm not used to being an outsider, and I think, along with the loss of everyone and everything we love being so fresh..." her voice trailed off, and her eyes looked to the floor.

"Lue, you're not a selfish person, and you have every right to be wary after what we've just been through," Raelia reassured, "but I need time."

The confusion etched in her friend's face prompted her to continue.

"I don't know how to tell Papa. I don't know how to tell Caias. I don't know how to-" her throat tightened, a sob welling within. She did her best to speak around it, but nothing could keep the tears from trickling down her cheeks. "I don't know how to tell them I'm all they have left..."

"Oh, Rae..."

"And I get why you want to go, but I don't know how to get us there safely! We don't have the means to travel on our own, and even if we did-"

"You want to know more about the power you have, and the people who share it," Luella finished for her, a knowing look in her eye.

She nodded, not sure what else she could say.

"I thought about this all night. I barely slept a wink," Luella told her. "I don't want to stay here, but I also don't think it's fair to take you away from the opportunity to learn more about your gift. So I have a proposal."

Raelia looked at her friend with questioning eyes. "Go on..."

"How long until your father and Caias are supposed to return home?"

She had to think about that for a moment. How much time had passed since they left for the Taevidian Empire? A week? 10 days?

"Probably six to seven weeks yet," she answered. "Though it might be less. I'm not really sure. Why?"

"Then let's agree we stay here for six weeks," Luella said, a sad smile touching her lips. "That will give you plenty of time to learn more about your Mark, and the gift it allows you. At the end of the six weeks, though, I will be returning home and I would like you to come with me."

Raelia mulled this over for a few moments before she responded. It was a fair compromise, and Luella had been right the night before — Caias and Eloi deserved to have an explanation when they returned home, no matter how hard it was for her to think about. This really was the best solution for them both.

She looked into her friend's bright blue eyes and flashed a grateful smile. "It's a deal."

Luella smiled and squeezed Raelia's hand. "Good."

On her second morning waking up in the Paodran forest, after a deep and much more restful sleep than the first, Raelia woke to Zayric sitting on her chest, looking down at her as if expecting something. She smiled groggily up at him and ran a hand over the soft fur along his spine. He licked her cheek happily and, in the blink of an eye, transformed into his fine white smoke, evaporating and quickly disappearing from sight.

After he was gone, she stretched, throwing the blankets off of herself, and got dressed. A soft knock echoed through her room as she was tying up her boots.

"Rae? You up?" called Luella from the other side of the heavy door. "Ready for breakfast?

She laughed. "I'll be out in a few."

Raelia and Luella met at the small table. They'd both woken up early and taken full advantage of the magical menu Brixxi had allowed them to have. When she looked down at the meals listed, she noticed that while some meals were the same, some had changed to include more traditional breakfast items.

Raelia ordered herself some orange juice and toast, fried eggs and sausage, and, much to her delight, pancakes. Luella ordered much the same, and then ordered fresh fruit for them to share.

When it arrived, the girls went quiet, mouths hung open, gawking at the spread before them. It smelled delicious, and every plate overflowed with delectable looking dishes.

"I could get used to this!" Raelia exclaimed.

Luella nodded her agreement, and the pair loaded food onto their plates. They laughed and talked as they ate, only stopping when they felt stuffed to the brim.

Once done, Raelia pressed the small rose to say they'd finished, just as Brixxi had shown her, and the plates and leftover food vanished in seconds.

She stood and stretched, fully intending to take a nap, when there was a knock on the door.

"Who could that be?" Luella asked.

Raelia shrugged her shoulders and walked over to the door. When she opened it, she was surprised to see Vysha standing before her, a bright smile on her face.

Her hair was tied in a high ponytail, and the form fitting corset top of the dress she wore clung to her curves, flaring out at her waist and flowing down to the floor below. It was open in the front, revealing her tight black pants and matching red boots.

"Good morning, my dear!" she said, her tone bright and adoring. "May I come in?"

"Of course!" Raelia replied, moving to the side to let her pass.

Once Vysha entered, she shut the door and turned to the Red Lady, who was greeting Luella.

Her eyes shifted back to Raelia's as she asked, "How are you liking it here in Paodra so far?"

"We could never thank you enough for allowing us to stay here, Vysha," she said.

"Oh, my dear, *Aldaehima,*" Vysha said, a loving warmth in her eyes, "you are welcome to be here for as long as you wish. This is your home."

There it was again. *'Aldaehima.'* Dandelion. If she was going to say anything, now was the time, but she couldn't bring herself to. The kindness in Vysha's expression held her mouth closed.

"Thank you," was all she managed.

"Well, girls," Vysha started, eyes connecting with Raelia's. "Rokoa told me he's shown you around, so I thought today might be a good day for you to see what training will look like while you're here."

"Training?" Raelia's fingers entwined into the end of her braid, tugging down, as if her hair wasn't already covering the Mark behind her ear.

"Yes, dear," Vysha stepped closer to her, placing her hands on Raelia's shoulders. "You're eighteen now. The sooner you learn to use your gift, the more powerful it will be."

"Rokoa mentioned he-"

"He doesn't train Mark Bearers, normally, but, yes, he will help with yours and Luella's defense training," Vysha interrupted. "However, you need to train with your gift and a dandelion cannot be taught by a Drykuan. They know little of our power."

"You're a Dandelion too?"

"Oh, yes! You and I are the only two in existence!"

"How-how can that be?"

"Let's sit, shall we?" Vysha said, leading Raelia over to the oversized sofa. "I mentioned the night you got here the Dandelion Indicative Mark holds great power, touching on all powers that fall under the six elements. What I didn't tell you was that a Dandelion is only born every few hundred years. It's how the magic controls the gift of such great power."

"But if that's true, then how does the new one learn their power? If the previous Dandelion is gone when they are born, how do they learn?" Luella asked, coming to sit on the floor across the coffee table from them.

Vysha's eyes shifted to Lue. "Some don't. Some never try to learn the power they were gifted, and it dies, or, like in my case, appears when there is great need."

"Great need?" Raelia asked, curiosity getting the better of her.

"For myself, it was when King Nikolai executed my family for the crime of existing. My son, you see, he also had an Indicative Mark. They tried to say he..." Vysha looked at her hands, clearing her throat and shaking her head. "Well, that was a long time ago. No need to dredge it up now."

Raelia knew the story well. Or, at least, she knew the Dirythian side of the story. The son of the Red Lady committed an act of magical violence against a village child. The King called for the boy to be imprisoned, after which the Red Lady slaughtered the guards sent to retrieve him and the rest of her village. Clearly, the histories were biased.

"All of that to say, the Dandelion appears when needed, and adjusts the ability given to suit the need," Vysha finished, before clapping her hands together and standing up, flicking her wrist towards the bedrooms with a smile, "Now. There is training gear in both of your rooms. Go change, and we'll head over together."

Luella's face turned to shock, her voice a high pitch of panic, "*Both* of our rooms?! I must have misheard you... I don't have a gift to train with! I'm certain I don't need to accompany you!"

Vysha chuckled softly. She stepped around the table, and cupped Luella's cheek, tilting her chin up to look at her. "My child, you may not have been gifted with magic, but you have been gifted with beauty and that always needs defending."

❦ ❦

"We'll start you with the dagger," Rokoa said, handing the small blade hilt first to Luella, who was still a shade of red Raelia could only compare to a tomato.

It had taken a bit of convincing to get her friend to leave her bedroom in the sheathlike tactical pants and curve-hugging shirt of the gear that Vysha had provided them to train in, and it was even more difficult to get her out of their living space. The minute someone saw her without a skirt on, Luella's pale skin flushed scarlet, and it had yet to fade.

Raelia had to press her lips together, so as not to laugh at her friend's shock at being told she had to use a weapon. Only when Vysha called her over to a secluded part of the training room did the humor fade.

"You'll start defense training tomorrow," the elder woman clarified. "Today, while Rokoa works with Luella, I want to work with you one on one. We'll start with a cleansing ritual."

"Cleansing ritual?"

"Yes, child, it will help cleanse the darkness of your spirit. Allowing your inner light to guide your gift."

Raelia followed as Vysha pushed on a heavy door in the corner of the large training space. It opened up into a small, dimly lit room. There were no windows, and no furniture, only large, plush cushions littering the floor. Candles were placed strategically around the room, giving the cozy space an ethereal glow. In the very center of the space was an empty stone bowl surrounded by several smaller bowls, all holding different herbs and leaves.

When the door swung closed, an eerie silence enveloped them, and Vysha gestured for her to sit on one of the large cushions. After which, she sat on one herself across the bowls from Raelia.

They sat in silence for a moment as Vysha used a mortar and pestle to crush the various ingredients filling the bowls in front of them. When she looked closer, Raelia realized there were quite a few seeds, and dried flowers, along with spices, and chunks of different plant stocks. The floral, bitter, and musky aromas of all the different ingredients overwhelmed her senses, and she took to breathing through her mouth to avoid it.

The next moment, however, Vysha pulled out a flower, still attached to its stem, the scent of which she could taste on the air. She nearly gagged. The sickly, fishy scent was wretched. She watched intently as the woman used magic to shred the plant, only causing the stench to worsen.

Even with her extensive knowledge of flowers, plants, and herbs, she couldn't quite place this one. If it didn't smell as horrific as it did, she'd want to examine it closer. The thick, fleshy taproot grew into green leafy stalks that were attached to a flower. The deep darkness of the center crept to the outer edges of the yellowish, white petals with spider-like veins.

"What kind of plant is that? I've never seen it before."

"This is Black Henbane," Vysha explained, as she flicked her wrist, sending the shreds of the plant into the large stone bowl in the center.

"I've never heard of it. What is it for?" she asked.

"It brings protection, my *Aldaehima*."

Vysha's voice seemed strained when she answered, and Raelia couldn't figure out why. There was something in the woman's tone that tied her stomach in knots. She mentally scolded herself for letting Luella's judgements affect what she thought of Vysha. Surely she had to be imagining it. Right?

"Protection from what?"

"Never you mind, dear."

Being brushed off left her feeling even more uneasy, but she kept her mouth closed and continued to watch Vysha work.

After it seemed she'd ground or shredded or cut every ingredient in the room, Vysha waved her hand, palm down, over the shredded Henbane, mumbling something that Raelia couldn't quite hear.

Flames burst upward from the bowl, momentarily engulfing her hand, before shrinking back down. Raelia jumped, and reached for Vysha, pulling back when she noticed there wasn't a wound. Her skin looked as pristine as it had before the flames.

As she watched, Vysha added more ingredients into the bowl, still mumbling words Raelia couldn't hear. Smoke billowed up, putrid and thick. However, when she took a breath, expecting to choke, Raelia realized that while she could smell it, the smoke didn't seem to infiltrate her lungs.

There was a tang in the air. Something Raelia recognized, but couldn't place, and she didn't understand how, but instinctively she knew it wasn't from the burning items in the bowl.

It brought life to her skin. Sparking every nerve ending in her body. Her eyes fluttered closed, taking in the feeling, when she felt a zing of pain behind her ear. She couldn't make her eyes open, but her hand flung quickly to where her Mark burned. It traveled down her hairline to the base of her skull, causing her to gasp out in surprise.

"*Toik lisde rivu spol kiasde*," Vysha uttered, louder than before.

Raelia's hand seemed to fall back to her lap of its own accord, and a tingling sensation rushed up and down her entire body, as if a million spiders were fleeing for their life all over her skin.

She tried to cry out for Vysha to make it stop. She tried to open her mouth but her body wouldn't comply. In her mind, she screamed for her body, mouth, limbs, any part of her, to move, but there was no movement. No sound.

Behind her closed eyelids, Realia could see the light of the fire between them growing larger, brighter. The heat from the flames burned her skin and she wished she could make her body move away from them.

Vysha's loud voice rumbled through Raelia's entire being when she spoke next, "*Edsaik lops uvir edsil kiot!*"

When her voice stopped, so did everything else. The tingling sensation, the flames, the paralysis. Raelia's eyes shot open, but she could see nothing. Every candle extinguished itself when the flames in the bowl disappeared. She didn't know what she just experienced, and she had never been one to scare easily, but in the darkness, her hands began to tremble with fear.

"Vysha?"

Silence.

"Vysha? Where are you?"

More silence.

She could feel her heartbeat picking up its pace as the panic set in.

"HELLO?!"

Fingers trailed up her spine, and she screamed — quickly turning around. She stared into the inky blackness behind her, but there was nothing there.

The fingers caressed her cheek this time, and she felt tears fall as she screamed again, terror taking over every sense.

As she jerked away from the invisible touch, she felt hands grab her shoulders and shove her down. She fell hard onto her back. Her shrieks became more piercing, more desperate as she felt someone climb on top of her, pinning her to the ground.

Raelia tried to kick, but her legs were pinned under the weight of whoever — whatever — was on top of her in the darkness, so she used her next best weapon. She punched, slapped and scratched out in front of her, meeting no resistance as her hands flew through the air.

She didn't understand it. What was going on? Why weren't her hands connecting with this beast holding her down? She only had a moment to ponder that before she felt two hands wrap tightly around her throat, choking off her air supply.

She tried again to scream, but the lack of oxygen made it impossible. Dizziness blurred the edges of her vision and she felt herself grow weak as the hands tightened around her neck. "That is all we need for today, my dear," Vysha's voice was sharp above her.

Raelia's eyes shot open as she gasped for air.

The hands were gone.

The candles burned.

She was sitting, and in front of her, seeming to not have moved an inch, sat Vysha, watching her expectantly. Her smile kind.

A shiver ran down Raelia's back. She watched as Vysha stood, gesturing for her to do the same and moments later, they were out of the room and back in the training space.

Raelia jumped when Vysha put a hand on her shoulder. "I'm very proud of you, child."

She turned to the Red Lady, green eyes connecting with her dark brown. She opened her mouth to speak, but no sound came out.

"Don't worry, *Aldaehima,* it will be easier next time."

CHAPTER 14

"Next time?!" Luella practically shouted, after Raelia told her about the training with Vysha. "You have to do it again?!"

"Vysha says when someone's power activates is when the Bearer is at their most vulnerable," she explained. "Apparently, their spirit is more accessible to dark forces... So," she sighed, plopping down on the sofa in their living space, "I have to do it every few days for the next few weeks."

"Did you tell her what happened? Did you tell her it attacked you?!"

"She said that it was the darkness fighting to stay with me."

Raelia looked down, avoiding eye contact with her friend. That *is* what Vysha had told her, but something in the way she said it was unsettling. It also didn't feel accurate. If the darkness was fighting to stay in her, and the ritual drove it out, wouldn't she have won the fight? The invisible being she fought would have killed her if she hadn't woken up when she did. Was it really driven out?

With Luella so distrusting of the Red Lady already, Raelia kept her mouth shut. She didn't want to give her friend any more reason to want to leave. She pulled her knees to her chest, wrapping her arms around them, and changed the subject.

"How was your training? Did you learn anything?"

That was all it took for Luella to dive right in. She complained more about the gear Vysha expected them to wear, and how unlady-like it was, and then about Rokoa's antagonizing manner. She paced back and forth as she detailed the blows she'd dealt, and the ones she'd been victim to.

By the end of her monologue, Raelia was surprised to realize her friend, even though complaining, seemed to have enjoyed her training session with her Drykuan teacher. Even more surprising, when she realized Luella seemed excited to see what the next day's session would look like.

The day had been exhausting, so after eating, they quickly sent their plates back and started down the hall to their rooms.

"Hey Rae," Luella called, just before she shut her bedroom door.

"Yeah?"

"Thanks for not letting me run back home the first night. I'm glad we're staying for a bit."

Raelia smiled, happy to hear that. "I am too."

⊰⊱

The next morning, Raelia was woken by Zayric licking her cheek. She smiled up at the fox and rolled her eyes, as she croaked out. "Good morning, furball."

Zayric cocked his head, his dual colored eyes bright, and she swore if he could smile, the pup would have a grin from ear to ear.

She stretched and yawned before pulling the blankets off and forcing herself out of bed. She shivered as she made her way across the room and grabbed her training gear from the small wardrobe in the corner. Moving slowly, she headed into the washroom to ready herself for the day.

When she emerged, cleaner and much more awake, she was sur-prised to see Zayric waiting at the door for her. Leaning over, she gave him a quick scritch behind the ear, but before she could stand back up, he jumped into her arms. His fur was silky soft as he nuzzled into her neck. She tilted her head into his and gave him a peck before setting him down, only to be followed into the common area.

Luella's bedroom door was still closed, so Raelia assumed she must still be sleeping and did her best to stay quiet as she perused the menu on the table. She ordered something she could eat quickly, after which she sent back her plate and headed toward the main entrance. Once again, Zayric followed. His eyes watched her intently as she put her hand on the knob, and as soon as she opened the door, he scurried into the hall.

"What has gotten into you?" she asked, chuckling and shaking her head.

After closing the door behind herself, Raelia headed toward the stairs leading outside, and, once again, the kyloxis followed. It seemed she was going to have a shadow today, and she wasn't sure she minded in the slightest.

The morning air was crisp and cool. Once again, it seemed she was up before everyone else, as the sun had only just begun to color the sky. She rolled her eyes, glaring down at the reason she was awake.

"Hey!" Naz's voice called from behind her.

Raelia turned, noticing they again had their easel out. The corseted dress they wore was tight at the top, but flared out, flowing to the ground from their hips. It was a gorgeous deep yellow, truly suiting their dark sepia skin.

"Good morning! Drawing again?"

Naz nodded, waving her over. "As you can see, I've moved on from your friend. Finished her yesterday!" they grinned at her from ear to ear.

When Raelia approached, her mouth fell open. She couldn't believe her eyes – It was her on their pad, now dressed in her training gear from yesterday. The expression on her face was fierce and strong.

"Who's your friend?" Naz asked, looking down at Zayric.

Completely entranced by their art, she didn't even hear the question. "I didn't even see you when I was in my gear yesterday! How did you-?"

"I was headed to train when I saw you go toe to toe with Qiralst a couple days ago. We all mostly wear the same training gear, so it seemed the natural choice."

"Oh," Raelia felt her cheeks warm.

"That was really brave of you," they said in a soft voice.

"And stupid," she replied.

"I don't know if I'd go that far, but it would probably do you good to think it through before you step in front of anyone with a whip again."

"Hopefully, my brain is quick enough to remember that before my stupid legs walk me over next time!"

They both laughed.

"How was your training session yesterday? I hear you trained with the Red Lady?!"

Raelia opened her mouth, but before she could answer, the main entrance into Paodra opened across the square. Both she and Naz turned to see who could be coming in at such an early hour.

Shock flowed through her as she watched a young woman, bloodied and bruised, fall through the door. Her sobs echoed across the large space, and both Raelia and Naz ran to help her, Zayric in their wake.

She knelt down next to the new arrival, placing her hand on the woman's shoulder.

"I'm going to get help! Stay with her!" Naz commanded before running off.

The girl looked up at her with frightened eyes. "Is this... Did I make it to Paodra?"

Raelia was surprised by the question, but nodded and answered honestly, "You did." Her eyes roamed over her open wounds and tattered clothes. "What happened to you?"

"I need the Red Lady. I was told this was where I could find her. Is-is she here?" The girl's voice was weak. Desperate.

Raelia didn't think before answering. "Yes. She's here."

She let out a cry of relief, tears streamed down her face as her body seemed to relax. Her hazel eyes connected with Raelia's, looking surprised at what she saw.

"What is it?" she asked. "Why are you looking at me like that?"

Before the girl could respond, Naz returned with the help they promised. Raelia stood, moving out of the way as two Drykuan guards picked up the young woman and put her on a portable cot. When they lifted it, Raelia noticed a large tattoo-like Mark on the woman's stomach, only noticeable because of the torn material of her dress.

'She's a Mark Bearer,' Raelia realized. She couldn't see it in its entirety, but it was clearly an Indicative Mark.

She jumped when Naz reached over and took her hand. Her eyes shot to theirs, worry clear on both of their faces. The pair followed the Drykuan's carrying the young woman. She looked for Zayric behind them to see if he had followed, but he was nowhere in sight. She sighed, turning back as they headed across the square and through a door leading underground.

Raelia hadn't been through this area before. When Rokoa had given them his tour, he had only told her it was a rarely used space. Which, now that she was inside, she had a hard time believing. It was obviously some sort of medical ward. She couldn't believe with the type of training they did here in Paodra that it was 'rarely used.' However, she had to admit there were very few patients, from what she could see.

The men turned into a small room and transferred the young woman onto a small bed. It was the same kind of cot her mother used for the patients in her office, and emotion hit Raelia like a ton of bricks at the sight.

Naz continued into the room, only stopping when they met resistance from behind. They looked at her, eyes questioning, as Raelia stood, stuck outside the door, looking in. She let go of their hand and took a step back. The sight of the medical space brought on grief such as she hadn't let herself feel yet.

Her eyes welled up, still staring at the cot, and she stepped back once more. Naz stepped toward her, reaching their hand out for hers.

"Raelia!" a voice called from behind, pulling her out of the grief-stricken trance.

Vysha rushed down the last few stairs at the far end of the hall, the purple train of her overskirt fluttering against an invisible breeze. She was followed closely by Dhovina, who looked as grumpy as they had when Raelia first met them.

"I'm so glad you're here, *Aldaehima*," Vysha said kindly when she reached them. She placed her hand on Raelia's arm, squeezing it gently before continuing, "Please stay here while I speak to her."

Raelia nodded. She didn't know why, but Vysha's presence calmed her. She felt secure at the sight of her coming down the stairs and safe at her touch. She took a deep breath to further calm her anxiety as the Red Lady stepped into the small space, leaving Naz, Raelia and Dhovina on their own.

"What happened?" Naz asked in a hushed voice, "Are you okay?"

She nodded, not exactly sure how to explain the overwhelming grief and anxiety that had taken over.

"Nazario," Dhovina's penetrating voice spoke from behind them. "You are free to leave."

Naz looked at them with an incredulous look. "Leave? Why would I do that? I want to make sure she's okay."

"Your presence is not needed," they answered. "I'm sure your *friend*," they spat the word with disdain, "can fill you in after Vysha is done with her."

Between their tone and wording, it sounded as if Raelia should be worried about what Vysha wanted to speak with her about. At the mere thought of being afraid of the Red Lady, however, her body calmed, and she mentally scoffed at the thought.

"There's no reason for them to go," Raelia interjected. "Vysha didn't say they needed too."

"And they do not have to," Vysha's voice sounded from the doorway. Her eyes pierced Dhovina's momentarily before turning to Raelia with much more warmth. "Raelia, darling, please join me?"

Vysha gestured into the small room she'd just come from, and somehow, even though grief had crippled her minutes before, she was able to walk right in without another thought.

The elder woman shooed the Drykuan's from the room and shut the door behind them. When Raelia looked, the girl was watching her with a curious expression.

"Raelia, this is Ayla," Vysha introduced, "She asked to speak to you again."

"Oh?" she turned a questioning gaze on the brunette.

"I just wanted to thank you for helping me. You and your friend."

"Of course!" Raelia said, surprise coloring her features. She smiled in return as she continued, "No need to thank us. I'm just glad we were there when you needed us."

"So am I!" Ayla chuckled in response.

"Well, now that you're settled," Vysha interjected, "I need to speak to Raelia, but I will be back to check on you soon."

"Will you visit too, Raelia?" Ayla's hazel eyes seemed hopeful, but there was another emotion there—one that she couldn't quite place.

"O-of course! I'll come back a little later to see how you're doing, if you'd like?"

"Please do!"

Raelia returned Ayla's kind smile before she turned to leave the small space. She heard Vysha telling her to get some rest and the girl's promise to do so before the Red Lady followed her and closed the door.

"Dhovina, please escort Nazario back to the courtyard," Vysha instructed. "I'd like to speak to Raelia on our own for a moment."

A smug smirk spread across Dhovina's face, as they turned their gaze, jerking their head toward the exit. "Come on."

Naz looked as if they were struggling on what to do. Their mouth opened, looking as if they'd like to protest, but seemed to think better of it and followed without a fuss.

She watched them go, only turning back to Vysha when the woman hooked her arm through the crook of Raelia's elbow.

"Come, *Aldaehima*, we have much to discuss."

They walked in silence through the underground hallways. Raelia knew she should feel anxious about being singled out for a meeting with the Red Lady, but, for some reason, she still only felt an overwhelming sense of calm at the thought.

Vysha walked the twisting halls with ease, turning corners and moving through rooms until Raelia had completely lost track of where they were. Rokoa had told her the underground hallways were all interconnected, but she had no clue there were this many of them.

Finally they made it to a long staircase—so long, in fact, Raelia couldn't see where it ended. That didn't stop her, however, from following Vysha up the elegant wooden stairs. They seemed to climb forever. Raelia's legs ached, and she opened her mouth to ask where they were going, but before she could speak, she finally saw a door at the stairs end.

When Vysha opened it, Raelia expected them to exit into one of the many small courtyards that were scattered throughout Paodra, however, she was surprised — the door opened into the sky.

They stepped out onto a balcony high up the side of one of the massive trees that made up the Paodran village. Without missing a beat, Vysha continued up the staircase that wound around the outside of the exquisite evergreen's trunk. It took Raelia a moment to follow, stunned at the beauty of the world in front of her.

The branches of the giant trees were thinner here than they were from below, and it allowed her to see further out than she could see from any of the village squares. The large, snow-covered mountain range that extended the width of Dirythia stood proudly in the distance, and she realized in amazement that only a few trunks away, every tree was covered in a thick layer of snow. She looked at the line across the trees where the snow started — it was distinct and unnatural.

"Paodra is protected from the elements," Vysha's voice interrupted her confusion. "The line you see is where the magic barrier ends, allowing the snow to fall freely."

"Is that why it seemed colder outside than it does within the *Triseyule?*"

Vysha nodded as she hooked her arm through Raelia's and gently guided her up the last flight of stairs. She stopped in front of one of the treehouse homes Raelia marveled over when they first arrived and opened the door.

"Welcome to my home," she said with a smile, gesturing for her to enter. "Take a seat."

Raelia smiled in return as she walked in and sat on the firm, floral patterned sofa in the living room. It reminded her so much of her home in Frayis, and she had to shove the thought down before grief could overtake her.

Vysha disappeared for a moment, returning promptly with a tray. A beautifully painted teapot with matching cups sat in the center. The rich cream color was overlaid with vibrant flowers of all colors, sporadically placed along what seemed to be ivy vines.

"Now, let's you and I have a heart to heart," Vysha said with a smile, as she poured the hot liquid into a cup and handed it to her guest.

"Okay... Did I do something wrong?"

"No, no, nothing like that!" Vysha assured her with a friendly smile, "I just wanted to see how you're getting along? It's been a busy few days, and I just want to make sure you're settling in okay."

"Oh!" Raelia said in surprise. She hadn't been expecting there to be such a simple reason for Vysha to bring her all the way up here. Though, she hadn't really known what she was expecting if she was honest. "I think we're settling in okay. Lue is excited about her training with Rokoa, and I... I'm just..."

Her voice trailed off as her eyes looked down into the cup she held with both hands. The ceramic was burning hot, and yet she held onto it as if her life depended on it, her tight grip the only thing keeping her hands from trembling. Her brows furrowed in thought. She wasn't sure how to answer the question presented. She didn't really know what or how she was. On the outside she seemed fine, as long as she wasn't left alone with her thoughts. There seemed to be an empty chasm where her heart once was — chiseled out as she watched her family slaughtered.

Vysha reached out and placed a supportive hand on her arm. "It's never easy to lose the ones we love."

Raelia's lip trembled, her eyes welling. She did her best to hold the tears at bay, but it seemed an impossible task. She tried to swallow down the sob that rose in her chest, but once again failed at repressing her grief. Before she realized what was happening, an agonized cry ripped from deep within her, and she lost complete control of the emotions she was trying so desperately to contain.

Without a moment's hesitation, Vysha grabbed the cup from her hands, setting it on the table, before wrapping Raelia in a tight, comforting embrace.

For the next few minutes, Raelia sobbed into her shoulder, unable to contain the emotion that broke free. Vysha rocked her maternally back and forth, as she ran her palm up and down her back in a soothing motion.

"You are not alone, *Aldaehima*," Vysha whispered soothingly, "You will never be alone again."

When Raelia finally calmed herself enough to speak, Vysha released her hold. She handed the teacup back to her, before picking up her own.

Raelia sniffled, looking into the golden liquid. "I'm so sorry. I don't know what came over me."

"There is no reason for you to apologize, child. None whatsoever," Vysha assured her. "Your entire world has completely changed in a matter of only a few days."

She sniffled once more before looking at the woman with a watery smile. "Thank you for understanding. I don't want you to think I'm not grateful for everything you've done for us..."

"And I don't."

Raelia lifted the teacup to her lips, sipping gently the fresh, earthy liquid. She had never tasted anything like it before, and she made a mental note to ask what kind of tea it was before she left.

"Does it ever stop hurting?" she asked in a shaky voice.

"No. The hurt will always remain," Vysha sighed deeply, "but one day, their deaths won't be what you focus on. One day, the pain won't be where your mind rests."

Looking at the woman, Raelia hoped her words were true.

"One day, you'll be able to remember more than their last moments."

She stayed with Vysha for a while longer. They ate and drank their tea, and the conversation became lighter after that. Raelia became lighter. She hadn't realized how heavy the burden of her grief had become, until she could finally get some of it out.

Chapter 15

By the time Vysha dismissed her, it was close to midday. Raelia carefully followed the directions she'd been given to get back to the ground level, and, thankfully, it wasn't as difficult as she expected. She quickly found the main square where she and Naz had been laughing together that morning.

Her plan was to head to the shared living quarters and look for Luella, but before she opened the large door leading underground, a familiar voice called out to her.

"Rae!" Luella called from across the open space. "Rae! Over here!"

Turning around, she found her best friend running in her direction, her long blonde hair billowing out from behind her. She seemed relieved as she approached.

"Where have you been? Rokoa went to search for you a couple of hours ago!"

"I was with Vysha. It's been, um, an *interesting* morning..." she chuckled awkwardly.

"What do you mean?"

Raelia explained to Luella everything that happened that morning; from being woken up early to her interrupted conversation with Naz. She told her of the girl, Ayla, who had appeared bloodied and bruised, and how she and Vysha spent the rest of the morning talking over tea.

"I was thinking of going to visit Ayla again," Raelia said. "She seemed like she wanted company."

"Oh, okay," Luella replied. "I thought we were going to train together today?"

"Come with me to meet Ayla first and then we can head over!"

"I don't know..." Lue hesitated, "I wouldn't want to intrude..."

"Oh, come *on*," Raelia whinged, dragging out the last word, making it sound like she was begging. "You haven't met anyone yet! And she's new too, so you could meet each other!"

"Oh, alright!" she agreed, hooking arms with her friend, and looking more excited than she had in the time they'd been in Paodra. "I'm following you!"

Raelia guided her friend to the medical ward, and then down the hall to Ayla's room. She knocked on the door, and was surprised when Naz answered it.

They smile brightly at her and Luella, ushering them inside at Ayla's persistent request from inside.

"I didn't expect you to be here, Naz," Raelia returned their smile with one of her own before gesturing to Luella beside her. "Naz, Luella. Luella, Naz." She chuckled and turned her smile to the brunette laying on her cot, "And this is Ayla."

They all greeted each other with welcoming smiles and words. Nazario and Lue took the two chairs meant for visitors, while Raelia stood, eyes locking with Ayla's.

"How are you feeling? It looks like you were able to get cleaned up a bit, at least."

"I'm feeling much better," the girl grinned, eyes sparkling. "Hot food to eat, water to drink, and, best of all, an indoor bed? I'm living the life!"

She seemed so much more full of life than she'd been earlier today. Raelia had a hard time convincing herself the girl from this morning and the girl sitting before her were the same person.

"Do you mind if I ask... What happened to you?"

The laughter died on Ayla's lips, though her smile remained as she looked into her lap. The atmosphere in the room shifted, becoming thick and anxious.

"The village where I've lived for the last few years..." she cleared her throat, "Well... I couldn't stay there any longer."

Worry and confusion colored Luella's expression, and even though she asked a question, her tone was knowing, "Why?"

"My Mark was discovered."

Raelia stifled a gasp, knowing full well what happens when that happens. She had lived in fear of it happening her whole life, and now most of her family was dead because of hers.

"How did you get away?"

"It's a funny story, actually. One that involves your family," Ayla told her with a crooked grin. "Your extended family, at least."

Her eyes narrowed in confusion. "My family?"

"Do you know a woman named Juniper? She lives really far south in-"

"Truliach," Raelia finished for her. "She's my father's cousin. I've met her only a few times—You know her?"

Ayla nodded. "Yes! She owns a small apothecary. She knew who I was and knew of my Mark when I came through town. She sought me out a little over a year ago now—I live with, or rather, I *did* live with her—before they came for me."

"Who came for you?" Naz asked.

"When I spoke to Vysha earlier, she said it must have been the royal guard..."

"It sounds like there's a 'but' there," Raelia pushed.

"*But...* They weren't dressed like royal guards." Ayla's brow furrowed in concentration. "There were five men in leather armor that came to the door, but the odd thing was they all looked almost identical."

"Like they were related?" Luella clarified.

"Not exactly... It was more like they were all the same person," the brunette explained, "only they had different scars or wounds."

As Ayla described their physical traits, an image flashed in Raelia's mind. A large man clad in leather armor. His eyes were dark, hair even darker, with skin as pale as a ghost. She twisted the ring on her finger and felt fear's clammy fingers crawl up her spine as she realized the men her new friend described were the same men that attacked her village.

"It can't be..." Naz's voice was a quiet whisper, only Raelia was close enough to hear them.

She looked at them closely. "Can't be what?"

Nazario returned her gaze, eyes connecting, and she saw confusion there. They turned back to Ayla. "These men, were they all the same height and build?"

"Yeah," Ayla answered as her eyebrow quirked up. "They even carried weapons that seemed to be the same. It was so strange."

More images flashed through Raelia's mind, sword after sword, all identical as they tore through the bodies of villagers during the attack.

"It sounds like... well...," Naz chewed at their bottom lip and began pacing the small space, "but it can't be... The King wouldn't... He couldn't."

"You know we can't hear your thoughts, right?" Luella joked.

"Grushik."

The three girls looked at each other and then back at Nazario. Confusion evident on every one of their faces.

"Care to explain what that means?" Ayla asked.

They sighed, and plopped down in their chair. "Grushik is a term used for copies of a person who is held in an enchanted state. The ritual is outlawed among the tribes, though it's an ancient magic and most have never even heard of it. Even fewer know how to perform it..."

Nazario's eyes seemed to glaze over, lost in thought as they were.

"And you're certain they said they were with the royal guard?" Raelia asked, eyes focusing back on Ayla, who nodded.

"They said it multiple times, in fact. A couple times when they came for me, and a few before I escaped them and headed here," Ayla told them, "I remember because I thought it seemed like they were trying to convince themselves."

"It does seem strange they'd repeat it over and over like that," Luella chimed in, brow furrowing.

"If it's such an ancient ritual," Raelia's eyes turned back to Naz, "how would the King know it?"

Their eyes focused on Raelia. "That's what's so strange. For someone who hates all magic, and is slaughtering innocent children just because of a birthmark... Well... It does seem strange he'd even know about it..."

"How do you know about it?" Luella asked.

Their eyes turned to the blonde sitting in the chair next to their own, and sighed. "The ritual originates from the tribal lands in the Taevidian Empire."

Raelia nodded. "Most magic does."

"Yes, but this specific ritual comes from a specific tribe. The Vixuln Tribe," they explained. "My tribe."

The news that Nazario hailed from the Taevidian Empire shouldn't have surprised her. Most, if not all, Mark Bearers either came from or had a parent that came from the tribal lands. It's how she had her Mark, after all. For some reason, however, she hadn't expected it.

"Your tribe?" Ayla asked. "You're from Taevidia?"

"Originally, yes," they answered, "but I left nearly five years ago now."

"Can I ask...?"

"Why I left?"

Raelia nodded. "If you don't mind sharing, of course... It seems strange to leave a place where you were safe and magic isn't illegal, is all."

"I don't mind," Naz replied softly, "It may seem strange, but, well... You... Can I assume you recognize I'm not... Well, I'm not a..."

Raelia knew without needing them to finish their train of thought. "You're Fludrian, right?"

They nodded, seeming relieved she knew what they meant. "In the Vixuln tribe, and quite a few of the others, we, Fludrian's I mean, are considered extraordinary. We are expected to rise into positions of power within the Tribe — to become leaders and teachers — and as such, they teach us much more about the tribe's history, magic, and legends than they do the others."

The three girls waited for them to continue, watching with expectant eyes.

"That's how I know about the ritual... but I never wanted to be in power," Naz informed them. "It was something I dreaded, and was never comfortable with. I left... well, because as the grandchild to the Vixuln Preeminent, I was not only to rise into a high position, but they expected me to inherit the Preeminent title. They wanted me to rule the Vixuln tribe. I..." the sadness in their voice was so clear as they continued, "I watched as my Grandparent worried and bore the hardships of leading us. I didn't want that for myself. They didn't want it for me either. They told me I'd be happier if I went somewhere I could be myself without all the expectations of the tribe."

"So you just left?" Luella asked in utter disbelief.

"Yes, and I haven't been back since."

"I'm so sorry," Raelia said as she put a comforting hand on their shoulder. "I'm sorry you had to leave your home to lead the life you wanted for yourself. That's not fair."

"Thank you," Naz said in return. "It's no less fair than being forced from your home for your safety. I'm sorry you had to experience that." Their eyes looked at Raelia and then to Ayla and finally settled on Luella. "That you all had to experience it. None of you deserved it."

The atmosphere in the room became heavy, thick with sorrow and loss. Grief seemed to swell within her chest, until Raelia felt weighed down, and needed to sit. With no other chairs in the room she had to plop herself onto the ground.

Luella gave her a quizzical look before turning her eyes back to Nazario. "Why is the ritual outlawed?"

Naz looked at their hands twisting in their lap. "Because it's inhumane. The ritual itself calls for the forcible detainment of whomever you wish to clone. It is a painful process involving physical, mental and emotional anguish that doesn't end until the wielder of the magic releases them."

"Releases them how?" Ayla asked, her voice wary, as if she didn't know if it was an answer she really wanted to hear.

"The clones must return. The magic holds power over them, so when the wielder calls them they cannot defy the order. Once they've all returned," Naz continued, "it's a simple spell to release them into the nothing once more. The main problem is that the person on which the magic is cast has to remain in a very specific position held in pretty brutal ways, and has to remain alive for the clones to survive."

"That sounds awful..." Luella said in a disgusted tone.

"It is. That's why the tribes outlawed it and made it punishable by death."

Raelia's eyes were unfocused, lost in thought over the conversation around her. Images continued to flicker in her mind of the attack on Frayis. There were so many men attacking, but all of them looked the same, at least the ones she'd seen did.

"I think it was Grushik that attacked our village, as well," she blurted out.

Three pairs of eyes turned to her, looking at her with varying degrees of alarm. Luella's eyes stared through her, as if running over her own memories and coming to the same conclusion.

"I can't imagine that's possible," Naz replied. "To create that many Grushik would take a lot of time and *so* much power..."

"She's right though," Luella chimed in. "The men that attacked Frayis... They were all nearly identical. I escaped from two of them, and they looked the exact same."

Raelia watched her best friend as she spoke. Her heart aching and anger bubbling in her stomach at the thought of someone hurting her. She couldn't believe someone had come so close to doing so.

"How do you know it wasn't the same man the second time?" Ayla's tone wasn't accusatory, just curious.

"My father killed the first man. It's how I was able to escape... My father saved me..."

Luella's blue eyes welled and looked down. Raelia got to her knees and shuffled over to her friend, sitting back down between Naz and Luella's chair. She reached up and entwined her fingers with her friends, squeezing her hand tightly.

She remembered Luella sobbing in the stable, and she mentally admonished herself for not comforting her then. She was so caught up in her own grief, in her own trauma, she couldn't be the friend Lue needed — she wouldn't let it happen again. Luella looked down, giving her a shaky smile, and squeezing her hand in return.

"Do you really think it was the Grushik in your village?"

Raelia looked at Naz and nodded.

"That's so bizarre... Do you know why they attacked the village?"

She looked down, eyes focusing on the grain of the wood flooring, when she felt Luella give her hand a reassuring squeeze.

"Vysha told us the night we got here... The King ordered it," Raelia felt her lip quiver, and throat tighten. She wanted to tell them more, but she couldn't speak around the emotion building in her throat.

"She said the King discovered Raelia's existence... And he..." Luella's voice trailed off.

A tear slid down her cheek, but Raelia hastily wiped it away, refusing to let her emotions win her over again today. The room went silent once more. She wanted to say something — anything — to lighten the mood, but she couldn't bring herself to speak.

The door opened, startling all four of them. Rokoa peered down from the doorway, a smirk appearing on his face.

"You're all a lively lot, aren't you?" He chuckled at his joke, but quickly fell silent when he noticed no one joined in. "Geez... What's going on?"

Raelia sniffled and wiped furiously at her eyes, making sure no other droplets had escaped. "Nothing. We were just talking about what brought us here, is all."

Rokoa gave her a knowing look, sympathy clear in his eyes. "Ah. A topic that could bring any room down around here."

As if only just noticing her, Rokoa stepped forward, and held his hand out to Ayla. "Vysha mentioned we had a newcomer today. Welcome. I'm Rokoa."

The brunette shook his hand, offering him a warm smile. "It's nice to meet you."

He returned a surly nod, and turned to look at Raelia, still sitting on the floor. "We were supposed to train today," his eyes flickered to Luella. "You both were."

"Oh, yeah!" Raelia exclaimed. "We got kind of caught up, is all..."

Rokoa shook his head, smirking at her before turning back to Ayla. "Vysha tells me you've had your Laanias Juice?"

"Is that the gold stuff Ekry gave me earlier?"

He nodded. "She asked that I show you to your room." He stated before looking back down at Raelia. "Then we can talk about training."

They all stood and followed the Drykuan out into the hall. Ayla seemed to be completely healed, though her clothes were still torn and shredded. It didn't seem to phase her though, and she walked with a confident stride behind Rokoa.

Once up the stairs and in the main square, Rokoa began explaining things to Ayla, just as he had when he arrived with them a few days ago. Raelia looked around, not really listening as she, Naz and Luella followed. The people around them distracted her eyes and thoughts.

Just as they'd done when Raelia and Luella arrived, the other Mark Bearers huddled in groups, talking in hushed voices as they watched their progression across the square, and after that, the common area.

"Do they do this with every new arrival?" She asked, leaning over so Naz could hear her quiet question.

They chuckled, nodding. "Absolutely! You'd think it'd get old, all the speculating, but for most it never seems to."

As they made their way back down into the earth, and across the common area where most of the Mark Bearers seemed to hang out,

Raelia had to fight the urge to yell for them to stop staring. Thankfully, they turned the corner before she gave in to the desire.

"Vysha had this one prepared for you," Rokoa said, gesturing to the door across the hall from where Raelia and Luella's living quarters were. He opened the door, and gestured for Ayla to enter first. "It's a single room, and there are clothes for you in the wardrobe."

When she entered, Raelia noticed it was almost identical to their own apartment. The only difference being there wasn't a hallway, just a door leading into the bedroom.

"Raelia?" Rokoa called, turning his eyes to meet hers. "I think we can train tomorrow. It's been a long day for all of you."

She nodded, doing her best to hide her disappointment. She had been looking forward to her training with Rokoa — the training she had with Vysha wasn't at all what she'd thought it would be. She supposed, however, he was right. It had been a long day.

"Our room is right across the hall!" Luella told Ayla, smiling. "You can come visit anytime!"

Raelia stifled a laugh. Luella had always been the more social of the two of them, but she hadn't expected her to brighten towards anyone so quickly here, especially after what Vysha told her the first night. It made her happy her friend wasn't moping and hiding away. She loved being around people, much to Raelia's dismay. They were polar opposites in that way, and yet, somehow, they seemed to make their friendship work.

Her heart swelled while she watched Luella. She and Ayla chatted about the comfortable sofa, and how meals were ordered, and Raelia couldn't help but smile at her best friend's kindness.

Nazario cleared their throat beside her, pulling her from her thoughts. They watched her with knowing eyes, but didn't comment on what they saw. Instead, choosing to ask, "So, your room is across the hall?"

Raelia nodded, just as Rokoa said, "I'm going to leave you three to help Ayla settle in." He gave her a stern look before stepping back into the hallway. "Training tomorrow. Don't think you're going to get out of it again!"

After he left, they hung out in Ayla's room for the next few hours, talking about a little bit of everything. They talked about their families and their gifts. They talked more about the Grushik, puzzled at the thought of the King using what Nazario called, 'some of the darkest magic there is.' They even talked about their family pets.

After a while, Ayla's stomach growled loudly, causing the other three to laugh, and admit she wasn't the only one who needed to eat.

"We have a decent sized table, and one of the menus in our room!" Luella told them. "Would you both like to come over and have dinner with us?"

Ayla nodded, excitedly, but Nazario looked at them both as if they were crazy. "You took one of Brixxi's menus?! You better put it back before she realizes!"

Raelia laughed. "Brixxi gave it to me! Said I could use it from my room, and as the dining hall is quite a hike from here, I plan to keep ordering my meals from there!"

"Well, if that's the case..." Naz's face relaxed into a smile, and they quickly agreed to accompany them for their meal.

Dinner with Luella, Ayla and Nazario was joyful. They avoided heavy topics, yet still were able to get to know each other better. She felt comforted by their presence, something she hadn't felt since she'd been stuck in her room recovering from her near drowning a few weeks ago — when she sat in her room laughing with Alister and Luella and her younger siblings. For the first time since arriving in Paodra Raelia felt completely at ease. For the first time since her birthday she didn't feel weighed down by grief and pain.

CHAPTER 16

"Come on, Rae!" Rokoa gruffed, as he pushed his blade against hers. The clang of steel reverberated through the empty training arena. "You're stronger than this!"

Her breaths were heavy in her chest. They'd been going for almost two hours straight, and her whole body ached with exhaustion.

It was the morning after dinner with Ayla, Luella and Nazario. Rokoa woke her up before sunrise, demanding she get dressed. She told him she hadn't gotten to bed until after midnight, but he ignored her, dragging her to the arena without even letting her eat.

With her stomach empty, and body aching, she didn't know how he could believe her any more capable than he was already seeing.

"But I'm starving!" she whined. "You could have at least let me eat something!"

He laughed and pushed his blade against hers with such ferocity she stumbled back a few paces. "Do you think someone attacking will be kind enough to let you eat before they swing their sword?"

His tone was mocking, and she wanted nothing more than to wipe the arrogant smirk off of his face.

"You never know when you'll be attacked," he continued, holding his sword with ease as she got back to her feet. She wiped the sweat from her brow, and once again got into the fighting stance he'd taught her. "You must train in all conditions."

When he came at her again, Raelia was ready. He jabbed at her middle, but she twisted to the left, avoiding his blade by mere inches. Tucking her knees to her chest, she rolled deftly across the padded training area, coming up behind him.

She smirked at his surprised look, but, caught up rejoicing in her swift move, didn't see his leg, swinging low and knocking her feet from under her. She thudded to the ground, hard, but stifled her pained cry, as her blade skidded away from her.

"Don't get full of yourself after one good move," Rokoa scolded, pointing his sword down toward her. "That's how you get yourself killed."

Rolling her eyes, Raelia pushed herself up and went to retrieve her sword. Hunger forgotten as the desire to prove herself swelled in her chest, and she stepped in front of him once more.

"Again," she told him.

They squared up anew, and for the next few hours, it continued like that. Raelia pushed herself relentlessly. Frustration and a desire to be stronger drove through her hunger and exhaustion as she was knocked to the ground repeatedly.

"Again. Let's go again," Raelia urged, stepping into her defensive stance.

Rokoa chuckled and shook his head at her. He stepped off the mat, leaning his sword against the wall before turning to look at her once again.

"I think it's time for a break."

"Absolutely not!" she responded. "You dragged me here at the crack of dawn, so you're going to keep going until I say I'm done!"

Raelia lunged toward him, sword in hand, making him grab his once more. He twisted around, avoiding her blade, and swung his around to meet her. She ducked and rolled out of his reach, popping back up, swiftly. Once again, she aimed her sword at him, only to be met with a reverberating clang as he turned to block her attack.

Annoyance colored his features as he looked at her through the gaps between their blades. "You're quite annoying, do you know that?"

She shoved on her weapon, pushing him back, only to attack once more. Again, he blocked her swing.

"No one would suspect it either," he continued, this time pushing her back a few steps. "You look so kind and fragile on the outside."

"Oh, come off it!" she demanded, rolling her eyes.

"No truly," he told her. "No one would guess how powerful you are. With a little more training, you could be lethal. It will be to your advantage in the future."

She swung once more, and Rokoa again blocked her. This time, when she fell to the ground, he put his foot on her blade, refusing to let her pick it up.

"It's time for that break, Bumblebee," he told her.

That distracted her and when she stood, she turned bewildered eyes to the Drykuan. "Bumblebee?"

He laughed. "Because you're adorable, but pack a sting no one would see coming!"

Raelia rolled her eyes at him, and headed toward the arena door. "You're not calling me that! It's awful!"

"And yet, you are now Bumblebee," Rokoa howled, as he picked up her sword and leaned it against the wall. "Or maybe just Bumble? Or, wait!" he exclaimed, excitement radiating from him, "Even better! BeeBee!"

She sighed exasperatedly as she stepped into the hall, followed quickly by Rokoa. He smirked amusedly at her, his voice taunting. "What's wrong, BeeBee?"

Running a hand down her face, Raelia rolled her eyes. "You're insane."

⁕

After they'd eaten an early lunch, Rokoa walked her to the massive room where she'd met Vysha on her first night. Instead of sitting upon the throne, the Red Lady was standing, hunched over a massive table against the back wall. They walked up the dais and past the throne, stopping behind her contorted form. She didn't notice them as she muttered to herself over the documents in front of her.

Rokoa cleared his throat, diverting Vysha's attention. Her expression was serious, irritated even, when she turned around, but it cleared when she saw Raelia, to whom she offered a bright smile.

"*Aldaehima*, my sweet child," her kind tone as sweet as honey. "I'm so glad you're here! Are you ready for your first real lesson?"

Raelia took a step forward. "I am," she admitted, not just to them, but to herself as well. "What are we going to-"

Her voice cut off sharply as she caught sight of one document on the table.

It was a map.

A map of somewhere she recognized.

"Is that... Is that Frayis?"

Her eyes scrutinized the parchment as she stepped closer to the table. It looked like some sort of battle plan, or at least what she'd seen depicted in books as battle plans. She took another step toward the table, trying to get a better look.

"No, dear one, no, of course not," the elder woman assured, stepping between Raelia and the table.

"But it really looks-"

With a wave of Vysha's hand, all the documents vanished, and a smaller table appeared in the center of the room behind them. "*Aldaehima*, this is nothing to worry yourself over. Come child," she grabbed Raelia's hand, and led her away from the now empty table. "I think we should begin." Her eyes turned to Rokoa then. "Leave us."

He nodded stiffly, and walked out quickly, shutting the door behind him.

"Today, I want to work on your ability to recognize and call forth the power within you," Vysha explained. "As we talked about before, the dandelion gift presents differently in every person, and the magic it provides can be elusive. It has its own natural instinct to protect you, but there are so many different ways to wield it outside of just protection."

Raelia nodded as she watched the woman remove a small vial from her pocket and uncork it.

"Close your eyes, *Aldaehima*. Breathe deeply."

Once again, she did as she was told. She didn't know what the substance in the vial was, but she picked up the aroma quickly, noticing the slight hint of rose among a bitter citrus. It was intoxicating, and she felt slightly lightheaded.

Focusing her mind on the aromatic essence, she began to warm where the scent entered her body. Her mind switched its focus, and the heated sensation began to spread — first down her arms, then over her head. Her mind followed the warm progression across her chest, then stomach, then slowly down her legs.

A smile tugged at Raelia's lips. It was the safest and most comfortable she'd ever felt in her entire life — as if someone threw her truest identity over her like a cozy blanket, and it provided the shield she needed to be who she was meant to be.

Vysha's voice was soft when she spoke again, "I want you to focus all the energy you're feeling. Push it to the palms of your hands."

The reaction was instantaneous, as if the magic only needed to hear the thought. Within mere seconds, the warmth she felt encompassing her entire body had shifted to her hands.

"Now open your eyes."

When she did so, surprise flickered in her eyes when she saw a soft yellow light glowing in the palms of her hand.

"Test your limits," came Vysha's next command.

Raelia looked at her with confusion. "What do you mean?"

"You only had to think about my earlier direction, did you not?" the woman asked. "Your own imagination is the true test of what your powers can do."

She thought about that for a moment, watching the delicate light dance on her hands. Nazario's face appeared in her mind's eye, as she remembered their gift.

Suddenly, she was on the beach they'd put her on the first time they met. The colors were muted, and the sounds were muffled. There was no breeze blowing, and she still wore her training gear. And yet, she knew it was the same place.

A small gasp of surprise sounded next to her. She turned to see Vysha, shock coloring her features, as she stepped toward the water's edge. When the tips of her fingers dipped into the sea, Raelia felt her muscles tense and her knees buckle.

Suddenly, her body ached, and her eyes closed against the flood of exhaustion. Every limb felt heavy and a wave of nausea hit her like a punch in the gut, as she heard Vysha's voice.

"This is... unexpected," she said, an unfamiliar gleam touching her dark eyes. "Tell me, *Aldaehima*, do you only have one Indicative Mark? Only the dandelion?"

When Raelia opened her eyes once more, she offered the woman a confused look, and nodded slowly. The movement caused her vision to blur, and even breathing became difficult.

"Vysha?" she called in a tiny voice, "Something's wrong... I think I might be sick."

The woman stepped closer to her, taking Raelia's hands in her own, and squeezing tightly. The instant their skin connected, it was as if the weight of a hundred bricks was lifted from her shoulders.

She sighed in relief.

"Let it go," Vysha told her.

She looked at her with confusion and panic. She didn't know how to do that. How did one take off their own self after only just finally putting it on?

"How?"

"Take a deep breath, and focus on releasing the energy from your hands."

Raelia pictured the soft yellow light running up and out the tips of her fingers. When her mind's eye could no longer see the light, her body felt pulled backward, though her feet never moved. It was a strange sensation, as if a giant rope hooked behind her navel, flinging her backward through the universe. The nausea came back tenfold.

When she opened her eyes this time, she once again stood across the small table from a grinning Vysha in the large throne room. Her head was spinning, only making the nausea worse, and her body ached with exhaustion.

"Why do I feel so awful?" she asked the Red Lady. "It feels as if I'm coming down with a flu... Is that normal?"

Vysha nodded, coming around the table and placing an arm around Raelia's waist. "In the beginning, yes... Magic has its limits, and you're only just learning. It will take time for your body to adjust, but it will get easier the more you practice."

"Will the exhaustion stop as I get better?"

"Unfortunately, using our gifts takes its toll on our bodies," Vysha answered. "With prolonged use, it will drain your energy."

Raelia nodded her understanding, then swayed on the spot. She needed to sit down. Her body ached terribly, and the exhaustion started giving over to dizziness.

"Oh, *Aldaehima*, let's get you back to your room," Vysha walked slowly, tightening her grip on her waist, as she guided her toward the door. "You need to rest."

Walking back to her room was a slow affair, though once they hit the fresh air, Raelia perked up. Vysha's grip remained on her waist until they reached her shared living quarters.

Before she could open the door, Naz and another person who Raelia hadn't met before came around the corner. They were laughing, though when they spotted the Red Lady supporting her, the smile dropped quickly.

"Raelia? What's wrong?"

"Oh nothing, Nazario," Vysha answered for her. "She will be fine. She just needs to get some rest. Training took a lot out of her today, is all."

Their eyes connected to Raelia's, looking for confirmation. She gave a small nod, and turned to their friend, saying a rushed goodbye.

After their friend disappeared, they came to Raelia's side, placing their hand on her elbow. "I can help her," they offered. "I'll make sure she gets some rest."

Vysha looked at them with a grateful smile. "Thank you, my dear." Her hand released Raelia's waist. "We'll work some more tomorrow afternoon, after your training with Rokoa."

Raelia nodded, offering a small, exhausted smile. In the next moment, the woman was gone, and Naz was ushering her inside onto the plush sofa. Her body ached, and her eyes felt heavy. She leaned her body back, sinking into the pillowed cushions, as Naz sat down next to her, worry touching their eyes.

"What happened? I thought you were training with Rokoa?"

She sighed, and let her head fall back, closing her eyes. "I was this morning, but he told me that Vysha wanted to work with me today too, so he took me to her afterward." Her head fell to the side, her face toward them as she opened her eyes. "Is it always like this?"

"What?" they asked, confused. "Magic?"

She nodded.

"It can be tiring, especially in the beginning, but..." Their eyes raked over her, scrutinizing her slumped form. "I've never seen it be like this. You look like you're on the verge of death!"

"I don't feel much better," she chuckled lightly.

"It's not funny, Rae!" Naz chided her. "Magic isn't easy, and it takes a toll on our bodies if we overexert ourselves."

"I didn't realize, that's all. I'm sure I'll be fine. I just..." she let her voice trail off, not sure how to finish her sentence. "Why does it take such a toll on us, but not on other creatures that use it? Rokoa uses his all the time, and it never seems to-"

"Rokoa is a Drykuan, Rae. They are made of magic," they told her, rolling their eyes before falling onto the back pillow next to her. "Their bodies don't have the same limitations ours do. They don't exhaust the way ours do."

"Never? Are they really that powerful?"

"I'm sure they tire eventually, but it would take a lot for them to exhaust themselves."

She went quiet for a moment, thinking on their words when an image flashed in her mind. A memory from only a few days ago.

"What about the Zarhaish? Are they the same?"

"I would think so," they answered, seeming unsure. "They're similar to the Drykuan in most ways, from my understanding, but, if I'm honest, I know little about their magic."

"Hmm..." Raelia's mind combed over all she could remember reading about the two mythical races. There was little on the Drykuans, but what she'd gotten her hands on taught her quite a bit about the silvery iridescent beings. On the other hand, there had been next to nothing about the shimmery golden beings.

She knew they were immortal and considered the counterparts to the Drykuan's — being their opposite in most ways. The one blurb she'd read made it sound as if they were meek and shy, never being seen by mortal eyes. Raelia thought about that for a moment. Dhovina had been the exact opposite. They'd been confident, albeit rude and condescending. In the square, Qiralst had been loud and abusive. Neither of them seemed to fit the descriptions she'd read.

"Do you know many of the Zarhaish?" she asked Nazario. "I haven't seen many of them since I've been here. Mostly I've only seen Mark Bearers and Drykuan's... Where are all the Zarhaish?"

They sighed and looked at her. "The Zarhaish aren't the kind of creatures you want to spend a lot of time with."

At her quizzical look, they continued.

"They keep their distance. They are, by nature, quite cruel, and Vysha wants them separate from us to keep us safe."

The image of Qiralst swinging his whip down at her flashed in her mind and a shiver went down her spine. Then another image, Privina, the Drykuan he'd been attacking.

"Why didn't she fight back?"

"Who?" Naz's expression was puzzled.

Raelia laughed when she realized her question had been out loud. "Sorry. I mean, Privina. The Drykuan from the other day with the mad Zarhaish. Why would an immortal and powerful being like a Drykuan take that sort of abuse from a Zarhaish?"

"WOW! You really *are* out of the loop!" Naz chuckled before becoming serious once more. "Paodra belongs to the Zarhaish race. They only allow us here because of Vysha. She's lived here for a few hundred years now, and..."

"And?" Raelia pushed.

"And... I'm, well, I'm not really sure why... It never truly made sense to me."

She waited for them to continue with their story, and when they didn't, she pushed once more, "What does that have to do with the Drykuan's though?"

"What do you know about the Drykuan's?"

Raelia thought about that for a moment. In all the research she'd done through the years, she still knew very little. "Mostly just that the world thinks they're extinct."

"Have you heard of the immortal war?"

Raelia shook her head.

"I'm not surprised. Most haven't," they smirked before continuing. "The two immortal races used to live harmoniously. They shared Paodra. From my understanding, they built the city together."

"What happened?"

"I'm not totally sure, but eventually the Drykuan's and Zarhaish went to war against each other. It lasted a really long time, from what I've read, but ultimately the Zarhaish won control over Paodra – forcing the Drykuan's out of the forest."

"How did they end up back here?"

"King Nikolai's ban on Indicative Marks included wording that allowed for the execution of magic creatures and beings. They were forced into hiding."

Raelia was quiet, lost in thought – until she realized they hadn't answered her original question. "So... Privina didn't fight back, because...?"

"When the Zarhaish allowed them back into the forest, it was for their own gain," Naz explained. "I don't know all the details, but from what I've seen they have some sort of control over the Drykuan's. All of the mundane, everyday tasks that have to be done seem to be done by Drykuan's. The Zarhaish rarely leave their treetops and when they do, it's almost always to demand something from them."

"Why would the Drykuan..."

"I don't think they have a choice," they interrupted.

"Because they don't have anywhere else to go?"

"Actually, I think the Zarhaish are using some sort of magic to make them stay. I overheard Ekry talking to another Drykuan a couple years ago. The guy said something about wishing they could leave, but knowing the consequences of the magic. That's when I realized there's only a few of the Drykuan's that I've ever seen leave. Most of them never leave the village, let alone the forest."

"Hmm..." Raelia's eyes unfocused as her mind raced through this new information, twisting around memories of her time in Paodra and the interactions she'd had with the Drykuan's.

"Raelia, I-"

Before Naz could finish, the door popped open. Ayla and Luella were giggling as they walked in, shutting the door behind them.

Suddenly, she felt Nazario's hand on her arm, squeezing reassuringly. "Let's talk about it later," they said under their breath, only loud enough for her to hear.

In her eyes was a question, but she nodded in agreement.

"Rae!" Lue beamed at her, excitement shining from her entire being. "You'll never guess what I did today!"

"Tell her *after* we get some food!" Ayla groaned, as she made her way to the small table on the other side of the room. "I'm starving!"

CHAPTER 17

The week following her conversation with Naz passed by in a blur. Most days Rokoa woke her for training in the early morning. They'd usually eat breakfast before heading to the training area, but if they didn't, they always had lunch together. She realized he was much less surly than she'd originally thought. It surprised her at how kind and gentle of a soul he actually seemed. He laughed easily when it was just the two of them. They cracked jokes back and forth, and picked on each other — he quickly became a comforting presence for her. When others were around, however, his laughter became obscure. Even getting him to smile was difficult if it was more than just the two of them.

She felt stronger than she had before, and more agile. He worked her hard in their training sessions, but never became impatient — always insisting that he knew she was strong enough to handle whatever he threw at her. Figuratively and sometimes even literally. She could never take her eyes off of him while they trained, because she could never be sure he wouldn't throw a knife or an ax in her direction. The first time he did this, she'd been so surprised she tripped after jumping back, twisting her ankle on a mace someone neglected to put away, and slicing her calf open on one of the sharp spikes that protruded from the iron ball at the top.

She could only continue training that day after he brought her a cup of warm, shimmery gold liquid. He told her it was called Laanias nectar, and was used for healing wounds. She was skeptical, but drank the liquid as instructed, and in mere seconds, the deep cut on her leg stitched itself together. The only evidence of the wound was the now dry blood stuck to her leg. Not only did the cut and sprained ankle heal, but she also noticed her body didn't ache, the exhaustion she'd felt moments before vanishing quickly. She looked at Rokoa in fascination and made a mental note to find out where she could get more laanias nectar.

Some days, other Mark Bearers would train alongside them. Most would train their physical abilities, but others came to practice the power afforded them by their Indicative Marks. It was exciting for Raelia to witness some of the other magic, and to learn about the different Marks. Even more than that, it was nice to meet some of the other Mark Bearers, if only to feel less like a newcomer.

She learned so much about the magic that the Indicative Marks afforded them in the first week. The first day they'd been in Paodra, Rokoa told her a bit about the elements, and that each power coincided with a specific one, but she had never imagined the type of powers that existed.

On her third day of training, she met Nira. She was much shorter than Raelia, no more than 5'2", if she had to guess. Her long, thick brown hair hung over the fawn skin of her arms like a blanket, coming just short of covering the large cornflower Mark that wrapped around her forearm above her left wrist.

Nira arrived with Casen, who seemed almost her exact opposite in looks. Tall and slender, his porcelain skin seemed to shine, and his blonde hair was shorn close to the scalp. His Indicative Mark wasn't visible at first — not until he took his shirt off, causing Raelia to blush and avert her eyes momentarily — that the King Protea flower became visible between his shoulder blades.

Raelia had been fascinated to watch as Nira sped around the room from point to point at a speed which made her nearly invisible to the naked eye. She didn't believe Casen's gift could compare, until he threw his head back, and his body shifted. It looked as if his bones stretched and bended in impossible ways, and before she knew it, a lion stood in his place. He chased Nira, not being able to keep up. As the lion ran, in the blink of an eye, it transformed. Once a large, muscular king-of-the-forest shifted into a thin, aerodynamic cheetah. He still wasn't able to keep up with Nira's speed, but the fast cat came much closer than the lion.

On another day, Raelia met Collette. Sweet and bubbly, she chattered on about all sorts of news and gossip from around Paodra. They sparred together that morning. She was strong, and much more advanced than Raelia was, and yet she held her own. It wasn't until Raelia was about to overtake Collette that she got an idea of what her gift was. Her words were like butter when she told Raelia to swear her loyalty. Commanding she lay her sword down, and take a knee to declare the end of their fight. Her mind melted and wanted nothing more than to comply — she couldn't stop herself.

Not until Rokoa came over and told Collette to "cut it" did she even realized she wasn't acting on her own accord. After another second, the strangest sensation flowed through her. As if strings wrapped around her body in various places were being pulled taut, before one by one they were cut loose, causing her to fall back.

Collette's gift, Rokoa explained later while they ate lunch, was the ability to force devotion or loyalty on others, which was given by the Violet Indicative Mark. From her experience, Raelia knew it was a powerful gift, and clearly useful during a battle, but she couldn't help thinking that it would be dangerous in the wrong hands.

The conversation she and Nazario had, echoed around in her mind that first week. She wanted to ask Rokoa what the facts were, but even though she had plenty of opportunity to bring it up, she could never work up the nerve to broach the topic with him.

After her morning training sessions with Rokoa, he always escorted her to the throne room to train with Vysha. Raelia quickly learned using her own magic, while still draining, was nowhere near as exhausting as using other people's. During her second session with the Red Lady, she was surprised to learn Dhovina would be helping with her training. She wasn't happy about it, but it didn't seem the Zarhaish was either, so she didn't complain.

This time she'd been instructed to put up a barrier between herself and Dhovina using the soft yellow glow in her hands. When she envisioned the barrier, it was once again as if the magic read her thoughts. A delicate shimmer of yellow blurred Dhovina's form from in front of them.

Without warning, the Zarhaish flung a rock the size of their fist at Raelia. She flinched, but the barrier held steadfast, sending the stone tumbling to the wooden floor with a scattered thud. Excitement coursed through her and she beamed proudly at Vysha before the Red Lady directed her attention back to Dhovina, who began preparing an arrow to fire. Once again, Raelia flinched as it hit the barrier, but as it skittered to the ground, she was elated at the strength her power gave her.

During her next training session with Vysha, she was told it was time for another cleanse. Raelia's whole body tensed at the thought, afraid of what would happen this time around.

When she once again felt the paralyzing effect of the magic, she readied herself for attack. This time, however, she gained the upper hand early on, and while the invisible figure did eventually pin her down, she was proud of herself for holding her own, even if only for a little while. Confusion washed over her, however, when she realized Vysha seemed less than happy about her success.

Her days continued that routine through the first couple weeks. Training with Rokoa in the mornings, sometimes joined by other Mark Bearers. Wielding her magic in the afternoon with Vysha, being 'cleansed' every few days, much to her dismay. The cleansing always seemed to drain her, and she still didn't fully understand how it was helping. She always struggled controlling her magic after the cleansing days, and if it wasn't for Vysha insisting it was normal, she'd have demanded to stop them all together.

Dinner with Ayla and Nazario became a nightly event, and by the end of that first couple weeks, she was surprised to realize she felt at home. It wasn't Frayis. It wasn't the same as sitting around a table with her mother, father and siblings, but somehow, she'd found another family here. Even Luella seemed happy. She and Ayla became close — even training together most days.

Raelia knew that the six-week cutoff she and Luella agreed on was still in place, but she was happy they were both enjoying the short time they had in the magical forest.

⥀⥂

By the third week, things shifted. Something came up that took Rokoa and Vysha's time, so her training routine looked different. She asked what was going on, but neither the Drykuan nor the Red Lady confided in her, which was frustrating.

On the plus side, it offered the opportunity for her to meet other Mark Bearers, and to train with her friends more frequently, which she was grateful for.

She particularly liked training with Ayla. Being the Bearer of the Zinnia Mark gave her the ability to communicate telepathically, and she used it to her benefit during a fight — scaring the daylights out of her opponents.

'Raelia... don't attack Ayla... she's your friend...' Raelia jumped at Ayla's voice, echoing around in her own mind, causing her to miss the chance to dodge her friend's attack. She took the swift punch directly in her gut, bending over from the force of it as Ayla chuckled.

"What *was* that?!" she demanded between deep gasps for air. Her head lifted to look at the smirking brunette before her.

"You asked what my power was!" she laughed. "Now you know!"

Luella was in the corner, watching the pair of them, and giggling uncontrollably at the circumstances. Raelia turned to look at her best friend.

"Did you know?!" When Lue nodded in response, a feigned look of betrayal crossed Raelia's features. "Why didn't you tell me?! I could have been at least a *little* prepared!"

"It's more fun to watch you learn this way!" Luella uttered between giggles. "Just like I did!"

"Traitor!" Raelia laughed as she stood up, and turned her attention back to Ayla. "How does it work?"

"It's pretty easy, actually," she told her. "I have to focus on who I want to talk to, and then open a line between our minds." She looked down, embarrassed. "I know it sounds crazy, but I literally just imagine a thread connecting us, and the words travel from my mind and across it. If I'm waiting for an answer, I leave the line in place until they've responded."

Raelia looked at her, intrigued. "Interesting. How far away can the person be for it to work? Do you have to be able to see them?"

"Not at all!" Ayla smiled, excitedly, "If it hadn't been for my gift, I never would have known how to get to you! I told Juniper that the soldiers were talking about Paodra, and asked what she knew. If she wouldn't have helped guide me, I never would have found this place."

"Wow! Truliach is thousands of miles away! And she was able to talk back to you?"

Ayla nodded.

By that point, Luella's giggles subsided, and she strode up to the pair intrigued. "How long are you able to keep the lines open? Can you open multiple lines at one time?"

"I've only ever tried to keep three lines open at once, and it did work, though it was a bit...uh..." Ayla scrunched her nose up, looking for the right word. "Noisy? It was a constant stream of voices, and it made it difficult to focus on each one individually."

"And what about time? How long are you able to keep them open?" Raelia asked, curious about the answer herself.

"I'm not sure, if I'm honest," Ayla answered. "I suppose indefinitely, but I would have to be able to rest more often than I normally would, especially if there was more than one line open."

"Does it drain you?"

"Slowly, but yes."

"We should test your limits!" Luella exclaimed with a bright smile.

'Test your limits' had become a sort of motto for Luella over the last few weeks. Apparently, Rokoa told her she needed to test hers during their first training session, and she really took it to heart. She told Raelia, every time she trained she repeated those words to herself, and was convinced they were the reason she'd come as far as she had. She became much stronger and coordinated than she'd been before coming to Paodra, and Raelia noticed.

"How so?" Ayla asked.

"Well, you could keep a line open for an undetermined amount of time," Luella explained. "That way you'll be able to see how long you can keep it open and still function as a human being."

Ayla laughed, but the gleam in her eye showed her piqued curiosity. "I think I'll try that!" she blurted out, before turning to look at Raelia. "Would you mind if I kept a connection with you?"

Her jade green eyes widened. "Me? I-uh-I don't think it'd be a problem..." Raelia chewed on her bottom lip as questions ran through her mind. "I don't necessarily think anyone needs to be in my head all the time though..."

Ayla laughed. "Oh, I wouldn't be there all the time! I can't explain it to you as well as I can show you."

Before Raelia could protest, she felt a strange sensation in her mind. As if there was a knock on her door, only there was no sound, only the impression of it. She hadn't felt that during their fight, though, it could be because she was so focused on their sparring.

"Why didn't I feel this before?" she asked Ayla. "This... uh... sensation?"

"It's a different type of connection than before," she answered. "To project into someone's mind, I don't need permission. To open two-way communication, the person has to willingly accept it."

Confused, Raelia looked at her. "Accept it? How do I do that?"

"I... I don't know..." Ayla told her. "I've never connected like this with anyone but Juniper, and she just did it."

Raelia closed her eyes, focusing on the sensation in her mind. She pictured a large, heavy door, and twisted the handle. Once open, a tingling sensation traveled through her mind and down her spine. She didn't know how, but she knew it worked.

"Can you hear me?" she asked while her mind's eye looked through the open door.

Ayla grinned, nodding in front of her as a resounding, *"YES!"* echoed into her head.

After she'd finished training with her friends that morning, Raelia headed to the throne room to meet Vysha. Upon arrival, however, she was surprised to find Jamina instead.

"I thought... uh... Where's Vysha?" she asked, confused.

"She told me to let you know that something came up," Jamina answered, as she shuffled through scrolls on the table against the back wall. "Said to tell you to come back tomorrow at the same time."

"Oh," Raelia replied before turning to head out the large door once more.

Jamina ignored her as she stepped into the dimly lit hallway, and soon Raelia found herself pushing open the heavy, ornately carved door that led back into the main square of Paodra. Her eyes stayed on the ground as she walked, and she was completely oblivious to what was going on around her as her mind wondered what had happened to Vysha.

A sudden bump from the left caused her to stumble. Losing her balance, she fell to the ground, wincing as her hip hit in such a way that pain shot through her entire right side. She twisted to sit on her butt and looked at the tall, inky haired woman who had run her down.

"Cerissa?

She met Cerissa a few times in the training arena, but they had been brief. The only things she knew about her, outside of her name, was that she possessed the Spider Lily Mark, and it granted her the power to raise the dead.

Now, Raelia thought it was a pretty amazing gift, but when she'd unexpectedly witnessed the power for the first time while Cerissa had been training against another Bearer, it terrified her to see skeletons rising through the floor and walls. Human and animal remains not only appeared, but fought in their beckoner's stead.

"Raelia! You really should watch where you're going," the girl replied, holding her hand out for Raelia to take.

She helped her back to her feet with a smile.

"Sorry. I was lost in thought," Raelia told her. "Guess I should look up and not at the ground, huh?"

The two of them laughed lightly before Cerissa spoke once more. "Where are you headed?"

"Oh! I'm just headed back to my room. You?"

"Well... I uh... I was looking for you, actually."

That took her by surprise. They barely knew each other. "For me?"

"I heard a rumor that you have a kyloxis staying with you. Is it true?"

"Oh! You mean, Zayric?" Raelia laughed, "Yep! He's a little pest! Wakes me up at the crack of dawn every day!"

"Do you think... Well... Do you think I could meet him? I've never seen a kyloxis before," Cerissa smiled sheepishly, "and, well, they have fascinated me ever since I came across them in a mythical beast book years ago."

Raelia smiled and nodded as she held up a finger and closed her eyes. Picturing Zayric in her mind's eye, she released tendrils of invisible power all around them, as Rokoa showed her in one of their recent training sessions, and called his name in her mind.

"Zayric? Can you hear me?"

Without further prompting, Raelia opened her eyes to find a swirl of white mist had appeared before her. It swirled down to the ground, and in a blink disappeared, leaving the familiar fuzzy fox in its place.

Zayric looked up at her with expectant eyes, and she reached down, allowing him to jump into her arms. He scaled up her arm, and perched on her shoulder, as he was fond of doing, before he looked at the other woman.

Cerissa gawked at the creature, but a smile crept across her face, stretching her olive skin. "He's beautiful! Can I touch him?"

Raelia peered at Zayric who gave her a small lick on the cheek in approval before she nodded. "I think he'd be okay with that."

Without a moment's hesitation, Cerissa reached out and scratched him behind the ears. Her brown eyes glowed with excitement as she pulled her hand back.

"Hey Rae!" Ayla exclaimed from behind as she and Luella stepped up beside Cerissa. "I don't think I've met you yet," she smiled, holding her hand out. "I'm-"

"Ayla," Cerissa finished for her with a kind smile. "Naz has mentioned you before. And you're Luella, right?"

Lue nodded, and shook Cerissa's outstretched hand after Ayla.

The conversation lulled for a moment and Raelia's stomach decided that was the time to let out a loud grumble. She placed her hand over it and chuckled. "I clearly need to eat something."

"We were just headed to the dining hall," Ayla exclaimed. "Wanna head there now?"

With a nod of agreement, Raelia turned to Cerissa, who'd resumed scratching Zayric behind the ear. "Would you like to join us?"

"I wish I could!" the girl replied, sounding disappointed. "Unfortunately, I have to meet Privina for combat training before I eat."

Raelia nodded her understanding, and after a brief farewell, the group parted ways.

The three friends made small talk on their way to the dining hall, Zayric still perched on Raelia's shoulder. She'd only been here a handful of times with Rokoa, and there'd been very few people each time. This time, however, it was crowded. As if every being in Paodra had decided that exact moment was the perfect time to eat. Mark Bearer's and Dykuan's mingled amicably at nearly every table in the room.

Ayla led the charge, stealing one of the paper menus along the way. They found an open table in the corner and hurried to sit down before anyone else did.

"Hmmm... What do I want to eat?" Ayla mumbled to herself as she stared at the paper with intense eyes.

"Why did we have to come here?" Raelia asked in a hushed whine. "There's so many people! We would be so much more comfortable in our room..."

Luella tried to hide her smile, as Ayla looked up to answer, "You have *got* to stop hiding away! I get you've always had to before, but now you don't! Not here. Paodra is safe for us! We don't have to hide who we are and avoid people for fear of discovery!" She smiled brightly at Raelia before continuing, "With the exception of our little LuLu here, everyone has a Mark so there's nothing to hide!"

"You know, that might not be the only reason I avoid people! What if I just don't like people? Maybe that's the reason...," she told her friend. Though, if she was honest, Ayla's pronouncement hit a little closer to home than she'd like to admit.

"Then why are you still wearing this braid?" Luella asked, gently picking up the thick braid and bringing it into Raelia's line of sight.

She yanked it back. "Because it's what I'm used to! I'm not trying to hide anything. I know I don't have to anymore."

Ayla chuckled. "Either way, it's good for you to be here around the other Mark Bearers. The more you are, the less of a fascination you become. You were complaining just the other day about feeling like you're on display, always being stared at, right? Well, this is how you fix it!"

Raelia rolled her eyes, and pulled the menu to herself. She looked down, perusing the meals available, and decided quickly on a seafood dish she hadn't tried yet. After pressing her finger to the little blue rose, she decided she also needed some liquid courage if she was going to sit around all these people while she ate, and added a cup of Gristoa berry juice.

Her friends watched on with matching smirks of amusement when the juice arrived, and Raelia immediately took a massive gulp from the tall glass.

"What?"

"Do you really hate people so much that you have to be a drunkard just to be around them?" Ayla asked, trying to stifle her laughter.

Raelia rolled her eyes once more, and picked up her fork. She speared a scallop and popped it in her mouth, just as Luella pressed her finger onto the paper to order her own meal.

They sat in amicable silence for a bit while they ate the delicious food from Brixxi's kitchen, and Raelia would have been happy for it, but the incessant conversation of others around her put her on edge.

She'd spent her whole life avoiding crowds, mostly because of her Mark, but also because of the overwhelming feeling that struck her when there were multiple conversations happening at the same time. The constant mumbling voices, never being able to fully follow the conversations, and most of the time, not being able to fully under-stand what was being said, set her nerves on edge. It made her mind feel muddy.

"Hey!"

Raelia jumped, her fork clattering against her plate. She looked up to see Nazario's smiling face, and sighed. "Don't sneak up on people like that!"

They laughed and looked to the person standing next to them. A tall, lanky man with tawny brown skin smiled softly. His gray eyes smiled with him, and he lifted his hand in a small wave. Under his left eye was a small flower Mark Raelia didn't recognize.

"Sorry, Rae," Naz smirked unapologetically. "I just wanted to introduce you to someone. Guys, this is Galys."

After the newcomers took their seats, and introductions were made, Naz and Galys ordered meals for themselves.

The conversation was lively amongst the small group, and when Naz told her Galys was a fellow bookworm, the next thing she knew, they were lost in their own conversation. The other three talked amongst themselves, as Raelia and Galys talked all about their passion for books. Books they loved. Books they hated. He told her about the wonderful books he'd found here in Paodra telling all about the legends of the world, and it took everything in her to not run off in the direction he pointed when he told her about the massive library no one had shown, or even mentioned to her yet.

There were books in the lounge room, she knew, but she'd been so busy since arriving, she hadn't taken the time to peruse the shelves. She'd been itching to get her hands on a good read the last few days, so when Galys offered to take her to the library the following day, she jumped at the chance.

"I would *love* that! We could go today, if you have time! Now even!" Raelia beamed at her new friend. She knew she probably sounded desperate, but didn't care.

Galys laughed, a low, rough sound that came from deep in his chest. "A little eager there, don't you think?" He didn't wait for a response before continuing, "I can't today, as I have combat training with Ekry this afternoon, but maybe tomorrow?"

She nodded in response before asking, "Do you train with Ekry a lot?" she asked, suddenly curious about more than only books.

"Not anymore. When she first brought me here, we trained together every day, but now it's only every couple weeks. I train with others like us much more frequently now. I miss our old routine, though. She taught me a lot." Galys flashed her a grin. "You're training with Rokoa, right?"

Raelia nodded.

"How do you like him?"

"I - uh - I like him okay," she answered, confused by his question. "Why do you ask?"

Galys shrugged. "I've been here my whole life and never seen him work with a Mark Bearer before," he explained. "He isn't even very nice to most of us. I think he's only said maybe five words to me in my whole twenty three years, and none of them were particularly kind words..."

"Really?" Surprise crossed her features. She knew Rokoa tended to be more reserved when it wasn't just the two of them, but it was hard to imagine him being unfriendly to anyone.

"Has he been as preoccupied as the rest of the Drykuan's?"

"Yes! He's canceled quite a few of our sessions, actually," Raelia answered.

"It seems all the Drykuan's have been preoccupied as of late. Do you have any idea what's going on? Ekry has been less than forthcoming."

"I have no idea."

"Galys?" Naz interrupted. "Have you seen Nira lately?"

"Nira? The one with the cornflower Mark?" Raelia asked, turning her gaze to Nazario.

"That's the one! Little Miss Speedy," they smiled. "She's supposed to show me a defense move she's been working on, but I haven't seen her for a few days."

"I haven't seen her for three or four days, actually." Galys told them.

"Isn't her room right next to yours?"

"Yeah, it is. It's strange, to be honest. Most mornings we have breakfast together, but she sort of just stopped showing up..."

Raelia noticed a look of concern flash across Nazario's features, but they neutralized it quickly with a grin. "I'm sure she's fine. I'll go check on her this afternoon. She's probably found a new beau, or something."

"Yeah," Galys agreed, forcing a chuckle. "You're probably right. I'm sure she'll turn up."

A hint of worry was apparent in his tone. Raelia noted he seemed to be trying to convince himself, just as much as he was everyone else.

"He's worried. Naz too." Raelia jolted at hearing Ayla's voice in her mind, and her eyes connected with her friend's.

"But we're in a safe place," she sent back. *"There's nothing to worry about, right? I mean, what could happen to her here? Vysha protects us."*

Sitting across from her, Ayla slightly shrugged and turned her gaze back to her meal, before her reply flowed through the open door in Raelia's mind, *"If that's true, why are they so worried?"*

Chapter 18

After lunch, the small group headed toward the Mark Bearer's living quarters. Galys promised to meet Raelia the following day to show her the library and then with a quick goodbye disappeared down a dark hallway.

When they turned the final corner into their own hallway, she was surprised to see Rokoa leaning against the wall next to their door. Even more surprising, however, was Zayric, sitting on one of the Drykuan's broad shoulders.

"There you are," Rokoa said, pushing himself up to stand. "Got some free time?"

He didn't specify who he was talking to, but his gaze met Raelia's eyes.

"Yeah. Why? What's up?" she asked.

Luella reached out, pushing her way in front of him to get into their room. Rokoa stepped back to allow the others through and, in a moment, all three of her friends disappeared behind the heavy wooden door.

"Come with me."

Without waiting for a response, Rokoa, along with Zayric on his shoulder, walked around her and headed back the way she'd come.

"Wait! Where are we going?"

Raelia hurried to follow, and soon he had led her past the lounge room, and back up the stairs to the main square outside.

"I want to swing by the training arena to grab a few things, and then I want to show you something."

Somehow she knew he wouldn't answer, but couldn't keep herself from asking, "What is it?"

He only smirked and continued along his route.

It didn't take them long to reach the training area, and he told her to go grab a bow and quiver of arrows from the loft. She did as instructed, and by the time she returned, he was slinging a rucksack packed with other weaponry on his back.

"Do I get to know where you're taking me yet?" she asked with a chuckle. "Should I be worried we're taking an entire arsenal?"

Zayric sat on the ground near him, and ran to her as she approached. He rubbed on her leg, much like a cat would, and she smiled as she crouched down to scratch behind his ear. "Do you know where we're going?"

"He knows as much as you do," Rokoa told her as he headed back toward the door. "Come on, BeeBee."

Rolling her eyes at the nickname, Raelia picked up Zayric. He crawled up her arm, and wedged himself between her neck and the arrows on her back, lying around her much like a scarf, as she hurried to catch up with him. "Do you really have to call me that?" she asked. "The novelty has really worn off."

"Maybe for you," Rokoa answered with a smirk.

She scoffed, as he led her down a dark staircase she hadn't been down before. The sound of their footsteps echoed off the wood walls as they made it further into the darkness.

"How do you know where you're going?" Raelia asked when her vision gave out almost completely.

"You are a magical being, are you not? Can't you produce your own light by now?" Rokoa laughed. "What's Vysha been teaching you if you can't even do that yet?!"

Feeling rather foolish, she focused her mind for a moment, before the soft yellow glow of her magic appeared in her hand, illuminating the hallway around them.

"Now was that so hard?" Rokoa smirked down at her.

She felt Zayric shifting his position on her neck, his back paws stretching over her shoulder as he lifted his head. Raelia looked at him from the corner of her eye, but wasn't able to make much of him out in the dim light. His dark fur blending seamlessly with the shadows being cast in the hall, only the white speckles of his muzzle stood out.

The hallway ahead of them seemed endless, just as the one they'd arrived through. After a few minutes, she realized they were going up a slight incline. Her breaths came quicker as they continued up their path, and she found herself wondering where on earth he was taking her.

"Look," Rokoa said, pulling her from her thoughts.

Her eyes followed the line from his pointing finger, curiously. Not far ahead of them, the glow from her hand extended over a doorway in their path. Rokoa put his hand on the knob, but turned to look at her before opening it.

"Be on your guard. It isn't as serene as it seems," he told her.

Before she could question what he meant, his hand twisted the knob. Bright sunlight flooded the dark hallway, causing Raelia to squint her eyes against it. She dropped her hand, letting the glow evaporate into the new light, and stepped through the doorway.

They were in the forest.

She heard birds chirping all around them. The sound of fluttering wings threaded through the dense branches above, and Raelia couldn't help but feel calmed, surrounded by the familiar sights and sounds. The sunlight had a green hue as it filtered its way through the leaves, and pine needles above, and somewhere in the distance, Raelia heard the babbling of water.

Rokoa watched her closely, as she took in their surrounding sights. He smiled down as she looked up. "Where are we?"

"This," he started, gesturing around them with his free hand, "is the Forest of Paodra."

Without warning, he turned and started down a narrow path winding through the trees. Raelia hurried to follow.

"I thought where we lived was Paodra...?"

He laughed. "We live in a pocket of the Paodran forest. We've called it Paodra to ease confusion," he told her. "If we want to be technical, we live in a village within the Forest of Paodra."

"Ah..." She wasn't exactly sure what the difference was, and she was pretty positive he knew that, but she had other questions on her mind. "And what are we doing out here?"

"We're going to do some training," he explained, smirking down at her. "Well... *You* are going to do some training."

"Just me? You know it's kind of hard to-"

Her words were cut off by a gasp as the path brought them into a clearing so beautiful it made her heart swell with joy.

On the far end, a creek bubbled happily along its bed. Between it and where they stood, a small meadow filled with wildflowers of all colors, sizes, and shapes. Butterflies fluttered among them, and birds flew through the sky above. It was as perfect as a painting, and she felt so light and happy at the sight.

Rokoa stepped into the clearing, dropping his rucksack next to a mossy log on the ground, and took a seat. One by one, he pulled out the weapons he'd brought. The two broadswords she'd seen sticking out the drawstring top. She hadn't, however, seen the mace, swing blades, daggers or throwing knives within the bag's depths. Raelia's eyes widened as she looked at the arsenal he laid out on the log.

"You realize we're only two people, right? Are we really going to need all of those?"

"I think it's time for you to have some real world training," he answered, "and I think it's best to have every option available to you. That way, you know which weapon you're most comfortable with."

"Uh... Real world training?" Raelia wasn't sure how she felt about that and was even less sure how she would get it in an isolated clearing in the middle of a forest.

Rokoa smirked, understanding her hesitancy. "Maybe not exactly real world, but as close as you're going to get while staying here. Now, get that pup off your shoulder."

She completely forgot Zayric still sat on her, and she turned to smile at the curious kyloxis who cocked his head to one side. Without even having to be shooed off, he stood and jumped down, running to the log where Rokoa sat.

Raelia watched as her furry friend stretched and then curled back up. She assumed he would go back to sleep, but as always, Zayric surprised her. His head may have laid down, but his eyes watched her with an alertness only a fox could convey.

"I want to start with the bow. You've mentioned you like to shoot, so I'd like to see what skill level you have."

Suddenly nervous, Raelia pulled the bow from over her shoulder, and then reached for an arrow. Her father showed her how to shoot when she was young, but he was the only one who'd ever seen her practice, and the idea of someone else watching made her jittery with nerves.

"What am I shooting at?" she asked, before adding, "And don't say birds or any other animal! I'm not killing anything!"

Laughing, Rokoa waved his hand, and across the clearing, on the opposite side of the creek, a target appeared. "We can start with this."

She sighed, relieved, as she notched her arrow, and pointed it toward the target. She closed her eyes, focusing on the slight breeze blowing tendrils of her hair across her face. She opened her eyes, adjusting her aim for its direction. Tightening her grip, she pulled the arrow back. The muscles in her shoulders and upper back protested after so much time of not shooting.

Once again, she focused on the breeze, and keeping her eyes on the center of her target, let the arrow fly. She knew at once she'd screwed it up. The arrow flew in the right direction, but swerved just far enough to the right that it zipped past the large target.

Rokoa laughed. "I thought you said you were decent?"

"I am! I just haven't practiced in a while!" she protested. "Besides, this is a completely new bow for me! I'm used to my old one!"

"Excuses, excuses," he replied. Before she raised the bow once more, the Drykuan stepped up to her, placing his hands on her hips and turning them just slightly. She felt heat flood her cheeks as his hands moved down her legs. Raelia stifled a nervous gasp as he repositioned them. "Try again."

Her eyes were wide when he stood up. At the sight of the smug smirk on his face, however, they narrowed – glaring at him as she pulled out her second arrow and notched it.

"This time, listen to the wind. Don't just feel what it's doing, listen to it."

"Listen? To the wind? It's not like it's going to tell me how quickly it's going to gust through here, is it?" She rolled her eyes, and looked back at her target.

Once again, she closed her eyes. Noticing the feel of the breeze against her skin, she also did as Rokoa told her. She listened. She heard the rustling of the grass and the whisper of the leaves as the wind blew through.

When she pulled back on the bow a second time, she adjusted her aim to consider not only what she felt, but also what she heard. She let it fly once more, and brightened as she heard the thud of her arrow sinking into the target.

It didn't hit the center, but it wasn't at the edge either, and if she was honest with herself, she was just happy she hit the target at all.

"Not bad, Beebee. Not bad at all."

She beamed at him as she pulled another arrow from her quiver. Raelia turned her attention back to the target and let it fly. Once again, she hit the mark. It was closer to the center this time, but still far enough off she wanted one more go.

The next time she watched the arrow fly through the clearing, she knew before it hit that she had done it.

Thud.

"Nice work!" Rokoa smiled as he looked at the arrow protruding from the center mark. "Now that you're warmed up a bit, let's try your hand at something moving."

"I told you I will not be shooting any defenseless animals today!"

Rokoa barked out a laugh and waved his hand. "No one asked you too."

She turned back to the mark, and understood why he laughed. The once stationary target now moved. First to the left, and then back the way it came. She watched the side-to-side movement, and nerves fluttered in her stomach once more. She'd never shot at anything moving before.

He stepped up to her, and reached for the bow, which she handed over without complaint. "With a moving target, the key is to be able to anticipate the movement, and shoot with it in mind," he explained, pulling an arrow from her quiver.

He notched it, and with no hesitation, let the arrow fly toward the target. Raelia was certain it would miss, and yet, it hit the exact center with ease, knocking her previous arrow out of its way.

"As you can see, it's really quite simple."

"Says the immortal being with hyper speed and super vision," Raelia replied, rolling her eyes as she took her bow back.

She retrieved an arrow, and notched it, as he watched her with intense eyes. She hesitated for a moment, but did her best to focus as she had before.

Her first shot missed. By a lot.

As she notched her second arrow, Rokoa was stifling laughter.

Missed again. Though not by quite as much as the first.

Third, fourth, fifth and sixth arrows all flew right past the shifting target, causing her frustration to grow with every shot.

Her seventh arrow grazed the edge of the target as it flew by, and even though it wasn't exactly a hit, she still grinned to herself.

On her eighth shot, the thud echoed through the small clearing, and she jumped up with excitement. "I hit it!" she exclaimed. "I hit it!"

Shaking his head, Rokoa chuckled. "Don't get too excited. You hit the very edge. It's barely stuck in the target!"

He kept her shooting for a couple hours. Any time she emptied her quiver, Rokoa waved his hand and arrows would fill it again. When she hit the center three times in a row, he'd declare she mastered it, and switch it up once more. The side-to-side movements became zig zagged, then up and down, and then a combination of all three.

"Now for the real world application," Rokoa said with a wave of his hand.

Suddenly, the target disappeared. In its place stood a group of people. As if acting out a scene from a theater production, a woman screamed as a man grabbed her satchel and ran through the crowd. When he disappeared into the trees, the scene replayed.

"Take down the thief," Rokoa told her.

A look of horror spread over her features. "You can't be serious!" she all but shouted. "I can't shoot people! What if I miss him?! What if I hit an innocent bystander?!"

"Raelia, they're not real," he explained. "You won't hurt anyone. Not really. And this will help you to not harm anyone in the future when you're among real people."

Her muscles tensed, but she knew he was right. This was the best way for her to practice, and if they truly weren't real, then what was the harm?

The first arrow she shot hit the woman screaming about her satchel. When the arrow sunk into her chest, there was no reaction, and then the scenery reset.

Again she shot at the thief, and again she missed. This time hitting a bystander, but only just missing the running man.

The third time, her arrow sunk deep into the thief's thigh. He screamed as it hit him, and blood poured from the wound.

Raelia jumped at the man's reaction. No one else reacted in the slightest, and yet the thief screamed in agony. Even knowing it was fake, her heart rate sped up, and an overwhelming grief came over her.

She turned to Rokoa, about to ask what was happening, when the screaming cut off and the scene reset once more.

He made her run through it over and over. Changing the scene slightly every time she hit her Mark. By the time he allowed her to put down her bow, her arms, shoulders, and even her chest ached, and she worried what other tasks he could possibly have for her.

"You catch on quicker than I expected you too," Rokoa told her as he walked over to the arsenal he'd laid out earlier. He picked up a small swing blade and when he returned held it out for her to take. Then he removed a sheathed dagger from inside his vest, and waved his free hand, making it disappear.

In the next moment, Raelia felt her belt become heavier. She looked down to find the dagger hanging at her hip. She looked at him with questioning eyes.

His returning smile was gentle, only confusing her more. "This time," he continued, as if nothing happened, "you'll need to be a bit more cunning. I won't stop or reset the scene until I see you're in danger."

"Dan-" Rokoa snapped his finger and her surroundings vanished, "-ger?"

Raelia looked around. She stood in the center of a busy market square. Much like the one she remembered from her childhood visits to the palace with her father. She spun around on the spot, her eyes following up the high peaks of the castle, confirming her location.

Suddenly, she jolted forward as someone bumped her from behind. Her weapon clattered to the cobblestones below. She reached for it quickly, stowing it away in one of the many pockets her training attire afforded her.

"You! Stop right there!" someone shouted from behind.

As she spun around, she heard the telltale thud of heavy boots and spotted three of the royal guardsmen heading in her direction.

Dread spread through her, tingling in her arms and legs, as she watched their progression. She felt frozen in place as fear consumed her, and could do nothing but watch with terrified eyes as they came closer.

"You should hurry, lest they catch you with that blade," an ancient voice said to her right. Her eyes shifted once more, landing on a small woman with eyes that seemed to tell the tale of millennia. The lines on her face were deep and gave her eyes a sunken quality only one who had seen the passage of generations could.

Pulled out of her paralysis, she shot her gaze back to the guards, coming closer by the second. With a nod of gratitude to the old woman, Raelia twisted around and ran at top speed through the crowd. People grumbled as she bumped into them, others spotted her coming and moved out of the way to let her pass.

She continued running, only looking behind her to check she was still far ahead of the guards pursuing her. Finally, it seemed she'd lost them. When she turned to look, their forms had disappeared in the ever massing crowd, and excitement flooded through her.

'Thump'

Pain flowed through her as she hit a massive, fleshy surface, causing her to fall back, hitting the ground hard. From somewhere above her, loaves of bread fell. Hitting her in the head, and legs, and thunking to the ground, just as she had.

When it stopped raining loaves, she looked up to see a large, thick man glaring down at her with rage.

"What do you think you are doing?!" he screamed. "You destroyed it! You destroyed every loaf!"

People around them turned their heads, looking for the source of the commotion. The man took a step towards her, and Raelia scooted back, fear replacing her excitement.

"I-I'm sorry," she stuttered, scooting back once more and making to get on her feet. "It was an accident. I-"

Without warning, the man's chubby fist whipped out, grabbing her by the collar and yanked her upward. "How do you intend to pay me for the loaves you ruined?!"

"P-pay?" Raelia's eyes went wide. She didn't have any money. How could she pay him?

If possible, the man's face contorted with even more rage than before. "You do not intend to pay?!"

"I-I-I d-don't have-"

"GUARDS!" the man screamed into the crowd. "Guards! Thief!"

Raelia wriggled, trying to break free of the man's grasp, to no avail. "Please! Please! I'll pay! I'll pay!"

When she felt hands grip her from behind, she knew it was too late.

"This mongrel destroyed my bread! She refuses to pay!" he shouted, as he released her to the guard's hold.

"Thought you could get away?" the guard closest to her asked in a mocking tone.

She twisted and turned, trying to free her hands. She needed her weapon. If she could only reach it, she could fight her way out of this. With every movement, their grip on her arms and wrists became tighter.

The unmistakable clink of shackles echoed behind her. She fought even harder to free herself, knowing that once they slipped on her wrists, there was little chance to escape them.

Knowing her options were limited, she kicked her heel back blindly. They hadn't expected it, and when she connected with some part of one of them, she was relieved to feel his grip lessen, even if only slightly. But it was enough. She yanked her arm out of his grip, and quickly grabbed for the weapon she'd stowed away.

The guard's shouted. She didn't hear their words as her hand tightened around the handle of the small swing blade and she pulled it from her pocket, completely forgetting about the dagger at her hip.

The blade was small, and yet deadly, curving back from the hilt where Raelia's hand gripped tightly, arming her with a razor-sharp edge atop her knuckles.

When she felt the hands reach for her once more, Raelia swung her arm toward the man, and winced as she felt the blade meet his flesh.

A scream of agony flooded the square, as Raelia brought her hand back around and twisted to face the other two guards. One still held her other arm like a vice, and she knew she needed to free herself.

Once again, she swung the blade. This time towards the wrists of the man still holding her. It was different this time, and even though fear coursed through her, she couldn't bring herself to cut into him, and her swing became hesitant.

To her relief, before the blade could come in contact with the second man, he released her, reaching for the sword at his waist. She stepped back, eyes wary as she watched their advances. A loaf of bread mushed under Raelia's foot as she turned, darting around the beefy baker, who reached for her too slowly as she ran. Within moments, she was being chased once more.

The crowd was of no help this time. As so many people had stopped to watch the ruckus, they weren't shifting and moving as they'd been before. She twisted and cut around them, but hiding among them was no longer possible.

Suddenly, a scream ripped through the air. A terrified, agonized scream. Raelia couldn't help herself. She knew she needed to keep running, but she turned just in time to see the first guard fall to the ground.

CHAPTER 19

The guard writhed in pain, batting his fists at a black, silky smoke that enveloped his face.

Raelia gasped, freezing in place as she recognized the magic of her kyloxis immediately. "Zayric?"

Before she could say or do anything else, the smoke shifted. Rising from the now dead guard and weaving through the crowd toward her. Raelia reached out her hand and felt tendrils of the soft vapor wind around her fingers.

Abruptly, her vision blurred, and her body seemed to evaporate into a whirl of colors and sounds. She couldn't tell which way was up or down. She wasn't able to distinguish the people or voices around her. Everything seemed to mush together.

In the next second, just as abruptly, the world around her formed once more as her feet hit the ground. Her knees buckled, but surprisingly, she kept herself upright. The dizziness she'd felt before seemed to expand, and she bent over, afraid she would be sick.

When she looked at the ground beneath her feet, she realized that there were no longer cobblestones. Thick green grass was being crushed under her heavy boots, and when she peered around, she didn't know where they were. In the distance, the castle protruded from the horizon in all its regal glory. She didn't understand how she'd gotten out of there so quickly.

Something soft rubbed against her leg, startling her. When her eyes landed on Zayric, she smiled. "Did you do that?"

"Yes," came a booming response in a familiar lilting accent. "And it wasn't supposed to happen."

Following Rokoa's words, a snap echoed, and she suddenly stood in the small clearing once more. Zayric pawed her leg, begging to be picked up, which she obliged.

"How did he do that?" she asked, snuggling her face into the fox she held. "Everything around me just evaporated and then we were in some field!"

When she didn't receive a response, she turned expectant eyes on Rokoa. His chin rested in his fist giving him a confused air as he thought through what just happened.

"Hello? Dirythia to Rokoa! Are you in there?" Raelia smirked when he finally looked at her, still looking dazed. "Are you going to share whatever you're thinking so hard about, or do I need to guess?"

"I was thinking maybe we're going about your training wrong."

That took her by surprise. "What do you mean?"

"I didn't know a kyloxis could share its powers with a mortal. Knowing it's possible, well," he stepped forward, reaching a hand out to scratch the top of Zayric's head, "it seems irresponsible not to train you together."

"Oh, very funny," she laughed, sure he couldn't be serious.

"Do you hear me laughing?" Rokoa's eyebrow quirked up. "It's only logical! A kyloxis is an immensely powerful being, and if you can share in its gift, you will be *very* hard to beat in hand to hand combat. He's still young. His powers are still developing."

She thought about it for a moment. She hadn't exactly seen much of Zayric's powers. Only his ability to turn into a mist, and suck the life out of people — or at least she thought that's what happened when the smoke touched them — What other powers could the small fox have?

"How could we train together if his powers aren't fully developed? Doesn't he have to learn how to use them first?"

"Not exactly. You see, a kyloxis learns to use his powers based on instinct. When the instinct clicks, they master it the first time out," Rokoa explained. "When they're bonded with an immortal being, the knowledge is transferred through connection. I assumed since there was no knowledge transfer, it meant you weren't able to share in his gifts. It appears I was wrong."

"If there's no - uh - knowledge transfer? How can I learn to use his gifts?"

"You, unfortunately, will have to learn through trial and error, which is why it will be so important for you two to train together."

Over the next couple of hours, Raelia was swirled into blurry nothingness over and over. It was much more tiring than she thought it would be, considering she didn't really do anything herself — All the power being used was Zayric's, and yet, she felt a deep exhaustion, making it harder and harder for her to land on her feet when she came back to a corporeal form.

She did her best not to let on how difficult it became, but when Rokoa spoke, she knew her efforts had been in vain.

"Once more," he urged. "You need to get used to it now, so it isn't so draining. It will take time, just like your other training, but you're getting better each time."

The constant swirling of colors and smells and sounds was making her nauseous, which made it hard to keep the irritation from her voice when she responded, "Maybe if we started with this instead of hours of combat training, it would be easier!"

He only laughed in response before repeating, "Once more," in an amused tone.

Raelia sighed before standing upright again, and looking down at Zayric sitting next to her feet. For a moment, he watched her with worried eyes, as if trying to convey he understood how difficult this was for her, but when she gave him a small grin, the look passed. Zayric stood, leaping up toward her awaiting arms.

At the moment his fur connected with her body, the world liquified around them and she felt the now familiar sensation of evaporating into mist. Minutes felt like hours as the scenery swirled, and somewhere in her smokey form she felt her stomach churn.

When her feet came back to the earth, she stood on the opposite side of the clearing, right next to the creek. She fell to her knees, panting. "I think I'm going to be sick," she croaked under her breath.

Rokoa laughed as he walked toward her. "You'll be fine." He sat down in the grass next to her, holding out a small piece of hard candy. "Try this, it should help the nausea."

Taking it gratefully from him, Raelia popped the small treat into her mouth as she shifted to sit cross-legged. As always, he'd been right. The fruity little candy instantly cleared up the sick feeling in her stomach.

She smiled brightly at him. "Thanks!"

He nodded and reached for her hand, eyes looking intently at the ring her father gave her a few weeks ago. Raelia felt heat rush to her cheeks, but she didn't pull away as Rokoa twirled the trinket around her finger. Her skin tingled under his warm touch as he looked closely at the tribal mark engraved in the silver. He didn't comment or ask about it, but she could tell he wanted to.

As she pondered on it, a glint of sunlight caught the dark lines of the Mark on his hand. The one she'd seen during their trek north.

Completely forgetting the strange emotion, and before she could stop herself, she'd pulled away from his grasp – grabbing his hand in both of hers as she gazed down at the tattoo-like Mark.

"What is this?" she asked as her fingers lightly touched the bold lines of the flame.

When he didn't answer, she looked up at him, surprised to see a tinge of red high on his cheeks. He cleared his throat and answered in a rush, "It's the Mark of the Drykuan's. We all have them."

She nodded before turning her eyes back to his hand. Her fingers traced the lines of the curling flame before following the stem it sat upon down to his wrist. "It's beautiful."

A few quiet moments passed as she continued to trace the dark lines on his pale skin.

When the sun began to lower behind the tree's, Rokoa cleared his throat once more. His voice seemed nervous when he spoke in a gentle tone, "We should head back. It's not safe to be in the forest after dark."

"Oh!" she said, releasing her hold on his hand. "Sorry…"

Raelia stood quickly. Too quickly. The moment she was on her feet, dizziness overwhelmed her and the nausea returned.

It didn't take long for Rokoa to pack up the arsenal he'd brought with them, and soon they were walking back along the same path. The light faded with every passing minute and she was glad for the quiet, still focused on holding down the urge to vomit, as she was.

"You know, for the first time out," Rokoa started, "you did quite well. Better than I would have imagined."

"Mmm," was the only response she felt capable of, afraid if she opened her mouth, her lunch would end up on their feet.

He looked at her quizzically. Whatever he saw in her expression must have answered his question though, because he held up a finger silently, indicating for her to wait.

Abruptly, he veered off their path, and disappeared into the thick brush surrounding them. He was only gone for a few moments, but in the ever fading light, it felt much longer.

When he reappeared on the path, a few steps behind her, he held a large golden orb in his hand, and if she had been confused before, she was even more confused now. Raelia quirked up an eyebrow at him, as he held it out for her to take.

"It's a Laanias berry," he explained. "Just take it and hold it out."

She lifted Zayric to her shoulder, and he made himself comfortable between her neck and the arrows sticking out of her quiver, then did as she was instructed.

Once the large berry was in her hands, she inspected it closer. It reminded her so much of a blueberry in shape and texture, even down to the crumpled underside. The size, however, was closer compared to a cantaloupe. It shimmered gold, much like the nectar Rokoa gave her a few weeks back, and tiny flecks of silver lined it in a pattern much like seeds on the outside of a strawberry. It was the prettiest berry she'd ever seen.

"Okay, hold it out," Rokoa instructed once more, bringing her gaze to him. He held a hunting knife in one hand, and placed his other on the underside of hers, holding them in place. Without a word, he stabbed the dagger downward, causing her to flinch as the sharp tip sunk into the berry's flesh with a ripping sound. He twisted the blade around in a circular motion a few times before yanking it out and wiping it on his pants. The motion wafted a floral scent in her direction, and her eyes lit up. It smelled delicious.

"Now, drink."

She nodded and did as told. It tasted as good as it smelled, and in seconds her nausea cleared. When she pulled the large fruit away from her mouth, she felt the sticky nectar run down her chin. She smiled up at Rokoa as she hastened to wipe it away. "I really would have loved that a couple hours ago! I feel like I could train for hours now!"

He laughed and took the berry from her, tossing it in the bushes before he began walking once again toward the doorway into Paodra. She hurried to catch up, realizing her body aches had vanished.

By the time they made it through the door into the dark hallway, all sunlight had disappeared from the sky, and she could feel Rokoa's relief when they closed it behind them. She lit up the corridor as she had before, and they quickly made their way back down the hall.

Raelia said goodbye to Rokoa in the main square and hurried passed the busy lounge to her living quarters, sighing in relief when she closed the door behind herself. It had been a busy day, and she felt peopled-out. She shooed Zayric off her shoulders and leaned her quiver and bow against the wall near the door, promising herself she'd take it back to the training arena first thing in the morning.

"Rae! Is that you?" she heard Luella call from somewhere down the hallway.

"Yep! Just little ol' me!" she chuckled as she walked over to the small dining table. "Have you eaten?"

"Not yet," came a softer response as her friend appeared in the living space with a smile. "I was waiting for you."

"Great!" Raelia exclaimed. "I'm famished!"

She held her finger down on the blue rose next to a dish she hadn't heard of before. In the last few weeks, Raelia had taken it upon herself to try as many local foods as she was able before leaving Paodra, and she had yet to be disappointed. Tonight's meal was called Iridilias. The description said it was a local delicacy, and when it arrived, the tantalizing aroma made her mouth water.

The pair shared their meals while they discussed how their days had gone. Raelia told her friend about the back exit Rokoa took her through, and the beautiful clearing in the forest. Then informed her of all the training she had endured. The 'real life' scenes that the Drykuan put her through, which seemed to fascinate Luella. When she told her about the work she'd done with Zayric, Lue's jaw dropped open.

"You mean, you turn into the smoky mist stuff too?!" she asked in disbelief.

Nodding, Raelia chuckled. "Don't ask me how though, because I have no idea!"

When it was Luella's turn to share her day, Raelia wasn't exactly surprised to hear it had consisted mostly of training with Ayla. The two of them had become fast friends and it seemed nearly anytime Raelia wasn't with her, Luella was with Ayla.

Suddenly, Lue's eyes went wide. "OH! I forgot to tell you!"

"What?"

"Galys stopped by!" she smiled. "He dropped off a book for you. I put it on your bed."

"Oh, great!"

After they finished dinner, and sent the dishes back to the kitchens, both girls called it a night. Raelia ran her hand down Zayric's back and then changed into her nightgown. Just as she turned down her bedding, she heard a soft rap on the door.

"Come in," she called, smiling when she saw Luella's face peek in.

"Galys said it was a book of fairytales."

Raelia chuckled knowingly. "It is indeed," she replied, gesturing to the large, leather-bound book now sitting on her nightstand. "Would you like to borrow it?"

Luella grinned shyly and shook her head.

"You want me to read it to you, don't you?"

Nodding, the blonde rushed into the small space and threw herself onto the bed that Raelia had so neatly made only moments before.

Her landing had barely missed Zayric, who looked put out by the surprise attack. He glared at Lue before jumping from the bed to the small cushioned chair in the corner.

"Hey!"

Her friend only giggled and patted the bed beside herself. "Come on! You're taking too long, Rae! I want to hear some stories before I can't keep my eyes open!"

Raelia rolled her eyes, and shoved Luella to one side so that she could get under the blankets. Not wanting to waste any time, Lue followed suit, pulling the thick comforter up to her chin as she snuggled in.

Before she knew it, Luella burrowed into her shoulder, laying her weight against it so she could better see the open book in Raelia's lap. A nervous energy flowed through her veins as she rested her cheek against the top of her friend's blonde hair. She did her best to ignore it, trying to just appreciate the closeness they shared.

Her voice was soft as she began reading a tale she'd never heard before, but her mind was elsewhere. Unsure of where the nervous energy came from, she did her best to keep her mind off of it. Focusing on keeping her lips moving. The detailed sketches within the pages helped, but didn't completely quell what she was feeling.

Page after page she read, not taking in a single bit of the story. Her body was tense, and her muscles felt stiff as she tried her best not to disturb Luella's comfort by moving. She was thankful when she realized she had reached the end of the story, because she didn't think she could handle not stretching soon.

Raelia closed the book, expecting Lue to get up, and head to her own bed. When she didn't, she tried to peer at her friend's face, but the angle made it impossible.

"Lue? The story's over... You can go to bed now," she chuckled softly.

When there was no response, she watched her form under the blankets, rising and falling in a slow and steady pace.

"You fell asleep, didn't you?" Raelia asked softly, letting her head fall back onto her pillow.

Once again, there wasn't a response, so doing her best to be gentle, she put the heavy book back onto the nightstand before twisting one arm around Luella's back while using the other to push her delicately off her shoulder and onto the pillow behind her.

Raelia sighed in relief when she pulled her shoulder free, amazed she hadn't woken her friend. Lue's face was so peaceful, so calm, when she slept. Just by looking at her, Raelia relaxed too.

Ever so gently, she reached over to brush a strand of hair off Luella's forehead. At the touch, butterflies seemed to dance within her, and she jerked her hand away quickly. Too quickly.

"Rae?" Lue sleepily looked up at her friend. "Is the story over?"

Startled by her racing heart, she only nodded in response. After which, Luella sat up and stretched. "I'm going to head to bed," she told her, as she got up and clumsily walked across the room and out the door.

After she was gone, Raelia stared at the ceiling lost in thought.

'What in all the gods names was that?!' she wondered. *'She's your best friend! You've slept in the same bed with her dozens of times! Why are you so nervous?!'*

Question after question flowed through. Questions she wasn't sure she had answers for — or at least answers she was ready to give.

It had been such a wonderful evening. The two of them hadn't been alone much since their first couple days in Paodra, and she was so happy to just sit comfortably with her friend.

'My best friend,' she thought to herself. *'My best friend.'*

She ran over those words a few more times in her mind, as she turned over and snuggled into the blankets. They felt wrong. They tasted like lies on the tip of her tongue, even when she didn't speak them out loud. It felt as if she was trying to convince herself of some alternate truth. She thought it was a truth she'd always known. Luella is her best friend. She'd been her best friend since they were seven years old!

Her eyes were heavy the last time the words repeated, and just as she realized what truth she was fighting, sleep stole her mind.

CHAPTER 20

The following morning, when she awoke, Raelia hurried to dress and ready herself for the day. She wasn't sure she was ready to face Luella with the epiphany she had before falling asleep the night before, so she quickly crept into the hallway, grabbing her bow and quiver as she did.

The lounge room was empty as she passed, and she realized she must have, once again, gotten up with the sun. As she hurried up the stairs, she wasn't sure if she should hope for Naz to be in their usual morning spot or not. They seemed so much more intuitive than most and she wasn't sure she was ready for them to read her quite yet. Not before she'd made sense of her feelings.

When she pushed open the door to the outside world, relief flooded through her as she noticed Nazario's easel wasn't set up. An audible sigh escaped her lips as she continued along her path toward the training arena.

It was a quiet, pleasant walk. She slowed her pace, letting the knowledge she wouldn't have to talk to anyone for a while calm her nerves. Somewhere in the thick canopy above, birds whistled a sweet melody. The fluttering of wings made her look up. She couldn't see them, but the joy in their song was contagious, and the nerves from the night before flitted away with the melody. Leaving the music of nature made her sad as she pushed through the thick, heavy door leading into the training center, but knew practicing her combat skills would help to keep her mind off of other matters.

Raelia went directly up the spiral staircase that led into the loft above. Her intention, to return the bow and quiver, was sidetracked as she spotted a large glass door. She had seen it yesterday when she had retrieved the gear, but only now she remembered Rokoa telling her that there was an archery range up here. She pulled the door open before stepping out. Once again, she was able to hear the birds singing, seeming even closer now than they had before.

The range was set in a large, grassy field, in which three different types of targets were set up. On the north side, stood half a dozen coiled straw targets of different heights, much like the one Rokoa had used to help her shoot in the clearing the day before.

The grouping on the west side consisted of training dummies that looked like they had not only been hit with arrows, but also sliced and stabbed by swords and daggers. Some were in worse shape than others, with chunks missing and the insides becoming outsides in places.

The set up on the eastern side of the field was one she hadn't seen before. A large wooden frame protruded above the horizon line. It was as wide as it was tall and stood on four legs, the tops of which were bound, leaving the bottoms splayed. It appeared the end of each leg was buried in the earth below. A long wooden beam at the top kept the large triangles together, and along that, in random places, were straps of leather. Some were thick, reminding her of a belt someone would wear to keep their britches in place. Others were thin, braided strings. All were various lengths, and at the end of each hung a fist sized leather ball. A smirk spread across her lips as she saw puncture holes in every one of the spheroids and she realized they were targets as well.

Quickly, she grabbed an arrow from the quiver on her back and notched it. She pulled back on her bow, muscles still aching from yesterday's training, and aimed at the center target.

"Don't get ahead of yourself," Rokoa called from behind her, causing her to jump and release the arrow by accident. It flew only a few feet and buried itself in the ground. He laughed as he walked up. "These are much harder to hit than you'd think."

"Don't you know it's dangerous to startle someone with a notched arrow in their hands?"

"Seems the only danger was to the poor earth," he smirked.

Raelia rolled her eyes and pulled the arrow out of the ground. She started cleaning the fragments of dirt from it.

"I went to collect you for our training, but you were already gone." It was worded as a statement, but she could hear the question in his voice. He wanted to know why.

"Sorry. Thought I'd get an earlier start today," she answered, keeping her tone light and her eyes on the arrow.

"Uh-huh."

She let the silence hang between them as she continued to pick the dirt from the metal tip of the arrow. She could feel his eyes burning into the back of her skull as if fire shot from them.

"For the sake of all the gods! The arrow is clean, Rae!" He growled out in frustration.

The sudden outburst caught her off guard, causing her to flinch and run her finger along the razor sharp tip. Blood bloomed immediately, and she sucked in a gasp of pain.

Rokoa rushed over and crouched down next to her. Pulling her hand towards him, he looked at her finger with practiced eyes. "It's not deep, but we should get it cleaned before giving you the Laanias nectar."

She nodded, and stood up, taking her hand from him.

They were silent as he led her back down the stairs and to the small medical room on the far end of the arena. She didn't mind the quiet, and wasn't going to open conversation when she didn't feel like talking.

Rokoa made quick work of cleaning the cut, then pulled out a small vial of golden liquid from one of the cupboards and held it out to her. She recognized the laanias nectar immediately and popped out the small cork before downing it in one swift gulp.

The wound on her finger slowly closed. It was an eerie feeling to watch a wound stitch itself together — as if she was watching the injury in reverse — but she was glad it was done.

"Thanks," she said softly.

"I think we should try something different today," Rokoa told her, a grin spreading across his features.

Raelia's eyes were confused when she looked at him. "Different like yesterday? I'm not sure I can do that two days in a row! I'm still exhausted!"

Laughing, he shook his head. "Not exactly," he said, jerking his head to one side. "Come on."

When the stables came into view, Raelia's smile brightened and excitement glowed in her eyes. She ran, leaving Rokoa behind her.

Bursting through the large barn doors, she startled a young Drykuan boy, who jumped and stepped back. Rokoa came through before she could apologize.

"Are Prickle and Onyx in their stable?" he asked the child, who nodded in response.

"Excellent. Thank you."

The two strode past a number of large stalls where other horses were housed, but Raelia only had eyes for her boys. She couldn't believe that in the nearly four weeks she'd been in Paodra she'd only seen them once, the day after they arrived. She felt guilty she hadn't at least thought to check on them.

Quickly, she unlatched and slid open the door to their stable. Both horses recognized her immediately, and it was obvious they were happy to see her. Prickle reared up, prancing in his elation to meet her at the door.

She hugged his neck tightly, kissing his forehead before walking over to do the same for Onyx. "Well it looks like you're being taken care of, at least!" she laughed, noticing Prickle had filled out since she'd seen him last.

"How about we take a ride? It'll be good to get some training in on horseback," Rokoa told her.

Raelia nodded excitedly as she bounced on the balls of her feet. It felt as if years had passed since she last rode. Most of her days before arriving in Paodra had comprised at least a short ride, and that she hadn't even thought about it before now surprised her.

The two of them set about saddling her boys up, which elicited an excited bray from Prickle, and before she knew it, they were walking them out of the stables. The sun was bright and high in the sky as Raelia pulled herself into Prickle's saddle and she could feel the colt's jittery excitement.

Raelia clicked her tongue, and without any other encouragement, Prickle took off. She laughed at his antics, and pulled back on his reins.

Once she had him turned around, she looked at Rokoa smiling on top of Onyx.

"Where are we headed?"

He clicked his heels on the large stallion's flank, guiding him south toward a trail peeking through the dense brush. "This way."

Following closely behind, Raelia guided Prickle down the narrow path. Pine needles and leaves grazed against her bare arms, but she paid them little heed.

A few minutes after following the trail, it opened into a large meadow. The grass was long, and rustled as the wind blew through. In the distance, Raelia could see a couple of deers grazing. When she looked closely, the clearing was teeming with wildlife. There were squirrels scurrying up and down trees, birds flying above their heads. Once again, Rokoa brought her to a place she couldn't imagine the beauty of even in her wildest dreams.

"Well, go ahead, run that colt!" he laughed, gesturing for her to gallop around.

Laughing, she clicked her tongue and tapped her heels into Prickle's side. He didn't need any further urging. The speckled horse took off further into the field., startling the roaming deer and a flock of small birds that had been hiding in the grass. He ran to the far end of the meadow before Raelia turned him around and he headed right back. Rokoa waved his hand, gesturing for her to follow him as Onyx galloped across the field and onto another small path.

The branches whipped past as they raced through the dense forest path. Raelia leaned down toward Prickle's neck, avoiding being hit by most of the foliage. She didn't know where they were going, but she didn't ask, enjoying herself too much to care.

Their path remained level at first, but eventually, started up an incline. In the distance, Raelia could hear the sounds of rushing waters, and a few moments later, they burst through the trees and into another clearing. The water she'd heard was a river, much like the one near her home. This break in the forest was much smaller than the meadow they'd been in before, but it was just as beautiful.

Rokoa swung his leg over Onyx's back, and let it drop to the earth, and she did the same. Prickle's speckled fur was slick with sweat, and his breath was heavy after the long run.

Raelia grabbed onto his lead and walked him to the riverbank. Patting his neck as he leaned down to drink the fresh water, Raelia looked behind her to see Rokoa bringing Onyx, as well.

"You're a better rider than I would have thought," he told her as he reached the river's edge.

"Do you have to be surprised every time I'm good at something?" she laughed. "Besides, you've seen me ride before," she reminded him.

"That was different. We were escaping then. Riding in that type of situation requires less skill and more motivation."

"Sure it does," she said, rolling her eyes.

She fell quiet, watching as the horses drank. The air was cooler than it would be back home, but the sun glistening in the sky gave bits of warmth in it's direct light. Raelia let her mind wander, thinking about how different Paodra, and the forest surrounding it, was from her home — from Frayis.

The thought of home left her heart aching. She was enjoying her time in this mystical place, but still, she wished for home. She wished for her own bed, and the warm spring air. She wished to see her family again...

'Stop,' she mentally scolded herself. *'There is no reason to follow that path.'*

"Are you going to tell me what's going on with you today?" Rokoa's voice broke through her thoughts. "There's more than just wanting to get an earlier start. I know you better than that by now."

Raelia sighed, knowing she needed to explain herself, but not knowing exactly what to say, she blurted out the first thing that popped into her mind.

"Luella and I made a deal."

"A deal?" this clearly wasn't what he'd expected, given his quizzical look. If she was honest with herself, she hadn't expected it either.

"The second night we were here, we agreed we'd go home in six weeks... It'll be four weeks in a couple days..."

"Ah," came Rokoa's only response.

"I think I'm just concerned about what it's going to look like... with... uh... Vysha." Now that she was saying it out loud, the worry about her feelings for Luella seemed miniscule in comparison. "I haven't told her about it yet..."

"Maybe you shouldn't." His voice was serious, but his eyes didn't meet hers and she couldn't be certain he wasn't joking.

She scoffed, and chuckled. "Right. We'll just disappear in the night! I'm sure that'll go over well!"

When he turned his gaze to meet hers, the laughter died on her lips. The intensity she saw was muddled with... fear... maybe? Or was it something else? It was hard to say. He was always so hard to read.

"Maybe that's what you should do," he said. "I could help you. Make sure you make it out."

This pulled her up short. "Make it out? Why wouldn't we make it out? We'd only have to walk out. Wouldn't we?"

The anxiety in his eyes made her wonder what he wasn't saying. It was scaring her in a way he hadn't done since he rescued her in Frayis — his silence only making it worse.

"Rokoa?"

In a flash, the intensity in his gaze faded, replaced with a hard look that Raelia had come to believe was his everyday expression. "Of course you can just walk out! No reason to believe otherwise! I'm just messing with you," he forced a smile that didn't quite meet his eyes, solidifying his dishonesty.

"Rokoa, what aren't you telling me?"

"It's nothing," he told her, turning his attention back to the horses, who had both finished with their drink. "I just think it will take Vysha by surprise," he said as he led Onyx away from the riverbank.

Raelia followed with Prickle's lead in hand. "She has to know I'm not going to stay here forever, right? I mean, my brother and father are still out there. They don't yet know that... that..."

"I've been of the belief you're happy here. She is, I'm sure, of the same belief," he replied, once again avoiding eye contact as he released Onyx and walked back toward the river's edge.

"But surely, she would expect us to leave, especially since Luella isn't a Mark Bearer?" Raelia followed him back to the river and plopped next to him in the grass. "And the fact that I have my Papa and brother to think about..."

"It's hard to say what she is expecting," Rokoa stated. "When you approach Vysha, maybe it would be better approached if you *ask* her instead of telling her."

"Ask? I have to ask to go home?" she questioned. "And what if she says no? Will I have to sneak out in the dead of night?"

Another forced chuckle. "Not at all! I don't know why I said that. There's been a lot of attacks and violence happening all around Diry-thia, and she's worried about you. About all of you. We're protected in this place. The magic keeps us hidden and safe," he explained. "You don't have that protection if you leave, so she won't understand why you would risk it."

Raelia guessed that made sense. She knew something had been going on outside of Paodra, though didn't know exactly what it was, and she knew Vysha would want to keep her and the other Mark Bearers safe from it. Somehow, though, his explanation didn't settle the sinking feeling in her gut.

"This isn't my home," she said softly.

Intensity returned in Rokoa's eyes, but a gentleness was there that hadn't been before, as he replied in a gentle tone, "But it could be."

The ride back was slower, yet just as fun. Prickle and Onyx both looked exhausted by the time they returned to the stables, and Raelia felt quite the same. The stable boy hurried to collect the horses when they dismounted. He explained Vysha had sent word Raelia would train with her this afternoon, so after the young boy assured them he'd tend to the horses, they started their journey back to the village.

"I think you should ask her today," Rokoa told her. "Then she can think about it a bit before the six-week mark has arrived."

She had to concede he had a good point. The more time she gave Vysha before the deadline Luella set, the more time they'd have to discuss it and come to an agreement.

"You're probably right," she agreed.

They walked in silence for the rest of the journey, and Raelia was glad for it. She ran over different ways to bring up the topic with Vysha.

Rehearsing how she would ask and what points she needed to make in her head the whole way.

Lost in thought as she was, Raelia was surprised when she found herself in front of the large, carved door leading into the throne room, and she stopped Rokoa's hand before he could open it. He gave her a questioning look, but she ignored it, keeping her hand on his, and closed her eyes. She took two deep breaths, calming her nerves, and then released his hand, allowing him to open the heavy door.

Vysha smiled at them as they entered the room. "Ah, my *Aldaehima*. There you are! I was beginning to worry you hadn't gotten my message." Her eyes were kind when connected with Raelia's, but when they darted to Rokoa, they turned accusing.

"My apologies, Vysha. I want to start her horseback training, so I thought it would be a good idea to get an idea of how she rides. We were gone longer than I expected."

"Which is my fault!" Raelia chimed in. "I wanted to let my horses run. It's been so long since they've had the freedom they're used to."

"It's quite alright," Vysha assured as she stepped down the stairs in front of the throne to walk over to them. She smiled kindly up at Rokoa. "You may take your leave. Raelia and I have much to go over today."

He bowed in a silent gesture of acknowledgement and made his way out of the room, flashing an encouraging look in Raelia's direction before he closed the door behind him. Vysha watched him go and then looped her arm into her pupil's.

"In the month you've been here," Vysha started, pulling Raelia across the room, "you've learned more than I would have expected possible. Your Mark allows for gifts that should be impossible, and yet, you have mastered every one of them."

"Impossible?" She looked at the Red Lady, confusion clear on her face. "I thought the gift given by the dandelion exhibited differently for every person...?"

"Well, yes, it does," she replied, seeming more flustered than Raelia had seen her before. "but it... well, it rarely affords the bearer gifts that aren't an in-the-moment kind of power."

"What do you mean?"

Vysha led her to two plush sitting chairs, and they took a seat. "Well, for example, when you faced Qiralst in the square. Do you remember what happened when he brought the whip down?"

"I-" Yes. She did remember — The only reason she hadn't walked away with her back bloodied and torn to shreds was because of the barrier her gift erected between them. "I didn't know what it was doing... it just kind of happened..."

"And that *is* usually how the power of the dandelion works. It's only with years of training and using the gift that it usually wields its will to it's bearer."

"So... It reacts to situations around me and protects me in the way it knows best?"

"Yes... and no," Vysha smiled, sounding amused at Raelia's oversimplification. "It tells you before you need it, so you can use the power it's allowing you. For instance-" with a quick flutter of her hand, all light in the large room vanished, leaving them both unable to see anything. "Now, don't do anything, but what is your instinct at this moment?"

"I want to bring the light back. Put it in my palms, like we've practiced."

"Yes. Now I want you to close your eyes and focus on where the instinct is coming from in your body. I want you to pay close attention to *what* is telling you to do that."

Raelia swallowed down a laugh, knowing the Red Lady wouldn't take kindly to it. This whole exercise seemed ridiculous, though. What more instinct could there be other than just wanting to see the room again?

Despite feeling foolish, she closed her eyes as she was told and focused on every sensation she was feeling throughout her body — starting at her toes. She wiggled them, feeling the muscles curling and uncurling in her boots.

She slowly slid her consciousness up the length of her legs, and then torso, noticing how hungry she was when it stopped on her stomach. Once again, she'd forgotten to eat something today.

When her focus spread across her chest, over her heart, she felt a flicker of something she didn't know how to explain. It was a strong yet soft sensation, seeming to glow in her mind's eye. As her mind zeroed in on it, she recognized another, even stranger feeling.

It felt like it was connected to a string, pulled taut and running up her chest. She followed the string slowly, consumed by the strange sensation, as it flowed past her collarbone and up her neck, stopping behind her right ear.

Stopping at her Indicative Mark.

Now with her mind focused on it, she couldn't believe she hadn't felt the throb of power there before.

"It's-It's a cord running from my Dandelion Mark into my heart. Like they're... tied together," she said in a soft voice. "The power-"

"Lies in your Mark," Vysha finished for her.

With her eyes still closed, Raelia pulled at the cord within herself. She pulled the energy she could feel pulsing through her Mark, draining it, and flushing it out to her palms.

A bright light pushed through the darkness behind her eyelids, and when she opened them, she realized it was coming from her palm.

Her glow brighter than it had ever been before, and she had to squint against it.

"Now, I want you to throw the light across the room," came Vysha's voice from beside her.

She wasn't sure how, but when she once again focused on the pulsing energy behind her ear, instinct took over. Once again, she forced the energy into her palm, only this time she flicked her hand towards the wall opposite of them.

In a flash, a ball of light shot from her fingertips and flew across the room at an immense speed. It hit the stone wall and broke into smaller glowing spheres all along it.

Raelia's eyes were wide as she watched, shocked at the speed and willingness of her gift to do her bidding. "So the power builds based on what my instinct says I need?" she asked, turning her gaze to Vysha, who nodded.

"When you were about to be whipped, what was going through your mind?"

She had to think about that. It happened so fast. The memory of that day seemed a blur. "I - uh - I'm not sure. Probably about trying to get free or not being hit..."

"In that moment, your Mark was teeming with power, only you didn't know how to ask for it, so it forced it's protection on you," she explained. "Tell me, did you feel any pain before the shield went up?"

"I... Yeah," Raelia replied, remembering how she thought his first swing had connected behind her ear and around the base of her skull — where her Mark was, she realized now. "It felt like something ripped open the skin where my Mark is..."

"Sometimes, when we don't draw from it, the energy builds up, the Dandelion Mark will force its power on us. It is painful, as you now know, which is why it's so *very* important to learn how to let your instincts speak to you through your gift."

Vysha stood then, gesturing for Raelia to do the same. With a flick of her wrist the chairs vanished, and Raelia remembered what she wanted to talk to the Red Lady about.

"Before we continue," she started, "I wondered if I could ask you a favor?"

"Of course, *Aldaehima*. What is it you need?"

Raelia clasped her hands together, wringing them silently in front of herself as she cleared her throat. Her jade green eyes connected with Vysha's and her voice was hopeful when she spoke.

"I want to go home."

Chapter 21

Over the next few days, Raelia's anxiety peaked. Her conversation with Vysha hadn't gone as well as she'd hoped, and she began to think Rokoa might have been right about disappearing in the night.

The Red Lady was vocal about her disapproval of the trip, and didn't understand why Luella couldn't just go by herself if she wanted to leave so badly. Raelia did her best to explain that wasn't the only reason, but once she heard Lue's name, there was no convincing her there was any other.

It was frustrating to know how little Vysha thought of Luella, and even more aggravating to know that nothing she could say would change her mind. She was not a Mark Bearer, and, in Vysha's eyes, there was no redeeming that.

Either way, she finally brought it up, and did as Rokoa suggested — she asked for permission. Raelia worried about what would happen if the answer was no, but she did her best not to dwell on it.

"Hey! Raelia, right?" asked a petite brunette about her age, pulling her concentration from the training session she'd been watching.

To keep herself distracted, Raelia took to haunting the training arena when it was busy. She usually avoided people, but she discovered quickly it was fascinating to watch others training with their gifts.

"Yes, I am," she answered, reaching out to shake her hand, "and you are?"

"I'm Zaira," the girl replied, smiling brightly as she gripped tightly onto her outstretched hand.

"It's nice to meet you."

"You're the new dandelion, right?"

Raelia nodded. It was common knowledge now that she had the Dandelion Mark, and yet every new person she met had asked her the same question. It felt as if they were trying to confirm rumors. "And what flower does your Mark represent?"

"Well, it's not a flower, actually."

That surprised her. "I thought all Marks were flowers?"

"Most are, but there's a few of us whose Marks represent a plant of some sort. Like mine. It's a papyrus."

"I... I've never heard of a papyrus before."

"Neither had I," Zaira chuckled. "but when I showed Vysha she explained it's native to the tribal lands, which is why I hadn't heard of it. I've never been."

"Interesting," Raelia said thoughtfully. "Can I ask what your gift is?"

"Oh! Of course! I'm a hydroporter."

If possible, Zaira's smile became even wider, and her eyes were expectant. She clearly thought Raelia should know what the term meant.

"I-I'm sorry. I'm not sure I know what that means..."

"She has the gift of Hydroportation," came a voice from behind them. Raelia looked back to see Galys grinning at her. "It means she can transport herself to places using water."

"Hey Galys!" Raelia smiled before turning back to Zaira. "Really?! How does it work?"

"I can show you if you'd like?" she offered. "Is that water you're drinking?"

Raelia looked down at the mug in her hands and nodded as Galys sat beside them on the floor.

"Do you mind?" Zaira asked, reaching for the cup, which Raelia excitedly handed over.

"Hey! What are you guys up to?" Naz asked as they approached. Galys opened his mouth to respond, only to be cut short before any words formed.

"Shhh! Zaira's going to show me how hydroportation works!" Raelia informed them in a hushed tone.

"Ah! That explains the giddy gleam in your eyes," they laughed, sitting down next to her.

They went quiet then, watching and waiting on Zaira. She scooted back and dumped a small amount of water from Raelia's mug onto the floor before she handed it back to her. Slowly, she reached one finger out to touch the puddle.

Raelia gasped as she watched first Zaira's finger, then her hand and arm, then her entire body quickly disappear into the water as if being sucked in. The water splashed when the last bit of her — the tip of her boot — finally submerged and disappeared with the rest.

"Where did she go?!" Raelia gawked, staring at the small pool of water with fascination.

"I'm over here!"

Raelia jumped, being completely focused on the water, she hadn't seen Zaira appear across the room. She watched in awe as the woman pulled herself out of a small glass of water. She gawked, not knowing what to say in response to seeing a person sucked into a small pool of water, and reappearing on the other side of the room.

"Pretty neat, huh?" Naz said, eyeing Raelia with amusement.

"To say the least!" she laughed in response, joined by the other three.

When their laughter died down, Galys looked at her with a grin. "Did you still want to see the library today?"

"Oh! Yes!" Raelia exclaimed, jumping to her feet, "I completely forgot!"

Naz stood with them, as did Zaira who smiled apologetically. "I have more training to do, but," she looked at Raelia, "it was so good to finally meet you!"

"You too!" she smiled in return.

And she meant it. Every day she surprised herself more and more. She still became overwhelmed easily, and needed a break from being around people once in a while, but things were different now. With the constant fear of her Mark being found now a thing of the past, she realized she sometimes enjoyed meeting and getting to know new people.

As she, Galys and Nazario walked out of the training arena, Raelia waved once more to Zaira before turning to look down the long hall-way.

"Where is the library, anyway?" she asked, not sure how she hadn't come across it already.

"It's a bit off the beaten track," Galys answered.

When he'd spoken the words, she thought he just meant not in the main hallways, but after almost 20 minutes of walking through the tunnel-like halls, and winding down a few spiral staircases into other hallways, she began to wonder if the library was in Paodra at all.

Her eyes flickered to Naz, the question in her gaze.

They chuckled. "Another five minutes."

"Where are we?"

She scoured their surroundings and realized she didn't recognize anything. The brilliant wooden floors and mossy walls of the common areas she frequented in Paodra were a big step up from their current surroundings.

Heavy bricks formed the path under her feet and matched the stones of the walls and ceiling. She'd seen buildings made of stone before, but there was something different here. The craftsmanship was different. It was well built, clearly sturdy as the tunnels weren't collapsing around them, but an aura permeated the air here. An ancient aura. She couldn't even imagine how many millennia these stones had seen.

Their footsteps echoed around them. An aroma of mildew permeated the damp air, and Raelia was certain if she touched the walls her fingers would come away wet. Suddenly, she was very aware of the position she had put herself into. She didn't know Galys well, and though he seemed friendly enough, she found herself thankful that Nazario joined them.

"Certainly the library isn't down here... The moisture in the air would destroy the books."

Galys grinned at her and opened a door revealing a tall staircase. "Of course it's not down here. It's just... well hidden, is all."

Feeling sheepish at having the obvious confirmed, an embarrassed chuckle rolled out on her breath. "What *is* down here, then? Anything?"

"I think there's a dungeon of some sort," Naz chimed in, "but that might just be rumors. Hard to say."

Raelia's expression turned curious, but she didn't speak as they started up the stairs. They were all quiet as they climbed in the near dark. The only light coming from sconces on the walls in wide, staggered placement. The soft green flames, the same as she had seen Rokoa pick up in the *triseyule*, danced merrily in their places.

At the top of the stairs a door came into view. It was another of the heavy wooden affairs that were used throughout the mythical city, and had its own magnificent carvings. When they came closer, Raelia saw that they were very different from the others she'd seen. Instead of flowers or leaves or vines, this door's ornate carvings could only be described as religious in nature. She didn't know much about the beliefs of the Drykuan's — or the Zarhaish for that matter — but the symbols reminded her of the runes she'd seen in books about the old gods the churches in Dirythia used to worship before they fell a millennia ago.

Nazario held the door open for her, and she gasped when she stepped through. The room was cavernous, nearly as large as the library in the palace. The times she'd visited, she remembered thinking nowhere else in the world could possibly have as many books. Paodra's library, however, proved her wrong.

Not only were books lining every wall from floor to ceiling and shelves scattered around the room that overflowed, but there were also various stacks in random parts as well. Some stacks leaned against the shelves on the wall, and Raelia's hands itched to shift them around and discover the titles hiding behind them.

She had no words for the joy sparked by looking at the massive collection. The only thing she was able to manage was a dropped jaw and wide eyes. Her friends watched her with amused expressions.

"It's magnificent, isn't it?" Galys said, eyes turning from her face to look out into the enormous room.

"Are-Are we allowed to read all of these books? Do they have to stay here or can I bring some back to my room?"

Nazario laughed. "I've brought them back to my room many times." They held out a satchel to her. "Though, I've never asked. I just make sure the books are returned and in a bag between locations."

Her eyes lit up with excitement as she took the bag from them, gratefully. "How many books does this fit?"

"Varies," they answered. "Depends on the size of the books. I've gotten seven total in it before, but they were smaller than most of the editions in here."

She nodded her understanding and began scrutinizing the different titles within her line of sight. "Is there any organization for them? Or are they piled at random?"

Galys perked up at the question and pointed to one side of the library. "There's a bit of organization, but not a lot. That side over there are works of fiction and art. This side is mostly non-fiction. There's a lot of history about legends, and Mark Bearers as a whole. As the two sections merge you get a lot of mixture," he explained.

"As Galys here can tell you," Naz interrupted, smirking at him, "you have to pay attention to what it is you're reading, because sometimes in the mixed areas you'll think you're reading something that's real and only find out you were mistaken when you try to tell someone who knows the histories better than you."

Without a word, Galys turned and walked down an aisle to get away from the teasing, though Raelia noticed the blush rising on his cheeks before he swiveled out of sight behind a stack of books. She slapped Naz's arm, who chuckled, and then she turned to the nearest shelf and started perusing.

The three of them went in different directions, and no one made a peep. A few hours later, the only sound Raelia could hear was the pages she turned in front of her, and she was more content and calm than she'd felt since the attack on her village.

Her father's study had always been the place she felt safest and at peace. She'd always believed it was because of her connection to Eloi, but the same sensation flowed through her now.

Instead of wandering over to the fiction section, she let her curiosity in myths and legends keep her near the entrance. She read about all different mythical beasts, some she'd heard of and some she hadn't.

The creature she was reading about at the moment was called a *Weialdin* — a strange beast that didn't look like a beast at all, by the sketches in the book. Its natural form was that of a tall white oak tree. It had no grayish bark, as a normal white oak would, but it was bare. Its branches were few and tattered. It didn't produce leaves, and, from what she thought, it looked like it was dying.

"Raelia!" Naz's voice rang out from somewhere a couple of shelves over, startling her. She jumped, smacking her head on the shelf behind her before she crawled to her feet with the book in her hand.

"I'm over here!" she hollered back, spotting the side of their head. She waved an arm in the air to get their attention, and once they spotted her, she looked down at the pile of books she had surrounded herself with. There were entirely too many for her to smuggle out in the satchel Nazario had given her, so she knelt back down to look through and decide which titles were coming back with her.

"Are you ready to go?" Naz asked as they approached.

"I just want to pick a few to bring back with me."

⁂

"I've given a lot of thought to your request," Vysha told her the next afternoon during their training session. Her voice reverberated off the wooden walls of the throne room, making her words sound louder than they were.

Raelia's concentration on the task the Red Lady had set for her vanished at those words, and the beam of yellow light coming from her palm disappeared with it.

"And?"

"Well, I'm not exactly sure it's a good idea," Vysha told her, "but Rokoa made a compelling case for you."

She nodded, not sure what to say. She hadn't had a clue Rokoa spoke on her behalf.

"He thinks it's important for you and Miss Luella to return home to help process the trauma dealt to you both. And I can't say I disagree with him."

"You... You don't?"

"My sweet *Aldaehima*," Vysha crooned, stepping closer to place a hand onto Raelia's cheek gently, "I want nothing more than your happiness, and if seeing your home again will make you happy, then I want to make that happen for you."

She sighed, relieved, as a smile crept across her face. "Thank you, Vysha! Oh I can't wait to tell-"

"That being said," the woman interrupted, "I cannot allow you to go unaccompanied. It is a long and treacherous journey, and I want to make sure you stay safe on the trip there and back."

"Well, I know Nazario and Ayla both intend to join us, so we won't be-"

"What?" Vysha seemed surprised, her tone angry. "That's not a good idea. Besides, they aren't nearly the kind of protection I am referring to."

"Then who...?"

"Rokoa brought you here, and he will escort you home as well. He knows the way and is strong enough to keep you both safe."

"And what about Nazario and Ayla? You've said we can leave at any time... Are you going to deny them a journey they wish to take?"

Vysha's eyes flashed red at her question, causing a shiver to race down her spine. It was brief, but the effect was lasting. The room seemed to chill, as Vysha thought over her response.

"Of course I will not *deny* them," she replied, her voice snippier than it had been before, "but I don't understand why it is necessary."

Unsure if she was being asked, or if Vysha was simply making an observation, Raelia kept her mouth closed, waiting for her to continue. The woman eyed her as if she suspected there was something more she wasn't being told.

"If they insist on accompanying you, then I must insist on Ekry joining as well."

Raelia wasn't sure she liked that idea. She'd spent little time with Ekry since arriving in Paodra, but every time they'd been in the same room she got a feeling the Drykuan didn't exactly like her. She didn't relish the idea of her homecoming, sure to be emotional, being witnessed by someone she wasn't sure would understand.

Even with that in mind, Raelia nodded, refusing to let the opportunity to have her friends join her pass by. "I have no problem with that."

"Wonderful," Vysha clasped her hands together in front of her chest. She smiled brightly as she dropped them, and took a step towards Raelia, placing a hand on her shoulder, "Before we make arrangements, I have one request. I'm afraid your answer will determine when and if your trip can take place."

Raelia looked at her with confusion. "But you just said-"

"That I want to do everything in my power to make it happen, yes," she paused, seeming to think about how to continue, "but there are things that have been happening, plans that are to go into effect soon, and you... well you are needed."

"Needed for what? What plans?"

"*Aldaehima*, you remember our talk about who was behind the attack on your village?"

She nodded, unsure where Vysha could be going with this line of reasoning.

"The Royal family has long since been fighting for the genocide of our people. They've slaughtered our kind for centuries, and the attack on Frayis has set things in motion."

"What things?"

Vysha waved her hand, conjuring up a small sofa to sit on and gestured for Raelia to sit next to her. Once seated, their eyes connected.

"Sweet child, the world is changing. Dirythia is changing. We can no longer sit idly by as King Calyx continues to slaughter all people of magic blood," Vysha reached out and cupped her cheek gently. "It is time for us to take up arms. We *must* fight back."

"Fight back?"

"We are only weeks away from a battle for our freedom. A battle that will bring down the King and his reign of terror against magic."

"Are you saying you... you're...-"

"Paodra will march against the Kingdom of Dirythia."

Raelia's mouth dropped open in utter shock as her heart picked up its pace. She knew things were bad, and there was something major going on behind the scenes, but she had never dreamed war was on their doorstep.

"King Calyx has *thousands* of men at his disposal. There's less than two hundred Mark Bearers in Paodra. You can't possibly think we can win?!"

"It's not only us, but the Drykuan's as well. The Zarhaish are confined to the forest, but they will send aid using their magic," Vysha's gaze was determined. Strong. "Magic will prevail against those who try to end it."

She didn't know what to say. She'd seen the King's forces, and they were great, but in the five weeks she'd been in Paodra, Raelia had also seen the power of Magic. With all she'd seen, she had to agree it would put them on more level footing.

"There's one thing I don't understand..."

"And what is that, *Aldaehima*?"

"What does this have to do with me returning home to Frayis?"

"If you are to leave, I need your word that you will return," Vysha eyed her once more. "Return and help us fight."

Raelia's eyes widened, startled at the request. "Fight?! You want *me* to fight?!"

"Your gift could help save countless of our lives. Your people need you, *Aldaehima*. Our people need the protection of their Dandelion."

Her gaze shifted to a knot in the wood at her feet, her mind racing. She fought for the first time in her life the day of the attack on her village. Other than that, the only fighting she'd done had been during her training here in Paodra.

She needed to go home. She promised Luella. She had to find her brother and father. They still didn't know about the attack on their village or the slaughtering of the rest of their family. She couldn't disappear and not tell them what happened. But... could she really fight in a battle against the royal guards? She didn't think so.

Keeping her eyes on the floor as she spoke, not sure she wouldn't crumble under the disappointed look the Red Lady was sure to have on her face, Raelia's voice was soft when she spoke, "I... I don't kno w..." She felt her hands tremble slightly with nervous energy. "I don't think I would be of much use in a real battle, Vysha..."

Luella told her. She had warned Raelia on their first night in Paodra. Why hadn't she listened? How did she not see the intent in their training? Of course Vysha had been training them all for battle. There had never been any other explanation — she just hadn't wanted to see it.

"I'm afraid I can't let you leave until this battle is over, Raelia. If you will not fight with us, you need to stay here for your safety."

She might have been imagining it because of her guilt, but Vysha's voice sounded colder than before. Harsher and tinged with the disappointment Raelia knew she felt.

"I promised Luella we would go home in six weeks," Raelia said, reiterating what she'd told the woman when she first requested going home. "And even more than that, my father and older brother are still out there somewhere... I can't disappear on them. They've lost everyone else – I can't let them think I'm gone too!"

"I understand your concern. We can send word to your father, but as I said, I will not allow you to leave unless you promise to return. It will be too dangerous for you to be out there alone when the battle begins!" Vysha stepped forward, lifting Raelia's chin with two fingers so that she had to look at her. "*Aldaehima*, I cannot let you put yourself in harm's way. You are too dear to me."

The brown eyes Raelia looked into were sincere, concern filled them. There wasn't a trace of the disappointment she'd feared, nor anger. Her stomach twisted in knots.

"Can I think about it? Maybe let you know in a couple days?" she asked in a trembling tone.

"Of course, child. We can talk again when you come back for training in a few days."

Before she could respond, Vysha wrapped her arms around her. She hugged her tightly, and Raelia returned it. The fierceness in the woman's hold reminded her of her mother, and Raelia found herself fighting back tears before she was released.

CHAPTER 22

Raelia took the long route back to her living quarters, moving slowly through the hallways, lost in her own thoughts. After she'd left Vysha in the throne room, the thought of what Luella would say when she told her of the Red Lady's request churned her stomach.

Lue warned her when they arrived Vysha was clearly planning something and there was a reason she wanted her to train in combat. Raelia, however, wouldn't listen. She loved Paodra, and felt at home here almost as much as she did in her home back in Frayis.

The friends she made here had become like family, and the thought of leaving them made her heart ache. Even more so when she considered the idea of them leaving for a battle where she should be fighting alongside them.

Would they be fighting, though? Would Nazario and Ayla? Would Galys and Zaira? She had a hard time picturing them marching on the castle and taking on the Kingdom of Dirythia alongside Vysha and the Drykuan's. The idea of what could happen to them scared her, making the image seem even more ludicrous.

She made her way up the stairs and across the square, completely lost in thought. Somewhere in the back of her mind she registered a voice calling out, but didn't hear the words or recognize it as someone familiar as she continued on her way. At least, until she felt a hand grip her shoulder.

"Raelia! Didn't you hear me calling you?" Her eyes went wide with surprise at the sudden contact. She turned to find Galys looking back at her, amused. "Where were you?" he asked before dropping his hand.

A chuckle escaped her, as she scratched her head awkwardly. "Sorry! I guess I'm a little distracted, is all..."

"A little?" he laughed.

She felt her cheeks warm. "So... uh... what's up?" she asked with an embarrassed grin.

"Oh! I have something for you!" Galys slapped the satchel at his hip, but didn't move to open it. He leaned in conspiratorially, lowering his voice to a whisper. "But I'd rather not - er - hand it over where there might be prying eyes."

Eyes lighting with understanding, Raelia nodded. "Okay, well, I'm heading back to my room. You can join if you'd like?"

With his nod of acceptance, the pair walked the rest of the way across the square and made their way into the common area — not stopping until reaching Raelia's door. As she turned the knob, the door across the hall opened and Ayla and Luella emerged smiling.

"Hey! We were just headed to look for you!" Lue said brightly, as the two approached them.

"I was going to get something to eat before I head out for training with Rokoa," she told them as she opened the door into her and Luella's living quarters.

Ayla's eyes turned to Galys, a question gleaming in them.

Before she could verbalize it, however, he held up his satchel with a grin. "I'm just here to drop something off."

Raelia gestured for her friends to enter, following them in and closing the door behind herself. Her eyes shifted to Galys. "So what is so hush-hush?" she smiled.

He sat down heavily on the plush sofa and opened his satchel, pulling out a large leather-bound book.

It looked ancient. Small dark stains and faded spots covered the dark brown leather. The pages looked weathered along the edges, having the distinct wave pages get when exposed to moisture of some sort.

When she took it from him, it took the strength of both arms to hold it. She plopped herself down next to Galys on the couch and ran her fingers over the worn leather.

"The Magic Mark?" she asked, curiously before opening it in her lap.

"It details all the different Indicative Marks," he explained. "There's a sketch of what each one looks like. It lays out which Mark falls under which element, and what power each one has."

"Wow..." Raelia's eyes were wide as she browsed through the first few pages.

"I've had it for a few years now," Galys told her with an anxious chuckle. "I couldn't ever seem to get myself to return it to the library, but... I guess I thought you'd like a chance to look through it. There's a section about the Dandelion!"

Her eyes lit up as she turned to look at him. "Really?!"

Ayla came to sit on the opposite side of her. Raelia's excitement mirrored in her eyes. "Is there much about my Mark?" she asked. "The Zinnia Mark?"

"There's a lot about every Mark, actually!" Galys answered. "It's really quite fascinating!"

Raelia closed the large edition and hugged it to her chest. "Why did it need to be so secret?" she asked. "Do I need to worry someone is going to come looking for it?"

An awkward chuckle escaped him. "It didn't really need to be, I guess, but about a year after I had taken it out, one of the Zarhaish came looking for it and... well, I never told them I had it," he admitted.

They all fell silent for a moment, and Raelia processed his words.

"Why - er - why didn't you just return it after that?"

"At the time, I was worried they were looking for it to harm one of us," Galys looked down, making it nearly impossible to read his expression. His next words came out in a rush, "It details not only our powers, but also our weaknesses. It tells the best way to harm us and nullify our powers... But even after it blew over, I just couldn't bring myself to give it back."

He sighed and his voice grew quiet as he continued, so much so that Raelia had to lean in to hear him properly. "I don't think... Well... I don't think the Zarhaish should have it... More than one of them has made it known how they feel about us — how they don't think we deserve powers... Maybe it's not my place to decide, but I... I just..."

Extending her arm, she took his hand and gave it a reassuring squeeze. His eyes lifted, connecting with hers as she spoke, "If that's the kind of information it has, I think you made the right call," she reassured. "I won't tell anyone you were the one I got it from. I promise."

Over the next couple days, Raelia tormented herself, trying to decide what answer to give Vysha. She wanted revenge against King Calyx for the destruction of her village — the slaughter of her family. Every time she thought about the attack, her insides knotted with rage and grief. When she recalled her mother sobbing for the lives of her siblings, or remembered the horrified screams Caeda made after watching their brother fall to the ground, she thought she knew her answer. She *had* to fight. She had to avenge them, right?

On the other side of it, however, she'd seen the royal guard before. She knew the massive numbers in their ranks. She'd walked through Vairek City and seen the castle. She had seen the thick, protective brick walls surrounding it, and couldn't imagine it being breached, let alone seeing it fall. It didn't seem possible an adversary as small as theirs, with or without magic, could ever defeat King Calyx's army.

She also worried about the citizens living there. Vairek City was the most populated in the Kingdom of Dirythia, and in a battle such as the one Vysha described, there was certain to be a vast number of innocent lives lost. The thought of children being orphaned, or worse, murdered, for her own revenge, didn't sit right with her. In fact, the thought haunted her.

The turmoil she felt over it all was stressful. Her stomach twisted in knots and made it nearly impossible to hold conversations with anyone. As such, she found herself holed up in her room more often than usual.

Thankfully, the book Galys gave her was a fascinating enough read it distracted her from the problem at hand. Part of her felt guilty for putting off the decision she had to make, but she reasoned that knowing more about her power could only help her in the end.

Three days had passed since Vysha's request, and Raelia curled herself into the corner chair in her room. The thick book was open and balanced on the arm of the plush seat as she read about the Indicative Mark she was born with.

The pages explained her Mark in detail. From what it looked like to where it could be found on the bearer's body. It was strange to read details about something that was on her body and felt so personal, but it was even more disconcerting to read about the powers it granted her.

'In nature, a Dandelion flower is known to be resilient. Even in the harshest climate, they are able to return over and over again. They represent renewal, regrowth, and abundant strength. They can withstand frost and freezes and tolerate crowding. Heat and insufficient moisture, while causing the leaves to bitter, will not kill the plant. It's very nature protects it's life.

With this knowledge, it is no surprise that the Dandelion's power is one of protection. It can be used in many ways depending on what protection is needed by the Bearer in the moment. The gift they are offered can vary greatly from Bearer to Bearer, but also from situation to situation. For example, some may manifest healing abilities, while others may only manifest destructive ones.

Throughout history, the strongest form of protection observed is the protective shield from physical harm. With practice, that shield can be extended to protect those around the bearer from physical attacks, as well.

If the Mark Bearer makes skin to skin contact with someone while their gift is activated, the protective glow can be pushed to extend over that individual. If focused, once the Bearer disconnects contact, the protection will remain intact.

This type of extension of their power can be very physically draining over long periods. The more training that the Mark Bearer undergoes, the easier and less exhausting it will become.

If the dandelion loses consciousness, the people their gift is guarding will lose the protection when the yellow glow fades from view.

In the event the Mark Bearer needs to protect someone they cannot physically connect with, the power can also be shot from the palm of their hand. With the right focus, the Dandelion can shoot a blast of power from their palm. Depending on their intent, this power can cause varying degrees of harm to the person threatening the individual they are trying to protect.'

Turning the page, Raelia couldn't help but peer at the sketch of the Dandelion Mark. Even though she'd seen her Mark before, she'd never seen the whole thing. It weaved in and out of the hairline along the base of her scalp, making it impossible to without cutting the hair it ran under. It was longer than she expected, and more detailed than she'd ever seen. Something about it seemed off to her eyes, but even with extended scrutinizing, she couldn't quite explain what. She struggled to pull her eyes from the photo, but with an effort, finally read on.

'The color of the Dandelion's glow indicates the kind of power they intend to use. While that makes hiding the type of attack impossible, little can be done about it.

A glow of Yellow

A yellow light is seen when the power used is protective in nature. This is the color of the glow extended to others when they need to be shielded from harm.

A glow of Green

When the Dandelion's glow becomes green, the power given is more defensive in nature. This glow when shot towards opponents has the ability to knock unconscious or divert attention from whomever is needing protection in the moment.

A glow of Red

If the glow of the Dandelion becomes red, anyone in the vicinity needs beware. This light of protection is offensive in nature. The attacks are violent and unpredictable. The shade of red can sometimes tell of the intent, but without extensive study or use of the gift, even the Mark Bearer will not always know what is to come. The lighter the shade generally shows the Bearer wishes to injure, but not kill. The darkest shade of red indicates the intent is to slay their opponent.

Light or dark, when the glow is red, only the Dandelion will know of their intent. Throughout history, even the lightest shades of red have been seen to slay an opponent. As such, no matter the shade, if the bearer glows red, the battle is already won.

The Dandelion's Weakness

Out of all Indicative Marks, the Dandelion has the fewest vulner-abilities. Though the ones they have tend to be more detrimental than those of other Marks.

First, and perhaps the most debilitating, is the power of the Mammillaria Indicative Mark. The nullification power granted to it's Bearer is able to temporarily stop the Dandelion from using their gift. To work properly, the Mammillaria Bearer must make direct skin to skin contact with the Dandelion.

The only other weakness known-'

"Raelia! Are you here?" Rokoa's voice called out, startling her so much the heavy book fell from her lap, slamming to the floor and closing itself. She jumped up, running to the door before he could make his way down the hall.

"I'm in here!" she hollered, putting her ear against the door. "I'll be out in a minute!"

There wasn't a response, but she waited listening to see if he would continue toward her. When she didn't hear footsteps, she quickly grabbed the book off the floor, and tucked it under her bed. She'd promised Galys she wouldn't tell anyone about it, but she figured it wouldn't bode well if it was found in her possession either.

After she felt certain it was safe, she headed into the sitting room where Rokoa lounged on the plush couch. He looked relaxed, almost sleeping, until he heard her footfall.

"You've been hiding," he said with suspicious eyes. "I haven't seen you in a couple days so I thought I better come check in on you. Up for a little training?"

For two days, she trained with Rokoa from morning until night. They spent most of their time in the forest clearing near the creek and only stopped to order food off the paper menu he brought with him. Zayric joined them, and Raelia repeatedly felt her body give way to smoke, swirling with the kyloxis from one place to the next in less than a blink.

It was exhausting and nauseating, but every time her feet landed on the ground, it became less so. She practiced over and over, learning how to let her feet fall in such a way that she could follow up her landing with an attack.

By the time the sun began setting on the second day, Rokoa beamed with pride. "It's hard to believe you're only human sometimes," he laughed. "You really have come a long way for someone who had no training before arriving."

Raelia smiled, her cheeks reddening. "And again you are so surprised."

The light shining through the canopy branches dimmed as they walked the path back into the enchanted city. The green shade reminded her of the forest behind her family's home, and she felt herself relax at the sight.

When Rokoa first found her, she never could have foreseen a friendship blossoming between them. For her, it seemed bizarre how the other Bearers reacted to him. They always seemed intimidated by his large stature and cold countenance, but she'd only known him to be gentle and warm. The burliness he presented never seemed as genuine as his smiles. She was grateful for his friendship and guidance. She wished others could see this side of him.

"Vysha asked me to have you visit her tomorrow," Rokoa's tone shifted, suddenly serious. "Do you have an answer for her yet?"

Raelia felt herself deflate as she shook her head.

"The answer will come to you," he said, placing a heavy hand on her shoulder. "It's a much easier decision than you think."

The next morning, as instructed, Raelia made her way towards the throne room, still unsure of what her answer would be. It felt like she'd gone over the options before her a thousand times already, but the pros and cons for each were close to equal across the board. After discussing the details with each of her friends, and even Zayric, she still didn't feel any closer to a decision. She wished she was still curled up with the book Galys gave her.

When she approached the large door leading into the throne room, she stopped and sighed. Her eyes followed over the exquisite carvings, closely eyeing the line of dandelion seeds wrapping around and through the other flowers.

'The other Marks,' she reminded herself.

She looked at the familiar blooms, picturing the faces she'd met belonging to the corresponding Marks. As she did so, she again followed the line of dandelion seeds, seeming to blow through the wind. The way they swirled around the other flowers gave a sense of protection. As if the dandelion was protecting the other Marks.

'The dandelion is meant to watch over the others,' Vysha had told her when she'd first met her. *'That's why it's not tied to any specific element.'*

Vysha had been kind in giving her an option, but she knew all along Raelia would concede. It was her duty. She is the new dandelion, and her Mark gave her a responsibility to protect the others.

Responsibility.

That word brought forth another memory. One that happened years before she ever came to Paodra. One she hadn't thought about since the dream she had the night before her birthday.

'My Glimmer,' her father had said, *'your Mark is one of power and of responsibility. You are more powerful than you know. Don't reject something that makes you who you are.'*

The sudden reminder of the duties her Mark bestowed upon her gave a sense of peace — a sense of understanding. The choice she needed to make suddenly felt simple. She didn't understand how she hadn't seen it before.

With a confidence only the right decision could give, Raelia opened the door to the throne room. Vysha smiled as she entered, her eyes expectant.

"Hello, *Aldaehima*," she greeted, stepping off the dais and walking toward her. "Are you ready for our training, child? I have a fair bit I want to go over with you and we need to do your cleansing today, as well."

Raelia nodded. "I am ready, but I wanted to speak with you before we begin, if I could?"

Vysha nodded, waiting for her to continue.

"I've given it a lot of thought, and I think you're right," she took a deep breath before continuing. "It is my duty, as the the Dandelion, to protect our people, so I will return after visiting Frayis to join the battle against King Calyx."

A bright smile spread across Vysha's features, and Raelia couldn't help but to match it. "I'm so glad, *Aldaehima*."

She hooked her arm through Raelia's and gently guided her back toward the dais, and past the throne she'd been sitting on when they first met, stopping at the table on the back wall behind it. Dozens of scrolls and a few large maps sprawled out over the surface of it.

Vysha's voice was softer, deadlier when she spoke once more. "I knew you'd come to the right decision."

The few days following her agreement were more chaotic than she'd yet experienced while in Paodra. She'd been given extra training, and every day was pulled out of bed before the sun rose.

Vysha decided training with Rokoa wasn't enough, so in addition to her sessions with him, she also worked with Jamina, who was a fiercer warrior than her petite structure would have led Raelia to believe. She would have enjoyed her time with the tracker, if it wasn't for the fact she clearly hated Luella.

Every time her friend came into view, Jamina's demeanor completely changed – becoming aggressive, and sometimes downright cruel with her words and fighting techniques. On top of that, the daggers she threw in her gazes toward the blonde, left little question as to how she felt about her presence.

The more time Raelia spent with her, the more she realized Jamina wasn't the only one who didn't appreciate Luella's presence. It seemed the people Vysha warned her about on their first night were real — they were just a bit more quiet about it when they didn't know whether the others they were with agreed with them or not.

A few of the people Jamina brought around for their sessions seemed to be the kind of people Raelia would have avoided in everyday life — even if she could have shown her Mark. They were angry, and aggressive, and most of them terrified her, if she was honest with herself.

One such Mark Bearer was a man who seemed to have more muscles than brains – whose enormous size would have intimidated even the best of warriors. A large Canna Lily Mark that ran down his spine, something he prominently displayed as he walked around bare chested. Raelia wished it was only in the training center he did that, but it seemed he never put a shirt on. She wasn't sure how she'd missed him, but after being introduced, she could always pick him out of a crowd easily because of his half naked appearance.

The first time Jamina pitted her against the muscular brute on the training mat, she hadn't been prepared for the flames he threw at her. She almost avoided the fiery ball, but it caught her elbow, and she shrieked in pain. The Mark Bearer's face held no remorse. His dark eyes seemed to glow with delight at her pain, and it infuriated Raelia.

Unfortunately, Jamina wasn't the only new recruit to help her train. Rokoa started bringing along Ekry for their training sessions. His reasoning being they should get to know each other before they all traveled to Frayis together. Raelia learned quite quickly into their joint sessions that she'd been right about the Drykuan woman not liking her. She didn't know what she'd done to make Ekry hate her, but she paid for it every time they crossed blades.

On one such occasion, the first one, Rokoa brought them, along with Zayric, to their normal meadow in the forest. He told Raelia she was to use the abilities she'd been working on with the kyloxis to disarm Ekry. Not attack. Disarm. His instructions to the Drykuan were to not attack, but to remain armed.

A few rounds in, Raelia still hadn't completed her task, and Rokoa decided to leave them practicing while he ran to retrieve something. The minute he was out of earshot, Ekry turned on her.

The clash of their blades echoed in the small meadow as the Drykuan growled under her breath. "I don't get why everyone is so impressed by you," she said through gritted teeth. "You are a waste of his time and energy!" On the last word, Ekry shoved her with so much force Raelia stumbled back a few steps.

Her eyes looked down at her feet, checking her footing for only a brief second, when she heard a whoosh of air.

"I'm done with you!" Ekry shouted just as she looked up.

The Drykuan woman now held a spear which she stabbed at Raelia's middle. She twisted quickly, barely avoiding being impaled on the sharp weapon, and jumped back out of Ekry's reach. The Drykuan stepped forward, threateningly.

Less than a second later, Zayric appeared at her feet and gave a warning growl, baring his teeth. Ekry glared down at the fox and then at Raelia, but she backed off.

Picking up the kyloxis in her arms, Raelia didn't wait to storm out of the clearing without another word.

Rokoa came to find her when he learned she'd left, but even after learning of what Ekry did, he still insisted they train together. Raelia only agreed after he swore to never leave them alone again, and yet she still dreaded the training sessions she knew Ekry would be attending.

On top of the extra training she was doing, Vysha thought it necessary to bring Raelia into the discussions of tactics and battle plans for the upcoming war. She'd been actively avoiding even thinking about it, so Raelia wasn't exactly happy about this new development.

During the warfare meetings, Dhovina and Qiralst, as well as a few of the other Zarhaish were in attendance. And while neither Rokoa nor Ekry ever missed a meeting, they were the only Drykuan's to ever show, which surprised Raelia. The knowledge that the Drykuan's would fight alongside the Mark Bearers when they reached Vairek City made her wonder why there weren't more of them in attendance.

On the day of her third meeting, she finally built up the courage to ask Rokoa as they walked toward the throne room together.

"Vysha mentioned that the Drykuan's would be a part of the war, but only you and Ekry have been coming to meetings. Why is that?"

He smirked. "Ekry and I are in charge of the soldiers. The General's if you will. We pass down the instructions. If the entire Drykuan army showed up to those meetings, there wouldn't be room for anyone else!"

Even though Raelia would have been happier if she could have skipped the war room meetings, she did learn quite a bit about not only the Mark Bearers and Drykuan's abilities and magic, she also learned a fair amount about the Zarhaish, as well.

The first thing she learned was when Vysha told her they were "restricted to the forest" she meant it literally. The Zarhaish couldn't leave the boundaries of the Paodran forest. When she asked Rokoa about it later in the day, he explained it was an ancient magic that cursed the Zarhaish to the confines of the trees.

He said a millennia ago, when the people of the Taevidian tribes were still only nomads, a group of Zarhaish warriors attacked and slaughtered a camp of the Vixuln's.

"One of the victims," he explained, "was the daughter of the Pre-eminent. If you believe the legends, she was the first ever Dandelion. The first ever human to bear an Indicative Mark."

Raelia's eyes were wide. She had never heard tellings of the original Mark Bearers. As far as she knew, they'd always existed.

"It's said she was born of a human and a Drykuan," Rokoa continued, "and the magic in her blood cursed the Zarhaish race. Forcing them into the confines of the closest forest so as to protect her people."

"The Dandelion... It-"

"The gift it offers is one of protection. Legend has it her death, and the magic's response to the violence, are the reason your power manifests the way it does. It's said the magic she possessed was greater than any being before her, immortal and mortal alike, and it is her magic that lives in every Mark Bearer still."

CHAPTER 23

The sun peeked above the mountains on the eastern horizon when Raelia and her friends began their journey south. It had been exactly six weeks since their arrival in Paodra, and she couldn't believe that much time had already passed.

The early start didn't bother Raelia, as she'd been getting up so early every day, and when she looked at Nazario, smiling at something Ekry said, she could see it wasn't a bother to them either. Ayla and Luella however, were sullen and cranky as they rode through the countryside.

Since the realization of her feelings, Raelia had done her best to avoid Lue, or at least avoid being alone with her. It was difficult, but with the increased training and battle meetings she'd been dealing with, she at least hadn't had to lie to her friend about where she was or why she hadn't been around.

They rode in pairs along the trail, Ekry and Naz in the front, Luella and Ayla in the middle on a cart pulled by Onyx and one of the large Drykuan horses. Raelia and Rokoa rounded out the back of the group.

In the time they'd been in Paodra, Raelia almost exclusively wore her training gear, and she was a bit disgruntled at being told she had to wear a dress outside of the forest. Luella hadn't minded, and took to being back in her frilly gown as if the last six weeks never happened. Nazario didn't even seem to mind being in traditional men's attire, though they had frowned at being told they couldn't wear their normal lip coloring. Then there was Raelia. She had always worn dresses in Frayis, and yet was uncomfortable and fidgety in one now. She wished for the much more comfortable attire Paodra allowed her.

The morning passed by without incident, and it wasn't until the sun was high in the sky that Nazario suggested they stop to eat. Zayric, who'd been riding in the cart amongst their supplies, seemed to enjoy the idea — hopping out when the cart stopped and running toward the nearby wooded area.

They ate in amicable quiet, all seeming to be lost in thought as they bit into the sandwiches Brixxi sent with them for the journey. They finished up fairly quickly, and took the horses to drink from the creek, where they found Zayric chomping down on what looked like a bird.

After they all loaded back up, Ekry and Naz started the procession south once more. Luella and Ayla livened up a fair bit after eating, and chatted amongst themselves, laughing and giggling at regular intervals.

A twinge of jealousy radiated through Raelia as she watched on. Mentally cursing herself for the sudden emotion, she tried her best to not watch them. It was difficult, though, as she and Rokoa still rode behind their cart. It felt like she couldn't get away from it at all.

"Are you ready to discuss your feelings for your friend?" Rokoa asked in a hushed tone after traveling for a few more hours. "I can see it's bothering you."

His voice pulled Raelia out of her reverie, and she felt heat touch her cheeks. "Am I that obvious?"

"Only to my trained eye." His following chuckle sounded forced, but before she could ask about it he continued more seriously, "She cares about you, Raelia. You should tell her your feelings. Get them out in the open. You will feel better for it."

Sighing, she pulled her eyes from Luella's blonde hair shimmering in the afternoon sun to look at him. "Do you think she will return my feelings?"

"It's hard to say," was his only response. When he turned his eyes back to the road, she felt she knew the truth.

"You don't think she will, do you?"

Now it was his turn to sigh. He turned his silver eyes back to hers. "No. I don't, but I still believe it's important for you to tell her."

"So she can reject me? So I can ruin one of the few friendships I've ever had?"

"So you can stop being weighed down by this burden."

She tore her eyes away from his, and looked up to the sky as a bird flew overhead. "But it's my burden. Telling her will only pass the burden on."

That evening when Gourdist came into view, Ekry and Rokoa decided against trying to find rooms at the inn. The group made their way to the forest behind the large town and set up camp for the night.

The following morning, they had another early start. Everyone seemed ready to go back to bed by the time they were climbing back on their horses, but continued their journey without complaint. Continuing south from Gourdist was an easier ride than the day before. They were able to break more frequently, and stop to eat midday in a small village along the route.

Everyone seemed in better spirits, though tired, when the last small village came into view.

"We'll camp again tonight," Ekry called from the front of the pack before veering off the road toward another small forest.

Everyone groaned, but no one commented. They didn't want to fight, they just wanted to get off their horses.

A few hours later, their camp was set up once more. Rokoa and Raelia took a short walk to the river and caught a surprising number of fish for their dinner.

By the time they'd all finished eating, the sun had set, and the canopy above was black except for where the firelight touched it. The whole group sat around the crackling flames, laughing and telling stories. For the first time since they left Paodra, Raelia didn't feel the weight of their excursion. And, even more, the weight of what would happen upon their return to the mythical forest.

Laughing along with everyone else at a joke Naz told them, Raelia's eyes caught sight of her best friend. She watched her for a moment. The smile on her face softened as Luella continued to laugh. Rokoa's advice from the day before echoed in her head as she watched Lue's slender fingers tuck a tuft of her blonde hair behind her ear, only for it to fall right back to her cheek.

Her heart swelled at the sight and she finally made up her mind.

"Lue?" Raelia said softly, the smile still bright on her face. "Can we talk for a moment?"

She stretched her hand out to her friend, who took it happily, still giggling. Raelia led them further down the trail, stopping when they reached the river's edge where she and Rokoa fished earlier in the day. The break in the canopy allowed them to see the stars above and the pale shine of moonlight covered everything around them.

Luella released her hand and it fluttered to her chest when she looked into the vast galaxy above them. "Look at all the stars! It's beautiful!"

"It is," Raelia agreed, though her eyes never left her friend. She felt her stomach twist into knots, as she reached for Luella's hand once more. "Can we talk?"

"Of course!" Luella exclaimed, a knowing look appearing on her face. "Is it about Rokoa? You two are so perfect together, even if he is hundreds of years old! I can see how much you mean to each other."

That took Raelia by surprise, and she momentarily fumbled for words. "Why?! What?! HIM?!"

Luella laughed, a melodious sound that echoed off of the surrounding trees. "Yes, him! I've seen how you two are together. I've seen how he looks at you. It's so obvious you care for each other!"

"I - I - I don't," was all Raelia could manage. Her face showed her confusion, and Luella's laugh faded.

"You don't?!" she asked, her smile faltering. "But you're always huddled away from the group, and talking in whispers. When you talk to him, you smile in a way I've never seen before... And the way he looks at you? I don't know... You always just seem so distracted when he's around..."

Raelia grabbed onto her friend's hand once more, and took a deep breath to help gather her thoughts. "It's not because of him that I'm distracted." Her voice was quiet when she spoke, and her eyes stared at their clasped hands, the pale white against her amber brown were at a stark contrast.

"I don't understand," Luella said plainly.

"It's not because of Rokoa that I'm distracted," she replied. "I seem distracted, because he knows that... that..." Her throat tensed with nerves, making the words difficult to get out.

"What does he know, Rae?"

She took another calming breath and swallowed the emotion building in her chest. "He knows that I... I..."

Luella squeezed her hand and stepped closer to her friend. Her cerulean blue eyes found Raelia's jade. "What is it Rae? You know you can tell me. You can tell me anything."

Staring into her friend's eyes seemed to give her the confidence to finally utter the words. "I love you, Lue."

"I love you too, Rae," Luella returned, confusion coloring her tone. "But that doesn't answer the question."

"But it does," she responded in a soft voice. "It explains why I'm always distracted when you're around. It explains why I can't focus when you laugh." Raelia gently tucked a strand of blonde hair behind Luella's ear, gently caressing her cheek as she did so. "You're more than my friend. You are my reason to keep going, to keep fighting. You know me better than any other person in this entire world, and you have never given up on me."

Luella's eyes grew wide, as Raelia continued, "You're the first thought in my mornings, and the last thought of my nights. My heart is full when you're around, and desperate to be near you again when you leave." She took a deep breath before finishing in a tender voice, "I've fallen head over heels for you, Lue. I... I love you."

Eyes still wide, Luella silently stared at her lifelong friend. Raelia felt hope growing in her chest. The expression on Lue's face flitted from shock to confusion to... fear?

Before she even realized what she was doing, Raelia reached out, placing a tender hand on her best friend's cheek. The affection she felt glowing in her eyes. Suddenly, Luella flinched away from the contact, looking flustered and disgusted.

Pain shot through Raelia's heart and she pulled her hand back quickly, looking down. She couldn't stand seeing the disgust in Lue's gaze.

"Rae-," Lue started.

"Don't. I understand."

Raelia stepped back, releasing her friend's hand — desperate to create as much space between them as possible.

"Raelia, please," Luella begged.

"Please what?" Raelia asked, a hard edge in her tone.

"I've never thought of you that way," Luella's voice was kind, but firm. "I've never thought of any... any woman that way. I don't... I've never..."

Raelia felt the telling pricks of tears in the corner of her eyes, but she refused to let them fall. All at once it felt as if her world were shattering around her, but she refused to give away how much pain she felt.

"It's fine," Raelia lied, interrupting the words she knew would destroy the little composure she strained to hold on to. "We should get back."

Before Luella could say another word, Raelia swiftly walked around her and back toward the trail they'd followed to the clearing. Her friend stayed a few paces behind and soon they were back in front of the glowing campfire where the others still laughed.

Raelia pasted a fake smile on her face when Naz looked up at her, and even though their expression showed they saw straight through it, they didn't comment. She moved past them and the spot she'd been sitting before and walked to the other side of the flames, dropping next to Rokoa with a thud. She grabbed the flask he held in his hand and took a deep pull from it. The creamy liquid had a cinnamon flavor and burned all the way down.

He watched her with curious eyes that flickered to Luella sitting down next to Nazario in Raelia's previous spot. When she took another swig from his flask, he took it back.

"You don't need more than two. It's too strong for you," he said in a hushed voice only she could hear. She expected gloating or teasing from him, but even in his soft tone, she could hear his worry.

Raelia glared at him, and reached once more for the flask, only dropping her hand when he pulled it out of her reach. Ekry watched on from her seat on the other side of Rokoa, snickering under her breath. Something about 'idiot mortals' caught her ear.

Anger rushed through her, and once again tears threatened to fall. Raelia stood abruptly. Her friends looked up at her, confused. "I'm going to bed," she said sharply, before turning on her heel and heading for her tent.

Once inside, she sat on the small mat and blankets making up her bed. She could hear her friend's muffled voices, and though she couldn't make out their words, knew they were worried about what changed her mood so suddenly.

She kicked off her boots and climbed under her blanket, burying her head underneath them before finally letting the tears fall.

CHAPTER 24

The next morning, Raelia busied herself. Helping pack up their campsite and hitching the horses back to the trailer. She was quiet as she worked, and avoided anyone who spoke. The pain she'd felt last night had now twisted into anger and she didn't know how well she'd be able to contain it if she opened her mouth to speak.

Last night hurt her deeply. She knew telling her friend of her feelings might result in rejection, but this pained her so much more than just a simple 'no' would have. It wasn't the fact Luella didn't feel the same way, it was the disgust that glowed in her eyes at Raelia's touch. As if what she felt was dirty. As if what she felt was vile.

Luella tried to approach her before Ekry called out for them to mount their horses, and even though she didn't like the Drykuan, Raelia was grateful for her impeccable timing. The last thing she wanted to do was have another conversation. Especially now that her anger outweighed her hurt.

The sun warmed them as it rose into the sky. Raelia was happy to only have on a lightweight cotton dress. She couldn't imagine how Rokoa and Ekry remained in their cloaks with the rising heat.

"We aren't affected by the temperature in the same way a human is," he told her when he caught her questioning gaze on his cloak. "Our body stays cool even on the warmest of days."

He reached out and pressed his fingers to the back of her hand. They were surprisingly cool, and Raelia found herself envious of this new information as a bead of sweat dripped from under her hair on the back of her neck.

They stopped for lunch in a small village only a few miles out of Frayis, but the anxiety Raelia felt about being so close to home didn't help her appetite. She wasn't sure why, but she was afraid to see her home again. In Paodra she'd been allowed a blissful ignorance of sorts — able to ignore what happened on her birthday. To her village. To her family... Able to pretend being in a mythical forest was only a coincidence when the reality was a life altering trauma.

Raelia's anxiety was at the pinnacle, when they loaded back onto their horses. She and Rokoa were once again in the back of the group, and though he talked about a wide number of things, she didn't hear a word he said. It wasn't until he placed a hand on her shoulder she even acknowledged his presence.

"Would you like to talk about what happened last night?" he asked, releasing her when he realized she was listening.

"What? I-" it took her a moment to process his question, and even though her mind had been on Luella for the better part of the day, she hadn't been thinking about her at that moment. Her mind had been churning over what awaited them in Frayis. She sighed. "I'm fine. Really."

Rokoa laughed lightly. "If that were the case, you'd have had something to say when I told you I thought Ekry was in love with you."

"WHAT?!" Raelia's eyes widened in shock, and she choked on the air she was attempting to inhale. "There's no way she's... Why would you think that?!"

"To get your attention!" he barked out a loud laugh. "You didn't even acknowledge it, so there's clearly something bothering you, Bee-

Bee." He paused for a moment, seeming to consider his words carefully before finishing in a nervous tone, "You can talk to me."

"It doesn't have anything to do with..." she let her voice trail off, hoping he'd get her meaning.

"Okay. Then what?"

A sigh of relief left her when she realized she wouldn't have to talk about last night's rejection. "I'm worried about... well... about what we're going to find when we get back to Frayis."

"Ah."

"We buried C-Caeda," she stumbled over her sister's name, realizing she hadn't spoken it since she'd said goodbye over her grave. "But we never — I never — went back for my mother and brother. What if I can't find their bodies?

"Find their bodies? Raelia, you did what you could when-"

"I *know* that!" frustration flooded to the surface. "In the moments I had before leaving, I did what I could, but... I... I have to bury them too. I can't leave them to rot somewhere."

"You know the intel we've recovered," Rokoa said kindly. "Frayis is just as we left it. No one-"

"But what if the information is wrong? What if we get there and someone has done away with all the bodies left in the village? What if the village has just gone back to normal? What if..." she stopped, unsure if she should even breathe the fear she held in.

"What if... what?"

"What if... What if the Grushik are still there?"

Rokoa's eyes widened in shock. "Grushik?! What do you... How do you even know... Why would there be Grushik?!"

Surprise colored her features when she looked at him. She hadn't expected him to be so flustered. "When Ayla first arrived, and we were talking with Naz, we told them about the men who attacked the village. I guess Naz's tribe is where the magic to create Grushik originated... We..."

"It is forbidden to create Grushik. It is punishable by death. Why would you think-"

"How would the King know of such magic, Rokoa? How would he know how to create them?"

"He wouldn't!" he asserted.

"But-"

"But nothing! There won't be any Grushik in Frayis! There weren't any in the first place!" he shouted, causing Luella and Ayla to turn around in the cart in front of them.

Without another word, Rokoa hurried his steed and joined Nazario and Ekry in front of the group. Raelia stared after him, bewildered. She'd never seen him act so irrational before. Why on earth would he be so angry about a theory? Why would he care if something was illegal? Both of their very existence was illegal, so why would the King completing the ritual elicit such a response?

Raelia realized she'd been staring at the back of his head, and it took her a while to notice the outline of Frayis growing larger on the horizon. Her heart started racing at the sight of her small village, and she knew she wasn't ready to go through it quite yet.

With a burst of speed, she overtook the rest of the group, veering Prickle toward the dense forest that led to the back of her family's home. She heard first Rokoa, then Naz call for her, but she ignored them.

Soon after, she heard hooves beating the ground behind her. When she turned to see who was following, she was surprised that they all were — even Ayla and Luella in the cart, though they moved slower than the others.

Naz caught up to her first. They didn't speak, but the question in their eyes compelled her.

"I want to go home first. I don't want to-"

"You don't have to explain, Rae. We're following you," they told her with a gentle smile. "Lead the way."

A wave of relief washed over her and she smiled in return. "Thanks."

A few minutes' ride was all it took to hit the edge of the massive forest and then the back of her family's pasture. As she rode through the field toward the stables, she looked at her family home just beyond the fence. It looked the same. Nothing changed, except the longer grass. Yet, as she looked upon her childhood home, it seemed completely different. It seemed smaller. Duller even. Her heart ached remembering the warmth she used to feel when she looked at it.

Her friends huddled around the cart, unhitching Onyx and the other horse from it. She hopped off Prickle and when she approached them, her eyes found Rokoa's concerned gaze.

"The back door is open," he told Raelia. "I think Ekry and I should go through and make sure there isn't anyone waiting inside."

She nodded, watching as he turned to the cart, lifting a sword from the back and holding the hilt out to her. "You should arm yourselves. Just in case."

Raelia took the sword from him and watched her friends as they each grabbed a weapon. At the rustling, Zayric popped his head from beneath a mound of blankets and jumped to perch on the side of the cart.

The fox watched her for a moment, but his eyes shifted as Rokoa and Ekry headed toward the house. Raelia followed them to the gate, each of her friends keeping close behind. Her eyes darted to the back door, only a few feet from where they stood. It was open, though looked in one piece.

When the Drykuan's disappeared into the dark house, Raelia looked at her friends, confirming they were all armed, before stepping forward toward the garden.

"Rae!" Luella called in a hushed tone. "He said to wait here! You don't know who might be in there!"

A sudden noise from the side of the house startled all of them, causing Lue to let out a small whimper. It sounded like an animal — like hooves on the cobblestone street out front.

Raelia couldn't resist hurrying around the corner to peek around to the front yard, Naz, Ayla and Luella following closely on her heels. Her eyes widened when she saw the familiar white horse hitched to a cart.

"Rae, isn't that-"

Before Luella could finish her question, a heavy 'bang' sounded out from inside, and a shout for help rang through the air.

"NO! STOP!" she screamed when realization hit her.

She ran as fast as her legs would carry her. Bee lining through the front door and down the hall where she could still hear muffled shouts for help. She burst into her father's study, screaming once more as she did so.

"NO! STOP! DON'T HURT HIM!"

Ekry paused mid swing, her blade aiming at the young man Rokoa held in front of himself, both of them looking at her with identical shocked expressions.

She hurried the short distance to his side. His blonde hair stuck to his forehead, and his blue eyes glowed with terror and confusion.

"Rae! Get out of here!" her brother screamed. "Run!"

Tears welled in her eyes as she pushed Rokoa's hands off of Caias and wrapped him in her arms. "I've missed you so much!"

Caias, still in shock and fearful for their lives, didn't understand what was happening. He grabbed her tightly, twisting his body in front of hers, pushing her against the wall as he looked at Ekry and Rokoa with a loathing that didn't fit his handsome features.

"Don't hurt her!"

"Caias!" Raelia tried to push him off of her, but he held his ground.

"Shut up, Rae! Let me handle this!"

Rokoa smirked, amused, before turning to Ekry. "Hear that? He's clearly got this under control. We're obviously not needed here."

Ekry rolled her eyes, and turned to leave just as Nazario, Ayla and Luella tumbled in through the open door.

"Caias! Would you get off me?!" Raelia shouted, shoving him once more.

"What..." Caias's flabbergasted expression was comical. "What's going on?" He stepped aside, letting Raelia out of the small gap he'd backed her into.

She grabbed his arm, turning him around so she could see his face. It was him. Caias was really there. Throwing herself at him, she felt tears flood down her cheeks.

Seeming to accept they would not be killed in that moment, Caias wrapped his arms around her, returning her hug just as fiercely. They stayed there, and not until the door clicked closed behind her did she realize the others left the room.

Tears streamed down her cheeks as she pulled back to look into her brother's eyes. She knew he'd been due home soon, but didn't expect him to be here when they arrived. Words couldn't express the gratitude she felt that he was.

"Raelia... What's going on?" he asked, concern coloring his expression as the fear dissipated. "Who were those people? Why are they here?" His eyes caught sight of the blade she still held in her hand, and they widened. "And why do you have a sword?!"

Of all the questions he could have asked in that moment, those were the easy ones, and she hurried to answer him. Stifling her tears and wiping her cheeks, she explained who each one of her friends were, surprising him when she told him Luella had been amongst them. She told him about Paodra, and how they had brought her back here to wait for him and Papa to return, but wanted to make sure the house was safe before they came in.

"Wait... Why... Rae, why wouldn't the house be safe?" Caias asked, a slight panic slipping into his tone. "And why were you in - uh - Paoda? Is that where Mama and the kids are? Why didn't they return with you?"

Raelia's eyes fell to the ground, her tears began again, splattering on the wood floor. She placed her sword on the small coffee table, backing away from her brother. She sniffled as she tried to find the words to tell him what happened.

"Rae?" his voice was softer now as he stepped toward her once more. "Rae, where's Mama? Where's Caeda and Blaze?"

She opened her mouth trying to speak, but no sound came out. Lifting her eyes to connect with her brother's, the worry in them broke the last bit of resolve she had.

Crumbling to the floor, she sobbed, "I tried to save them! Caias, I tried! I wasn't strong enough!"

He sat in front of her, and grabbed her hands in his. Before he could speak, she slumped her head into his chest as she continued, her words muffled against him.

"The men! They attacked during the festival! They shot flaming arrows! People were screaming and I ran to find Mama! I ran to the booth! But... I was too late... The man he... he..."

The image of her mother's head departing from her body flashed through her mind, and she shuddered. Unable to finish, she told him then about how she'd attacked him, and got Blaze and Caeda away.

"But then an arrow, it..." She watched again as the memory took her and she watched the light leave her younger brother's hazel eyes. "Blaze, he... he..."

Caias slumped against the wall, seeming to lose the strength to hold himself up. Raelia still cried against his chest as she told him how she had to leave Blaze's body behind.

"Caeda screamed for him, over and over, but he was already... I couldn't save him!" she sobbed. "I almost made it to the horses. I almost got Caeda out, but... the man... the man who killed Mama... he..."

Words failed her as sobs took her ability to speak.

"They... They're all... gone?" Caias's voice cracked with emotion, with pain.

Suddenly, his arms squeezed Raelia so fiercely, she thought her ribs might break from the force of it. He was silent as he sobbed, his shaking breaths the only give away of his tears.

They held each other like that for what seemed like an eternity. Sobbing and grieving the loss of their family. Raelia hadn't realized how badly she'd needed him — how badly she needed to grieve with him — until that moment. She'd cried with Vysha, she and Luella had cried together too, but this was the first time she felt as if her grief wasn't something to be ashamed of. This is what her heart needed. It needed to grieve alongside someone who felt the weight of her loss, because it was also the weight of their own.

Shadows crept across her father's study as the sun lowered in the sky. Eventually, Caias pulled back and wiped his cheeks with his hands, before reaching out to wipe his sister's eyes as well.

"How d-did you escape?" he asked through his ragged breath.

"Rokoa. He saved me just before..."

He squeezed her hands and his gaze met hers. "Thank the gods he did!"

Those words hit her like a punch in the gut, causing her to break down again. The guilt she felt about her failure to save her family had been eating her alive. Surviving what her mother and younger siblings hadn't, was its own kind of agony. And knowing the attack was her fault, made the guilt even thicker.

Caias rubbed her back soothingly. "Rae. I'm glad you're here. You did everything you could... It's not your fault."

"It is! It's all my fault!" she sobbed.

"No, Rae. You couldn't have known-"

"But they were there because of ME! They wanted ME!"

"I... I don't understand..."

Raelia did her best to get her emotions under control before telling her brother everything Vysha told her. How the only reason the attack happened was because the King learned of her Mark — of her existence — and wanted her dead.

When she'd finished, Caias was quiet. The only sounds around them were her stifled sobs. She couldn't bring herself to look at him, afraid she would see the hatred she felt for herself reflected in his eyes.

"Raelia," when he spoke again his voice was filled with grief, but it was soft, and kinder than she expected it to be, "you are not to blame for their deaths. For any of their deaths. If King Calyx sent them, then he's the one responsible. Not you. I will not listen to you blaming yourself for the actions of a murderous King."

That evening, after Raelia introduced Caias to her friends, she showed him where they'd buried Caeda's body. She told him she planned to retrieve Yaila's and Blaze's bodies as well, so they could lay them to rest next to the garden with their sister.

"It will be nice if we're all here for it this time. Caeda only had myself, Luella and Rokoa..." An image of what remained of their family looking down on the graves of their loved ones flashed in her mind. "When will Papa return?" she asked, realizing only then that Eloi should have been there too. "Why did you come separately? Is he still in Taevidia?"

Caias sighed heavily, and Raelia felt suddenly panicked. The pain in her brother's sigh telling her more than he probably realized.

"I don't know where Papa is."

"What?! But you were-"

"We were together, yes, but Ouma... she got sick, and Papa came here to look for the remedy in one of his books," he explained, sorrow filling his tone. "The healer told him what book contained the information, so he left to retrieve it from his study."

"Then where is he? He should be here!"

"I don't know... I thought so too, but I arrived only a little while before you turned up... and the house was empty when I got here."

Her father's smiling face flashed in her mind, and she felt the now familiar rise of anxiety in her chest. She took a deep breath, trying to calm herself before she lost herself in emotions once more.

"We'll find him, Rae," Caias reassured, squeezing her hand. "Juniper said he came through Truliach on the way back up, so at least we know he made it through the wastelands. That's the biggest hurdle."

"That's something, at least," she said, calming down slightly.

The wastelands, she knew, were the treacherous stretch of barren land connecting Dirythia to the Taevidian Empire. Truliach was the last southern stop before having to travel across them if one wished to make it to the other country.

She always wondered why more people didn't sail to Taevidia if going by foot was so dangerous. Before he and Caias left, Eloi told her the waters were even more perilous than the wastelands. He said in all of recorded history, only two ships had ever made it across the stretch of sea between their two countries, and only a few from each survived the journey.

He hadn't, however, told her why the sea between them was so dangerous, and now she may never get to ask. The thought pained her, but she shoved it down.

She sighed, looking at her brother, so happy he was home, yet so scared for their father. She smiled through her fear. "You're right. We'll find him. Maybe you two crossed paths and didn't even realize."

"Maybe..."

Before anymore could be said on the subject, the back door opened. They both turned to find Nazario and Rokoa coming through.

"It's getting late," the Drykuan said. "We should leave early if we're to find your mother and brother. It will be harder work if it is as warm tomorrow as it was today."

"Ekry and I made dinner for us all," Naz informed them. "You should come in and eat. It's been a long day, a long trip really... We could all use a good night's sleep."

She and Caias both nodded, and followed them inside.

Dinner was a quiet affair. Caias and Luella chatted softly, catching up on the events since they'd last seen each other. Raelia felt her stomach tense with envy as she watched Luella's eyes light up with affection when looking at her brother. It had always kind of bothered her, but now she recognized why, and her jealousy was at its peak.

Raelia picked at her plate, not as hungry as she probably should be, but with her stomach in knots, every bite made her nauseous. A scratch on the back door drew her attention away from the table, and she felt relieved for an excuse to get away from it.

When she opened the door, Zayric sat on the other side. She hadn't seen him since he'd bounded out of the cart near the stables, and a wave of emotion hit her when she looked at him. Scooping him up, she excused herself and said goodnight. They all looked at her with curious or confused eyes, but she paid them no heed.

At the top of the stairs, a few tears escaped down her cheeks, and she hurried into her room. The emotions that had been building in her flooded down her cheeks the moment the door was closed.

Zayric, seeming to understand, twisted around to nuzzle into the crook of her neck as she made her way to the bed. When she plopped down, it groaned under her weight. Placing the kyloxis on the bed, she pulled her boots off and climbed under the blanket, fully sobbing by the time her head sunk into the pillow.

<hr>

The following morning came much earlier than Raelia would have liked, but as the sun peered through her window, she resigned herself to getting up.

Her dress was rumpled and twisted after a night filled with tossing and turning. She mentally cursed herself for not changing out of it before crawling into bed. Pulling back her blankets, she stretched and placed her feet on the ground, yawning as she did so.

Zayric stretched along with her before jumping onto the window sill next to her bed and looking at her expectantly.

"I know, I know..." she said sleepily.

She cracked the window open for the fox to slip out, watching him hop from it to the tree outside and then down to the ground. She shook her head before turning around and heading to the washroom down the hall.

When she returned, face washed, and hair brushed and braided, she changed out of her rumpled dress and into her Paodran training gear. Rokoa told her they weren't to wear it on the road, worried it would draw too much attention to their group, but he said nothing about not wearing it once she got home. Besides, if they were going into town today, she didn't know what to expect and she wasn't going to let her guard down. She wanted to be ready for anything, even if it was unlikely that anything would happen.

CHAPTER 25

When she got downstairs, Nazario was the only one awake. They sat at the small kitchen table, with a steaming cup of tea in their hands.

"Glad to see you're back to dressing normally," they said with a bright smile. "You want a cup?"

She nodded, returning their smile and sat down quietly.

"How are you doing, Rae?" they asked, voice concerned, as they handed her the steaming mug. "You had me worried last night. The way you just disappeared..."

She breathed in the warm, sweet aroma that had just a hint of char. A special blend of green tea only found in this part of Dirythia. It was her mother's favorite.

Dropping her eyes to the mug in her hands, she sighed. "I'm okay," she lied. "This has all been a lot to take in, is all. A good night's sleep was just what I needed."

"Are you sure?" they asked, eyeing her suspiciously. " You seem... off."

She mentally cursed herself, she knew better than to try and pull the wool over Naz's eyes. They were only slightly less perceptive than Rokoa. She opened her mouth to speak, but before she could, the back door opened and Rokoa walked through.

"Good morning!" he said brightly. "Everybody sleep well?"

His sudden appearance would have been surprising enough, but she couldn't fathom what he'd been doing outside when the sun was only barely coming up from the horizon line.

"What were you doing out there so early?" she asked. "I figured you'd still be sleeping."

"Don't you know me at all, BeeBee?" he chuckled. "I've been up for a couple hours already." He put his arm in the air, showing her a long chain with a few fish dangling from it. "Thought we could use some breakfast before we head out."

A smile spread across her face at the proud air swirling around him. Something in him seemed different here. He seemed relaxed, and almost jovial, something she never thought she'd say about the usually serious and stoic Drykuan.

"As if we haven't had enough fish on this trip?" she joked, smiling, as she stood up. "We have some rice in the cupboard. I'll start washing it while you clean those and get them ready." She turned to Naz. "Could you get the fire going? The tinderbox should be on that shelf," she said, pointing to a built-in row of shelves a few feet from the wood-burning stove, "and there's a wood crate just outside the door against the house."

As the three of them hurried to prepare breakfast, the rest of the house woke. The others slowly made their way into the kitchen and were promptly pointed toward the dining room, where Raelia had set plates and cutlery. By the time the food made it to the table, everyone was ready to eat and get their day started.

When the plates were emptied and the table cleared, Raelia and Caias walked to the stables to ready the horses for the ride into town. They'd decided on having Marah, their family's white mare, pull the cart, so once the other two were saddled up, they readied the small wooden wagon for her.

While they worked, Raelia couldn't help but notice the odd looks Caias kept giving her. She tried to catch him at it, but when she would look his way, he quickly averted his gaze. It was driving her mad.

Once Marah was hitched, she grabbed her brother's arm before he could walk away. "Why do you keep looking at me like that?"

"Like what?" He tried to pull from her grasp, but she only tightened her hold.

"I don't know! It's like you've never seen me before or something!" she chuckled, trying to lessen the frustration she felt at his odd behavior.

Finally, he managed to yank his arm free of her fingers and sighed. "I... You just... You're different." He gestured to the clothes she wore, then to the dagger holstered on her hip. "Since when do you dress like a man? Or carry weapons like a man? You were carrying a sword yesterday, and now this?"

Suddenly a movement behind Caias caught her eye. Swiftly, she shoved him behind her and pulled out the dagger in question, and held it up threateningly toward the cart, sighing in relief when Zayric popped up from inside, sitting on the edge as he watched her happily.

She laughed. "You scared me half to death!" Shoving the dagger back into her holster, she turned to see an incredulous look on her brother's face.

"What in the world was that?!" he nearly shouted. "Who *are* you?!"

She felt a defensive anger rise in her chest, but shoved it down, not wanting to fight with him. "I'm the same sister you've always known, Caias," she told him, "but I'm trained for battle now. I'm trained to protect myself and those I love. I... I..." She felt her lip tremble as a sudden wave of emotion washed over her. "I don't want to be weak again. I don't want to watch the people I love die because I can't protect them."

Somehow, she managed to keep the tears from falling, but he knew her too well. He wrapped his arms around her, hugging her tightly. His voice was quiet in her ear. "You don't have to protect anyone anymore, especially not me. I'm your brother. I'm here. *I* will protect *you*."

Raelia let out a shaky laugh, muffled by his shoulder. "I don't need you to protect me." She pulled back, her jade green eyes serious when she found his. "I can protect myself now."

"Is the wagon ready to go?" Ekry called out from the gate, startling both of them.

"Uh... Yeah!" she hollered back, walking away from her brother. "And the others are all saddled."

Ekry's silver eyes scrutinized her for a moment before nodding her acknowledgement. She walked to where her horse stood, saddled and ready, in the pasture.

Raelia hurried to open the front gate. When she peeked back, Caias still stared as if he'd never seen her before. She felt ashamed, and felt her cheeks burn with embarrassment.

By the time she'd tied open the gate, everyone else had made their way out into the pasture. Caias climbed up on Onyx while Luella climbed into the cart, taking Marah's reins in her hands. Naz, Ayla and Rokoa climbed atop the remaining horses and soon after, they headed out.

They kept at a moderate pace and reached the edge of town fairly quickly. Rokoa put his hand in the air, stopping them before they entered the small village. "I think we should take it in teams," he told them. "We're here to find your family members," his eyes shifted to Raelia, "but we also need to explore the area to make sure it's safe."

Collectively, they all nodded in agreement and Rokoa proceeded to split them into two groups. Caias, Luella, Ayla, and Ekry in one and Raelia, Nazario and himself into the other. He had Naz and Luella swap positions, knowing they would need the cart for Yaila and Blaze's bodies, and soon they were hunting through the narrow roads and alleyways of Frayis.

Raelia felt relieved to be in a separate group from her brother and best friend. The stress of this situation was hard enough without the emotional strain she felt around them both.

She led her small group down an alley that opened up on the end of the street her family's stall was on, knowing her mother's body still lay within. However, when they came out the end of it, she stopped, frozen in place at the scene before her.

Six, nearly seven, weeks had passed since the attack on her village. The first six weeks of spring, which was wet and warm in this part of Dirythia — conditions that would quicken the decomposition of a human body, and yet, none of the surrounding bodies seemed to have decomposed at all. If it wasn't for the fact the blood pooling around each was a dried, dark brown, she would assume they had only just fallen.

The hair on her arms raised as fear licked up her spine. "Rokoa? How... What..." she didn't even know how to word the question in her mind and her eyes turned to find his, completely unperturbed.

"Something has settled over Frayis," he told her. "Vysha had reports back from scouts in the area that everything looked as if the attack just took place. I guess this is what they meant."

"Grushik..." Raelia heard Naz mutter under their breath. Rokoa's eyes flitted to them, but he didn't comment.

"What else did the reports say?" Raelia asked as she urged a hesitant Prickle forward slowly.

"They said no one was left alive. Either all the residents left or were slaughtered."

If she hadn't spent so much time with Rokoa, she was certain she'd have missed the tinge of shame in his tone. Or was it guilt she heard?

"You couldn't have saved them all," she reassured him in a soft voice. Her tone kind and understanding. She didn't want him to feel the same guilt she did for not being able to save anyone else. "You did all you could do. We both did."

Her words seemed to startle him, and the emotion in his eyes betrayed his heart. He looked away quickly to fix his face into its normal stoic expression. He didn't respond in words or gesture, just spurred his horse forward, letting the conversation end.

She would have called out to him, or caught up with him, but her gaze fell on a familiar face. It was one of her neighbors. She hadn't even known the young man's name, but the weight of what they were doing settled on her once more, and she couldn't find her voice.

As they made their way along the cobbled road, they passed different booths and carts. Every few feet, another body would present itself, and the longer she looked at them the more her stomach twisted into knots.

Raelia lifted her head, looking outward instead of at the bodies around them and saw the booth where her mother tried to protect her children. When her eyes lowered, a sob caught in her chest. There was her mother. Her beautiful yellow dress covered in dried, brown blood.

Yaila's body was exactly where Raelia remembered it falling. Her head nearly six feet from it, and the memory of the squelching thud it made when it hit the ground overwhelmed Raelia's senses. She squeezed her eyes shut. Trying to block it from her mind.

When they approached, the sound of hooves sounded behind them, all three turned to see Caias coming their way, Onyx trotting distinguishably.

Through the sob building in her chest, she choked out, "What are you... doing here?"

His eyes were sad when they found hers; his voice colored in grief. "I couldn't leave you to do this on your own."

She didn't have to ask what he meant. She understood completely. Physically, she wasn't alone. Rokoa and Nazario were with her. But Yaila and Blaze... They were their family. They would grieve their losses in a way no one else here would. He was offering something to her no one else *could* give her, not really.

A partner in grief.

He jumped down from Onyx, and reached his hand out to her, helping her down to the ground. The pain in his eyes as he looked down at their mother was more apparent than anything Raelia had ever seen on her brother's face before, and it mirrored the grief in her heart.

They brought sheets for the bodies, one for Yaila and Blaze and one for each of Luella's parents. Nazario brought one to her now. Caias's eyes hadn't moved from Yaila's severed head, and the look of horror on his face grew.

Raelia reached out, placing her hand on his arm, and squeezed reassuringly. She couldn't blame him for his reaction. She hadn't explained the details of her mother's death, only that they'd killed her. At least she'd known what to expect.

"I'll get her... her... head," Raelia choked out as she handed him the sheet.

He nodded, numbly and lifted the ball of fabric from her.

Tears threatened to fall as Raelia knelt down next to her mothers head. If it had still been attached to her body, Raelia could have believed Yaila was only sleeping, and the thought unsettled her.

Her hands trembled as she reached out and lifted her mother's head, the dirty blonde hair soft against her fingertips, making her shudder. It was lighter than she expected, but the weight of her grief didn't allow her to think on that long.

When she walked over to where Caias was — just laying their mother's decapitated body onto the clean white sheet — she set the head alongside it. They quickly wrapped their mother tightly and put her in the back of the cart.

Rokoa and Naz watched on as the pair worked. Neither wanting to intrude on their grief. But once Yaila's body was put into the cart, the Drykuan cleared his throat.

"Where is your brother?"

She thought about what happened after her mother fell. It felt so fresh, and her heart raced in response to the images flashing in her head. She looked up the street, only two doors down, and saw him.

His body seemed so small in death. He was crumpled on the ground, and his blonde hair blew in the light breeze. She lifted her finger to point to him, the other three following the line. She knew the instant Caias spotted their brother, a quick intake of breath giving him away.

He didn't say a word, only turned to go grab another sheet. He brushed past her, and Raelia watched with a heavy heart as Caias knelt down, pulled the arrow from Blaze's chest, and wrapped him just as they'd done Yaila. He easily lifted the small bundle. As he walked back, Raelia could see him struggling to hold back his tears.

After placing him next to Yaila's bundled body, Raelia, Rokoa and Caias climbed back onto their horses, while Naz climbed back into the wagon. They rode back the way they came, turning down a side road and following it to the main square.

Raelia was about to ask where they should look for the others when an angry shout cut through the air. Her blood ran cold. Memories of the solitary scream at the beginning of the attack on Frayis flashed in her mind, as Rokoa gestured for them to follow.

They raced their horses down the small road, the cart rattling against the cobblestones behind them as they turned into an alleyway barely wide enough for it to fit through. When they came out the other side, Ekry, Ayla and Luella sat on their horses facing a group of royal soldiers.

"Who are you?! What are you doing here?!" one of them yelled, his voice proud and forceful. He seemed to be the leader, older than the rest by at least a decade and his chest more decorated with medals and insignias than the others. His beady eyes shifted to Rokoa, Caias, and Raelia as they walked their horses forward, followed closely by Nazario. "By order of the honorable King Calyx Prilot, ruler of the illustrious Kingdom of Dirythia, I order you to tell us what happened here!"

About fifteen soldiers stared at them with barely veiled malice in their eyes, all holding the swords at their hips. Only two were on steeds of their own, the one making demands on the largest, while the rest of them were on foot.

"We are only here to collect our dead," Rokoa called out in an amicable tone. "We will be on our way now."

Ekry turned to look at him, and he gestured with his eyes for her to pull back. She nodded, but before she reacted, the soldier yelled out once again.

"I have ordered you to tell us what happened here!" In one swift, sudden movement, every soldier on the ground shifted to a defensive position. "If you do not answer me you will be taken into custody for further interrogation!"

A voice echoed in Raelia's mind at his pronouncement. Vysha's voice. A story she had told her the night they met, about Williana, the woman who had done the council review shortly after her birth. The woman who saved her life by lying about her findings.

"Under their torturous interrogation, she revealed your identity to the King. She told him about your Indicative Mark."

Raelia's blood boiled with rage. It took every ounce of self control she possessed to not lash out at the soldier as the memory of Vysha's voice continued.

"They attacked the village in search of you. In the eyes of the King, the villagers have been harboring you. He made an example out of them."

Blood pounded in her ears, and before she could stop herself, she was screaming, "Do not *pretend* you do not know what happened here!"

"Raelia! What are you *doing*?! Keep quiet!" Caias scolded in a hushed tone.

She ignored him as she continued, "King Calyx *ordered* the attack on this village!"

"I was not speaking to you, woman!" the head soldier spat, rolling his eyes as if he thought her nothing more than a silly, insignificant child. "You have no idea what-"

His voice stopped at the same moment she felt a heat flood her body. It was completely foreign. Not until she heard Caias's startled gasp beside her did she look down at herself, realizing her entire body glowed a deep, brutal shade of red — a color she'd never seen from her power before.

The eyes of the soldiers widened fearfully, and she noticed a few of their hands seemed hesitant on the hilts of their blades now.

"What matter of being *are* you?!" their leader demanded, taking her much more seriously than before.

Raelia turned to look at Rokoa, whose expression surprised her. While she knew her face must have shown the confusion and fear this unknown power caused her, his eyes seemed... knowing. As if he knew exactly what she was ready to do.

The head soldier walked his horse a few steps forward, diverting Raelia's gaze back to his. Her fear and confusion withered as she felt hate rise in her chest. The skin all over her body seemed to vibrate with the intensity of her rage. The emotion bubbled in her midsection, forming a ball and swelling within her — threatening to pop and throw forth a weapon of power.

"Don't come any closer," Rokoa warned the man in a threatening tone, lowering the hood of his cloak and allowing them full view of his pointed and unnaturally silver ears. More than a few of the soldiers gasped at his appearance, but the leader didn't flinch. His eyes only narrowed further, and as Ekry followed Rokoa's lead, lowering her hood as well, the man laughed.

"Do you believe we, the soldiers of the honorable King Calyx's royal regiment, could be afraid of you?" His smirk was sinister as he continued, "We do not fear unnatural beasts."

"We only wish to retrieve our dead. We do not wish to fight you," Rokoa stated, "but if you push our hand, we will not hesitate to cut every last one of you down."

Laughing, the leader's eyes grazed over each of their faces before finally landing on Raelia once more with a menacing look. "Remove yourselves from your horses, and lay down any weapons you have," he told them all. "You are officially under arrest. You will be-"

Whoosh.

Thump.

Before the man could finish his sentence, an arrow hit his chest with a sickening thump.

Raelia looked around, having no clue where it came from until she saw Ekry lower a bow she hadn't been holding the second before.

"You talk too much," the Drykuan grumbled, as the soldier's body slumped and slid off his horse and onto the ground.

The sound of blades being unsheathed ripped through the following seconds of silence. Luella's eyes widened, and she was the first to move, bringing everyone else back to reality. She pulled the reins of the massive Drykuan steed she sat on, and the beast moved with unnatural and unexpected speed as he turned around.

As her horse raced to get behind the cart, the soldiers seemed to come to their senses. The man on the second horse yelled for the foot soldiers to attack, unsheathing his sword in the process, and before she had half a second to understand what was happening, the shouts of attack rang through the air.

CHAPTER 26

Raelia didn't even have to pull the sword from her hip. The anger within her still raged, and the glow over her body became brighter with every blade she saw swing.

In only seconds, Ekry and Rokoa had cut down half of the soldiers attacking, but hooves beat on the ground in the distance. When they looked up, another dozen soldiers rode their way, drawing their swords as they got closer.

Raelia lifted her glowing fingers to her face, wondering what would happen if she used her power. She only had a moment to think about the consequences, however, before the second horse approached, the soldier on top lifting his blade. In the blink of an eye, Raelia stretched her palm towards the man and pushed a bolt of red light toward him — hitting him square in the chest. He froze, eyes wide as blood began dripping slowly from his nose and eyes and ears. Slumping out of the saddle, he fell to the ground, unmoving.

Fear struck her heart. Had she just killed a man?

"Rae, we've got to get out of here!" She heard Caias yell as his hand reached over to grab her horse's reins.

A shout rang through the air as the new group of soldiers reached them. She watched as Ayla, on top of her horse, barely moved out of the way in time to avoid a fatal blow, and she felt her rage grow once more.

Ripping the reins from her brother's grasp, she raced Prickle toward her friend, raising her palm at the soldier who'd swung at Ayla. With very little urging, she felt power surge down her arm and shoot from her skin. The blast of light flew past her intended target, hitting another of the soldiers behind them. Anxiety coursed through Raelia's body, as she sent another bolt of light toward the man.

This time the light hit her intended target, directly in the face. The blood oozing from the soldier's orifices was no less a shock than the first time, but she couldn't bring herself to hesitate as she watched her friends fight.

"Raelia!" Caias called, panicked, behind her as she rode closer to the oncoming soldiers. "Raelia! Come back!"

Ignoring her brother's pleas, she charged at one of the newcomers. Unsheathing her sword, she brandished it at one rider. The clash of steel on steel made little noise compared to the battle raging around them. She felt the strike reverberate down her blade into her hand painfully. He pulled back and swung his sword once again, this time aiming for her neck. She parried the blade, but only just.

"What *are* you?" he asked through gritted teeth, eyes roving over the glow of her skin.

She didn't answer, refusing to give the royal army any information about herself or any of her friends.

The soldier swung his blade once more, and once more she blocked. The reverberation in her palm was less surprising and painful now that she was expecting it.

"STOP!" a deep voice bellowed, echoing against the small buildings on either side of them.

All of them, soldiers and Raelia's friends, looked up at the command. Ekry pulled her blade from her opponent's chest, and a wicked grin spread across her face when she spotted the source of the demand.

Raelia's expression changed as well when she saw the familiar face watching her with horror from across their small battlefield.

'Alister?'

In the half second it took her to realize who yelled, Ekry let out a maniacal laugh, racing toward Alister, who's gaze was still locked on her. The Drykuan raised her blade, and Raelia felt panic rise in her chest, as she rushed Prickle forward.

The crowd resumed their fight as Raelia burst through the other side, running toward her once savior. At the same time, Alister spotted Ekry racing toward him with her sword drawn. He drew his own in response, and before Raelia made it even half of the way to where he stood, she heard their swords connect.

"Ekry!" she yelled. "Ekry! Stop!"

The Drykuan still laughed maniacally as she swung toward the newcomer once more. Raelia was surprised at Alister. He held his own better than she'd ever done against the mythical race, especially on her first encounter. Never having pegged him for a fighter, she couldn't help the small bit in the back of her mind that was impressed as she continued to scream at Ekry to stop.

It wasn't until she drew her own blade, swinging it in between the pair, swiftly blocking Ekry from cutting Alister down, that the Drykuan stopped, piercing her with mutinous eyes.

"What are you doing, girl?!" she growled, pulling back her sword.

"The royal soldiers are our enemy!" Raelia yelled. "*Not* Alister! He is my friend! He's not with them!"

"The hell he isn't! Don't you know who this is?!" Ekry's voice burned with hatred.

"He's my *friend*," she shouted again, unsure why Ekry was so determined to fight Alister when there were plenty of others for her to go after. "That's all that matters!"

Alister reached for Raelia's arm, but the moment his fingers gripped on, Ekry launched herself off her massive horse. She slammed into him, forcing him to fall backward.

"Ekry!" she yelled. "No!"

In that moment, the world seemed to slow. Raelia watched in slow motion as the pair dropped to the ground with a thud, both their swords clattering to the ground.

They scuffled, rolling around in the dirt. Alister had somehow gotten on top of Ekry as Raelia jumped to the ground. Before she could intervene, however, the Drykuan laid him on his back, slamming him down. With an unnatural speed, she pulled out a small dagger from her sleeve, pressing the tip against Alister's throat with a sneer.

"Stop! Please! Stop, Ekry!"

Alister raised his hands in surrender as Raelia pulled at the Drykuan's cloak, trying to pull her back.

"DO NOT KILL HIM EKRY!" Rokoa's voice demanded from behind them.

All three turned their heads, and to Raelia's surprise all of the soldiers had been defeated — their bodies laying on the ground. Their horses mostly scattered, though a handful still meandered in between her friends, looking cautiously around themselves.

Ekry sighed, and shoved Raelia, who hadn't been expecting it, and fell back hard onto the ground. Without so much as even acknowledging her, Ekry stood, yanking Alister by his collar to his feet. His face was unreadable, though his eyes showed worry when he looked down at Raelia on the ground.

"Why shouldn't I kill him?!" she shouted to Rokoa, who spurred his horse in their direction. "He deserves to die!"

"No, he doesn't!" Raelia yelled as she got to her feet. "He's not involved in this!"

She reached for Alister's hand, yanking him toward herself. With a look from Rokoa, Ekry released him with a grimace.

"Your highness," Rokoa's voice was low and venomous, "I believe you're in the wrong place at a *very* wrong time."

Raelia's laugh came out shrill, almost panicked, but before she could say a word, Alister's deep voice sounded behind her.

"How do you know who I am?" he asked the Drykuan, still sitting atop his horse.

She gasped at the admission, turning to look at him in shock. "What?!"

"I am one of ancient blood, and can smell a royal from a mile away," Rokoa laughed, "and even if I couldn't, I would be a fool to not recognize the face of a man whose family has been slaughtering innocents for generations."

Tightening her grip on Alister's hand, Raelia's jade eyes watched her friend's response to Rokoa's words. First shock, then defiance, flitted across his expression before his brown eyes connected with hers.

"Raelia?" he said softly, squeezing her hand in return, though she could barely feel it in her shock.

"You? Alister? You're?" she yanked her hand from his grasp and stepped back.

"Alister? Who's Alister?" Ekry let out a laugh. "Don't tell me you really don't know who he is? I thought he was your friend?" she said in a mocking tone. "And yet you have no clue who he really is?"

Hooves clip-clopped behind her against the ground, but she couldn't bring herself to look at who joined them. Anger flooded through her. Embarrassment and betrayal followed close in its wake.

"Who *are* you?!" Raelia demanded in a low, lethal voice.

"Prince Alton, son of King Calyx of the Kingdom of Dirythia," came the answer from a voice she wasn't expecting.

When she turned to look at its source, Caias stood there. He had a few minor cuts, and his shirt was destroyed; he must have hit his head on something, because she could see a matte of his blonde hair clumped against a bloody spot on the side of it. Overall, however, he seemed to be whole and had clearly held his own against the soldiers.

"Caias?"

"With all the books Papa has on the royal family... You don't recognize him?"

She looked back at her friend, eyes questioning. He seemed so familiar when they met. She remembered him being disappointed she didn't know who he was. She remembered suspecting he wasn't being honest about who he was on the ride back to her house — she hadn't questioned it again, however. When he came back to visit her, she didn't even think about it even once.

"You're?"

"My name is Alton Prilot. I am the first born son of King Calyx Prilot," he answered in a solemn voice as sorrow touched his eyes. When he spoke again, his voice was quiet, remorseful, "I never wanted to lie to you... When you didn't-"

"Enough!" Ekry shouted, stepping forward to grip tightly onto the front of Alton's tunic. "Time is up! I want to kill the royal!"

"You will not kill him, Ekry," Rokoa commanded.

Looking at him in disbelief, the Drykuan's eyes bulged. "What do you mean, I won't kill him? Why shouldn't I kill him?! It's better than he deserves!" Ekry pulled out her small dagger, and pointed at the Prince's face. "Besides, why should she care now that she knows he's a filthy liar?"

A green light glowed in Raelia's palm as she watched Ekry inch the tip of her dagger closer and closer to Alton's eye, a smirk spreading across her face.

"Stop, Ekry," she commanded in a calm voice.

When the Drykuan woman looked at her, it was with disgust. Seeing the light glowing in her palm, fury replaced disgust. "How dare you! You dare threaten me?! What do you think we're going to do? Leave him alive, so he can follow us home and bring his armies?!" she rolled her eyes before turning back to Alton. "No! This filthy royal is going to die right here before he can cause any further harm to our people!"

"I will *not* let you hurt him, Ekry!" Her voice was commanding and strong as she raised her hand, palm pointed at the Drykuan woman.

"It will not come to that," Rokoa chimed in, swinging his leg off his horse and to the ground. "Ekry, back away."

Her silver eyes shot to his, incredulity written there as if permanently etched in the lines of her face. She opened her mouth to protest, but at the look he gave her, seemed to decide against it. After sheathing her dagger, Ekry reached down to retrieve her sword, and stomped, like a child, to her horse.

A hand on her shoulder, brought Raelia's eyes back to Rokoa. His face grim as he looked down at her. "Ekry has a point," he said. "We can't simply let him leave here only to bring his armies back for us."

Raelia's eyes shifted to Alton's. There was sadness there, and she felt a pang shoot through her heart.

'He lied to you. You are not allowed to pity him,' she mentally lectured herself.

"Raelia?" He said her name like a caress, gentle and caring.

Her jade green eyes hardened. "You lied to me! You knew who I was this whole time!" she accused. "I can't even look at you!"

She turned then, storming back to Prickle and pulling herself up.

"Raelia," Rokoa called. "We cannot let him go."

"We're leaving. We'll be gone before he can return."

"We can't take that chance, and you know it."

He was right, she realized. It wasn't safe for any of them if he followed. Her eyes found the silver eyes of her friend, and she realized he was giving her the opportunity to decide Alton's fate. An opportunity to take charge. "I'm not killing him!" she nearly shrieked. With effort, she forced down her panic, before speaking again. "We can't kill him, Rokoa. He may have lied to me, but he saved my life."

The Drykuan nodded his understanding and looked at Alton's brown eyes with a piercing gaze. To the Prince's credit, he looked ashamed. The words behind his eyes as he watched her, spoke more of sorrow than fear.

"We'll take him back to Paodra," Ekry shouted from behind them, drawing everyone's attention. "We'll let Vysha decide his fate."

Raelia's eyes widened as a strange fear took hold of her heart. She turned to look at the Drykuan. "What?! Why would we do that?! That would lead him straight to-"

"You will not kill him," Rokoa reasoned, pulling back Raelia's attention, "and we cannot leave him. She's right. It's the only other option."

"But Vysha... She might-"

"She will see use in his life. In the information he may provide," he replied in a calm voice.

Ekry scoffed in response, but didn't speak again.

Again, he was right. Vysha would be pleased to have a member of the royal family to feed her information before they marched on the capital, but... would he provide the information she needed? What would she do if he didn't? She wouldn't hurt him... would she?

"Okay..." she answered, her voice giving away her trepidation.

Alton remained silent during their exchange, still watching Raelia as if unable to look away, until Rokoa silently waved his hand and ropes appeared around his wrists. The look of shock on his face when he looked up at the Drykuan would have made Raelia laugh if the situation wasn't so serious. With another wave of his hand, Alton momentarily disappeared, reappearing just as suddenly on the top of his horse, looking bewildered.

Rokoa took the reins to his steed, pulling him along as they headed back to their waiting friends.

"The Prince will return with us to Paodra. Vysha is seeking information, and he is the perfect person to provide it," he announced as they approached.

Ayla nodded, Ekry sneered. Luella and Caias both looked scared and somehow flabbergasted at the same time. It wasn't until Raelia's eyes fell on Nazario's worried expression that she felt the weight of what she'd agreed to.

"Luella, do you know where your parents are?" Rokoa asked, before Raelia could give it much more thought. "We should collect them quickly."

After a short back-and-forth, they continued on as if nothing happened. They already collected Yaila and Blaze, so all they needed now was to collect Lue's parents and return them home before returning to the Kesby's farm.

"Naz, Ayla, I would like for you to accompany Ekry back to Raelia's home with the Prince," Rokoa instructed. "See to it he is put in one of the upstairs rooms and locked in."

"What?! No! She," Raelia pointed to Ekry, "can't be trusted! If we send him back with her, there will have been no point in-"

"We need to continue our day," he interrupted. "I do not think it wise to trot around with the heir to the Dirythian throne tied up and clearly being taken prisoner. It will be hard enough if we come across more guards. If those guards feel the need to protect-"

"Fine!" she agreed, before turning to glare at Ekry. "But you are *not* allowed to kill him!"

Ekry rolled her eyes, spurring her horse forward to take the reins from Rokoa. "Whatever you say, *Dandelion.*"

Rokoa hopped down from his horse and told Naz to take it before stepping into the cart. They did as instructed, and before anyone said another word, the three, and Alton, were on their way out of the small village.

CHAPTER 27

It wasn't a long journey home from Luella's, and as lost in their thoughts as they all were, it seemed to go even quicker than expected. Rokoa guided Marah to the side of the house closest to the garden and was silent as he stepped down from the cart.

Once they were unmounted, Luella grabbed the reins and led the horses toward the stables. Rokoa came around the back of the cart and reached for Yaila's wrapped remains, only stopping when Caias stretched his arm in front of him.

"This is our family. We will be tending to our loved ones."

Rokoa nodded, silently, stepping to the side to let him pass.

"Thank you," Raelia said quietly when she reached the back of the cart.

She lifted Blaze's small body into her arms. He was heavier than she'd remembered, but she didn't complain. She wouldn't. The enormity of their loss washed over her like a tidal wave, but she held back her tears as she followed Caias down the path toward their mother's garden.

Toward where Caeda was buried.

It took a few hours to dig the graves for their mother and brother — both Raelia and Caias were covered in dirt and sweat when they'd finished.

She reached her hand up from the deep hole she dug for Blaze, and was pulled out swiftly by Rokoa. She stumbled forward when her feet hit the ground, falling into his chest. He placed his hands on her waist, to steady her.

"There are a few hours of daylight left," he said back and Caias climbed out of their mother's grave. "You should clean yourself up before we bury your loved ones."

Raelia knew he was right. She didn't want to lay her brother and mother to rest covered in tears and dirt and sweat. She turned her eyes to Caias, silently asking for his approval.

"That's a good idea," he answered, emotion clinging to every syllable, "We should both clean up. Then..."

Reaching out to grab his hand, she squeezed reassuringly. Her eyes welled up, but she choked back the tears.

"Sometimes we have to do the hard things," Raelia sniffled. "That's what Mama would say."

His stormy blue eyes connected with hers and he nodded, "And even if it doesn't feel like it, we can all do the hard things," his voice was tight, raspy with his grief.

"That's right."

After cleaning themselves up and putting on fresh clothes, brother and sister met outside once more. Luella, Ayla and Nazario joined them, all of whom wore matching expressions of sorrow.

Raelia, once again, raided her sibling's bedroom, this time bringing a teddy bear Blaze always said he didn't need, but slept with every night. She also clung to a small blanket she'd given him when he was only an infant. One she'd made, with the help of her mother, especially for him.

Not wanting to make Caias get back into the earth in his clean clothes, Raelia looked to Rokoa, who nodded at her. Without a word, he hopped into the deep hole and reached up toward her brother.

Caias gave him a grateful nod and then gently picked up Blaze's small, broken body, still wrapped in the sheet they brought him home in, and handed him down to the Drykuan. After he gently laid the child down, Rokoa reached up to take the items from Raelia, and placed them delicately with her brother.

A moment later, Rokoa pulled himself up and hopped back down into the grave meant for Yaila. As Caias handed their mother's body over, Raelia looked down at the small portrait she'd taken from her parent's room. It was drawn by her mother's father on the day she and Eloi married, and more than once her mother told her it was her most prized possession. She handed it over to Rokoa. After he set it on top of the sheet covering Yaila's form, he hopped back out of the earth to stand next to Raelia.

Caias's eyes searched his sister's, a question there. He didn't know what to do, she realized. Reaching out, she squeezed his hand tightly, as a tear ran down her cheek.

"You were both taken much sooner than should have been possible," Raelia said around the knot in her throat, her eyes on her mother's form in the earth. "Mama, you were better to us than we could h-have ever asked, and we miss you more than words could ever s-say."

Raelia sniffled, and looked to Caias, not sure she could continue without breaking down. He nodded and cleared his throat.

"Blaze, you were the best little brother anyone could ask for. You loved deeply and fiercely, and made all of us proud every day. We miss you, Blazie, and we hope you are watching over us. We will never forget you."

A hand grabbed onto Raelia's shoulder from behind, and squeezed gently. She turned, seeing it belonged to Nazario, and she was so thankful they were there. She'd done her best to contain her emotions, but at the look in their eyes, her composure disappeared and a sob escaped her. Naz wrapped their arms around her, hugging her close, before they relinquished her to her brother.

Caias held her tightly to him. She couldn't hear his cries, but his body shook as much as her own as they sobbed into each other's shoulders.

It had been nearly seven weeks since the attack on Frayis, and still, after all this time, it didn't make sense to her. How had her family been taken in such a short amount of time? Why did the King murder an entire village when he could have executed just her? Why didn't he just execute her?

When their sobs settled, Caias released her. His hands moved to either side of her face, gripping tightly. He looked into her eyes with an intensity she had never seen from her easy-going, quick-to-laugh brother before.

"We'll make it through this, RaeRae. Mama wouldn't have wanted us to give up, and we're not going to. We're going to do the hard thing. We're going to do the hard thing for her."

She sniffled, and nodded, "For her," she croaked out.

Caias let his hands fall, and she felt Rokoa's strong hand on her shoulder.

"I'll finish up here. You and your brother should spend some time together before dinner."

"Dinner?"

"Ekry is cooking. It will be ready soon."

"Thank you, Rokoa," Raelia said, sincerity radiating through every word as she looked into his silver eyes. "I couldn't have done this — any of it — without you."

His eyes widened, seeming shocked by her gratitude. "You don't need to thank me," he replied, looking down, before letting go of her and stepping away to retrieve a shovel.

Caias watched the interaction with curiosity, looking at her quizzically when she turned back to face him.

"What do you mean 'any of it'?" he asked.

"Vysha wasn't exactly keen on us coming back here, is all," she explained, as they walked lazily toward the pasture. "Rokoa convinced her I needed to see home after being away for so long... I think the only reason she approved of me coming at all was because he spoke up and offered to come along."

Caias cleared his throat before speaking, "Why does this Vysha person get a say in where you go? Frayis is your home," he told her. "Not Paodra."

"Frayis will always be my true home, Caias," she started, trying to figure out how to continue, "but Paodra... Well, it's become like a second home. I have... family there."

"They're *not* your family, Rae." The frustration in his voice rang loud and true. "I'm your family! Papa is your family! Hell, even Luella is more your family than any of them will ever be!"

She placed a hand on his shoulder, and he seemed to settle at her touch. He looked into her eyes, seeming to seek an answer to a question he hadn't asked. Whether he found it, she didn't know.

"I'm sorry," he said in a quiet voice.

"It's a lot to take in. You don't need to apologize."

"It doesn't matter," he said, more to himself than her. "None of this matters. In a few days-"

"Dinner is ready!" Ayla called from the house, pulling both of their attention.

Caias's gaze found hers once more, all emotion seeming to vanish with the interruption. "Let's go eat. We can talk later."

When they walked into the kitchen, everyone else gathered around the small table in the middle of the room, grabbing plates from the pile someone set on the surface. Caias grabbed his, and then handed her the last from the stack, prompting her to look around for any others set out. When she realized there were none, she looked toward the Drykuan who'd cooked their meal.

"Where's Alis-uh... Alton's plate?" Raelia asked, looking expectantly at Ekry.

"Why would we feed that scum?" she asked, disgust coloring her features.

"Why wouldn't we?" Luella demanded. "You can't really expect him to go without food?!"

"I can, and he will," Ekry responded plainly.

"Absolutely not!" Raelia shot back, her anger and grief getting the better of her. She yanked Ekry's fully loaded plate from her hands, and turned on her heel, shouting back as she stomped down the hallway, "You do not get to force us to take him hostage and then refuse to feed him!"

Her chair scraped noisily on the floor, as Ekry jumped to her feet. "You wretched little-,"

"Hush, Ekry," Raelia heard Rokoa's voice start. "We cannot expect..."

But what they couldn't expect, Raelia never heard, his voice fading as she swiftly stomped upstairs.

She stood in front of her bedroom door for a few moments, not sure she should be the one bringing this to the Prince.

'You have every right to be angry at him!' she thought. *'He lied to you! He's part of this oppressive monarch and wishes you dead!'*

That's what she told herself, but no matter how many times she'd repeated those words in her mind, it never felt right. If it were true, why would he have saved her that day in the river? Why would he sit with her for a full day while she recovered and talk to her as if... as if...

'As if he cared...'

Raelia shook her head, trying to free it of confusion, before knocking on the door.

'This is your bedroom! Why are you knocking, idiot!' she mentally cursed herself, as she turned the knob and walked in.

It took everything in her not to gasp. Raelia hadn't seen Alton since the village, and what she saw now made her sick to her stomach. His hands were tied tightly above his head, attached with wire to what appeared to be a stake driven into the wall. The thin silver strand wrapped around his wrists multiple times, cutting into his skin. The blood running down his arms, shoulders, and sides, soaked into his once cream-colored tunic, causing the fabric to cling to his skin all down his torso. His busted open lower lip, only adding to the bloody red mess he already was.

His skin was pale, and when his eyes found hers, they were darker than she'd ever seen them. His dirty blonde hair, usually brushed and neatly tied back, was loose around his face, clumped with dirt and blood. Bruises littered the parts of his body she could see, his face, even his neck, where it looked Ekry had tried to strangle him.

"Oh, gods!" Raelia quickly set his food down, hurrying to undo his bindings.

"Hey... Rae..." his voice was weak, but when his feet rested fully on the ground, they held his weight.

She wrapped her arm around his waist, careful not to touch any open wound, and guided him to the bed. She gently pushed on his shoulder, making him lie down, "Don't move! I'm going to get the medical kit."

Not waiting for a response, she ran into the hallway and down to the small washroom at the end. She grabbed the medical basket, thankful her mother always made sure it was fully stocked for any injury, and filled a small basin with warm water.

She hurried back to Alton's side, being careful not to spill the contents of the basket or the water, as she did so. The bed groaned under her weight as she sat down next to him. Without another word, she undid his shirt, stifling a gasp as she pulled it back. The left side of his body was a deep purple, the color running from under his arm down to his hip. There was a cut from his right shoulder, across his chest, stopping just above his hip. It wasn't deep, but she realized it was the main source of blood, not the wrists, as she'd previously thought. Though, looking at his wrists, they were bleeding their fair share as well.

"Did Ekry do this to you?" Raelia asked, already knowing the answer.

"Is that the woman with the silver glow?"

She nodded.

"Then yes."

Emotion was thick in Raelia's voice when she spoke once more, "I'm so sorry, Ali- Alton. She wasn't... You weren't supposed to..." she sighed, frustrated that the words she wanted to say weren't forming, "I'm so sorry..."

They sat in silence after that. Raelia cleaning and tending Alton's wounds as best she could, as his gaze followed her careful movements.

Using a clean, wet cloth, she was able to clear the blood from him, allowing her to see the actual injuries.

A while later, once she finished cleaning and dressing his wounds, she remembered the reason she came up in the first place. Raelia picked up the plate of food from the small table she'd left it on, and walked it over to him. He took it from her gratefully, and lifted the fork to his mouth. She left the room, walking the mess of bloody rags and other supplies to the washroom.

She stood in the doorway for a moment upon her return, watching him wince with every movement. Anger flared in her, but she held it down, determined to take it up with Ekry later.

"Do you need anything else?" she asked from the doorway. "I can come back a little later for your plate."

"I... I don't need anything," Alton said, watching as Raelia's hand touched the knob. Panic colored his features as she began pulling the door closed, and he called, "B-but would you stay with me for a while?"

She froze for only a second before nodding and stepping back into the room. She shut the door behind her, and walked over to sit at the end of the bed as Alton continued eating.

It felt awkward, sitting there like that. She was technically his captor. She couldn't understand why he would want her there at all, considering the situation.

Silence overtook them as Alton ate. Raelia was lost in her own thoughts, until a light tap at the window pulled their attention.

Both of them smiled as they recognized Zayric through the clear pane. Raelia hopped up and opened the window for him to come in, before closing it once more.

"Is that Zayric?" Alton asked, as the kyloxis hopped onto the bed and sniffed his plate. "He's gotten so big!"

Raelia laughed and sat back down next to the fox as Alton cut off a chunk of his pork steak and fed it to Zayric.

As he ate it happily, Raelia was distracted by the furry creature between them. She could feel Alton's eyes watching her movements, and when she looked up, was surprised to see a wistful expression

"Do you remember when we first met?" he asked, his voice soft.

Her eyes lifted, connecting with his. "Of course I do! How could I forget you saving my life?!"

A glimmer of pain flashed in his eyes, before he continued. "That's not actually the time I meant."

That pulled her up short, and confusion colored her features. "Then I'm not sure what you're referring to..."

"When I was young, I used to spend hours in the palace library. I'd wake up, and before I could even eat breakfast, I'd be surrounded by piles of books," he told her, a small smile touching his lips. "My mother used to love to read, you see. I only have a few memories of her, but in every one of them, she was reading. Either to me, or to herself, but there was always a book in her hand. 'Reading is the only path to power,' she used to say."

Raelia smiled at his shared memory.

"After she died, reading was the only way I could feel connected to her. My tutors would always comment that I needed to be around other children, or be outside, but..." his voice trailed off for a moment, eyes unfocused, seeming lost in thought, "but I didn't want to be anywhere but near my mother's precious books."

"Books are a safe haven. For more reasons than I think people realize," Raelia said, "but - uh - I don't understand what this has to do with me?"

"Your father... He's the book binder. He tends to the royal library. He's spent a lot of time there," he explained. "He was one of the few people I knew outside of those I had to see every day. I always looked forward to his visits."

"I didn't... You know my father?"

Alton nodded before continuing, "When he would tend to the books, he'd bring me ones that he thought I'd enjoy," he chuckled lightly. "He was never wrong."

"Papa always knew the right book for the right moment," Raelia said, her heart aching at the thought of her father, as she twisted the ring he'd given her around her finger. She missed him terribly.

Suddenly, a flash of memory came back to her. A small boy with white blonde hair surrounded by a pile of books. Her eyes widened as Alton continued.

"The first time I saw you, you were carrying a tattered old book. He was telling you he wanted to fix it, but you said he couldn't because-"

"It would lose its magic..." Raelia finished.

He nodded. "You came with him every day that trip and I was so intrigued by this tiny girl that so desperately clung to the tatters of a book."

The memories of the time they'd spent together exploded in her mind. They had been so young, only six years old. Caias had been severely sick with naxictilitis, and her mother had been worried Raelia would catch it too, so she sent her along with her father on his annual trip to the palace.

Alton was shorter than her then, only by an inch or two, and his hair was short, shorn almost to the scalp along the sides. His eyes, however, were the same soft brown, radiating kindness as they did now. The two of them read together for hours, and when their eyes would ache, they'd play imaginative games, all based around the stories they'd read.

It had been the best three weeks of her life. She cried and cried when her mother refused to let her return the next year.

He was her first friend.

"You followed me around for the first few days..." she added. "You only talked to me because-"

"You hid under the table where my books were and tied my boot-laces together, so I couldn't run away from you!"

They both laughed at the memory, until Alton winced and placed a hand over one of his many bandages.

"Why didn't you tell me you were a part of the royal family?"

Raelia's eyes searched his swollen ones, wanting so badly to understand how he could keep such a huge secret from her. She hadn't known when they were children, and she obviously didn't know after his rescue.

"I never dreamed I'd happen across you that day at the river. I recognized you immediately when I pulled you out of the water," he told her. "I couldn't believe my luck to have found you on the first day I went searching."

"Searching? You were searching for me?"

Alton nodded. "I never forgot you, Raelia. I waited for your father's annual trip every year, just hoping you'd be with him again," he looked down at his plate. "You never were, though."

"My mother needed my help at home," she explained. "Blaze was only a couple weeks old the next time Papa was due at the Palace, and she had such a hard labor with him. She couldn't tend him on her own..." Raelia sighed, sadly. "I wanted to be there. Honest I did."

He looked back at her, a small smile touching his lips. "I know. Your father told me. I think I just needed to hear it from you."

Outside the window, clouds shifted, allowing rays of the setting sun to stream through the window, lighting up Alton's bruised eyes. A sadness filled her at the sight, and she sighed.

"How did we ever get here?"

Alton reached for Raelia's hand, squeezing it gently. He opened his mouth, but before he could speak, the bedroom door opened, revealing Rokoa and Caias in the hallway.

"You've been up here a long time," Rokoa said in his deep lilt. He spoke to Raelia, but his eyes did not leave Alton. He didn't look shocked, as she'd been at his appearance, but a flicker of concern touched his eyes. "We wondered what was taking so much time."

Caias squeezed past the large Drykuan man, but before he said a word, his eyes fell on Alton's blackened eyes. "What happened?! Raelia! What did you do?!"

Her eyes went wide, mouth dropping open in shock. "I-I didn't do anything!" she yelled, standing up in her frustration. "You really think I'm capable of-"

"It wasn't her," Alton interjected. "She's been cleaning and bandaging my wounds."

Caias looked as if that information was a relief to him, and Raelia's heart dropped. It hurt that he thought her capable of such brutality, and once again, she wondered if they'd all just been waiting for her to be violent.

Tears pricked in the corner of her eyes, but she refused to let them fall, choosing instead to storm past her brother and Rokoa without another word.

CHAPTER 28

Over the next couple of hours, Raelia holed herself up in her father's study, glad no one came looking for her as she calmed down. The sun set behind the mountains, leaving the only light the fire she'd started in the grate.

The musky smell of the books, and the cedar smell of the shelves and desk mixed in a way that always brought her comfort. The firm leather of the chair she curled up on squeaked as she shifted her weight and set the book she had been attempting to read on the coffee table.

She sighed, wishing her mind would just be quiet, if only for a moment or two. Everything that happened in the last twenty-four hours was overwhelming, and when she added in the last couple months, it all felt impossible. She pulled her knees to her chest, the leather screeching in protest, and rested her forehead on them, closing her eyes.

"You know, you can't hide away in here forever," Caias's voice called softly.

Raelia groaned, and turned her head, cheek resting on her knees as she looked at her brother in the doorway.

"I can try," she said dully, rolling her eyes. Her gaze shifted to the flames in the fireplace as Caias closed the door behind him.

"I'm sorry for jumping to conclusions," he told her, plopping himself on the sofa on the other side of the coffee table.

"You're not the only one who seems to think me capable of such atrocities." Raelia kept her gaze on the dancing flames, her throat constricted as she tried to contain the venom she felt, "I just wish I knew how you've all hidden what you really thought of me so well."

"Rae... I have never thought you capable of anything that-"

"Don't feed me that crap!" she cut him off, standing to pace in front of the fire. "If you never believed me capable, *why* would you think I was capable only a few hours ago?!"

"Please don't raise your voice," Caias sighed. "I'm not here to fight with you."

The defeated tone in her brother's voice gave her pause. Anger still swirled within her, but she'd never heard him sound so agonized.

She looked at him, his blue eyes connecting with her green. "I never wanted to be born with this... this thing! I never wanted this *'gift.'* You *know* that..." she plopped herself back into her seat.

"*Of course* I know that, Rae! How could I not? You've never exactly let it be a secret."

His eyes were honest and loving. She didn't doubt his sincerity for a moment.

"Everything that's happened in the last couple days... it just... just. .." Caias was at a loss for words, another thing his sister had never seen before.

"I know," Raelia said quietly. "It's a lot to take in."

"Everything about our lives—about who we are—seems to have shifted," he sighed once more, "Rae, it's like I don't even recognize my own sister anymore, and I don't know if that's because *you've* changed, or because my world has changed so much that *nothing* is recognizable."

"Or it could be both," she offered.

"I think it is both," Caias sighed, turning his eyes to the flames. "You've changed. Of course you have... No one could be the same person after watching what happened to... to..." He let his voice hang for a moment, unable to finish his sentence, before continuing, "It will be better when we get back to the tribal lands. Ouma will know-"

"What?" Raelia's muscles tensed, her voice a panicked whisper. "Why would you think I'm going to Taevidia?"

His eyes widened, shifting to his sister's. "Why wouldn't I? Of course you're coming back to Taevidia with me! You and Luella both are! That is where our family is! It's where Papa knows to look for us!"

"Caias, I-"

"You what?! What, Rae?!" For as much as he didn't want to fight, he was quick to raise his voice, anger coloring his tone. "You can't honestly think I'm going to let you go back to Paodra?!"

"Let me?!" Raelia's voice rose, matching his, as fury flared up in her chest, "*Let* me?! I am eighteen years old, Caias!"

"Your age is of no consequence!" Caias shouted back, meeting her rage with his own. "Mama is gone! Papa is missing! As the eldest brother, it is my *duty* to protect you! It is my *duty to-*"

"I can protect myself!" Raelia shouted. Her voice echoed in the small space. "I am not your defenseless little sister anymore, Caias! You saw me! I don't need you to rush to my aid, because the village boys called me names anymore! I am more than capable of protecting myself!"

He was silent for a moment as he breathed deeply, seeming to contemplate his next words before sighing. He plopped back down on the sofa and looked up at her with pleading eyes.

"Raelia, you're my little sister," he said, the softness returning to his tone. "I know you can take care of yourself. I saw how you fought in the village. You've clearly trained hard."

Raelia sat next to him on the couch. "I have."

"But training or no training, we have to find Papa."

She sighed, nodding and looking at her hands twisting in her lap. "I promised Vysha I would come back. I gave her my word I would help in the battle to come."

"Battle? You mean she actually *is* planning to attack the Kingdom? To march on Vairek City?" Caias looked at her astonished, "Rae! You've been training for what? Six - seven weeks? That's not long enough to have the skills you'll need to take on the entire royal guard!"

Reaching out, Raelia grabbed his hand, squeezing it reassuringly. She kept her voice neutral as she continued, "I won't be alone. Naz, and Ayla. Vysha, Rokoa, Ekry. And all of the other Mark Bearers and Drykuan's! It's not just me going against them. It's all of us! "

"This isn't your battle, Rae. It doesn't have to be!"

"Of course it does!" She had to fight the urge to shout at him again. She couldn't believe he didn't understand! "Caias, he killed Mama! He killed Blaze and Caeda! If it hadn't been for Rokoa, you would have been burying my body along with theirs today." She took a slow, calming breath before continuing, "You didn't have to watch as the people you loved died one by one at the hands of a mad King, only to find out that you being there was what got them all killed in the first place!"

"That's not true," Caias insisted. "There's no way that King Calyx sent the order to kill an entire village because of one young girl! It doesn't make sense, Rae! You see that, don't you?"

Her jade-green eyes connected with her brother's ocean-blue, and she sighed. "Caias, it's not the first time he's done something like this. They've all done things like this! Ever since Nikolai, every King that has sat on the throne has done everything in their power to wipe out magic of any kind. They've been killing innocent children for five hundred years, Caias! Not even children! Babies! Infants!"

"I know the history, Rae, you don't have to remind me."

"Do you? Do you know the *true* history of our Kingdom? The royal families all have blood on their hands! They're steeped in it!"

"What about Prince Alton?" Caias questioned. "Luella told me he saved your life not even a week before the attack on the village! Why would he have done that if..."

Her heart ached. She didn't want to think about that. She didn't want to think about Alton and whether or not he was just pretending to be her friend when he could have let her die in the river that day. Everything would have been different then. Even if they were grieving for her, at least her loved ones would still be alive.

She didn't want to talk about this anymore.

"Caias," she sighed, "there is nothing you can say that is going to change my mind. I'm returning to Paodra. I won't go to Taevidia. Not right now. Maybe after the war is won..."

Her eyes drifted back to her lap, and she heard him sigh deeply next to her. "I hate this..." he reached over and squeezed her hand, "but... you're right. You're eighteen, and I can't stop you."

Releasing her hand, he stood up, stretching his arms above his head before looking back down at her.

"I do hope you'll change your mind, though."

⋆⋅☆⋅⋆

The next morning was a quiet affair. Raelia slept in her father's office, and though she loved to curl up and read on the stiff leather, sleeping on it was uncomfortable and made for a restless night. Though, her mind racing with the day's events hadn't helped either.

When she rose, it was later than normal, and she could hear voices in the kitchen. Her stomach grumbled at the smell of food cooking. The delicious fragrance of bacon filled the house, and her mouth watered, but she couldn't bring herself to join the others. She didn't have the energy to face anyone at the moment.

Silently, Raelia crept down the hallway and out the front door, confident no one heard her exit as she walked around the side of the house toward the pasture. When she stepped through the large barn doors, she felt calmer. She'd always found solace here with the horses, and as she crossed her legs on top of the tack table, she realized she was happy that, at least, hadn't changed about her.

The conversation with Caias the night before swam in her memory, surfacing more frequently than those of the fight in the village or Ekry's anger at Alton. His judgment of her actions, his accusations, his disappointment in her — his rage — seemed to swell into a massive beast in her chest, picking at her very existence until she wasn't sure there was anything of herself left she knew to be true.

Everything that had happened since her birthday seemed to irrevocably alter who she was down to her core. In her mind's eye, she watched on repeat as she let the red glow fly from her hands toward the soldiers. She saw again the blood pouring from them as the lights left their eyes. She should feel guilt. She should feel shame. She couldn't, however, find either.

When she remembered the terror in her mother's voice as she tried to protect her youngest children, when she remembered Blaze, croaking out her name one last time before he crumpled to the ground... The only feeling she could conjure within her was a sense of justice being done as the soldiers died.

"Is that wrong?" she asked herself, drawing the attention of one of the large Drykuan horses. "They might not have swung the killing blow, but they were still a part of it. Weren't they? They help uphold a system that calls for the slaughter of innocents... And-"

"And they would have killed all of us, if we hadn't protected ourselves."

The sudden sound of Nazario's voice caused her to jump and almost fall off the table she was perched on.

"Naz! You scared me!"

They chuckled, but the light of amusement in their tone didn't meet their eyes as they made their way over to lean against the table. "You did what we all had to do," they continued. "We protected ourselves. Each and every one of us would have been interrogated until our hearts stopped beating if we hadn't fought back. You know that, Rae."

"Of course I do. I just..." She sighed, looking at the dirt floor. "It's just... Shouldn't I feel guilty about it?"

Her response seemed to surprise them. "You... uh... you don't feel guilty? I thought that's what you..."

She smirked. "Well that's what you get for interrupting a person's private conversation."

"Private conversation with themselves?" They laughed. "If you want the thoughts in your head to remain private, maybe you shouldn't verbalize them."

Raelia punched them in the arm, grinning as she hopped down from the table. Dust bloomed around her feet as they struck the dirt and she headed toward Prickle's stall.

"So what's the plan for today? Are we heading back to Paodra? Or staying another night?"

"Considering we're holding the Crowned Prince of Dirythia hostage, Rokoa thinks it's best we leave this morning."

She hadn't considered that. She'd been hoping for one more day before they rode north again, but she knew Rokoa was right. They needed to leave before people came looking for Alton.

"Right."

"Don't you think you should eat something before we go? It's a long trip."

She nodded. "I'll make sure to eat something before we leave."

"How about now?" Caias's voice rang out from behind them.

When the two turned to look at him, he held out a plate of eggs, bacon, and toast toward her.

"I'm going to... uh... ready myself for the journey," Nazario said uncomfortably before hurrying past Caias in the entryway.

"Rae, can we talk?"

She nodded, leaning against the tack table.

His hay colored hair blew around his face as he walked over, putting the plate of food into her hands. "I don't like the idea of leaving you alone," he said, his worry radiating in his tone.

"I won't be alone, Caias," she sighed. "I have..." she paused, catching herself before she said 'family' — knowing the use of that word could undo the tenable peace they had this morning. "I have friends."

"Luella and I spoke last night, and she wishes to travel with me to the Taevidian Empire. She says she doesn't feel safe back in that place. She doesn't trust this Vysha person," he explained.

Raelia could hear the frustration twisting with his concern, and the last thing she wanted was to fight with him before they parted ways. "I know she doesn't, but if we're being honest, Lue never gave Vysha a chance. She hasn't trusted her since the moment we stepped foot in

Paodra," she tried to reason. "If she doesn't want to return, that's fine, but it will not change my decision on the matter."

His eyes were angry when she looked at him, but his voice remained calm when he replied, "I wish it would. You've always trusted Lue's opinion and judgment. I don't understand why that's changed..."

The memory of the first night they spent in Paodra flashed in her mind. Her best friend's voice admitting that maybe all Mark Bearers were violent and evil by nature. The pair discussed it later, and she'd forgiven her friend, but those words had hit Raelia hard. She wasn't sure if she'd ever fully recover from them and she knew she'd never forget.

She did her best to control the frustration she felt rising within her when she replied, "Luella's true opinion about people like me became *very* apparent while we were in Paodra. Her judgment can't be trusted when it comes to Mark Bearers."

Caias sighed and leaned next to her against the tack table. "What about yesterday?"

She tensed, her fork freezing in midair, halfway to her mouth. "What about yesterday?"

"Ekry. What she did to the Prince... You can't justify that. He's innocent in this, and she almost gouged his eye out when we were in the village," the disgust was clear in his tone, "*and* that's not even to mention what she did to him after we parted ways. Nazario and Ayla were there, why didn't they stop her?"

"I don't want to talk about this anymore, Caias," she said, feeling her frustration giving way to rage when he brought in Naz and Ayla. "I don't want to fight with you before we go our separate ways. I don't want that on my conscience before heading into a war."

He sighed, eyes shifting to the dirt below his boots. "I just wish you'd change your mind."

"But I won't. I gave my word. You know what Papa says..."

"A person is only as good as their word," he said dryly before letting out a small chuckle. "Why do our parents have so many mantras? You'd think they were walking oracles or something!"

Raelia laughed, accidentally spitting bits of egg onto the ground, causing Caias to bend over, laughing as well.

***

The rest of the morning went by quickly. Raelia told Alton of their plans and then set about packing some of her belongings to bring with her back to Paodra. She was surprised to learn that Zayric slept in her room with the Prince overnight. In the entire time since Raelia rescued the fox, he'd slept with her, and if she was honest with herself, she was a bit jealous.

Zayric watched her closely as she went around the room, figuring out the things she wanted to take with her. Alton watched her, too.

"Raelia?" his voice was soft when he spoke, almost timid.

She stopped, turning from her closet to look at him. "Yes?"

"Where are you taking me?"

"Paodra."

The look of shock on his face was nearly comical. "Paodra? You mean the forest up north? Why would you... What's there?"

"I don't think I should tell you. If you escape, I can't be-"

"I'm not going to run, Rae. And I wouldn't do anything to hurt you or your friends."

She thought about that for a minute, not sure if he was being honest, but wanting so badly to trust him. He saved her life. Why would he have done that if he meant her harm?

Plopping herself down next to him on the bed, she sighed.

"You don't want to take me there, do you?" he asked, though his tone made it sound like more of a statement than a question.

Raelia's eyes widened, not sure how he had read her so well. "Why... Why would you say that?"

"It's written all over your face."

"It's more that I'm not sure I can protect you if we do," she admitted. Saying the words out loud let them resonate in her heart more than just the errant thoughts, and the truth in her fears was undeniable.

"Well after that woman... Ekry was it? After she... you know... I can understand why, but it seems like that other silver guy-"

"Rokoa," she told him.

"Rokoa. He seems to be able to keep her in line, at least."

"They're not really the ones I'm worried about..."

"Oh?"

Another sigh emitted from her lips as she let herself fall back on the bed behind her. "Vysha's family... Do you know the tale of the Red Lady?"

He nodded.

"Vysha is the woman from those tales."

Alton burst out into disbelieving laughter. "Raelia! That was over five hundred years ago! There's no way she-"

"She is," she said sternly. His laughter stopped when faced with her stony features, realizing she wasn't joking. "King Nikolai had her family executed unjustly. Her children were around the same ages as Blaze and Caeda. And he killed them for no reason."

"He wouldn't have executed children for no reason! Nikolai was a fair man, by all accounts."

"And by all accounts, Mark Bearers are vicious murdering monsters!" she spat. "Every book ever written in Dirythia, every book in the palace library on the subject, writes us as such!"

"Rae..."

"The histories are wrong, Alton! The books are written to make the royal family look better than they are! They're written to make us look like monsters!" She felt tears welling in her eyes, but she refused to let them fall as she yanked her braid back, exposing her Mark, making sure he could see it. "I didn't *choose* this! I didn't choose to be born with this hideous Mark! I *never* wanted it! And yet your father sent his bloody Grushik to slaughter not only my family but my entire village! He signed the death warrant of every person at that festival, all because I existed!"

When she finished emotions hung heavily between them. Alton looked confused, and sorrowful, and grief-stricken all at once. He opened his mouth to speak, and then closed it.

Silence hung in the air, and for a few minutes, the only sound was Raelia's shaky breathing.

When he finally spoke, confusion won out in his tone. "What is a... grivish?"

"Grushik."

"Grushik? What is it? My father didn't order an attack on Frayis, Raelia. He knew I was going to be attending the festival the next day! He never said a word to me about an attack or any G... Gr...Grushik."

Before she could answer, her bedroom door swung open. Ekry stood there, her disgruntled expression told her she hadn't expected Raelia to be in the room.

"It's time to load up the prisoner," she explained, stepping into the room.

"I don't think so!" Raelia's tone was fierce, commanding, as she stood and squared up to Ekry. "You are not coming near him! Get out of my room!" she demanded.

"I do not take orders from you, girl. Sit down!" Ekry reached around Raelia, stretching her fingers towards a terrified Alton.

Without warning, Raelia shoved Ekry back with every ounce of strength she possessed. The Drykuan tumbled back, falling to the ground. Before she could even react, Raelia pulled the dagger from her hip, and directed it at Ekry's face.

"I will prepare him for the journey. You will not lay so much as a finger on him without my say so. Do you understand?"

Ekry glared up at her, fury rolling off of her in waves. With lightning speed, she stood, and twisted her fingers into the hair on the top of Raelia's head.

"Ekry!" Rokoa's voice startled them both as he came into the room. "Let her go!"

She did as she was told, throwing Raelia away from her and storming out of the room without even a glance at the larger Drykuan.

When Ekry was gone, Rokoa held out a rope. "He has to be tied up, Raelia, and we need to get going." She reached for the rope, but he pulled it back. "I would feel better if I tied the knots. I'm not sure I can trust your skills at the moment."

She rolled her eyes, and then looked down at Alton with a reassuring gaze. "Just be gentle. He's still hurting."

"That's why I brought this," Rokoa gave a half smile as he pulled out a small vial from somewhere in his long, green traveling cloak. Inside shimmered a golden liquid Raelia recognized quickly.

"Laanias nectar?" she exclaimed, surprise evident in her tone. "I didn't know you had any."

"I never leave Paodra without a few vials," he explained, reaching around her to hand Alton the shimmering liquid with a command, "Drink."

The Prince did as instructed. Within seconds, every wound on his body healed. The look on his face was comical, and Raelia couldn't help but laugh.

"Good stuff, right?" she said with a wink as she grabbed her bag and walked toward the door. "I'll see you both downstairs."

Caias was waiting for her when she walked out of the house — Luella standing only a few feet behind him. He kneeled between their younger sibling's graves, a hand on each.

"I don't want to leave them," he told her. "Any of them," he added, eyes on the mound of dirt over their mother's body.

Raelia knelt down, placing her hand upon the pile with a sigh. "I know."

She heard her brother sniffle and watched as he wiped his cheek before turning his stormy ocean eyes on her.

"I don't want to leave you, either."

Without a word, Raelia reached over and grabbed his hand tightly. Her eyes were rimmed with tears when she looked at her brother. She wanted to beg him to come with her to Paodra. The idea of separating from him was excruciating, but she knew he would never join her. Not when their father was still out there somewhere.

The door to the house opened behind them. Rokoa waltzed out followed closely by Alton, whose hands were bound in front of him. Anger flashed in her brother's eyes at the sight, but he kept his mouth shut.

"We should get going. Where are the others?"

"They're in the stables," Luella chimed as the siblings stood.

They followed quietly behind Alton and Rokoa toward the pasture. Outside the barn doors, they found Marah and Onyx hitched to separate carts. Prickle and the Drykuan horses were saddled and ready for the journey, it seemed.

"About time!" Ekry complained, huffing as she pulled herself up onto her chosen steed.

Raelia rolled her eyes at the Drykuan and watched as Rokoa waved his magic over Alton, sending him into the back of the cart. She turned to look at Luella, standing on the other side of her brother.

She hadn't properly spoken to Lue since a few nights ago. She was still hurt and angry, but it didn't feel right to let her go off without even saying goodbye.

"Be safe, Lue," she said, eyes connecting with her friend's.

Luella nodded, and without a word rushed Raelia, wrapping her in a hug so tight she thought her ribs may break. "I'm sorry..." the apology was muffled against Raelia's shoulder, but she understood all the same.

Returning the hug, she replied, "I'm sorry, too."

Her heart ached when Luella pulled away, turning around without even a glance at her friend, and hurrying to seat herself in the cart hitched to Marah. Raelia sighed, turning her gaze to her brother, who watched their interaction with curious eyes.

"Find Papa. You have to find him, Caias," her voice was insistent, but kind, aware of the burden she was placing on him.

He wrapped his arms around her, squeezing even tighter than Luella had as he whispered in her ear, "There is a pouch of gold in your bag. Do not give it away, do not use it on this trip," his tone was harsh and his breathing quick, "If you find you need to run, do not hesitate. Use it to get to Taevidia. Juniper will give you supplies to cross the wastelands if you can make it to Truliach. Do not *die*."

When he pulled away, a tear ran down his cheek. He wiped it furiously, before locking his gaze on hers. "I love you, RaeRae. You better make it home to me. I need you, sister."

She pulled him in for another fierce hug. "I will. I promise," she half said, half sobbed into his shoulder. "I love you too, Caias."

CHAPTER 29

The journey back to Paodra was quieter than the trip to Frayis. It felt like the joy had been sucked out of all of them. Ayla, Naz and Raelia rode a ways back from the cart Rokoa drove and Ekry rode leading the charge the entire way.

Not only was it quieter, but the road seemed rougher this time around. Having the Crowned Prince as a hostage made it impossible for them to travel in the open. Instead they opted for riding through the dense forests, and avoiding any other rider they came across. Thankfully, Rokoa made the same journey before, so at least they had someone who could keep them on the right path.

Ekry seemed to be trying to get her hands on Alton at every turn, and it made Raelia paranoid. She barely slept, afraid if she let down her guard for even a moment, the Drykuan woman would take the chance to bury her blade in his heart.

The nights were the hardest.

Rokoa, Nazario and Raelia took it in turns to watch over their hostage. Ekry offered, but Raelia refused to let her be in charge of him again. Not after what she'd done the first time.

When she wasn't on watch, Raelia laid in her small tent, tossing and turning. Sleep was an elusive beast, and before it ever washed over her, the sun began to rise.

Alton mostly kept quiet on the journey, only speaking when spoken too, and even then only giving one-word responses. Not until the last night of their journey, while Raelia kept watch, did he finally decide he needed to say more.

"Do you remember when I pulled you out of the river?" he asked, his voice barely above a whisper as he watched her sitting at the end of the cart.

"Not exactly," she chuckled softly. "I was kind of unconscious."

"Oh, yeah," he smiled. "How could I forget?"

In that moment, she remembered how comfortable she'd felt with him before knowing who he actually was. They'd laughed and teased each other, talked about books and legends when he visited. How did she forget that?

"When I recognized you on that riverbank," he started, "I was terrified you would die. I remember seeing your Mark while you laid there unconscious and-"

"You saw it?"

He nodded. "I knew what it was right away. There are books in the palace library that have sketches of Indicative Marks. None of them were yours, but... I knew. I remember thinking when I saw it that someone with a power like the Dandelion gift couldn't die of something so mundane as drowning."

"It doesn't make me invincible," she laughed, darkly.

"Doesn't it?" he asked in a serious voice. "It's the Mark of longevity. The Mark of protection. The Mark of rebirth. It's supposed to protect you from things like that, isn't it?"

His knowledge about her Mark surprised her. He seemed to know more than even she did. "How... How do you know about my Mark?"

"I told you, I saw it."

"No... I mean, how do you know it's called those things? How do you know it's the Mark of protection and rebirth? I didn't even know that until a couple weeks ago..."

"Oh... I read about it..." He looked down with a nervous chuckle. "My... my mother, she... was from the Taevidian Empire. Did you know that?"

Raelia shook her head.

"Her father was a Dirythian merchant who met her mother on a trip to the tribal lands. As the story goes, they fell in love, married and then my mother was born barely nine months later," he shared. "She lived there until she was twelve years old. They only moved here after a trip my grandfather was on where he happened along the then Prince Calyx — only fifteen. Apparently, he ditched his guards and soon found himself being robbed by a group of miscreants. My grandfather happened along just in time to save his life. He was able to fight off the group and reclaim most of my father's belongings, which, in turn earned him a knighthood, and ultimately set him up to offer his daughter for marriage."

Raelia had never heard this story before, which surprised her. She thought she knew most of the histories of the royal family. Though, when she thought about it, there weren't ever mentions of the histories of the women who married into royal life. The books only ever spoke of their existence. It seemed historians weren't generally interested in a woman's life, unless they were the villain of some tale.

"I never got to meet my mother's parents, they died before I was born. But... When my mother died, I was allowed to keep the small collection of books and diaries that had been handed down to her. Most were of Taevidian legends. They're very old, and speak of the magic."

"Your mother... was she... did she...?"

"No. She wasn't a Mark Bearer... but..." Alton's eyes shined in the moonlight as he added, "my grandmother was, according to her journals."

Raelia's eyes grew wide. She never considered the idea there could be Indicative blood in the royal line. How brave his grandmother must have been to put herself in the line of fire that way.

"Really?" she sat up, leaning toward him with intrigue. "Do you know what Mark she had?"

"An Everlasting Flower."

"I... I've never heard of that one," she said with confusion. "What gift does it allow?"

"She called herself a Memory Walker," he told her. "Her journals spoke about living in other people's memories. As if she can watch them replay, but there's not a lot of information about how it works."

"Interesting..." Raelia's voice faded. She rested her chin in her hand, lost in thought for a moment. "Your father didn't know her lineage? He didn't know your grandmother was a Mark Bearer?"

"Not at first. If he had, all three of them would have been executed. I think she told him in the end though... Before she died, I mean. He's never admitted as much, but..." Alton hesitated, watching her with an intensity that startled her, "but he's become much less fanatical about keeping Dirythia free of magic... That's why... why..."

Raelia sighed, understanding why he began his story in the first place now. "He's not as understanding as you seem to think, Alton."

"He didn't order the attack on your village, Raelia. I know he didn't."

"I know he did. Vysha told me what happened, and I believe her. Our kind have been persecuted for centuries over something we can't control. There's no reason for her to lie to me."

He sighed. "I guess, I just want you to understand... I know that being born with a gift doesn't make you bad or evil or a monster. I know you aren't any of those things, and... I know you were only trying to protect your loved ones in the village. I don't blame you for fighting back. The guards didn't give you any choice."

"Alton... I-"

"I'm here," Naz's voice sounded from the darkness surrounding the little clearing. They stepped forward into the moonlight, looking exhausted. "Go get some sleep, Rae. Rokoa said he wants us out of here early tomorrow."

She turned to Alton, surprised to see a soft smile cross his features when his eyes connected with Nazario's. She nodded, not sure if either had noticed and headed into her tent. She kicked off her boots, and bundled herself up against the cold northern night. She squeezed her eyes closed, knowing she needed sleep, but Alton and Naz's voices drifted in. The words weren't completely clear, but the gentleness in both their tones surprised her. They sounded familiar and comfortable. She did her best to ignore them, trying so hard to sleep, but to no avail.

⧫

The sun rose earlier than Raelia would have liked the next morning. Her conversation with Alton kept replaying in her mind. Something about it unsettled her. Instead of sleeping she tossed and turned running it over and over in her mind.

Ayla came to get her when breakfast was ready, and soon after they started on the last leg of their journey.

"How far out of Paodra are we, Rokoa?" Raelia shouted up to her friend.

"We should arrive by midday if we keep this pace," came his response.

Nazario watched her closely, though they had yet to say a word since they left their last camp. Ayla too was quiet, though Raelia had figured out by now that might just be because she's not a morning person.

"Is there a reason you won't stop staring at me?" she finally asked, smirking over at her friend.

"Was I that obvious?" Naz asked in return.

Ayla snorted. "I could feel your stare and it wasn't even directed at me!"

Both of them joined in her laughter for a moment, and it was the lightest Raelia felt since they'd taken Alton hostage.

"So? What is it?"

Nazario's eyes flicked ahead of them, landing on Rokoa and then on Ekry. They seemed wary of expressing whatever was bothering them, until Ayla cleared her throat.

"I'm a useful tool, you know?" she smirked.

Confusion colored Raelia's features, though Naz seemed to know exactly what she meant and a moment later their voice echoed in her head. Her eyes widened, looking at her friends, who burst out laughing at the expression on her face.

"Wait! How is that possible?! I thought I could only hear you! How can I hear them?!" she looked to Ayla waiting for an explanation.

Instead she heard Naz's voice again.

"She can connect all of us. It's like we're in our own little meeting room, isn't it?"

And they were right. In her mind's eye a small room connected them all. It may not be their physical forms, but their voices represented themselves with flashes of specific colors. Green shimmered when Nazario spoke. Raelia wondered what color she would give off.

"A little warning would have been nice, though," she sent back with a burst of yellow.

"This is kind of draining, so maybe you should get to the point?" Ayla's voice reverberated with a splash of purple

"Sorry..." Naz replied.

Raelia could hear the trepidation in Nazario's thoughts, though she couldn't make out the thoughts themselves.

"Rae? How are you doing?"

She laughed, unable to help herself before speaking out loud. "That's all you wanted to talk about? You could have asked it out loud!"

"Rae!" Ayla's voice echoed in her mind. *"They're building up to it, dummy!"*

Sighing, she focused again on the small, colorful space in her mind. *"I'm fine. Why do you ask?"*

"Because you're not fine," came Nazario's reply. *"You haven't been fine since the night before we got to your village. You got worse while we were there, and... Since we took Alton prisoner, you've been acting down right bizarre. We're worried about you, Rae."*

Her eyes found theirs. The rich sepia tone of their skin shined in the morning sun, and the stormy gray color of their eyes seemed to sparkle when the light hit them. She pulled her thoughts into her own mind, leaving the small space created by Ayla's gift, so she could think how to answer them.

After a moment, she heard Ayla's soft voice calling in her mind, *"Raelia? You can trust us. You know you can, right?"*

"Of course I know I can trust you both," she answered, appearing back in the colorful space. *"It's just... I'm worried, is all."*

"Worried about what?" the green color flashed.

"About what's going to happen when we get back to Paodra..." She felt her heart sink. Admitting it to herself was one thing, admitting it to her friends felt sharper somehow.

"You mean about the war we're walking into?" the purple asked.

Raelia looked at her friend, concern woven into her expression, before returning, *"Not that, no... I'm worried about Alton. About what Vysha might... What she..."*

"What she'll do to him," Naz's voice finished for her. It wasn't a question. It was a statement and their tone seemed more understanding than Raelia expected.

"You are too, aren't you? About what she's going to do?"

They nodded.

"Why though? I think that's what's bothering me the most! I don't know why I should-"

"We should go the rest of the way to the *Triseyule* on foot," Ekry called from the front of the group. "It's Weialdin season. They will be harder to avoid on horse back."

"We'll finish this later," she told her friends in the small space within their minds. A second later the space vanished, leaving only the door connecting her to Ayla.

The trip through the Triseyule didn't seem as magical as her first. She'd been through it before, yes, but that wasn't what took away its appeal. Every step closer Alton got to Vysha, the worse Raelia felt. Her stomach twisted into knots, nausea overwhelming her as they stepped into the main square.

Alton let out a tiny gasp of awe upon his first view of the magnificently magic city, and even though she'd seen it before, Raelia too was taken aback. Her mind was so lost in everything that happened in the week they'd been gone, she'd nearly forgotten its beauty.

A peace settled over her now she was back. It might not be the place she grew up, but Paodra had become a kind of home for her. It wasn't her family home, where her father's books filled up all the nooks and crannies, but instead was a home she felt she could call her own.

They walked across the square. Mark Bearers, Drykuan's, and even Zarhaish watched their progression. All of their eyes on the hostage, hands still bound in his front, walking in the middle of their group. They walked the same path as before — headed to the throne room — where Vysha would most likely be. The feeling of peace Raelia felt when they walked into the main square, vanished as they descended down the long staircase into the winding tunnel halls below.

Rokoa's gaze found hers, a hint of worry touching his silver eyes, before he turned his gaze forward once more. Her heart beat faster with every step, and she wanted nothing more but to grab Alton and run as far away from the Red Lady as they could.

"Ekry and I will go in and let Vysha know we're back," Rokoa told them when they walked up to the large ornately carved door leading to the throne room. "You three stay here, and watch him," he finished, pointing at the Prince.

They all nodded, though, Raelia's eyes were following the progression of the dandelion seeds carved into the door. The way the seeds wrapped around the other flowers never ceased to bring her a comfort she didn't understand.

"Rae?" Ayla's voice called softly from behind her, pulling her focus from the large door. "Something doesn't feel right..."

Turning to look at her friends, she nodded. "I feel it too."

It was then she noticed the dark circles under both Ayla and Nazario's eyes. They matched her own.

"What do we do?"

She sighed. The same question had been running through her mind since they'd taken Alton in Frayis, only getting louder the closer to Paodra they traveled.

"There's nothing we can do at this point. We're here..."

Before anything else could be said, the door opened, drawing all of their attention. To her surprise, Dhovina stood in front of them, a wicked smile spreading on their face.

"And here I thought your trip south was useless," they crooned, an evil joy lighting up their golden eyes. They reached for Alton's bound hands, and fear kicked Raelia into gear. She stepped in front of the Zarhaish, blocking their view of the Prince.

"There's no need for you to touch him," Raelia told them. Her words coming out sharper and stronger than she actually felt. "He can walk in on his own."

Dhovina glared and without another word, shoved Raelia to the side. The attack surprised her, and she stumbled, tripped over her feet and fell to the ground with a painful thud.

When she looked back up, the Zarhaish grabbed onto the rope bounding Alton's wrists, dragging him into the throne room.

Her friends quickly helped Raelia back to her feet. Ayla's eyes shooting daggers in the direction Dhovina had gone. The three of them rushed into the large room just in time to see the Zarhaish throw Alton to the wooden floor, cackling as they watched him struggle to get to his knees.

Raelia looked around the room, spotting Jamina, Qiralst and a couple Zarhaish she didn't recognize, but the faces she was seeking weren't there.

"Where is Vysha?" she demanded. Her eyes flitted to where Ekry stood, leaning against the wall with a disgruntled expression. "And Rokoa? Where did he go?"

"Rokoa went to collect Vysha. They will be along shortly," Qiralst answered in his slimy tone.

She walked further into the cavernous room, heading toward where Alton was kneeled on the floor. However, before she reached him, Dhovina spun around, kicking their leg out. Their heavy boot slammed against the Prince's side, throwing him to the ground once more. His head cracked against the hard floor, and he let out a pained cry.

"HEY!" Raelia ran, putting herself between the Zarhaish and their victim once more. "Don't touch him!"

Another cackle emitted from Dhovina. "Get out of the way girl."

"NO!" she shouted in reply. "He is not here for you to torture! Walk away!"

They continued to grin, an evil twinkle in their golden eyes, until Nazario and Ayla stepped up to join their friend. Their amusement faltered, and rage colored their expression, as Qiralst stepped up next to them.

"How *dare* you!" he spat at the three of them. A puff of smoke appeared at his hand, the smell of singed hair emanating from it, leaving only a bullwhip in its place. Qiralst gripped the thick leather braid threateningly in his fist. "Step aside or face the consequences!"

A powerful green glow erupted from Raelia's body in a flash of light. She hadn't even thought about using her gift, but at that moment, it seemed to have a mind of its own. The light was translucent, and formed a wall between the two Zarhaish's and the Mark Bearers.

"We will not!" Her voice was strong, not even a glimmer of fear in it as she faced them down. Inside, however, her heart pounded erratically, and she was sure her face must be giving away the fear she felt.

At that moment, the door swung open faster than Raelia expected for such a heavy thing. Rokoa marched in with a curious expression as he looked upon the scene before him.

"Vysha will be here shortly."

Qiralst took one last look at Raelia, a look of pure hatred in his eyes, before he swiftly turned and moved back to dais. Dhovina, however, looked at Rokoa as he approached, seeming to lose interest in her all together.

"Did you tell her?" Dhovina demanded.

Rokoa shook his head then bowed forward. "No. She didn't give me a chance."

Dhovina rolled her eyes, as if irritated by his answer, but chose not to say anything else before turning and heading back up to the dais with the others.

It was quiet while they waited. The only sounds to be heard were the quick paced breaths of the Prince who sat on his knees behind her. Raelia let her protective wall drop, reasonably certain the onslaught from the Zarhaish had finished.

A few moments later, a sudden whooshing sound fluttered around them. Raelia squeezed her eyes shut against the wind swirling around her, and when she opened them again, Vysha was there.

Shock colored the Red Lady's features, but faded quickly, replaced with a look of malicious glee the longer her eyes remained on Alton.

Raelia had never seen the woman look so evil, and fear trickled down her spine in response.

"Oh, my *Aldaehima*," the Red Lady exclaimed, her smile twisting darkly, "if I had known you would be bringing me back a gift, I would have sent you sooner."

CHAPTER 30

At the look Vysha gave Alton, Raelia wished she hadn't let her protective barrier vanish. She mentally scolded herself at the thought.

'She's one of us,' she reminded herself, trying to calm the growing fear in her chest. *'She's not one of those blood hungry Zarhaish.'*

Raelia wanted to believe that, but the look on the Red Lady's face made it increasingly difficult.

"My dear, Prince Alton," Vysha began, gently pushing Ayla, Naz and Raelia out of the way, "you have to forgive my associates. I did not know you would be joining us. It clearly is a shock for them, as well."

Suddenly frozen in terror, Raelia could do nothing but watch as Vysha stepped forward and helped the Prince stand. He looked at her with trepidation, but was cordial when he thanked her.

The atmosphere in the room was tense. Raelia felt slightly calmer now that it seemed Vysha didn't mean any harm to him, but she kept her guard up. Terrified it would change.

Vysha reached for the ropes bounding his hands together and with a mere touch they fell to the ground. He rubbed his wrists as the Red Lady hooked her hand in the crook of his elbow with a strange smile. It seemed malicious to Raelia, but her actions seemed so soft and kind, she thought she must be reading it wrong.

"I didn't hear the details," the Red Lady said before turning to look at Rokoa. "How exactly is it that the Crowned Prince has come to be in our beautiful forest?"

The Drykuan bowed his head, clearing his voice before he spoke, "There was a bit of trouble in the village when we went to collect the bodies of Raelia's family. There were royal soldiers, and a battle ensued. Prince Alton turned up toward the end, and it turned out they knew each other."

Vysha's eyes widened in surprise, and she turned them on Raelia. "*Aldaehima*, you never mentioned you knew any of the royal family."

Her mouth opened to speak, and yet nothing came out. Thoughts racing, she wasn't able to collect them quick enough to respond before-

"She was unaware of his title and real name, Vysha," Rokoa explained, still bowing his head. Concern colored his tone, and Raelia could tell he was trying to protect her. From what, she didn't know.

"That's... interesting," the woman said, her voice seeming darker than before. "How is that possible, *Aldaehima*?"

Raelia cleared her throat, giving her time to form the explanation. "He saved me about a week before the attack on Frayis," she explained. "He didn't want to expose himself, so he didn't tell me his real name."

Vysha's gaze shifted back to Alton. "Is this true?"

He nodded, not daring to speak.

"And you learned who he was during this skirmish on your trip?"

She hurried to nod. "Ekry recognized him by sight, and we thought it would be best to bring him here instead of letting him go free."

"Letting him go free?"

The look that took over Vysha's features made Raelia recall the legends of her viciousness, and again fear trickled down her spine.

"Why would you ever let him go free?" she asked, looking at Raelia with shock, as if she'd never seen her before.

"I... I..." How could she answer that question? In her mind, bringing him here was uncalled for as it was. Letting him go seemed logical to her in the moment back in Frayis.

"I wanted to kill him, as his family has done to our kind for centuries, but the *Dandelion*," Ekry said the word like a curse, "refused to step aside! This was the only reasonable solution we could come to."

"*Kill him*?!" Vysha seemed as appalled at the thought as Raelia had been in the village. "Killing him would be just as idiotic as letting him go!"

Ekry blanched. She obviously hadn't expected that response.

"Who's idea was it to bring him here?" Vysha asked, walking Alton toward the dais. "Rokoa?"

The Drykuan cleared his throat, but before he could speak, she continued.

"Of course it was you," Vysha laughed, letting go of Alton's elbow and stepping up to sit on the throne. "You always know exactly what I need."

As she sat upon the throne, looking down at Alton where she'd left him a grin spread across her face. Raelia took a step forward, but Vysha held up her hand.

"Stay there, *Aldaehima*," she instructed, never taking her eyes off of the Prince. "Your Majesty, I assume they have made you aware of the coming events?"

Alton shook his head, though Raelia had told him enough bits and pieces that she was sure he'd figured it out.

Vysha clicked her tongue. "Tsk. Tsk. Did you not wonder *why* you were being brought here?"

Alton didn't respond, seeming to decide silence was the best option.

Pursing her lips, Vysha stared at him for a moment, seeming to determine her next words. Her voice was sickeningly sweet when she asked, "How many soldiers does King Calyx have on a normal day in Vairek City?"

This question surprised him. His eyes were wide as he shook his head. "I... I don't know. That's not something my father and I have ever discussed."

A derisive cackle erupted from Vysha as she clicked her tongue once more, shaking her head as she did so. Without warning, she flicked her wrist. Her fingers flitted toward Alton, and in less than a second, he began screaming in agony as he fell to his knees.

"Vysha! Stop! Don't!" Raelia screamed, trying to run to her friend, still writhing in pain on the floor. With a blur of speed, Rokoa appeared at her side, grabbing onto her arm to stop her progression. She looked at the Drykuan, the betrayal she felt clear in her expression. He looked down, remorseful, but didn't loosen his grip.

The Red Lady looked at Raelia with rage in her eyes — a look she'd never seen from the woman before — and in the next second she flicked her wrist once more.

Alton's screams stopped as Vysha stepped back down the dais toward him. She stopped in front of his panting form, watching as he tried to sit up.

"Now..." she said slowly, deadly, "Let's try that again, shall we? How many personal soldiers guard your father every day?"

"You can... ask... as many questions... as you want..." Alton told her between his labored breaths, "the answer won't... change."

With a wave of her hand, a slap echoed around the large room, and Alton's body flew to the side as if he'd been struck, though Vysha never touched him. A small dribble of blood flowed down his chin.

Raelia restrained her scream of frustration, but pulled at Rokoa's vice-like grip. Nazario and Ayla watched the scene play out, horror coloring her expression, while disgust colored theirs. Anger brewed in Naz's eyes, and they looked like they wanted to step forward, but then she glimpsed Ekry, hands raised at the pair.

'She must be putting up a barrier.' The thought confirmed when Nazario pressed their shoulder against something Raelia couldn't see, as if trying to force open an invisible door.

"Let's try something easier then," Vysha continued, stepping closer to him. "Where are the weaknesses in the city's defenses?"

Alton spat blood at her feet, a look of loathing in his eyes as he said, "I have nothing to tell you!"

The Red Lady's eyes glowed a faint red with her rage as she flicked one hand and then the other, causing Alton's body to flail this way and that. She raised her hand, magically lifting Alton's body a couple of feet into the air. He hovered there for a moment, seemingly paralyzed from the neck down, until Vysha slammed her hand back down and with it Alton's body.

The thud his body made against the hard wooden surface was deafening. He yelled out in pain, but spoke no words. Vysha would not get the information she was seeking. Not from him.

With that realization, Raelia's already pounding heart became thunderous. Her struggle to free herself seemed futile, but she would not stop trying.

Again, Vysha flicked her wrist and Alton's beaten and bruised body flailed.

Flick. *Thud.*

Flick. *Bang.*

Flick. *Crunch.*

Blood spurted from the Prince's nose when he lifted his face from the floor. It was misshapen, and very clearly broken. His body so beaten, so bruised, he struggled to lift his own weight from the ground. Alton turned to face the Red Lady, cheek pressed to the floor, as he tried, unsuccessfully, to push himself up.

"Stop! Please, stop!" Raelia shouted, tears overflowing from her welling eyes. "Vysha! Please!"

"I have no... information... for you..." the Prince gasped out, pained.

"Well then," Vysha's mouth twisted into an evil, smug smirk, "I guess you've worn out your usefulness."

When Vysha's skin glowed red, Raelia's heart nearly stopped. She watched as Vysha's lips moved once more, but the blood pounding in her ears didn't allow for her to hear the words spoken.

Everything seemed to slow as Vysha's hand raised, palm pointed at Alton. Raelia felt herself scream, but heard no sound. Turning her head, she sank her teeth into Rokoa's hand. His blood tasted metallic, with a hint of sweetness she couldn't place as it burst into her mouth. He let out a shriek of pain and loosened his grip. She yanked herself free and with a speed she never knew she possessed, Raelia wrapped her arms around her friend as her skin burst into its protective yellow glow.

When their skin connected, Alton's flesh glowed just as her own. As if he had his own Dandelion gift. The burst of red light left Vysha's hand at the same moment, and Raelia squeezed her eyes shut, preparing for the pain.

None came.

Vysha's enraged eyes stared in disbelief at the pair on the floor in front of her. Qiralst stepped forward, lifting his whip as if to strike, but the Red Lady waved him off, eyes never leaving her *Aldaehima*.

"Take the protection off of him, Raelia!" she screamed. "This *filth* does not deserve your protection!"

She'd never seen Vysha behave like this before. The glow of her rage flowing out of her fingertips, her eyes, her arms. Every bit of her body was glowing a deep, vibrant red, and appeared to leak that light into the room in waves.

Raelia choked down a sob, fear coursing through her. "He doesn't deserve this, Vysha! Please! He saved my life! If it wasn't for him, I never would have made it to Paodra! I never would have met you! I wouldn't be able to help you fight King Calyx! He's not like his father!" Her voice was shrill, but her words were clear as she continued, "HE KNEW ABOUT MY MARK AND HE STILL SAVED ME!"

That seemed to grab Vysha's attention. She stopped, chest rising and falling rapidly with the intensity of her anger.

"Of course he knew about your Mark!" she yelled. "Calyx knew who you were and where you lived! Of *course* his son knew!"

With great effort, Raelia forced her tears to stop falling. She wiped her cheeks on her sleeve and took a deep breath, calming herself before she spoke again. "Vysha," she began in as calm a tone as she could manage, "he saw my Mark when he pulled me from the river and again when he helped me home. That was a week before the festival."

"Don't be so naive, *Aldaehima*! He knew all along!"

"No," she replied, becoming calmer with every breath. "You said they only found out who I was a day or two before the festival at most. Alton knew before then."

"Well then maybe *he's* the one who told his father of your existence!" she shouted, seeming pleased with herself for the logic she presented.

Raelia thought about that for a moment, eyes never leaving the Red Lady. She had a point. Alton very well could have told his father who she was, but...

'It was really nice to visit. I know there's a festival in a few days in the village,' the memory was clear as day. His voice rang in her mind. *'I've heard it's quite the spectacle to behold... Would - uh -would you be willing to show me around the festival one day?'*

The moment seemed so long ago, but it proved he hadn't told anyone. Didn't it? Why would he make plans to spend a day with her, if he was planning on telling his father who she was? Between that, and the new knowledge about his grandmother being a Mark Bearer, she couldn't find any logic in Vysha's argument.

"No! It wasn't him! He has shown me nothing but kindness, even knowing what I was! I will not allow anyone to harm him!" With Raelia's words, the yellow light shining from both of their bodies glowed brighter, causing Vysha to squint her eyes against it.

Without another word, the woman took a deep breath, closing her eyes as she did so. Little by little the red glow surrounding her dissipated, and when she opened her eyes once more, she was the Vysha that Raelia had come to know and trust in her time there. Her face was calm, her eyes caring.

"You can release him now, *Aldaehima.* I will not harm him," Vysha sighed. "Not if you do not wish it."

Raelia wanted to trust the woman before her, but after what she just witnessed, she didn't think she should. When she sat up, taking her weight off of Alton, her hand grasped his, keeping contact so her protection of him did not break.

A flash of irritation touched Vysha's eyes, but she did not comment on it. Shifting gears, she smiled sweetly. Too sweetly. It was as if she wanted to convince Raelia that everything she just witnessed hadn't even happened.

"Sweet child," she crooned, "I understand why you want to protect him. I acted rashly, and didn't take your feelings into account." Her eyes shifted to Alton. "I apologize, your Highness."

Suddenly, the door to the throne room burst open and all eyes turned. A Drykuan woman Raelia had never seen before rushed into the room. Her long black hair fluttered behind her as she hurried to Dhovina's side to whisper into their ear. Their eyes widened in surprise.

"Are you certain?"

The woman nodded and then bowed. Her voice was soft and high pitched as she answered, "Yes, Dhovina."

"Go back to the stables and ready the horses. I will meet you there." With a quick nod, the servant rushed out of the room.

"What is it?" Vysha asked. "Is it what we've been waiting for?" Dhovina nodded.

"Excellent," the Red Lady smiled brightly, a wicked excitement in her eyes. "Go now! I will be along shortly!"

Everyone in the room watched the interaction with varying expressions of curiosity. It seemed Qiralst, Ekry and even Rokoa were as clueless as the three Mark Bearers. Before any of them could ask for clarification, however, Dhovina disappeared through the door and Vysha turned back to the pair on the floor at her feet.

"*Aldaehima*, we will have to continue our discussion later." Her black eyes shifted to Rokoa. "Take him to the dungeon. Do not let anyone," her eyes flickered to Raelia as she spoke the next words, "including myself," she emphasized before looking back at the Drykuan, "harm him in any way. Take Raelia with you, so she knows where he is being kept. Provide him with whatever food he requires and make sure he is well taken care of."

Rokoa nodded, stepping forward as Vysha turned back to Raelia, still kneeling on the floor. "*Aldaehima*, you have my word no one will harm him." When she didn't let go of Alton, the Red Lady sighed. "I can understand why you're hesitant, but I have more important things to deal with now. Stay with him, if you'd like. I can even have a bed brought down to his cell, but I hope that won't be necessary."

"This is ridiculous!" Qiralst burst out in anger, causing everyone in the room to jump. "Why does this *child* get to dictate what happens to *our* prisoner?!" He stepped down from the dais, flicking his whip out, the tip of which hit an invisible barrier only inches from Alton's face. "If he will not provide information to help our cause, then he is not useful and should be executed!"

Vysha stared daggers at the Zarhaish as she spoke, "Rokoa, if Qiralst so much as enters the dungeon halls, you are allowed any force necessary to remove him."

"I..." Rokoa's eyes widened in surprise, and though his lips moved, no words came out. He seemed terrified at the very thought of the order. The Red Lady turned her gaze back to him, still attempting to speak. She eyed him with a ferocious gaze before lifting her hand, palm out, toward him.

There was no light, but the air between the two seemed to shimmer and bend in a way that Raelia had never seen before. She was about to ask what flowed between them, but Vysha spoke first.

"He will not be able to harm you, nor punish you in any way now."

"Now wait a damned minute!" Qiralst shouted. "You have no *right*! He will do as *I* say! Your words hold no power over him!"

Vysha turned to look at the enraged Zarhaish, smirking with an eerie calmness. "Stay away from the Prince. If I find out you have even looked in his direction, I will go straight to Yizark."

Raelia hadn't heard that name before. Clearly, Qiralst had, though. Fear flashed across his features before he let out a frustrated growl. With one last glance at Alton and Raelia, still on the floor, he stormed out of the room, his footsteps echoing the whole way.

"Now that's settled," Vysha started, turning her gaze back to Rokoa, "please escort our guest to his cell."

Rokoa nodded, and Vysha looked at Raelia once more. "I will find you later so we can discuss matters further," and then she was gone in the same blur of speed she'd appeared in, Ekry following in her wake.

Getting Alton to his feet after the beating he'd taken was nearly impossible. Eventually, Rokoa left the three Mark Bearers to watch over the Prince while he ran for some Laanias nectar. His injuries were severe enough that the healing drink didn't work as quickly, or as thoroughly as it usually did, but it was a start.

Once he was able to walk on his own, Rokoa, Raelia, Ayla and Nazario walked him through the winding hallways down, down, down into the earth, where they eventually came to the damp stone tunnels. They passed the staircase that Raelia knew led to the ancient library, and turned right not long after.

The tunnel opened into a long, narrow room. The only light that of a few flickering sconces on the wall at the entryway and at the end of the tunnel like space. There were doors every few feet. They were thick and wooden, with only a small barred window the size of someone's face. The sound of dripping water could be heard in more than one place, but in the dim light, it was impossible to find the source.

Rokoa led them further into the room, and as they approached the sconces on the other side, she realized a tunnel led off from each corner. He turned left, and Raelia realized the cell doors were different here than in the other part of the room. These seemed more in line with what she would expect — long bars from floor to ceiling.

A few cells down from where they turned, the Drykuan stopped and opened one of the barred doors. Alton stepped through first, closely followed by the three Mark Bearers.

"*This* is where he has to stay?" Raelia asked, disgust evident in her tone.

The room was small, cramped even. The walls were damp and Raelia could smell mold she assumed must be growing in the cracks of the stone bricks of the walls and floor. Near the back wall there were long, thick chains bolted into the ground, and her heart sank.

"You're not putting him in those!" she demanded.

"I'll be okay," Alton tried to reassure her. He forced a weak smile. Flakes of dried blood cracking away from the skin around his lips fluttered down into the darkness.

Raelia turned to Rokoa, pushing a yellow glow into her palm to light up the dark space. "There's not even any light in here!"

Rolling his eyes, the Drykuan waved a hand toward the wall across from the cell's door. One of the small sconces with light green flames appeared immediately, and she let her own glow vanish. The green hue against the stone walls reflected on their skin, making all of them appear sickly. The light the sconce gave off was dimmer than she would have liked, but she knew it was likely the best she would get.

"There's not a bed, or even a blanket," Nazario complained. "Where is he supposed to sleep?"

This time, Rokoa's eyes hardened as he grumbled under his breath. Waving his hand once more, a small mat appeared on the ground near the back wall where the chains sat. On top of that a thin, ragged blanket that Raelia knew would do him no good. A bucket appeared in the corner closest to the mat, and Raelia looked at the Drykuan in disgust.

"You have *got* to be kidding?!"

"He's a prisoner! He may be your friend," Rokoa's voice was bordering on exhaustion, but the frustration was clear, "but he is an enemy to everyone else here!"

"He's not *my* enemy! If R-mmph-" Ayla's eyes went wide as she seemed to choke on her words. She coughed and looked at Rokoa with a mixture of fear and confusion.

"Names aren't allowed here," he said, plainly. "The stone was dressed with the magic when Paodra was built. It only warps noises or voices, but names? It will choke the air right from your lungs if you try to even whisper one."

Ayla cleared her throat and took a deep breath before attempting to speak once more. "A little warning would have been nice..."

Rokoa smirked, but it faded quickly as Nazario spoke up — getting back on topic. "Be that as it may, *he*," they emphasized, pointing at Alton, "is not our enemy."

Ayla folded her arms across her chest, nodding in agreement.

Raelia felt so touched her eyes welled with emotion, though no tears fell. She looked at Alton, who was watching her closely.

"We won't let her hurt you."

Chapter 31

Over the next few days, Raelia, Ayla and Nazario all took turns checking on Alton. They brought him a warmer blanket and a few pillows — Raelia even swiped a menu for him to be able to order food.

Upon her first visit after the first night, she was furious to find the cuffs at the end of the large chains bolted to the floor were locked on his wrists. He told her someone he didn't recognize turned up in the middle of the night and put them on. When she asked if they said why, he shook his head.

"They didn't say anything, actually. Just came in, put them on and left."

Raelia stood, swearing to talk to Vysha and have them taken off, but Alton raised his chained hand.

"Don't. I don't want you to get into any more trouble. If this is the worst of the treatment I get while I'm here, then I'm luckier than most."

On day three, after arriving back in Paodra, Raelia sat in the training arena — her gaze shifting from the book in her lap to Nazario and Ekry battling against each other on the mats, when Galys turned up. He explained he'd been instructed to send her to Vysha for training.

She wasn't particularly keen on spending time with Vysha. Not after what she'd seen from her the night they arrived with Alton.

However, no matter how angry she might have been with the woman, she still needed her guidance on how to use her gift.

When she arrived in the throne room, she was surprised to see Rokoa there. Both he and the Red Lady were bent over a large table, searching through papers and maps. Raelia assumed it must have to do with the upcoming battle and cleared her throat to announce her arrival.

"Oh! *Aldaehima*!" Vysha crooned when she turned around. "I'm so glad you're here! We have much to discuss!"

"Galys said you wanted to see me?" Raelia did her best to keep her tone light, though after everything that transpired, it was an effort.

"Yes... I wanted to check in with you," Vysha set down the map in her hand and turned to look at her with a worried expression; grabbing her hand as she continued, "We haven't spoken since that nasty business with the Prince. I wanted to apologize again. I lost sight of the big picture in my own anger and grief. I'm so sorry I hurt your friend."

Her stomach twisted in knots as she looked at the Red Lady. She wanted to trust her apology, but there was an overwhelming feeling nagging in the back of her mind. Over and over again it hissed, *'she can't be trusted.'*

"It's done and over now," she replied instead. She looked down, and took a breath before bringing her gaze back to Vysha's. "Is that all you needed?"

"Do you wish to go already, *Aldaehima*?" Vysha asked, eyeing her suspiciously. "You just got here."

"Oh! No!" Raelia burst out, making the Red Lady's eyes narrow. She forced a nervous chuckle, doing her best to lighten the mood before continuing, "I just... You look busy, is all! I didn't want to interrupt your planning!"

Rokoa chuckled, looking at her quizzically, but it seemed to placate the woman, whose suspicious gaze shifted into a bright expression. "Oh, Raelia! You are ever so considerate. However, it wasn't the main reason, you see."

"Oh?"

"I'm going to be very busy over the next week before we begin our march on Vairek City, so I wanted to get one last training session in with you before then."

"I... oh! I didn't realize there was more to go over before..."

"There will always be more to go over with your gift, *Aldaehima*," Vysha crooned. "The Dandelion presents differently for every bearer, remember. You will be no exception. Also, Rokoa told me about your kyloxis. I'd like to see how he might interact with your gift."

"Oh! I can go get him!" she turned, stopping when she felt Vysha's hand grip her elbow.

"If you are bonded, as Rokoa says, you should be able to call him here," she explained. "No reason to run off!"

"OH! Yeah... I can do that," Raelia chuckled nervously.

She mentally reached out, calling for Zayric and a moment later, a white mist appeared at her side.

It wrapped around her shoulders, and in a blink, the weightless scarf shifted into a heavy one covered in fur.

Vysha's eyes lit up. "Oh how wonderful!"

The woman reached for the pup, as if to scratch his head, but without warning, Zayric growled. He twisted into a protective stance as Vysha pulled back her hand, startled.

"Oh my! He's not as friendly as Rokoa made him out to be," Vysha said, eyes locked on the small beast perched on Raelia's shoulder.

A few hours later, Raelia left the throne room exhausted. Zayric followed her along the path down the dimly lit hallway, as if he was just as tired.

Vysha kept them there until Raelia had successfully projected her gift through Zayric's mist. It was a bizarre sensation. As if a piece of her was leaving her physical form. She stood, watching as the black mist emitted a soft yellow glow and floated across the room to where the Red Lady stood.

The first few times, the glow never left her palm. A few other times, it snapped back to where she stood, as if thrown at her.

The last time, when it finally reached Vysha, the excitement in the woman's eyes was undeniable as she exclaimed, "This is *just* what we needed!"

All in all, it had been a productive training session.

She was halfway down the stairs leading to the common room when she realized she left her book on the table with the papers and maps Vysha and Rokoa had been going through. A heavy sigh escaped her as she turned around to head right back the way she came. Zayric looked at her with large eyes, curiosity clear.

"I'll meet you soon. I forgot something," she told him before pushing open the door to the square.

The journey was quick, though she felt like her feet dragged with every step, and soon she was turning the corner of the dimly lit hallway once more.

The heavy door was cracked open and Raelia could hear Vysha and Rokoa's voices from inside. She made to push it open, but stopped short of touching the wood when she heard her name.

"He's in the dungeon?!" Rokoa's voice sounded outraged, though she couldn't figure out why. He'd been the one to show Alton to his cell. "Raelia won't stand for it. Vysha, you have to-"

"*Raelia* will stand for what I tell her too!" the Red Lady's voice was irritated and she sneered her name like a curse. "That child will have to learn the way of our world soon enough."

"What do you mean?" Rokoa's voice was low, concern flowing through the four simple words.

"Oh, Rokoa! You haven't gone soft on me, have you?" Vysha returned, mocking. "You know as well as I that if she knows the truth, she won't fight against the Kingdom. I *need* her gift! We all do! We can't win without it!"

Soft footsteps echoed around the room, muffling the next few words. Raelia leaned in closer to the slivered opening, managing to catch the last bit of Rokoa's sentence.

"But the Prince-"

"The Prince is a means to an end! He will make good bait for his father's surrender, and then we will kill them both."

"But... Raelia... You made her a promise."

"Oh, the Dandelion won't know of this until the time comes. You will not breathe a word of it. Do you understand?"

There was a pause. Raelia assumed Rokoa must have nodded, because Vysha continued.

"I need her in this battle. Her gift is strong, and her being there will be the difference between win or lose. Especially if we figure in the kyloxis. We will be unstoppable with them. This is the only chance we have. We *need* her."

"She won't fight if she finds out, Vysha, and I'm not the only one that knows. Aren't you worried it will get back to her?"

"No. I'm not worried in the slightest."

"But she's down there every-"

"The Dandelion will know nothing of this!" Vysha shouted. "You will not breathe a word of it, and neither will Jamina or Dhovina. There will be no reason for her to not cooperate during the battle."

"Vysha, I-"

"There is nothing left to say. You have your orders. Now go."

It was quiet for a moment. Then footsteps echoed once more, this time headed toward the door Raelia stood behind. Her heart raced as she stepped back silently, then dropped her feet heavily, trying to make it seem like she'd just gotten there as she pulled the door open.

She forced a smile, and nearly ran into a surprised Rokoa at the door.

"Hey!" she said, a little too brightly.

He looked at her quizzically, before replying, "Hey. What are you-"

"I just forgot my book," she interrupted, pushing past him without even making eye contact.

She hurried into the room, picking up the large leather-bound book and hugging it to herself.

Vysha looked surprised, but pleased to see her. "I didn't even notice you'd forgotten it!"

"Sorry to interrupt. I just... I just wanted to read before I go to sleep, is all."

She kept her eyes on the ground as the Red Lady responded. "Don't be silly! You didn't interrupt anything. Rokoa was just leaving," Vysha turned her eyes to the Drykuan, still standing in the doorway. "Why don't you see her back to her room?"

"Oh! That's not necessary!" Raelia exclaimed, struggling to keep her voice at a reasonable volume.

"Is everything alright, *Aldaehima*?" Vysha asked as her brown eyes scrutinized her features.

"It's not a problem, Rae," came Rokoa's voice from behind her.

"I'm fine! Really!" she sighed, deeply, trying to calm her nerves. "I think I'm just overly tired."

"Well, let's get you to your room then, so you can get some sleep," Rokoa chuckled, extending his arm as if to say 'after you'

Raelia internally cursed herself as she nodded. The last thing she wanted to do was be around either of them. Rokoa, however, seemed the more dangerous option at the moment. He could read her so well. Suddenly, the short walk to her room seemed excruciatingly long.

She remained silent as they walked down the dimly lit hallway. It wasn't until he pushed open the door to the outside world that Rokoa finally spoke.

"Are you going to tell me what's bothering you?" His voice was kind, no indication he suspected she'd heard their discussion, but she knew she had to come up with something to explain her jittery behavior.

"There's not exactly anything to tell," she answered, keeping her eyes on the ground as they walked.

"There's got to be something," he laughed. "Come on, BeeBee, what's going on?"

The nickname made her stomach knot. How can he so easily joke around and smile with her, when he knew Vysha was planning to kill her friend? She forced a sigh, squeezing the book tighter to her chest as they started their descent toward the common room.

"I'm tired, that's all. A lot has happened in the last few days."

He eyed her closely, seemingly not convinced of her reasoning. "Are you sure that's all it is?"

A pang shot through her heart when she heard the worry in his voice. How can he seem so sincere when he is colluding with the Red Lady? He's supposed to be her friend.

"I'm sure."

Silence filled the space between them once more, and Raelia was thankful for it. She didn't know how to keep acting like everything was okay, when it was very much the opposite. As they turned the corner toward her room, she was grateful to see Ayla and Nazario waiting for her.

"There you are!" Ayla exclaimed when she saw her. "We've been looking all over for you!"

"You have?"

"I think you should both go. Raelia needs to rest," Rokoa told them, still clearly concerned for her.

Naz looked at Raelia with a curious look.

"I'm fine," she told them before turning to Rokoa. "Really. I'll get some rest. I promise." She could tell by the look on his face, he wasn't happy about it, but there wasn't exactly anything for him to do. Reaching for the knob on her door, she continued, "Besides, I still have to eat dinner."

It took a bit of doing, but soon Rokoa left, leaving the three Mark Bearers on their own to order their meals. Raelia and Naz sat on the couch as Ayla talked happily of the events of her day from the floor. Naz listened intently. Raelia, however, was distracted.

The conversation she'd overheard between Rokoa and Vysha replayed in her mind. Bits of it didn't fully make sense, but now that she knew Vysha's plan for Alton, she didn't think it mattered. She had to get him out of there.

"Raelia!" Nazario's shout pulled her out of her head.

"What?! Why are you yelling?!"

Both her friends laughed before Ayla replied, "We've been calling your name for ten minutes!"

"Where were you?" Naz added.

Raelia's green eyes connected to their brown. She didn't know what they saw, but it was clearly enough for them to worry.

"Rae?" they reached out, gripping her hand reassuringly. "What's going on?"

Her mind was tormented. She trusted her friends, but she had trusted Vysha too. Even more than that, she had trusted Rokoa. Can she tell them what she overheard? Should she?

She searched Naz's eyes, looking for the answers to the questions her mind was screaming. Tears pricked in the corner of her eyes, and in that moment, she didn't know how to keep her emotions in control. Ayla put her plate on the small coffee table and scooted forward, placing her hand on Raelia's knee.

Deciding she had to trust her friends, she opened her mouth to speak at the same time that Naz said, "You can talk to us. Tell us what's going on," in a concerned tone.

"I... Well earlier... I..." she struggled to figure out how to put into words what she'd overheard — the betrayal she felt. How could she tell them the woman they've put their trust into wasn't worthy of it?

"Earlier when you went to train with Vysha?" Ayla asked, squeezing her knee reassuringly.

Raelia nodded before continuing, "I... I overheard Vysha and... and... Rokoa," she choked out his name, the betrayal seeping into her heart hurting even worse when she figured in his role in all of this. "They were discussing Alton... and... and..."

"Vysha's going to kill him, isn't she?" Ayla asked plainly.

Naz's eyes widened at the implication and turned to Raelia, who nodded. "That was her plan the whole time! She's going to use him as bait to get King Calyx to surrender!" The words flowed from her lips as if a dam had been opened. "Then when she has control, she's going to use them as examples so the rest of the Kingdom doesn't fight back!

She didn't know I could hear them. Vysha swore Rokoa to secrecy! He didn't like it, but it was like there wasn't anything he could do against her..."

She took a deep breath, allowing Nazario to interject, "Of course he can't do anything... Even the Zarhaish are answering to her and they control the Drykuan. I imagine he'd be severely punished — maybe even killed — if he tried to stop her."

Raelia nodded before blurting out, "She's going to kill him! He saved my life and I brought him to someone who's going to kill him! I can't let her do it!"

Her friends nodded their agreement.

"Of course you can't," Ayla reassured. "He shouldn't have to suffer because of his family's wickedness."

Nodding once more, Nazario squeezed her hand reassuringly. "We'll figure something out. We'll help you."

At their words, tears of relief fell from her eyes. She stretched out her arms, wrapping one around each of her friends and hugging them tightly.

"I don't know what I would do without you guys! Thank you so much!"

She felt both of their arms weave their way around her as well, making them look like a giant ball of limbs.

When they finally pulled apart, Raelia smiled at her friends. She felt lighter, and she had them to thank for it.

"Okay... Now," Ayla started, looking sheepish, "Do either of you have any ideas about how we're going to protect the Prince and not bring about the wrath of the Red Lady?"

Raelia felt herself deflate. That was the hitch. How could they protect him from such a powerful being? And that's not even mentioning the gifts of the Drykuan's and Zarhaish. From what she knew of Indicative Marks, specifically the Dandelion Mark, Vysha's powers were nothing compared to those of the immortal races.

Naz cleared their throat. "If we're going to have any sort of chance, I think we need to do it before the march on Vairek City."

Both the girls nodded in agreement.

Raelia's mind raced with different scenarios as the three of them started coming up with different plans. They talked through every step of each, and every possible downfall.

Hours passed, and it was the wee hours of the morning when a plausible idea finally presented itself. After they discussed every step and drawback, Ayla stretched.

"I don't think discussing it further is helping," she yawned. "We either decide right now to do it, or we decide not to and move on to something else."

Raelia sighed, she was right. This plan had fewer opportunities to go wrong than the others they'd come up with. None of their ideas would be completely risk free, so it was time to call it.

"You're right. I'm in," she replied. Her eyes shifted to Naz, who nodded. "The sooner the better. Let's do it the day after tomorrow."

CHAPTER 32

R aelia was woken the next day by a loud knock on her bedroom door. Before she even had a chance to get out of bed, Ayla came in looking exhausted.

"Did you get much sleep?" she asked as she plopped herself down on the bed.

Raelia shook her head, falling back on her pillow.

"Not a wink. What's the chance we can just skip over this meeting and not be noticed?" she asked, closing her eyes and snuggling into her pillow.

"No chance," Naz interjected as they walked into the room and plopped down next to Ayla. "For you especially," they chuckled.

Groaning, Raelia forced her eyes back open and sat up. "Well, I better start getting dressed then."

"Are we still doing this tomorrow?" Ayla asked, worry flooding her tone. "Maybe we should wait unti-"

"No," Naz answered, "it needs to be tomorrow. We don't know when Vysha is planning to march south. We need to do it as long before then as possible."

"We all know what we have to do?" Raelia asked, tossing the blankets off of herself and stretching as her feet hit the floor.

"I think the hundredth time we went over it last night finally etched my job details into my brain permanently," Nazario smiled, trying to bring a lightness to the conversation that seemed out of place.

Ayla nodded, and stood, pulling them up with her.

"Get dressed. I want to eat before we head over," she said, dragging Naz behind her as she walked out of the room.

Raelia closed the door behind her friends and opened her wardrobe to prepare herself for the day ahead.

It wasn't long before they'd eaten and headed into the throne room where most if not all Mark Bearers were standing around chit chatting before Vysha came through the doors.

The meeting was long, and Raelia had a hard time staying focused. Her mind kept wandering to all the things she needed to prepare, and wondering if they'd be able to pull off the rescue they'd worked so hard to plan.

It wasn't until Vysha announced they would leave in two day's time for Vairek City that Raelia was jolted into paying attention. Her eyes shifted to Nazario who sat a few people away with Galys. They looked just as shocked as she felt.

"We can't wait until tomorrow night!" Ayla's voice rang through her mind. *"We have to do it tonight!"*

"Until we get out of this meeting, we can't do anything!" Raelia sent back through the open door in her mind.

"Just stay calm," Nazario, ever the voice of reason, replied in a flash of green. *"Everything will be fine. So we move it up a day. It won't be a problem."*

Raelia's eyes found theirs once more and she gave a curt nod.

"When this is over, let's meet back in your room," came Ayla's voice with a tone of finality.

The door in her mind closed, and once again, Raelia was left alone with her own thoughts.

The meeting ended quickly, after that, Raelia, Ayla and Nazario all completed their separate tasks – then the only thing left to do was wait for nightfall.

⊰⊱

The lock clicked out of the frame, and Raelia winced at the noise. In the dungeon's silence, it seemed as loud as a cracking whip. For some reason, the fire in the sconce was out, leaving the darkness pure and unyielding.

"Who's there?" From the other side of the door, Alton's deep voice sounded strange — unrecognizable. If she had any doubt about which cell he was in, she'd have sworn she'd gotten the wrong one. Even as it was, however, she could hear the terror in his warped tone.

"I said who's there?!" the Prince demanded once more as she stepped through the door, closing it behind herself. It wasn't until she was inside the cell that his voice returned to his normal bass. She pushed her power into the palm of her hand, the glow lighting the dark room.

"It's me," she called back in a whisper.

Relief flooded his features, and he visibly relaxed.

Quickly, she hurried across the small space, and pulled at the chains bolted to the stone floor. "Hold still," she urged.

She slid two fingers under the iron cuff on each of his wrists, wrapping the rest of her hands over the latches. Closing her eyes, she focused on the feel of the iron, and pushed the heat of her glow into it, just as Vysha had taught her.

At that realization, the glow emanating from her skin flickered, and her concentration floundered.

"What are you doing?"

"Shhh!"

When it was quiet once more, she again closed her eyes. She forced the thought of Vysha out of her mind, also shoving down the guilt rising in her chest as she did so. She focused her mind on the rough texture of the iron, opening her mind to the heat it would take to break the cuffs apart.

"Ouch!" Alton's cry of pain was hushed, but still echoed around the room.

Raelia froze, listening for any sounds from beyond the walls.

Silence.

Breathing a sigh of relief, she turned back to the task at hand. She could feel the raw skin of his wrists against her fingers, and realized that heating them up could cause more harm than good.

"Ice!" she exclaimed in a whisper.

"Ice?"

"It's going to get cold, but I think I can get you out of these easier than with heat."

She hadn't produced ice before, but Vysha told her it was the same process as creating fire, only with opposite instincts. Raelia focused her mind once more. Closing her eyes, she pictured the icy mountain peaks to the north of Paodra. She imagined the warm steel in her hands icing over and becoming brittle.

When she felt the cold slowly flowing up her arms, she looked down at the cuffs in her fists. The dark, almost black color of them had turned into an icy blue, and her eyes lit up at the sight.

"Come over here," she instructed, pulling him toward the wall behind him. "This might hurt a little."

Before Alton could respond, Raelia slammed the underside of his wrists against the stone wall. The following clatter was loud, but she felt the crack vibrate through both of the now iced cuffs.

She waited a moment, listening again for any sounds to indicate someone heard the noise she was making. When there weren't any, she slammed both again. This time, along with the echoing clatter, she heard the telltale sound of ice breaking, and felt the cuffs become loose in her grip.

"You did it!" Alton exclaimed in hushed amazement.

He rubbed his wrists, looking at her with an emotion Raelia couldn't quite place. Gratitude? Relief?

She knelt down, pulling a dagger from her ankle holster, and held it out to him, hilt first. "Take this. If we come against any trouble, use it," she told him. "I'm going to get you out of here."

Alton nodded, clearly not sure what to say in response. The gravity of their situation was not lost on him, if his expression was anything to go by, and she was thankful for it.

The heavy door creaked when she cracked it open to peer to the right and left. She sighed in relief when she realized there was still no one in the hall.

Alton gripped her hand tightly, bringing her attention back to him with a questioning look. "If anyone can get us out of here, it's you," he whispered.

A brief smile touched her lips. "Let's go."

They stepped into the hall, Raelia first, followed closely by Alton. Their steps were soft, making only the tiniest muffled noises. She knew a Mark Bearer wouldn't have the capabilities to hear them, but with the Zarhaish's and Drykuan's advanced hearing, she couldn't be certain it was silent enough.

Their movements were slow, calculated, as they moved through the winding halls.

Left.

Right.

Another right.

Raelia was thankful she had spent so much time walking the halls and exploring every nook and cranny in the labyrinth of Paodran hallways. If she hadn't, the chances of them making it out of here was slim.

Hallway after hallway after hallway they traveled, Raelia only using her glow when absolutely necessary, and even then she dimmed it as much as she could without letting it evaporate into the shadows.

"We're almost there," she whispered to Alton. "One more hallway."

He only nodded in response, the muscles of his jaw tense and pulsing as they took the final turn.

She reached back, grasping his hand as she hurried her steps to the door at the end of the hall, outside of which, if Ayla had done her part, Prickle would be awaiting their arrival.

Relief flooded through her as she wrapped her hand around the knob and pushed open the heavy door. Though she remained alert, she knew from where they were now, Alton should be safe.

The early morning sunlight burned their eyes after the abundance of dark hallways. Both squinted against it, but Raelia refused to slow down. She ran across the small clearing toward the path she walked with Rokoa only a few weeks ago, all but dragging Alton behind her, only slowing once they had entered the safety of the forest canopy.

Prickle's dark eyes watched them make their way down the path and seemed relieved when Raelia reached out to scratch his forehead.

When she dropped her hand and looked to Alton, the horse rubbed his head against her shoulder, begging for more attention.

"Can you get up on your own?" she asked, stepping to the saddlebag nearest her, and opening it up. She pulled out a canteen and held it out to him. "You should drink something before taking off. Naz set you up for the journey. There's food, water and laanias nectar on this side," she told him as he took the container off her, "and on the other, you'll find a bag of coin and a couple blankets. Take the dagger with you, just in case."

"Aren't you coming with me? Rae, you can't-"

"I can stay here, and I'm going too."

"The Red Lady," he started, worried as he stepped toward her and squeezed her hand, "she'll know it was you who let me out. You're not safe here anymore. Come with me, *please*."

"I can't. If I leave, Ayla and Naz will pay the price, and I won't have that on my conscience," she sighed, returning the squeeze. Releasing his hand, she pushed him gently toward Prickle. "You need to go quickly, before the guards realize you're not in your cell," she continued as he pulled himself into the saddle. "Head south. Gourdist is almost a full day's ride from here, but you're going to need the advantage in time if they send out a search party for you. The Drykuan horses are swifter than any others I've seen before."

Alton's kind brown eyes looked down at her and he opened his mouth to speak, but before he could, the sound of a twig snapping ripped through the air.

Raelia turned, spotting Rokoa as he came through the dense shrubbery. Terror coursed through her veins at the fury in his expression.

"Alton! Go!" she shouted, bringing her power to the surface of her palms in an instant, the green glow reflecting off the trees above.

"I can't leave you!" he yelled in return.

Before she could respond, Rokoa leapt toward them, swiftly pulling a dagger from the sheath at his hip. He was fast, but they'd been training together for weeks, and she expected the movement. In a rapid flick of her wrist, her own blade was drawn and meeting his mid strike.

"What are you doing?!" he growled, inches from her face.

"ALTON! GO NOW! HURRY!" she screamed, blocking the Drykuan's path as he attempted to sidestep around her.

Somewhere in the back of her mind, she registered relief at the sounds of hooves galloping away, but the rage in Rokoa's eyes as he watched the crown Prince disappear deeper into the forest kept her focused.

"I couldn't let Vysha use him as a pawn!" Raelia spat, pushing her weight into their crossed daggers. "She promised me she wouldn't hurt him! She swore it!"

"And she hasn't! Spending a few days in a dungeon cell won't-"

"I heard her! I heard you *both*," she screamed, matching his fury with her own. The betrayal she felt still burned within her. He'd lied to her. Vysha had lied to her. The ache of their deception wasn't soon to be forgotten.

His eyes went wide, realization dawning as he stepped back, pulling his blade from hers.

"You were outside the door? That's why you were acting so bizarrely... Why you've been avoiding me since...?"

"I will not let her use him like a pawn in this war! I won't! It's not right!" she raged, ignoring his words as she felt the telltale prick of furious tears in the corners of her eyes.

"Raelia, he is the enemy. He is *your* enemy." Rokoa's voice was hard, but the rage there only moments before seemed dulled.

"NO! He's not *my* enemy!" she shouted, anger still coursing through her. "He is my friend! He was my first ever friend! And Vysha promised me she wouldn't hurt him while secretly planning his public execution!"

The flame of rage had been completely extinguished in Rokoa's gaze — a look akin to guilt taking its place. "His family murdered her children, Rae. King Nikolai had them slaughtered and-"

"Alton is not Nikolai! He wants better for the magical community! He wants to stop the genocide against Mark Bearers! He can't do that if he's dead!"

Rokoa sheathed his dagger and held his hands up in surrender as he stepped toward her. His movement was wary, slow, as if approaching a wild animal. "Raelia, you don't know the royals like Vysha does. None of them can be trusted. Not even Alton."

"In this moment, after all that I have seen," she spat around the growing lump in her throat, "the people I can't trust are Vysha and you!"

He winced at her words like she'd slapped him, and he let his hands fall to his side in defeat. His eyes connected with hers, and she could have sworn the pain in them was real, but she wouldn't allow him to fool her again.

Raelia sheathed her dagger at her hip before stepping back to put more space between them.

"Bee-"

"Don't call me that!" she snapped. "My name is Raelia to you. Nothing else. Not Rae. Not BeeBee. Raelia."

Another flash of hurt, this time tinged with sorrow, crossed his features, once again making her question the anger she felt.

"No! He has proven he can't be trusted!' she mentally scolded herself. *'He is not your friend!'*

Without another word, she turned, hurrying back toward the entrance into the village. When Raelia pulled open the door, Rokoa looked up. Their eyes connected momentarily and it seemed like he wanted to say something, but she didn't give him the chance. Swiftly, she hurried through the heavy door and ran down the dark hallway. She brought her glow to the surface of her palm mid step. By the time she heard the click of the door opening once more, she'd already turned into a new tunnel.

She needed to get back to her room. She had to tell her friends what happened. Before Vysha came for her, they needed to know she wouldn't betray them.

Still running, she didn't stop until she slammed into the door at the end of the final corridor. It flew open, cracking against the outer wall with an echoing crash, but she didn't wait for it to close before taking off in the direction of her living quarters.

Her lungs burned and her muscles ached, but she didn't slow down until she came to the main square. Slowing to a hurried walk, she crossed the open area, trying not to draw attention from the few early morning risers.

Once through the door and down the stairs, she picked up the pace. Keeping her eyes on the ground, she ignored the hollered good mornings from her peers and made her way quickly to her room.

Nazario and Ayla paced in her small living space when she burst in. Both looked startled at her arrival.

"It's done!" she choked out through heavy breaths. "But you need to get out of here!"

"What? Rae what are you-"

"Rokoa. He found me! Alton's gone, but Vysha will come for me any minute!"

"Raelia, we're not going to-"

"Yes, you are!" she shouted, reaching out to Naz and pulling them by the elbow towards the door. "I will *not* have you two implicated in this! Go!"

Pulling open the door, she shoved them through it, before reaching for Ayla, who pulled out of her reach.

"We're not leaving you! This was our doing too! You can't take the blame when we were a part of it!"

"I can and I will!" she replied, finally getting a hold of her friend. "Please! I can't stand the idea of you two getting caught up in all of this! Please!"

Ayla yanked back on her arm, looking daggers at her friend as Nazario walked back to the pair, leaving the door wide open. The way they looked at her, Raelia knew they didn't like what she was asking, so when they spoke, their words took her by surprise.

"Ayla, come on. Nothing will be gained by arguing right now," they pulled a resistant Ayla toward the door, but stopped to look at Raelia once more. "We can protect you better if she doesn't know right now. I will not promise to keep this secret though, not if I think it will save you."

Without another word, they pushed Ayla through the door and closed it behind themselves. Finally, Raelia could breathe a sigh of relief.

It was done.

Alton was free.

Her friends wouldn't be blamed.

Now all she had to do was wait for her punishment.

CHAPTER 33

"Do you even understand the damage you have done?!" Vysha screamed, her voice reverberating around the room. She didn't give Raelia a chance to answer before continuing, "We no longer have the element of surprise! You've completely destroyed any opportunity to sneak into the royal city!"

The Red Lady looked down at her from the throne in the middle of the dais. Raelia was tied up before Dhovina dragged her out of her living quarters, and now she sat, hands still bound, knelt on the throne room floor. Vysha had been screaming for the better part of ten minutes and hadn't given her the chance to explain herself yet.

Behind the throne, Dhovina and Qiralst stood, glowering down at her. Rokoa and Ekry stood against the far wall behind them, leaning against it casually, as if neither had a care in the world. Though, Rokoa's eyes flickered to Raelia more than once and she could see the worry in his silver gaze.

"What would possess you to go against your own kind?!" the Red Lady continued, "You sent another monster who wants us dead back into the world!"

Raelia had so many things she wanted to say. She had so many answers, but Vysha wasn't giving her the chance. As the woman raged on, she made mental notes of her answers and the reasoning for her actions. She mentally rehearsed what needed to be said, just waiting for her chance to speak.

"What am I going to *do* with you?! How can I trust you after this?!"

"You can't!" Dhovina growled from behind the throne. "Dispose of her and be done with it! We have more important things to be dealing with!"

Vysha fell silent, eyes turning to look at the Zarhaish behind her throne. She didn't say a word, only watched Dhovina as if mulling over their words. When her gaze returned, Raelia knew this was the only chance she had to say what she needed.

"I didn't think there was a choice! You promised me you wouldn't hurt him," she yelled, desperately, "but then I overheard your conversation with Rokoa! You intended to kill him the whole time!"

"Of course I did!" Vysha's tone was venomous. "The royals have been killing us for millennia! Why shouldn't we kill them in return?"

"Alton is not like the rest of his family! He respects the magic! He wants to find a way to-"

"Respects the magic?! Is that what he was doing when he let his father slaughter your village? Slaughter your family?!" Vysha burst out, rage flowing through the very air around her. "He is a monster! A monster that would sooner skewer you on his blade than give you the respect you deserve!"

"No." Raelia's voice was low, forceful. Vysha was determined to believe the worst in Alton, and nothing she could say would change her mind, so she would not yell. Either she listened, or she didn't.

"No?! NO?! What do you mean no?!" Vysha's voice was disbelieving, and rising in pitch. "You have no idea the atrocities that-"

"That his family perpetrated against the magical community? I have an idea. But you don't know him."

Vysha fell silent, looking at Raelia as if she had only just seen her for the first time. Her eyes were calculating and furious. It seemed everyone in the room understood the gravity of the Red Lady's next words as no one moved a muscle. The only sound that Raelia could hear was her own heart beating against her rib cage.

"Rokoa!" Vysha called, snapping her fingers. "I want you to put the Dandelion in a cell down in the dungeon. She is allowed no visitors and I want her chained until I decide what to do with her."

Nodding his understanding, Rokoa stepped forward and easily lifted Raelia's bound form as if she were no heavier than a feather. He set her feet on the ground, and without a word, forced her into the dimly lit hallway.

The silence continued as they made their way down to the dungeon. Raelia kept her eyes on the floor. She wanted to ask for his help — wanted to ask him to release her, so she had a chance at escaping Paodra, but she couldn't bring the words forth.

If he helped her, his life would be in danger, and no matter how betrayed she felt, she still cared about him. Still thought of him as a friend. She wouldn't ask him to risk his life for hers.

When they finally reached the dungeon, Rokoa opened the first cell door they came to, gesturing for her to walk inside. Once she was chained to the floor, Raelia sat on the damp stone, leaning against the wall and closing her eyes.

The door to her cell creaked as the Drykuan closed it, and she heard the lock click into place before everything went quiet once more.

"I should have told you..." came Rokoa's warped, but soft, and remorseful voice from the other side of the door. "If I told you her plans before then maybe... maybe..."

Raelia opened her eyes. The cell was dark. The only light she could see came from the small barred window near the top of the door. Rokoa's face was shadowed as he spoke to her through it.

"It wouldn't have changed this," she reassured, lifting her chained hands and gesturing at the cell around her. "The second we decided we would bring him here, this was always going to be the outcome."

A heavy sigh escaped Rokoa as he pulled his face from view. She heard a heavy thud against the door and the tell-tale dragging sound of him sliding down to the floor.

"That doesn't mean I shouldn't have tried."

Silence hung thick in the musty air. Raelia wasn't sure how to respond. This wasn't his fault. If he'd told her, she would have done the same thing. It just would have happened sooner. Though, maybe if he had, she would have asked for his advice on what to do, instead of focusing so much on his betrayal.

Either way, though, she didn't blame him... and she didn't want him to blame himself, no matter how hurt she felt.

"What do you think she's going to do to me?" her voice was quiet and small. Knowing Vysha needed her in the upcoming battle was the only glimmer of hope she had of making out of this cell alive, but what would she have to do? What would Vysha make her do?

"I... I don't know..." came his response. "She... She needs you alive right now, though. I think it's best to focus on that. I won't let her kill you," his voice was warped, but sounded desperate — like he needed her to believe him. "I swear it."

It was cold in the dungeon. Especially during the night hours. She curled in on herself, pulling her legs to her chest and wrapping her arms around them — doing her best to stay warm — but the cold, damp of the floor soaked through her clothes, making it a wasted effort.

She hoped her friends would visit, but neither Ayla nor Nazario came. Rokoa came more than expected, bringing one of Brixxi's paper menus each time he did, so at least she was able to eat. He wouldn't leave it, though. He never said why, but Raelia got the impression Vysha couldn't know he was bringing it, so she didn't complain.

Being this far underground, Raelia couldn't tell what time of day it was or even how many days passed, but she tried anyway — counting every time that Rokoa visited her cell as a new day.

After his third visit, Raelia noticed sounds coming from the cell next to hers. A cough. A sniffle. At one point, she was sure the person was crying — the way the magic warped the noises, however, made it hard to tell. When Alton had been in here, she didn't look into any of the other cells. She'd never heard noises from anyone else, so she assumed there weren't any other prisoners.

That seemed foolish now.

The wall separating her and her neighbor had cracks in places and in one spot a gap between the stones. It wasn't large, but when she tested it, she would have been able to squeeze her hand through, had it not been for the large iron cuff on her wrist.

"Who's there?!" called a gravelly, warped voice as she pulled her hand back. The scratchy sound to the tone made it sound painful for them to speak, but she responded through the crack in a loud whisper. "Sorry! I didn't mean... I was just..." she sighed. "I was just testing this hole in the bricks, is all."

The telltale sound of heavy chains dragging against stone echoed. She heard a muffled thud and heavy breathing before the voice finally responded. "I didn't realize there was a gap here," came a rough, whispered response.

Long, emaciated fingers poked out from the hole, the movement startled her, but she smiled at the sight. Under normal circumstances, it wouldn't normally fill her with hope or relieve her anxiety to know a stranger was there, but it did. Knowing someone else sat just on the other side of the wall calmed her spirit. As she gripped the boney fingers in her own, she smiled softly.

It meant she wasn't alone.

A few more visits passed, and Raelia took to ordering extra food for her neighbor. Pressing through bits of chicken and potatoes or apples and carrots. It wasn't much, but it made her happy to be able to help him.

The two prisoners shared tidbits about themselves, usually while Raelia pushed bits of food through the gap between the stones. He would ask questions about her regular visitor, or how she came by the food she shared. With the magic warping their voices, and limiting what they could share with each other, they didn't have much of a choice but to keep their conversations to a minimum. It was frustrating at times, though, if she was honest with herself, she figured it was probably better for her to not get attached.

From what she could gather, he was more on in years than her, and didn't know where he was or even why he was there.

"I was sleeping when they grabbed me," he told her during the second meal they shared. "They bound my hands and feet, put a hood over my head and the next thing I knew," he sighed, "I was here."

"And no one told you why?! They didn't tell you anything?!" she asked, shocked.

"Nope! And I tried! Tried to get them to tell me anything at all! None of them uttered even one word!" he laughed abruptly. "I've learned more in the time you've been here than I have the entire time since they brought me!"

She couldn't imagine how scared he must have been. She couldn't imagine being dragged in the middle of the night to this wet, cold hellhole. At least she knew why she was here.

When she tried to explain to him he was in Paodra, and the people who brought him here were Drykuan's, he laughed in disbelief.

"Aren't those the magical beings that the King wiped out hundreds of years ago?" he continued to laugh, though the sound was muffled as he stuck a piece of chicken in his mouth. "I thought they were all gone? You're telling me they still exist?"

"All the history books talk about their extinction, but..." she sighed, as a memory attached itself to her next words, "most of the histories seem to be skewed in favor of Dirythia. Few stories seem to give accurate accounts."

Footsteps echoed down the hall then and she whispered hurriedly, "someone's coming!" before turning her back to the hole and going quiet.

Rokoa had been there only an hour or so ago, so she was surprised when the door to her cell opened and a large figure stepped in. As her eyes focused, however, she realized it wasn't him.

About the same height, but with eyes of gold rather than silver, Qiralst's short black hair was distinctly different from Rokoa's. The dim light from the hall made the golden sheen of his skin glimmer. Her body tensed at the sight, her heart picking up its relaxed pace from only moments before.

"Qir-" an invisible force clamped down on her throat, choking the name into oblivion. She coughed and cleared her throat. "Wh-what are you... Why are you here?"

The Zarhaish lifted his hand, his ever present bullwhip casting a shadow against the wall.

Fear rushed down her spine at the wicked light in his eyes.

"And why shouldn't I be here?" he smirked, enjoying every second of her terror. "You deserve to be punished for your crimes..."

Raelia pulled her knees to her chest, pushing her back against the wall so hard that it was painful. She'd never been alone with Qiralst before, and had never wanted to be. Her mind raced with ways to protect herself from his rage as he stepped closer.

Without warning, her soft yellow light burst forth, covering her entire body. So lost in her fear, she hadn't even thought to use her gift.

The Zarhaish glared down at her now glowing form.

"Okay! Fun's over!" came Dhovina's voice as they stepped into the door frame. "We won't hurt you. *She* sent us."

When Raelia didn't respond, her eyes never leaving the whip still held in Qiralst's raised hand, the new arrival smacked his arm. "She's not going to come if she thinks you're going to whip her!"

"That doesn't matter," Qiralst growled. "I won't be giving her a choice."

After being dragged through the tunnels, Raelia found herself once again knelt in front of Vysha upon her throne. They were alone this time, however. The Zarhaish having been told to leave as soon as they'd set her down, much to Qiralst's dismay.

In the dim light of her cell, she couldn't see the filth covering her body. Now, however, it made her cringe. She'd never been so grimy before, and if she lived through this, she would run to bathe as soon as possible.

Vysha sat silently as she looked down at her. The hate in her eyes Raelia had seen last time seemed muted. It was still there, but somehow seemed muffled by other emotions she couldn't quite pinpoint. Raelia squinted against the brightness, trying to let her eyes adjust, as the Red Lady cleared her throat.

"I have given a lot of thought to our... *predicament*," she explained, standing up from her throne and stepping down the dais. "While my anger is justified, I think my decision to imprison you was harsher than necessary."

Raelia's eyes widened with surprise. Was this really the same woman who, only days before, wasn't sure she even wanted to let her live? Deciding not to speak, she watched as the older woman paced before her, fingers on her chin as if in deep thought.

"What you did was detrimental to our battle efforts; however, I did lie to you and, if the roles were reversed, I can't say I wouldn't have done the same thing."

Raelia perked up. "Really?" she asked, her voice hopeful.

The Red Lady stopped her pacing and knelt down in front of her prisoner. "Yes. Really." Vysha's hand cupped Raelia's cheek in a maternal way. "You remind me so much of my daughter, Asmi."

With a wave of Vysha's hand, Raelia felt the rough, jagged tendrils of her magic wrap around her wrists. A moment later, her bindings vanished and she rubbed her raw skin.

"The fire within you is admirable," she said, reaching down to help Raelia to her feet, "but I need to be able to trust you going forward, and I don't know how after what happened. I need to know you won't betray my trust again, *Aldaehima*."

Her stomach twisted with nerves. Something didn't feel right, as if Vysha was trying to lull her into a false sense of security. The woman's eyes were expectant as she waited for Raelia to say something.

"How can I prove that to you?" her throat was scratchy, and her words came out rough. "I can't promise to not protect the people I care about, Vysha. And I care about Alton. He's my friend."

The Red Lady went silent for a few moments, her eyes scrutinizing Raelia's face. Her voice became less friendly than before, though she was clearly trying to maintain her composure. "I have taken care of you, have I not?" she asked, releasing her elbow and turning to face her straight on. "I took in you and your friend when you had nowhere else to go, correct?"

Raelia nodded.

"We have fed and clothed you? Given you everything you could ask for? I have mentored you and given you a shoulder to cry on. Yes?"

Once again, Raelia nodded.

"Then why is it that a deceitful and murderous royal gets your loyalty?

She didn't know what to say. This was the time to explain herself, but she didn't think Vysha would accept anything that she hadn't already told her.

"The other day, you said the Prince was your first ever friend," Vysha said slowly. "What did you mean?"

Raelia sighed. "I met him when I was six years old. I didn't know he was the Prince at the time. My father used to take me along when he worked in the royal library and we became friends on one trip."

"Your... Your father took you to the castle?" Vysha asked, astonished. "Didn't he know what you *were*?! How could he risk your life like that?!"

"He said it was the best kind of ruse," Raelia smiled to herself, remembering her father's explanation from years prior. "He said the best way to stay undetected was to be directly under King Calyx's nose. The way he looked at it no one would ever expect someone to bring a child that was Marked, so no one would be looking."

She'd always thought her father the bravest man she'd ever known, and that memory was only one of the many reasons. Her heart ached at the thought of him.

'I should have gone with Caias...' she thought to herself. *'I should be looking for Papa. Not here... A prisoner for doing the right thing.'*

A smirk appeared on Vysha's face, as if Raelia's explanation amused her. "Your father was a clever man."

"Is. He *is* a clever man. He wasn't in the village when it was attacked. He's still out there."

"Oh? Ekry mentioned he wasn't with your brother in Frayis. I guess I just assumed..."

"He went missing... Caias will find him, though. I know he will," Raelia asserted, sounding more confident than she felt.

"I'm sure he will," Vysha said, patting her arm. Her words seemed reassuring, but her tone seemed placating — like a mother assuring her child there were no monsters under their bed for the 10th time.

It set Raelia on edge.

"None of this solves the problem we are up against, *Aldaehima*," Vysha accused, as if it was Raelia's fault they ended up on this topic. "How can I trust you to fight with us in the battle with King Calyx?"

"I... I don't know..." Raelia answered. "I don't know what I can do to make you trust me. Maybe... It would be best to leave me out of this war all together, if you're worried about what I might do."

She didn't intend the words to come out as a challenge, and yet somehow it still sounded like one, and as fury flashed in the Red Lady's eyes, she knew that Vysha caught it as well.

Raelia hurried to cover her mistake, wanting to avoid the woman's wrath. "I mean, I want to avenge my family! I just... just..." she thought for a moment, wanting to choose her words carefully. "I don't think I can fight against Alton, but that doesn't mean I can't fight against anyone else..."

If she was honest with herself, she didn't want this war. Her words were true — she *did* want the King to pay for what happened to her family, the guilt over their deaths had been eating her alive, but... A war like this would only result in more lost lives — more of her loved one's deaths.

Vysha's eyes scrutinized her every feature, looking for any dishonesty. When she didn't seem to find any, she sighed. "*Aldaehima*, I just want what's best for all of you. I want you all to be protected."

Raelia nodded, as the woman continued.

"We will travel to Vairek City tomorrow. We need the Dandelion protection. We *need* your gift. You will come with us."

"I-"

"Ekry will be your guard, so you can focus on keeping your protection over as many of us as you can."

"Ekry?" Raelia's eyes widened. "Why not Rokoa? Ekry doesn't even like me! She'd rather watch a sword run me through than protect me against it!"

"Rokoa has a special task, and he is the only one I can trust with it," Vysha explained. "I'll speak with Ekry. She will do as she is ordered."

CHAPTER 34

After their discussion ended, Vysha allowed Raelia to go back to her room. It was a relief to know she'd be able to clean herself up and change her clothes.

On the walk back to her room, it seemed every pair of eyes she met were angry or hateful, so instead of heading to train, or looking for her friends, she stayed in her living quarters. A few of the books she'd brought from the library were still in her room, and she sighed in relief when she saw the menu Brixxi had given her still sitting on the small dining table.

She decided against going to look for her friends, afraid that their association with her would make them pariahs. It didn't stop them, however, from seeking her out as soon as they heard Vysha had released her. Naz didn't even stop to knock on the door before bursting in with their wide, toothy grin. Followed closely by a distressed looking Ayla.

"Thank the gods!" Nazario exclaimed, rushing to wrap her in a tight bear hug. Picking her up, they swung her around in a circle. "We've been so worried! No one would tell us what happened to you! All we knew was that Vysha punished you for releasing Alton!"

Ayla closed the door behind her and stepped into the room as Naz placed Raelia back on the ground and stepped back to give her some space.

Wasting no time, Ayla moved in quickly, hugging her as she whispered, "I'm so glad you're okay! Why didn't you answer me?"

The emotion in her friend's voice brought tears to Raelia's eyes and she hugged her back just as fiercely. "I couldn't hear you! I think the magic in the stones blocks the communication somehow..." Raelia sighed as she pulled back. "Are you two okay? Did anyone realize you helped me?"

They both shook their heads.

"No one even suspected us," Naz said in a hushed voice. "Or at least, no one came asking about it."

Ayla nodded in agreement before adding, "I expected for Vysha to call for us, but we haven't even seen her since before you released Alton."

Raelia plopped down on the plush green sofa and looked up at her friends. "She only let me go, because she needs my gift in the battle. I..." her voice trailed off for a moment as she ran over the conversation she'd had with the Red Lady. "I... don't think... if it wasn't for that, I don't think she'd have let me live..."

Ayla's eyes widened in surprise, as if she couldn't imagine it to be true. Nazario, however, their eyes looked serious as they sat down next to her. Their hands twisted in their lap as they spoke.

"I don't think you'd be the first one of us she's killed," their voice was barely above a whisper. "Galys and I... we-"

Suddenly, the door into her living quarters flew open. "Raelia?!" Rokoa called as he burst in.

All three of them looked at the newcomer with surprise as he stepped into the room, relief flooding his features at the sight of her. He hurried over and yanked her to her feet. Wrapping his arms around her in a vice-like grip.

"I heard Vysha called for you, and I waited in the dungeon for you to be returned to your cell," he explained. His voice was filled with an emotion that Raelia had never heard before. An emotion she couldn't quite place as he continued, "No one told me she released you! I thought... I thought..."

Raelia pulled back to look into his silver eyes. "Thought what?"

His features hardened as if suddenly realizing he'd said too much. "What I thought doesn't matter. All that matters is you're here and safe!"

Rokoa smiled, but it didn't reach his eyes as he released her and stepped back. He looked at Ayla and then Naz and his eyes became curious as he smirked, amused. "Did I come at a bad time?"

All three of them shook their heads.

"You just surprised us, is all," Naz explained with a smile as they got to their feet.

Watching her friend closely, Raelia wanted to ask them to continue their conversation. However, with Rokoa in the room, she knew they couldn't. She hated that she couldn't trust him anymore. She'd come to rely on his brutal honesty and insight into the inner workings of Paodra, but now she didn't know if that would ever return.

During her time as Vysha's prisoner, he'd been the only person allowed to see her. He'd brought a menu so she could eat. He'd made sure she wasn't alone. He'd shown her kindness... But it would take more than that to earn back Raelia's trust, and her stomach twisted with the thought.

The room fell into an awkward silence and Nazario's smile fell with it. Rokoa looked like he was going to ask something, but Raelia cleared her throat to speak before he got the chance.

"It's getting late," she started, eyes connecting with Ayla as she opened the door in her mind, "and I've missed sleeping in a bed..." she chuckled nervously as she pushed into Ayla's mind.

'I want you and Naz to give me thirty minutes,' she raced. *'Then meet me in my room.'*

'You got it!' came her friend's mental response, before she grabbed onto Nazario's hand.

"Well, then we should all leave you alone then!" Ayla said brightly.

The brunette turned toward the door, pulling Naz along with her. Stopping just before she turned the knob, she eyed Rokoa with confusion. "Aren't you coming? The poor thing needs sleep."

Rokoa scrutinized Raelia's expression before turning to follow the other two.

"Get some sleep, Rae!" Naz chimed in with a smile as they were pulled through the door.

She thought she was in the clear, until Rokoa stopped in the frame. His eyes were gentle with a warmth she knew he only ever showed her. A warmth that seemed at odds with the brisk silver color of his iris's. "I hope you sleep well," he told her. "You'll need as much energy as you can get for tomorrow."

And then he was gone. Vanished from view, as if he'd never been there at all.

⁂

"You have to explain, Naz!" Raelia pushed. "You can't say something like that and just expect us to drop it!"

She sat on her bed, Ayla sitting next to her. The two of them facing Nazario, who leaned against the door frame.

Once Rokoa left, Raelia hurried to bathe and ready herself for bed. It had taken longer than expected for her friends to return, and she'd almost fallen asleep while she waited. Now, however, looking at her friend and waiting for them to explain their theory, she was wide awake.

Nazario pushed themself off of the frame and began pacing.

"You two are newer here, so you most likely haven't noticed anything out of the ordinary," Naz started. Their words rushed out, only picking up speed as they continued, "Galys and I, however, we've been here for a long time. Longer than most. Do you remember a few weeks ago when we were eating all together and Galys and I were talking about Nira?"

The girls nodded.

"Neither of us ever found her. Before we left for Frayis, Galys told me he talked to Vysha and she said Nira left in search of her family. That she wanted to reconnect or something like that..." their voice trailed off, suddenly unsure of their next words.

"That's a good thing, right?" Ayla pointed out. "Most of us don't have families to reconnect with."

"The problem is she didn't *have* any living family..." Naz stopped their pacing and turned to look at them both. "Her mother was killed when Nira was only fifteen... She didn't have any other family. Her Dad died when her Mom was pregnant. I asked her a few years back if she had any other family and she said it had always just been her and her Mom..."

Raelia's eyes widened. "Wait... What are you saying?"

Shoulders drooping, Nazario plopped down in the small chair in the corner. Their eyes fell to the ground and their voice was low, hesitant.

"She's not the first to disappear..." they explained. "In the time I've been here, so many Mark Bearers have come and gone. Two, just in the time you've been here, Rae. But... well... none of them ever come back... and there's rarely a goodbye. They all just... suddenly disappear..."

Silence fell between them. Raelia opened her mouth to speak and then closed it. She was at a loss for words. It seemed they all were.

"Who left before Nira?" Ayla's eyes were worried.

"The day after Rae and Lue turned up, a woman named Driary left," they answered. "She had the Mammillaria Mark. It's a really rare Mark. I didn't know her well, but she was always happy and kind. Then one day she just... vanished."

"And what did Vysha say?" Raelia asked. The Mammillaria Mark sounded so familiar, but she couldn't place where she'd heard of it. It tugged at the back of her mind, but she ignored it, still having other questions. "Did she tell you where she went?"

"No... Vysha was so preoccupied with your arrival, it was hard to get a chance. I asked Ekry though," they explained. "She acted so... so... strange. She told me not to worry, that Driary just wanted to spread her wings or something. And when I mentioned I was going to ask Vysha about it, Ekry freaked out! Told me I was being paranoid, and it wasn't something I should bother her with, because she was already upset about it."

"Hmm... how bizarre."

"What is?" Ayla asked, turning her eyes to Raelia.

"Well, when we got here, Vysha seemed fine. I never would have guessed she was upset about anything... and she definitely mentioned nothing about it," she explained. "I've never even heard the name Driary before. If Vysha was so upset about it, don't you think she would have mentioned at least her name?"

"Maybe it was too hard for her?" Ayla offered. "Maybe she was really heartbroken over her leaving, so she didn't want to talk about it?"

Naz shook their head. "It made no sense that she was upset about Driary's leaving. The two never got along. From what I've gathered, Driary was terrified of Vysha and avoided her at all costs. Which is another reason Ekry's explanation never quite made sense."

"What do you think happened to her and Nira?" Raelia asked. "You said earlier you don't think I would have been the first one... You think Vysha killed them?"

Naz stood and began pacing once more. "See, that's the thing! I don't know! None of us do! As far as everyone is concerned, they just left, but Galys and I have been keeping track," they explained, turning around to walk back toward them, "and most of the people who've disappeared were people with gifts that were obscure. Ones that almost no one knows about or hears about, because people are born with them so rarely," Nazario fell silent in thought for a moment before continuing, "There have been a few who left under the same suspicious circumstances that had more common Marks, though. Not all are rare Marks, just *most*."

"That makes it sound like there's no pattern at all," Ayla pointed out. "If people with super common Marks and super rare Marks are disappearing, then doesn't it mean all of them are?"

"No," Naz said, stopping to face them. They let out a groan of frustration. "Galys is better at explaining it! He suspected something was up long before Driary disappeared, so he's done a lot of digging into records and put numbers to what he's found. There's a correlation between the rarity and which elements the powers fall under and how common they are in Paodra specifically."

Raelia watched her friend pacing, their hands waving around dramatically with every word. What they were saying worried her. She'd only known Nazario for a short time, but she didn't think they were the type to spout baffling conspiracy theories without having seen some sort of evidence.

Both Galys and Nazario, Raelia knew, had been here longer than most, and as such, had the opportunity to see more patterns than a lot of the others. Galys, specifically, told her he'd been here since shortly after his birth. His Indicative Mark being where it was, his mother ran with him after seeing it under his eye. He never endured the council's review, and had spent the entirety of his twenty-three years in Paodra because of it.

This was his home.

The people of Paodra, his family.

He would be even less likely than Nazario to spout off theories he didn't see real evidence for.

"Have either of you told anyone else about this?" Raelia asked.

Naz shook their head.

"Good. Don't. Tell Galys not to either," she instructed. "We need to be sure. Maybe get some sort of physical evidence to back up the numbers he has."

"How are we going to do that?" Ayla looked at her with wide eyes.

"I don't know."

The next morning, Raelia struggled to wake up. After the conversation she had with her friends, her sleep was restless and her dreams filled with fear and worry.

When Zayric tried to wake her up at dawn, she'd batted the fox away, determined not to open her eyes yet. He'd given her a reprieve, backing off and settling back down, but moments later, her bedroom door opened, startling her into consciousness.

Ripping upward, her twisted sheets pulled at her. Her eyes were foggy, still thick with sleep. She rubbed at them, and Rokoa's serious face became clearer.

"You need to ready yourself," he told her. "Vysha wants all Mark Bearers in the throne room in an hour."

Before she could respond, he turned and walked back out of her room, giving Raelia a moment to process his words and body language. He was upset. Angry even. What did she do?

She shook her head, doing her best to clear the thoughts, and stretched. In the next breath, she was out of bed and headed to the washroom to start the day.

After she was clean and dressed in her combat gear, she braided her hair back as she went to find her menu to order breakfast.

"Took you long enough."

Rokoa's voice startled her. She hadn't realized he was waiting for her, and she jumped back. "What are you doing here?! I thought I was meant to meet everyone in the throne room?!"

Hand on her heart, she worked to calm her breathing as she stepped over to the small table and looked over the menu.

"Am I really 'everyone'?" he asked.

She could hear the smirk in his voice and she chuckled. "I didn't mean it like that. I just didn't know you were waiting for me. I would have tried to be quicker."

Raelia pressed her finger down on the little blue rose next to herb buttered rice with fried egg, then mixed fruit, then hot tea, before turning back to look at him.

"Are you going to explain what was so important you couldn't wait for an hour?"

He stood from the sofa and walked over to stand next to her. "I wanted to make sure you're okay with the arrangement Vysha made?"

The confusion on her face must have been clear, because it only took a moment for him to explain.

"For Ekry to keep you protected during the battle. She said you seemed, er, *concerned* it wouldn't be me."

"Ah," she nodded as she sat down in front of her plate. "I'm not looking forward to it, if that's what you mean, but she told me that was the only option because — what job did she give you, anyway? Do I get to know? Or is that another secret I get to be kept in the dark about?"

She failed to keep the bitterness out of her tone, and even though she knew she had just cause to feel it, guilt churned in her stomach.

"Rae... I-"

"It's fine," she hurried to reassure him. "Don't worry about it. It's done and over."

Raelia shoved a large bite of egg into her mouth, keeping her eyes on her plate. Sighing, Rokoa pulled out a chair, and plopped himself down.

He watched her as she continued eating. She did her best to avoid eye contact, but it was hard to focus while being scrutinized like that. She wished he'd just say something already.

"What?!" she finally snapped. "Why are you staring at me?"

Rokoa jumped at her sudden outburst. "I... I don't know," he finally admitted, anger seeming to flood out of him. He stood and pushed the chair back under the table, before sighing. "I guess I'm just trying to make things right between us..."

She watched him with wide eyes. Only once before had she seen him this anxious — when she'd approached Qiralst in the square. He was so terrified then, and she understood why, but now? With her? It didn't make any sense.

"It's not something you can make right, Rokoa," she sighed, putting her fork down. "I'm fine. Really. I'm angry," she admitted. "But it's Vysha that I'm angry at. Not you."

It wasn't exactly a lie. Her anger was directed mostly at Vysha. It was the hurt and betrayal that made it difficult to be around him. The feeling she couldn't trust him felt like a punch in the gut.

"Is that why you were so angry when you woke me up?"

Annoyance flared in his eyes as he shook his head. His voice came out as a grumble when he spoke, "Vysha informed me of the plan for Ekry to protect you. The job she's given me is something any Drykuan could do, and it's infuriating she won't let us swap jobs. I think it's to punish me for visiting you, if I'm honest."

That took her by surprise.

"Were you not supposed to? I assumed she told you to keep an eye on me."

"Quite the opposite, actually," he explained. "She told me to have someone else do it. I just didn't find anyone else. She's not exactly happy about it."

"What does she want you to do?"

The question seemed to jolt Rokoa back into the reality of their situation. Something flashed in his eyes that Raelia wasn't quite able to place. Remorse? Guilt? Before she could figure it out, however, it was gone. Replaced by an icy look she hadn't seen from him since they'd first met.

"It's nothing important," he told her as he stood and pushed his chair back in. "Nothing you need to worry yourself about, at least."

Before she could reply, he turned and headed toward the door. Only stopping in the open frame to say, "I'll see you in there."

Then he was gone.

And she was left alone to process his strange behavior.

⊰✦⊱

"For too long, we have been forced into hiding!" Vysha shouted from where she stood atop the throne, her black boots smudging the surface of the stone seat. "They have killed us! Slaughtered our loved ones!"

The large space was crowded. Zarhaish, Drykuan, and Mark Bearer alike stood shoulder to shoulder, listening with rapt attention to the Red Lady's rallying cry. Some shouted their agreement, punching the air above their heads with an enthusiasm Raelia had rarely seen, at least from the immortal beings.

"Today is the day we take back our right to exist!" she continued. "We take back our right to walk freely among the citizens of Dirythia! Today is the day we avenge our fallen brethren and make the royals pay with their lives!"

Nearly everyone in the cramped audience cheered their approval. It was so loud Raelia had to fight the urge to cover her ears against the noise.

Once the shouts settled, Vysha spoke again, her tone commanding. "I want everyone to spend this morning preparing for our battle ahead. We will attack at dusk. Spend today resting, and preparing your weapons." Her dark eyes found Raelia's in the crowd, holding them with her next words, "Prepare your gifts."

She nodded to the Red Lady, understanding her command. Her gift, she knew, was how Vysha intended to win this battle. Her ability to kill people with her red glow and shield people with the yellow was intricate to the plans they'd gone over in the war councils. No matter how much Raelia hated it.

"We will return here an hour before to portal south," she explained before once again raising her voice to shout, "They may have more in numbers, but we have powers that they can only dream about!"

Once more, the voices cheered together, as if they'd already triumphed. When the shouts quieted, people moved toward the door and the crowd thinned. Raelia was bumped this way and that as she turned to follow the lines of people, but stopped when she heard Vysha shout her name.

The Red Lady's voice was loud as she called across the room, "I'd like a word."

"She wants you to what?!" Nazario nearly shouted. "That doesn't make any sense! Of course you need to be armed! We're going into a war against the most powerful man in the world!"

Raelia couldn't help but smile at her friend's outrage. It mirrored the reaction she had when Vysha made the request.

"She thinks if I'm armed to the teeth, the way everyone else is," she explained again, "it will distract me from keeping the protective barriers up and keeping people safe."

"But what does she expect?" Ayla interjected. "For you to just walk in with no weapons? The anxiety of that would be even worse, wouldn't it? Knowing you could be attacked at any moment and having no way to defend yourself?"

"'That's why Ekry's going to be there,' is what she said when I asked that," Raelia told them, rolling her eyes.

The three of them sat on the sofa in Raelia's living quarters, discussing the morning's events. The plates and utensils from the early lunch they'd just enjoyed sat in their laps or on the small end tables.

"What did you tell her?" Naz asked. "You didn't agree, did you? Ekry's good, but that doesn't mean she can't get distracted with one person while another is coming at you! You need to-"

"I know, I know. Don't worry," Raelia reassured, "I didn't agree to anything. I told her I'd give it some thought."

"And she just accepted that?" Ayla asked, her hazel eyes surprised.

"Surprisingly, yes. She was trying to be... um... nice? Maybe? Something seemed off," she admitted, "but considering there's no way I'm going into war without weapons, I'm trying not to think too hard on it."

Before either of her friends could respond, the door opened. Raelia wasn't surprised to see Rokoa enter the small space, though his eyes widened, seeming surprised to find her with company.

"Oh... uh... Sorry. I thought..." he started, looking nervous.

Raelia had seen the Drykuan worried. She had seen him scared. But nervous? Nervous was a new one. Rokoa's confidence exuded from him like a second skin, as if he knew he was the most capable being in any room — seeing that wall torn down was bizarre.

"Don't be sorry," she told him, deciding in that moment she didn't want to hold on to the betrayal when they were about to head into a battle they might never come out of. "What's up?"

"Could we, uh, could we talk?"

Nazario stood, stretching their arms above their head. "Ayla and I were just getting ready to go, anyway."

"We were?" Ayla asked, looking confused as she stood alongside them.

Chuckling, Naz grabbed her hand and tugged her toward the door, where Rokoa stepped further inside. Their eyes locked onto Raelia's with a knowing look, before swiftly disappearing into the hall.

Without a word, he sat next to her on the couch. He was closer than she expected, their knees touching lightly as he reached for her hand; she felt her muscles tense at the contact.

"I have something for you..."

He pressed Raelia's hand open, facing it upward, while the other rested underneath, holding it gently with his fingertips. With a small wave of his free hand, a heavy, coarse material pushed her knuckles into his palm.

A bag sat in her hand.

It was small, no bigger than the journal Caeda and Blaze had given her for her birthday. The dark navy blue color of the material faded in each corner and Raelia could see a woven strap tucked under the flap that kept the bag closed.

"A satchel?" she asked, confusion evident in her tone.

"It was my father's," Rokoa's voice was quiet and thick with an emotion Raelia had never heard from him before. "I want you to have it."

Her eyes widened at his words. She knew little about the Drykuan's past. Anytime she'd asked anything about it, he always shut her down without a second thought. All he had ever admitted was that he didn't have any family left.

All the air seemed to rush out of her before she was able to force her voice to work again. "Your father's?" she repeated in a hushed tone.

Rokoa nodded, keeping his eyes focused on the bag. "Well, it started that way, at least. His father made it for him when he was young. When he and my mother married, he gave it to her," he explained, quietly. "When they... they... died, this was one of the few things I was allowed to keep."

"Allowed?"

His silver eyes met hers briefly before he looked back at the bag. Ignoring her question, he continued. "They only let me keep it, because they didn't know what it was. If they'd known, they would have destroyed it along with most everything else."

Raelia wasn't sure what to say. Her eyes scraped over the worn material, trying to discern what could make this tiny keepsake worth destroying.

"It's called a *plisheiry*," he explained, releasing her hand and pushing it and the satchel toward her. "It means, 'innermost ample' in the ancient tongue," he chuckled lightly. "They're not common, and I've only ever known Drykuan's to know the word. It appears small, but the inside is expansive and can fit nearly anything."

Eyes widening, Raelia looked from the bag to Rokoa. "Is such a thing possible? How does that... How..." She struggled to wrap her mind around the concept, but it didn't seem possible. Besides, wouldn't a bag that carried anything and everything be too heavy for the bearer to lift? It didn't make sense to her at all.

"You should try it," Rokoa smirked, a hint of his normal self returning as he watched her struggling to understand. "It might be a better place to hide the book you keep shoving under your bed."

His chuckle burst into a bark of laughter at her expression. "You didn't honestly think I didn't know about that?!"

"But... how?!" she demanded, torn between feeling angry and embarrassed.

"Let's just say that my hearing is better than you'd believe."

Chapter 35

After Rokoa left, Raelia took a much needed nap and then packed everything she owned into the small satchel he'd given her. Admittedly, she owned little in Paodra, but she couldn't leave behind the journal her younger siblings had given her on her birthday, nor the hairpin she'd received on the same day from Luella. She also made no qualms about packing the books she'd been hoarding in her room. Specifically, the one Galys gave her about the Indicative Marks. It was the first one shoved in.

When she saw the opening for the bag and looked at the book, she assumed it wouldn't fit. Rokoa had told her, however, that anything could, so she started with just the corner, eyes widening in shock as the small hole seemed to suck the book in. She hadn't even had to stretch the fabric. Surprising her even further, even after the book was in the bag, it wasn't any heavier than it had been before.

Before he left, Rokoa told her he would bring weapons for her to pack in it, and when she woke from her nap, the weapons he promised covered the entire sofa. He'd instructed her to put them all in the bag, but even knowing she had to be armed, she knew it was entirely too much.

She holstered the dagger Rokoa had given her during their training session a few weeks ago. Next to it, she placed a sword with a curved end meant for one handed wielding and then pulled a full quiver of arrows over her head, resting it between her shoulder blades. After that, she shoved a broadsword and small scythe and a few more daggers into the bag and left the rest of the artillery on the sofa with a roll of her eyes for Rokoa's excessiveness.

When she stepped into the hallway, her friends were exiting Ayla's living quarters across the hall. She smiled at them, but the look of worry in Nazario's eyes made it falter.

"Have you seen Galys?" Naz asked in a rush. "I went to look for him last night, but he wasn't in his room, and I didn't see him at the meeting this morning, either."

Ayla took their hand in hers and squeezed reassuringly. "It was hard to see anyone at the meeting, because there were so many people."

The three of them made their way quickly past the common room and up the stairs.

As they stepped into the warm evening sunlight, Naz shook their head. "I... I don't think so..."

"Galys disappears sometimes!" Raelia added. "He loses himself in the library! You told me he disappeared for nearly a week before, just sitting in there reading. With this war," Raelia gestured around to the others in the square, all armed to the teeth, "he's probably been researching battle strategies, or the history of different wars or something like that."

Sighing, Nazario nodded. "Maybe..." they admitted, though they didn't seem convinced.

They fell quiet, following Drykuan's and Mark Bearers alike through the square, toward the throne room. Nerves seemed to get the better of all of them the closer they came to their destination, and Raelia felt her heart pick up its pace.

"Did you pack it all?"

The sudden sound of Rokoa's hushed voice in her ear caused Raelia to jump as her hand fluttered to her chest.

"All?" was the only word she was able to utter in response.

The Drykuan leaned down, putting his lips to her ear once more, as he clarified, "the weapons. Did you pack them all?"

His gift bounced lightly against the side of her hip, and once again Raelia marveled at how lightweight it was. If not for the steady tap it made in response to her movement, she would have forgotten it completely.

Ayla and Nazario looked at the pair with confusion, a smirk appearing on the former's face. Neither of them spoke as Raelia shook her head at Rokoa.

"I told you to pack all of it!" frustration colored his tone, but he kept his voice low.

"I'm sorry... All of it just seemed excessive! I got quite a bit of it though," she lied.

Rokoa grabbed her arm, stopping their progression and turning her body until she faced him. "We're heading into a *war*, Raelia!" He looked like he wanted to scream his irritation at her, but kept his voice low, so only she and her friends could hear. "She wants you there unarmed! I don't know why, but you need as many weapons on you to combat whatever she has planned!"

"Planned?" Ayla's eyes widened. "What would Vysha have planned?!"

Rokoa sighed, his eyes turning cold as he looked at Ayla, though only Raelia seemed to notice. "Nothing. She doesn't have anything planned. There's no reason to think she does," he told them in a voice that was entirely unlike his own. It was forced, and too optimistic, and it made her uncomfortable. "I just want to make sure Raelia is able to protect herself."

Without warning, Rokoa's hand roughly grabbed the small satchel hanging at her side. "Keep this out of sight!" he commanded, his normal gruff voice returning.

The fingers of his free hand were rough against her skin as he lifted the bottom of her shirt just enough to tuck the top of the seemingly empty bag underneath it. Her skin tingled where he touched and she twisted away just as his thumb looped behind her belt and into the waist of her pants.

"Ouch!" Rokoa yelped, bringing his thumb to his lips with a pained look on his face.

"What are you doing?!" Raelia demanded, stepping back from him.

The people pushing past them began to look on, and Rokoa's eyes drifted around, clearly worried about drawing attention.

He raised his hands, as if in surrender, and lowered his voice once more as he stepped closer. "Vysha knows what that is," he told her, pointing at the satchel still partially tucked under her top, as he leaned in to whisper, "She can't know you have it"

Raelia finished tucking the satchel under her clothes just as the three of them walked through the throne room door. She wasn't sure what she expected when they entered, but what she saw clearly wasn't it.

Two large, clustered lines were formed on either side of the room. At the front of each were two massive gaping holes in the once beautiful wooden floor. The holes opened into the very earth, the edges moving and growing wider.

Beside each, separate from the messy lines, stood a Mark Bearer, neither of which Raelia recognized, who knelt, eyes closed with both palms on the floor.

"They are Terraporters," Nazario explained when they saw the questioning look on her face.

Terraportation, she remembered, was a gift granted by the Mark of the Iris. In the book Galys gave her, it detailed the massive portals they were able to create, and how they opened into blackness allowing whoever entered to emerge from a similar hole where the Mark Bearer sent them. It made sense when she peered at the portals, then, that they seemed to open to nothing.

"Where will they-" she began to ask, just as a hush fell over the crowded room.

When she looked up, Vysha entered. Alongside her, stood Dhovina, and a Zarhaish she'd never seen before. The man was taller than both of his companions, but his strong features, and golden eyes were nearly identical to Dhovina, so Raelia wondered if they were related.

"Supreme ruler Yizark and Dhovina will be handling things from this side. I will be going through first," Vysha explained, "and they will oversee the rest of you coming through. Next to each portal," she pointed out two other unfamiliar Zarhaish, "either Sierrina or Mizic will make sure you are adequately armed before coming through."

She fell silent for a moment, looking out into the crowd as if wanting to make sure she had their full attention.

"We will win this battle!" she shouted. "Nothing will stop us!"

Cheers erupted, and Raelia fought the urge to cover her ears.

When the shouts died down, she heard Vysha once more.

"Raelia?! Please come up here," she instructed as she stepped down from the dais. Her eyes were roaming the crowd, but couldn't seem to locate her.

A hand grabbed onto her own, and gave a squeeze.

"See you on the other side," Naz said. "Stay safe."

She looked in their eyes, then shifted to Ayla's. "Protect each other," she offered, before flinging her arms around them both.

She turned away quickly after releasing her friends, and made her way toward the spot she'd seen the Red Lady disappear.

"Ah! There you are!" Vysha exclaimed when she spotted her.

"Was there something you needed before you went through?" Raelia asked.

The Red Lady's gaze raked over her, locking on the sword at her hip. "I see you decided against listening to my request to not arm yourself?" A flash of cold showed in her eyes, and Raelia felt the urge to shrink back. Before she could answer, however, Vysha continued, "I would like you to come through with Ekry and I first. It will be easier to discuss how to move forward on the other side."

She nodded her agreement, and jumped when she realized Ekry appeared beside her. The Drykuan looked grumpy, as she always did, and once again Raelia wondered why Rokoa couldn't be the one with her. She had faith that Ekry *could* do the job, but little faith that she *would*.

"Take my hand," Vysha instructed, releasing her arm, and holding her hand out.

Raelia did so and felt the Red Lady squeeze her hand in a maternal way.

"You don't have to be nervous," she said as they stepped closer to the huge portal in the floor. "This will be over quicker than you think."

Without another word, Vysha jumped, yanking Raelia forward and down into the swirling blackness.

Everyone made it through the portals in only a couple hours. The sun had set by that time, leaving the only light from a few fires someone had started. While she waited, Raelia learned they were in a forest only a few miles from Vairek City, and they'd be using the lake to portal into the large stone walls that surrounded it. The thought of using another portal made her queasy, but she knew she didn't have a choice. This was the plan Vysha set, and she just had to go along with it.

The fire was warm as they waited, but she was eager to get this fight over with so she couldn't seem to relax. Though, when Naz and Ayla showed up with Zayric, it helped quite a bit.

She started to fill them in on everything she'd learned about what would happen next, but before she could finish, Vysha's voice rang above the crowd.

"The city has gone to sleep! Our attack will be unexpected and swift!"

"You need to come with me," Ekry's rough voice said behind her as Vysha continued with her speech. "We can't get separated."

"I want to go through with Naz and Ayla too. I want to protect them," she replied.

"No," the Drykuan said simply. "They've already been given their groups upon arrival." Ekry eyed her friends with an accusing look. "They should be with their groups already."

Without a word of protest, Naz and Ayla shot off in different directions to find where they were supposed to be. Vysha was still jabbering off instructions, but Raelia was too distracted now that her friends were gone to make sense of what she was saying.

Before long, Ekry dragged her to the lake, and there, just as she remembered her, was Zaira, her expression grim, but focused. Her brown hair was tied back in a tight bun at the base of her neck, and she was dressed for battle as the rest of the Mark Bearers.

For Raelia, seeing the petite woman donning a sword and daggers, as well as a large wooden shield, made their situation more real than anything else.

They were really doing this.

They were starting a war against the most powerful man in the world.

Against King Calyx.

Against the Kingdom of Dirythia.

Fear began to bubble in her chest as Zaira raised her hands and the lake began to churn.

Just as in the throne room, a hole in the water appeared. It was small at first, but became wider and larger, until Raelia was certain it could fit at least ten people across it.

Zayric curled up on her shoulders as she watched people crowd around the edge. She felt Ekry's hand grasp her arm tightly as the Drykuan leaned closer. "Not yet."

Four large groups of Mark Bearers and Drykuan's jumped through the portal before Ekry's grip loosened and she shifted to grasp Raelia's hand instead. Without a word, she pulled her, jumping into the vast black hole.

CHAPTER 36

Clashing swords and screams of anger and pain rang out all around them as Raelia and Ekry rose out of the portal. The moonlight above illuminated the vast space, giving everything an ethereal glow. Before Raelia could even react, Ekry yanked her to the side and raced across the battle. With her unimaginable speed, they weaved in and out of the fighters until they were against a wall, ducking behind a bale of hay.

Raelia's heart raced, and her breath hitched in her chest as she pulled her hand from the Drykuan's grasp. "What are you doing?! We have to help them!"

"My orders are to keep you safe, so you can protect our fighters!" Ekry shouted over the din. "So do what you're supp-"

Her voice was cut off as a royal guard ran at them. He screamed as he swung his heavy blade at Ekry, but it took only two swipes of the Drykuan's sword before the man fell to the ground, defeated.

"What are you waiting for?!" Ekry screamed at her. "You have a job to do!"

Raelia nodded resolute and turned her eyes to the crowd in front of her. The square was as wide as the massive tree trunks in Paodra and the fountain they portalled through sat in the center, though she could barely see it beyond the mass of bodies clashing and colliding.

A terrified scream ripped through the night from her left. An unfamiliar Mark Bearer swang her sword, dancing just out of reach of the three guards surrounding her. They closed in, and with a twirl, the woman moved around one blade, but a second caught her, dragging along the edge of her hip.

Blood bloomed where the sword cut and without another thought, Raelia felt a tug on the internal cord connected to her Mark as a surge of power flowed through her. A green glow erupted from her skin as she raised her hand, palm pointed at the three men. One by one, she sent a blast of green light at each of them. Two collapsed, falling unconscious to the ground, but her bolt of light missed the third by only a couple of inches.

The man's dark eyes turned, finding hers across the crowd. He swung his blade at the woman before him, but she danced out of the way once more. A scream of frustration erupted from the guard and as he swung again, his gaze turned back to his original opponent. They continued their battle.

Raelia shot another ball of green light at him, again missing him by only inches. He twisted around, forcing his opponent toward her with every swing.

'He's bringing her this way,' she realized.

She unsheathed her sword, keeping the palm of her other hand pointed toward the guard as she forced out another orb of power in his direction. His face contorted in rage as he ducked around it. The dueling pair were only a few feet from her now, and she raised her sword.

The moment their blades connected, Zayric leapt from her shoulder. Claws extended, mouth open, the kyloxis attacked the man's face as he screamed. A moment later his body became smoke and the guard fell to the ground.

"Thanks!" the other Mark Bearer exclaimed, as she put her hand to the wound on her side.

"Sure..." Raelia said, worried as she saw blood drip between the woman's fingers. "I can help you with that."

Before waiting for a response, Raelia pushed her palm against the wound and focused her light. The green faded into the soft yellow glow of the dandelion and a warmth spread through her as she focused it on where they touched.

It was only a moment before she pulled her hand away, sticky blood squishing between her fingers. The girl looked at her now closed wound and then back at Raelia with awe. She opened her mouth to speak, but before she could utter a word, Ekry appeared at her side, breathing heavily.

"They're moving towards the castle!" she shouted. "We don't have time for this!"

Before she could protest, the Drykuan once again grabbed and dragged her through the fighting crowd. Zayric followed, hurriedly, growling at Ekry the whole way.

She'd been right, the battle moved closer to the gate of the castle, and the blaring sounds of the melee reverberated off of the stone walls around them. The tunneled path to the gate was wide, but much less so than the square they'd started in, causing the mass of fighters to bottleneck and slow their progression. The stench of sweat and blood overwhelmed her senses as bodies pushed against one another. Without releasing her grasp on Raelia's arm, Ekry drove her blade through man after man. The blood leaking from their bodies ran underneath Raelia's feet, causing every step to feel like she'd stepped into a puddle.

Raelia did her best while being dragged behind the Drykuan to shoot bolts of power at soldiers she could see. All of them were so focused on whoever their opponents were, they never saw it coming. Body after body dropped to the ground after her green light hit them.

She also laid a yellow hand on each Mark Bearer and Drykuan she passed. Forcing her protection upon them without asking. By the time they'd made it halfway through the tunnel, it glowed with the soft yellow light only shifting when she'd shoot a bolt of green.

She could feel the shared power draining her, and eventually stopped giving her protection to the others — afraid she would pass out from exertion. Exhaustion called her to sleep, but the adrenaline pumping through her veins kept her moving.

As they neared the large wooden gate leading into the castle grounds, Ekry forced her back against one of the tunnel walls. When Raelia looked up, Royal guards surrounded them, all with swords drawn. The Drykuan paused, breathing heavily and eyeing them maliciously as one man opened his mouth to speak.

"You will kill no more of us tonight, *Beast*," he spat at Ekry.

As the men each raised their swords to swing down against her protector, a surge of fear licked up Raelia's spine. Without even realizing she had done it, she raised her hand and a bolt of red light shot from it, hitting the man who spoke in the chest.

His blue eyes widened with shock, and fear etched itself in his companion's features as the glow stretched out from the spot it struck and tendrils of light reached out for each of them. Within a matter of only a few seconds, all five men glowed a viciously deep red as blood began pouring from every orifice. A few of them opened their mouths to scream, but no sound was heard as one by one they crumpled to the ground.

Ekry's eyes went wide as she turned to Raelia, still pushed against the stone walls. The disbelief in them was clear, but there was an underlying tone of fear that Raelia wasn't surprised by. It was a fear she felt as well. The power she'd just thrown was greater than any she'd wielded before. For one attack to encompass so many men at once? That wasn't like anything she had ever seen.

The crowd around them seemed to move forward, thinning in the tunnel. A familiar voice yelled out in frustration, and Raelia was filled with relief when she saw Nazario's face, even dirtied and twisted in concentration as it was. Her palm glowed a deep red as she aimed it at their opponent, hitting him in the center of his back. This time there were no tendrils, no stretching of her power to other enemies, but the man fell just the same — in a pool of his own blood.

Naz's eyes appeared black from this distance when they found hers. A grateful smile spread across their features as they ran at her.

"You're safe!"

"She won't be for long if we don't keep going," Ekry responded before Raelia could even open her mouth. "Come on!"

This time, the Drykuan didn't grab her, but she followed just the same, and Nazario ran alongside.

A thought occurred to her then and as she continued to follow Ekry she opened the door in her mind, reaching her thoughts out to Ayla.

"Where are you?" she sent through the doorway. *"Naz and I are just heading out of the tunnel toward the gate!"*

For a moment, there wasn't a response, and Raelia felt her heart race. Worry began spreading through her mind as a fire would spread through a bale of hay, until suddenly Ayla's voice echoed in her head.

"I'm... just... about through..."

When her voice disappeared, an image forced its way into her mind. A man was swinging his sword and connected with a sword held by a hand with Ayla's bracer on it's wrist. Raelia searched the mental image and saw the large wooden gate open wide just behind the guard her friend battled.

"It's open!" she yelled as she, Ekry and Naz approached the end of the tunnel.

Neither of them paid her words any mind as they approached the throngs of guards, Drykuan's, and Mark Bearers still fighting.

The end of the tunnel opened into a garden, and from there, the large wooden drawbridge of the castle led to the open wooden gates. She spotted Ayla there, at the end of the drawbridge, only steps away from the boundaries of the entrance.

Raelia's heart jumped at the sight of her friend, fighting against one guard, as another stepped toward her from behind.

"ZAYRIC!" she shouted, just as the fox jumped in front of her. The world twirled around her the instant she made contact. One moment, she rand alongside Ekry and Nazario and the next, her feet landed, solid once more behind the man approaching Ayla.

She didn't hesitate, forcing her sword through his back as he screamed, falling to the ground. Zayric's inky black mist floated to the man in front of Ayla, and soon his screams died just as quickly.

Ayla's wide eyes were terrified when she turned to see Raelia standing there, but before either of them could speak, Zayric's smoke came back, connecting with her and the world swirled again. When her feet hit the ground once more, Ekry's infuriated gaze glowered at her.

The Drykuan grabbed her arm and quickly took off once more. Before making it far, however, a royal guard stumbled into them. The metal of his armor clanged as she bounced off and backward to the ground. The loud sound reverberated in her skull. The stone was hard underneath her, but she had no time to consider the pain it caused before the guard turned around, aiming his sword at her.

She opened her mouth to scream, just as Ekry turned, swinging her blade upward at the neck of the guard. Blood sprayed in every direction from the wound. It splattered Raelia's face and hair. Her clothing and hands. It went in her mouth, nose and eyes as the man's head nearly separated from his body.

There was chaos all around them, but the sound of the melee faded as her heartbeat raced and the sound of rushing blood became the only thing she could still hear. The man's body fell, and she felt both Ekry and Naz pull on her, trying their best to get her to her feet. She was vaguely aware of their voices, shouting for her to stand, but she was frozen. Stuck in a memory.

What was she doing? Why did she agree to this? Why hadn't she gone with Caias when she had the chance? She didn't want this. She didn't want any of it.

Her body trembled, eyes unable to look away from the guard that fell in front of her. The smell of blood and sweat mixed with the scent of the grass and flowers in the garden. The sweet whirling with the bitter churned her stomach. She turned quickly, shifting to her hands and knees as she retched, losing her dinner on the ground below.

A gentle hand touched the top of her head as Naz leaned in to say softly, "You can do this. We have to do this. You *have* to get up."

In her mind, she heard her mother's voice, *'sometimes we have to do the hard thing.'*

Raelia sniffled, but nodded, doing her best to avoid the sick as she stood and looked around. Ekry battled two more guards, and behind them another dozen approached.

"Ekry!" Naz shouted, when they spotted the new group of enemies.

"Get her further ahead!" The Drykuan demanded. "KEEP HER SAFE! I will find you!"

Naz grabbed onto Raelia and dragged her further into the battle, away from the newcomers, their sword in the other hand — ready to fight anyone who got in their way. She unsheathed her own as she scoured the surrounding battle.

Harsh colors glowed all around, as bolts of light shot this way and the next. The singed smell of magic swirled in the air, mixing putridly with the stagnant blend of blood and sweat. She felt bile rise in her throat once more and swallowed it down, refusing to lose control again.

The bodies thickened around them, and her hand slipped from Nazario's grasp. She shoved her shoulder into the back of a guard battling an unfamiliar Drykuan, forcing her way past. The man seemed startled by the sudden shift in his balance, and when his eyes turned to locate the source, his opponent ran their sword through his midsection.

When he fell to the ground, Raelia looked for her friend and suddenly realized they were no longer outside. They passed into the keep and fighters filled the entryway. It amazed her to see how few Royal Guards still stood. The ones that did, faced three, four, or even five opponents. She knew there were other groups around the city, but from where she stood, it seemed the castle had fallen.

Abruptly, Ekry appeared at her side, grabbing her once more and dragging her further in. Instead of hiding, she dragged her up the stairs, stopping halfway up.

As they looked down at the fighting crowd, the Drykuan shouted, "You need to use your gift! You can get them from here!"

Raelia nodded, sheathing her blade once more and raising both of her palms. The light around her glowed a deep rich green, and one by one, she shot her power at the guards in the vicinity, only missing a few times out of the twenty or so shots she sent.

The men fell unconscious in heaps onto the ground. The opponents they'd been battling looked up at her with gratitude before turning to continue fighting.

When the last royal guard fell, shouts from the Mark Bearers and Drykuan's alike rang out in jubilation. The sound bounced off the stone walls, making it feel as if thousands stood in the space instead of only the couple hundred there.

"Well done!" Vysha's voice echoed from the entrance.

Everyone turned to see the Red Lady appear, looking just as pristine as she had at the lake. Raelia found herself wondering if Vysha had even been in the fray at all. Did she really not fight with her people?

Before she could consider it any further, however, the Red Lady's dark eyes found hers on the stairwell. "There is still much to do!"

Her voice was loud, and had Raelia not made eye contact with her, she wouldn't have known the comment was meant for her.

Nodding her understanding, Raelia turned to look up the stairs. No one was coming down, but if what they had discussed in their war meetings was correct. The people they were searching for would be found in the rooms above.

She and Ekry started moving up, when a shout rang out from above. A scuffle sound echoed down the stairs to their ears and suddenly three Drykuan's stood before them at the top. All three wore the draping green cloak Raelia had come to relate to the race, and each held a struggling prisoner.

The prisoner held by the warrior in the middle was easily recognizable. She'd met him more than once on her father's trips to the royal city.

King Calyx's hands were bound behind his back, but it didn't stop him from struggling. His curly black hair was thinning on the top of his head, his beady eyes widened as he looked down at the crowd below. His tunic rubbed against his captors side, causing it to bunch in on itself and lift up, letting his round midsection show underneath.

The Drykuan to the left of the King held a young woman, not much older than Raelia. Her dress was torn, and her blue eyes were frightened. At the sight of the fighters below, she froze in terror, seemingly unable to fight for her freedom any longer. On the opposite side, stood an elderly man. One Raelia had never seen before.

The Drykuan holding the King threw back his hood, and it took everything in Raelia not to gasp as Rokoa's face appeared in its place. His silver eyes were sullen, and he avoided her gaze as he looked down at the crowd. When his voice rang out, his determined tone spoke to Vysha directly.

"The upper levels have been cleared," his deep voice explained. "These three are the last left alive."

A pang shot through her at the thought. Alton's face flashed in her mind's eye, but she shoved it away. Maybe he never made it home? Maybe he's in hiding somewhere?

Vysha stepped through the crowd with a determined gait as she smiled. She walked silently up the stairs all the way to the top stopping in front of the King. Not a sound could be heard while she moved. It seemed as if everyone held their breath, waiting for the Red Lady's next words.

"King Calyx," her voice bounced off the stone walls. "For centuries, your family has slaughtered our kind. They have slaughtered those with the ancient magic running through their veins!" Vysha's voice was venomous, and the rage in her eyes palpable. "But after tonight, the only blood that spills will be yours!"

Celebratory shouts rang out from below in response to her words. Ekry cheered along with the rest, but Raelia kept quiet as she watched Vysha say something to Rokoa, who nodded. The surrounding noise made it impossible for her to hear the words, but something in the woman's eyes sent a shiver down her spine.

"We have won!" Vysha's voice rang above the echoing cheers. "Now is the time for magic to reign!"

The celebratory shouting continued, and while Raelia searched the crowd below for her friends, she suddenly felt Ekry's hand clamp down on her arm.

CHAPTER 37

Vysha stepped down the stairs, eyes on Raelia as she yelled out to her army below.

"Let us tend to our wounded and celebrate our victory with food and drink!"

Raelia pulled her arm, trying to get Ekry to release her grip. A few of the Drykuan's moved to the front of the crowd and led the fighters down the hallway, past the stairs. She pulled once more against Ekry's hold, and once again failed to free herself.

"You don't have to drag me anywhere now, Ekry," Raelia forced a chuckle, trying to keep herself calm. "So, can you let go, please? I want to go find Nazario and Ayla."

"That won't be necessary," Vysha's voice was pointed with a deadly sweetness, Raelia had only heard once before — after she'd released Alton. The Red Lady turned to look at Rokoa and the other two Drykuan's, still standing at the top of the stairs holding their prisoners. "Take them to the dungeon. Keep them separate. Then, Rokoa, I want you to come find us."

It was a long moment before Rokoa nodded his understanding. His eyes locked onto where Ekry's hand held on to Raelia's arm, and he didn't look like he wanted to agree at all. Despite his clear misgivings, however, after a moment of tense silence, he led King Calyx down the stairs, followed by the others.

As he passed Raelia, their eyes met. Shock pulsed through at the pain and worry in his silver orbs, but she shook the concern from her mind as the six people reached the bottom of the stairs and disappeared around the corner.

"Vysha?" Raelia's voice was more timid then she meant it to be. She cleared her throat as she continued in a stronger tone, "What's going on?"

A glitter of humor danced in the woman's dark eyes as she smirked and stepped toward her. "Did you really think I would forgive you for what you've done?" Her tone was amused, but Raelia could hear the venom in her words. "This should have been clean and easy! I should be able to kill the royal's and be done with it, but you let that stupid boy go and now there's still a royal out there!" The woman before her seethed with barely controlled rage, and she no longer seemed amused in any sense of the word.

Fear coursed through her at the look on the Red Lady's face and without thinking, her power glowed on the surface of Raelia's skin. Her entire body shined yellow and she heard a sizzle where Ekry's hand held her arm causing the Drykuan to wince.

"I don't think so," Vysha said sharply as she placed a cold hand on Raelia's neck.

A shudder rolled through her body. Her knees went weak and she suddenly struggled to stay upright as the Dandelion's glow flickered then died out, leaving Raelia confused and dizzy.

"That should give you plenty of time to take her where we discussed. I'll be there after I make an appearance in the great hall."

Without another word to Raelia, Vysha turned sharply and marched down the stairs. When she was out of sight, Ekry pulled at her arm, dragging her up the rest of the way.

"Where are you taking me?" Raelia demanded, still pulling against the Drykuan's vice like grip. "Why are you doing this?!"

Her answering snigger was derisive. "You've been a pain in Vysha's side since day one. It's about time you get what you deserve!"

That was all she said, as she dragged Raelia. She pulled and kicked against Ekry's hold as she dragged her down the hall, but she couldn't get away. She fought the urge to scream as Ekry threw her into a small room.

As the Drykuan disappeared behind the wooden door, latching it from the other side, Raelia took in her surroundings. There wasn't much in the room. A couple of tapestries hung on opposite walls, and what could only be described as a throne sat in front of three large arched windows. A couple of wooden benches sat on either side of the door she'd been thrown through, and tall vases with some sort of long, green leaves sticking out the top in each corner.

She froze when she laid her eyes on the fourth vase, noticing then that there was a second door. Raelia rushed to it, pulling and pushing on it as hard as she could, but it didn't budge.

Sighing, she turned and walked to the windows, looking out onto the green grass of the grounds around the castle. None of the windows opened, but when she noticed how close the ground below was, she realized what she had to do.

Racing to the vase closest to her, Raelia dumped the leaves out of the top and hurried back to the window. It only took one hit for the glass to shatter. Realizing she wouldn't be able to lift herself up on the jagged broken pieces, she ran to the tapestry. Using her dagger, she hacked at the fabric until she could detach a large enough piece to protect herself.

Raelia threw the rectangle of fabric over the edge of the jagged glass and hoisted herself up into the window frame.

"Not going to happen, Dandelion!" Ekry's voice rang out from behind her, and in the next second, Raelia felt hands on both her arms, pulling her roughly back into the small room.

She struggled against her and tried to bring her power to the surface, but she couldn't find it. She couldn't even feel a hint of the power she'd grown so reliant upon. She screamed in frustration when she couldn't free of Ekry's grip.

"Look what you've done to my new home," Vysha's voice was smooth and deadly when she spoke. She moved around Raelia's struggling form in a half circle, positioning herself on the throne-like chair in front of the windows. Ekry threw her down, leaving her to sit on her hands and knees in fear. The Red Lady looked down at Raelia as a hawk would a mouse — like prey that would soon be devoured.

"Do you know the history of the Dandelion?" Vysha asked.

The atmosphere in the room was tense, and Raelia kept her eyes on the stone bricks of the floor as she shook her head. Vysha stood. Slowly, she paced back and forth in front of the makeshift throne, eyes never leaving Raelia's cowering form.

"I guess I shouldn't be surprised," came the woman's response. "Not much is known about us, after all. Though, I did expect you to know a bit more than most, what with the hours you spent in the library. Did you really learn nothing?"

When silence fell, Raelia pushed herself back, sitting on her feet as she looked at Vysha. She had considered this woman her friend. Her mentor even. How had it come to this?

"I know we have the gift of protection."

"Yes. The gift of protection. The gift to protect ourselves and our loved ones," came her response, in a malicious tone as a smirk spread across her face. "And yet..."

Vysha gave a curt nod to someone out of Raelia's sight, and footsteps echoed off the stone walls. The door behind her opened and she fought the urge to turn around. A muffled voice and scuffling feet sounded, breaking her resolve.

Her blood ran cold as her gaze connected with a pair of familiar golden brown eyes. The man had a mop of auburn hair on his head. Hair that matched her own.

"Papa?" her voice croaked, heavy with emotion. Tears pricked in the corner of her eyes at the sight of him. He was dangerously thin, and his hair stuck out at all different angles. Face unshaven, clothes filthy and tattered, he looked at her as if she was the first ray of sunshine after the longest night.

"And yet you weren't able to protect your own father," Vysha said as she walked to where Ekry stood holding Eloi.

Her father looked as if a strong breeze would blow him off his feet, swaying as tears welled in his eyes. Vysha squeezed his lips into a pucker. He winced in pain as her nails dug into his skin.

"Let him go!" Raelia yelled, struggling to keep her emotions under control. "You-You've had him all this time?!" A sudden realization hit her and she had to choke back a sob. "This has nothing to do with Alton!" she accused. "My father has been missing since long before I went back to Frayis!"

The Red Lady released Eloi's face as a smirk appeared on her face and she began to circle around Raelia like a vulture would its prey.

"I was worried when Rokoa put you in that specific cell. I think he assumed you'd figure out who your neighbor was."

Raelia's throat went dry. Her eyes never left her father's. The man she'd shared her food with. The one that struggled to speak and didn't have a clue where he was or why. It was him? Even knowing the magic of the dungeon warped their voices, she couldn't understand how she didn't recognize his voice.

"Papa..." she whispered to herself. Heart aching as she watched him struggle to stay standing and yet pulling against Ekry's hold with the little strength he possessed.

His voice was barely a whisper — his normal baritone gone in the wheezing sound, "Raelia..."

The pain in his voice shot a rage down Raelia's spine such as she had never known. A tearing pain shot through her Mark and a red glow burst from her skin. She wasted no time raising her palm, and aiming it at Ekry.

Vysha's eyes went wide, seeming shocked at Raelia's gift appearing. She ran at an unnatural speed to Raelia and again, put her cold hand on Raelia's neck. The same shudder ran through her body and weakness overtook her as her glow flickered out. She fell to her knees before looking up at the Red Lady with tears in her eyes. "Why are you doing this, Vysha? What do you want from me? I thought-"

"Thought what? That we were friends? That I *cared* for you?" she spat. Her black eyes dangerous as she continued in a dark tone, "I have a proposition for you, *Aldaehima*."

'*Aldaehima*'. The word now sounded like a curse on Vysha's lips, and it made Raelia's skin crawl.

"What proposition? What do you want from me?!"

"Our little cleansing sessions. Do you remember them?"

Raelia's eyes followed Vysha's pacing form as she nodded. How could she forget?

"Those sessions have prepared you for the next step in a plan I have been putting together for the last two centuries. I want your word that you will cooperate and then I will release him."

"Cooperate how?" Raelia asked. Those sessions had been brutal, and she couldn't imagine what an extension of them would look like.

"Does it matter?" Vysha asked. "If you do as I say, your father will go free. Isn't that what's important?"

Raelia looked at her father — her kind, intelligent, loving father. He shook his head at her. She could see the plea in his eyes, begging her to not agree. But Vysha was right. If it meant saving her father's life, the answer was a moot point and it wasn't exactly like she could fight back with whatever Vysha was doing to her powers.

"No. It doesn't matter," she admitted in defeat. "Release him and I'll do whatever you need me to do."

"No!" Eloi gasped out in his broken voice. He pulled weakly against Ekry's grasp and the desperation in his eyes brought tears to Raelia's.

"Can I please just-just-" she started, trying to hold back the sob building in her chest.

"Just what?" came Vysha's response. Her tone was cruel and amused, as if she was enjoying every second of their suffering.

"Please, just let me go to him..." Raelia's eyes were on her father's as she felt a tear escape down her cheek.

Vysha laughed, loud and vicious. "Go to him? Maybe I would have given you that courtesy before you took my chance at a clean victory! Maybe if you hadn't let that wretched Prince escape!"

Before she could respond, the door behind Ekry opened, drawing her eyes from the Red Lady. Stepping aside, dragging Eloi with her, she revealed a forlorn Rokoa standing in the doorway.

"You asked me to find you?" he asked. His silver eyes stared directly at Vysha, seemingly oblivious to the others in the room.

"Yes, Rokoa. Please, come in," Vysha nodded, gesturing into the small room. "I don't think you've met Eloi Kesby. Raelia's father."

The Drykuan's pale face became even paler at the sight of Raelia's father. Shutting the door behind him, he stepped in further and his silver eyes shifted to Raelia's. The emotion she saw there was something she didn't expect. It was raw and remorseful.

As he turned his eyes back to Vysha, Raelia realized he'd known. He'd known her father was in the dungeon. He'd known he was the one next to her cell. He'd known and he let her go on believing that her father was missing... that Caias would find him.

Her mind whirled with emotions. She trusted him. After everything that happened with Alton, she was hurt, but it was nothing in comparison to the agonizing betrayal she felt now.

"You..." she seethed, bringing everyone's eyes back to her. "You *KNEW?!*" she screamed. "You were supposed to be my friend!"

"Raelia, I-"

"*Aldaehima*, you can't blame Rokoa," Vysha interrupted. "He only found out a couple weeks ago. Besides, he's never been your friend. Rokoa here has been my minion for nearly a century. Did you really think he'd return my trust in him with disloyalty?" she walked up to him, placing a hand on his shoulder as she clicked her tongue in disappointment. "No, child, you saw what I told him to make you see."

Raelia's eyes found his, and something flashed there, but it was gone so quick that she wondered if she imagined it. She shook her head, not wanting to believe the words. Rokoa was her friend. She didn't imagine it. She knew it couldn't have all been an act. Could it?

"Is-is that true?" Her voice was weak. She felt defeated as she watched him.

Pushing his shoulders back and tightening his jaw, he nodded. "I did as ordered."

The room fell silent as Raelia swayed on the spot, watching someone she trusted more than almost anyone else in Paodra. Sure, she'd

questioned that trust before she'd released Alton, but she thought...
she thought...

"I thought you were my friend."

Vysha cackled, joined by Ekry near the door. "Naive child," she said,
shaking her head.

Raelia's eyes found her father's, doing her best to tune out the
sadistic laughter. She tried her best to communicate with him that
she was going to get them out of this. Whether or not he understood
her, she couldn't be sure, but he didn't break eye contact for even a
moment.

It suddenly hit her, she could communicate with someone outside
of this room. She searched her mind, finding the door that connected
her to Ayla and opened it.

"Ayla! Are you there?" she shouted out the doorway. *"Ayla! I need
help! Please! Are you there?"*

"Take them to the dungeon," Vysha's voice broke through her
thoughts. "Keep them separated."

⊰••━━━━━••⊱

Two days had passed since Ekry threw Raelia into the small cell in
the castle dungeon. It was just as filthy and musty as the one in Paodra,
but this one, at least, had a small cot a foot above the cold stone floor.

No one came to visit her. The only time anyone appeared was to
slide a feeble meal of mushy peas and some kind of bread under a flap
on the base of the door. The first night there'd been a glass of water. On
the second night, however, there wasn't anything to drink, and Raelia

cursed herself for being so quick to guzzle down what she'd been given the night before.

Vysha instructed Ekry to keep Raelia and Eloi separated, and she'd followed her instructions to the letter. Even when Raelia called out for him, her father gave no reply. The idea of him rotting away in some cell all by himself was agonizing, and to think he'd already been doing that for weeks shattered her already broken heart.

Through the first day, she continued to call for Ayla in her mind, but no response ever came, and by the second day she had given up trying. Knowing the battle they just fought through, worry for her friend began to overwhelm her. Between that and her fear for her father and what Vysha had planned for her, she was riddled with anxiety, and found herself pacing more than she ever had in her life.

On the third day, she woke to the clatter of the lock on her door being twisted open. The screeching of the rusty metal echoed off the stone walls, and when the door opened, Rokoa stood in front of her with a blank expression.

"We've been ordered to bring you to Vysha," he explained flatly.

Briefly, confusion flickered across Raelia's face, until Ekry followed him in and she understood why he said 'we'.

The Drykuan's approached her from either side, each grabbing an arm as they dragged her from the small cell. Ekry's grip was vice-like, so painful Raelia was certain there would be a hand shaped bruise when she released her.

"Wh-where are we going?" Raelia croaked out, her throat achy from lack of use.

"Vysha wants to see you," was all Rokoa answered.

She looked up at him — the man she thought was her friend — but he avoided her gaze. She'd have given anything to see the expression on his face, but it was unreadable from this angle.

"Rokoa?" she called timidly, knowing she couldn't say what she really wanted to say with Ekry in earshot. "Was any of it real?" she asked.

His answering silence was painful. Sorrow flooded her heart and she looked to the floor, suddenly seeming very interested in the stones under her feet.

A large hand suddenly grabbed her hip. Rokoa's hand. She peeked up at him, but his expression was still unreadable and he stared straight forward as if nothing happened. His hand squeezed, digging his fingers into her side, before deftly slipping the tips of his fingers into the waistband of her pants. She stifled a gasp as she felt him pull at a piece of fabric, causing the satchel that had been tucked under her clothing shift.

She had completely forgotten about it.

He told her to keep it secret — to not let Vysha know she had it. Did he know she would need it? Had he known that this was Vysha's plan all along?

There wasn't much time to think on it before they turned and stepped forward into a lavishly decorated bed chamber. The walls were tall and draped in a powder blue fabric. A four poster bed stood against the wall between two long and narrow windows. A sheer white fabric created a canopy between the four posts and a curtain at the end of the bed.

Ekry and Rokoa released Raelia's arms, and without another word, disappeared behind the door they'd come through, slamming it shut behind themselves. The noise of it reverberated off the walls and caused her to jump.

She took a mental note of her surroundings, and realized the windows were too high to jump from. There was no other door that she could see, and when she tried to open the one they'd left through, someone stood in the way.

"Today is not the day you'll be escaping, *Dandelion*," came Ekry's voice from the other side, before she shoved the wooden door back in its place with a loud click.

Raelia paced around the lavishly decorated room, periodically stopping to search it for some clue of how to get out of it without using the door. She pondered on using the weapons she had in the satchel, still hidden under her clothes, but upon realizing she'd never make it from here to the dungeon to find her father and back out again, let it remain hidden.

Finding herself called to the windows, once she stopped searching for something she knew would never present itself, she stared out of them — watching birds fly across the sky and the wind blow the leaves on the trees. She could see familiar faces in the fields below, but as the windows didn't open, she didn't bother calling for them.

It wasn't until she heard voices in the hallway that she moved from her perch on the windowsill. Creeping over to the wooden door that kept her from freedom. It was Ekry's muffled voice she heard first.

"I don't understand why she doesn't just kill the petulant brat," the Drykuan was saying. "She has no use for her!"

"Vysha wants her power," came Rokoa's answering baritone. "She has to be alive for the *Veleshein Tiago*."

"But she *is* a Dandelion! Why does she need this little girl's power? There's no-"

"Every Dandelion manifests differently," he interrupted in an emotionless voice. "She wants the extra gifts Raelia possesses. I think she also believes her to have an elemental Mark. Besides, it's not our duty to ask questions."

"But she *eats* their *skin*!"

Ekry's loud cry of disgust earned her a hurried "Shh!" from Rokoa. "She eats their *Marks*. That's where the magic lies, so as unfortunate as it is, she has to for the *Veleshein Tiago* to work properly."

Raelia felt her mouth fall open, and her stomach twisted in disgust at what she heard, but she kept her ear pressed against the door as the pair continued.

"Do you think each of them has a different flavor?" Ekry laughed cruelly. "I bet that Galys guy tasted like a book or paper or even ink!"

As Ekry continued to laugh, Raelia's eyes filled with tears. Galys? Images of her friend flashed in her mind's eye. The fir flower on his cheek, underneath his rich brown eyes. His dark, frizzy hair that was always disheveled, no matter how hard he tried to tie it back. How could Galys be... be...

She stepped away from the door, mouth agape as she ran over the conversation she'd had with Ayla and Nazario only a few days before. Naz had been worried about Galys. They hadn't seen him, and she and Ayla brushed them off. Even knowing they had been worried about Vysha doing something to Mark Bearers. Why did they brush their concerns aside? Why hadn't they taken Naz seriously?

Raelia couldn't listen anymore. She sat on the floor against the ornately decorated bed and pulled her knees to her chest, squeezing them tightly. The world seemed to spin around her. A horrified sob built up in her chest, and tears welled in her eyes, but she choked it down and wiped them furiously before they could fall.

"I'm sorry for making you wait."

Vysha's voice was sickeningly sweet and startled her, causing her to jump to her feet. A lick of fear ran up her spine as she looked at the Red Lady standing in the doorway.

Rokoa and Ekry followed her into the room, the latter shutting the door behind herself.

"My dear," Vysha started when she noticed the stricken look on Raelia's face, "whatever is the matter?"

She did her best to regain her composure, fighting to make her expression into one of indifference as she shook her head.

"I see you're finally understanding the gravity of your situation," Vysha cooed as a malicious smirk spread across her features. "It is time to call in your debt."

"Wh-what-what do you mean?" Raelia's voice was weak, her fear evident in every word as she stepped back, pressing her legs against the bed.

"I told you your father would go free if you did as I said, and I'm here to tell you what I want you to do."

"What do you want?"

Vysha reached a hand into her pocket, pulling out a small vial filled with a deep red liquid. "I want you to drink this," she explained, extending the vial to Raelia.

"What is it?" she asked, as she took it from her. Lifting it into the air, Raelia looked closely at the contents. Grainy black swirls mixed with the deep red. It seemed violent to her, though she wondered if that was only because of her current predicament.

She shifted her gaze to Vysha who continued to look expectantly at her. "You may wish to lay down before you drink it."

"What is it?" she repeated.

"It will help you sleep, *Aldaehima*," the Red Lady explained, though something in her tone hinted it wasn't the full truth. "That is all."

"And all I have to do is drink this and you'll let my father go free?"

Vysha nodded.

"What will happen to me when I wake up? Will you let me go free too?"

"That's not a discussion I am prepared to have at this moment," she replied, before gesturing to the bed once more. "It's time to lie down, *Aldaehima.*"

Raelia did as she was told. She felt herself slowly sink into the plush bed as she laid her head onto the pillow and lifted the tiny bottle once more to peer at the contents.

"And you'll let my father go?"

Once again, Vysha nodded, watching her with expectant eyes.

Her stomach twisted into knots as she popped the cork from the vial and held it to the light. Terror flooded through her and she closed her eyes. Images of her mother, Caeda and Blaze flashed in her mind. She didn't want to die, but thought it would be okay if she saw them again. The idea of being able to hug her mother once more comforted her as she watched the black grains twirl in the red liquid. In the next moment, she brought the vial to her lips – downing the entire bottle in one gulp.

The liquid was bitter, but not unpleasant. She couldn't feel the tiny grains she'd seen, but that was the least of her concern as her hand fell heavily to the bed. The room seemed to vibrate, and her body became so heavy she couldn't even lift a finger.

Blinking slowly, Raelia's heart rate picked up its speed in panic at what she'd just done. She tried to fight the heaviness of her eyelids, but soon her thoughts became muddled and the world around her faded to black.

Chapter 38
Rokoa

"**Y**ou asked me to find you?"

Rokoa's voice was plain, emotionless as he stepped into the room. It was clear he had interrupted something, but he gave it no mind as he looked at Vysha.

"Yes, Rokoa. Please, come in," the woman replied. "I don't think you've met Eloi Kesby. Raelia's father."

His silver eyes flicked to his right where Ekry held a thin, disheveled red haired man, and he felt the blood drain from his face.

Closing the door behind himself, Rokoa stepped into the room, glancing at Raelia as he did so. It took him a moment to get his emotions in check, and the pain and rage he saw in hers made it take even longer.

"You...You *KNEW?!*" she screamed at him. The hate in her words and her tone shattered his heart. "You were supposed to be my friend!"

"Raelia, I-"

"*Aldaehima*, you can't blame Rokoa. He only found out a couple weeks ago," Vysha interrupted. "Besides, he's never been your friend. Rokoa here has been my minion for nearly a century," she explained, twisting the knife of his betrayal even deeper. "Did you really think he'd return my trust in him with disloyalty? No, child, you saw what I told him to make you see."

Emotion built up in him, but he shoved it down, just as Raelia's eyes connected with his.

"Is-is that true?"

Her voice sounded broken, defeated. It took every ounce of will power he possessed to shut down his feelings, letting his eyes go blank as he stood up taller and replied, "I did as ordered."

Raelia stared at him for a moment, a war of emotions building up in her jade green eyes — the eyes that held such power over him.

"I thought you were my friend," she said, every syllable sounding like it broke her more.

Vysha and Ekry's answering laughter was the only thing that kept him from running to her.

'Stick to the plan,' he reminded himself. 'Stick to the plan.'

He repeated it over and over in his mind, doing his best to keep his willpower in place and tune out any other sounds.

And then they were gone.

He stared at the spot where Ekry disappeared with the pair out the door, completely oblivious to Vysha watching him from behind.

"Do I need to be concerned, Rokoa?"

His name on her lips jolted him out of his daze, and he turned to face the woman.

"Concerned?"

"You've grown a soft spot for the girl," Vysha observed. "Do I need to be concerned about it, or do you have it under control?"

"I..." he straightened, looking down at her defiantly. "There is nothing to be concerned about. My loyalty belongs to you."

"Good. Make sure you don't forget it."

Two days later, Vysha gathered the citizens of Vairek City in the main square. Rokoa knew it was planned, and yet Vysha left out one minor detail — something he hadn't been expecting so soon.

"Here to convey what will happen if you don't accept this new change in rulership is King Calyx, Princess Adelaine, and Royal Advisor Remus."

Sweeping her hand to gesture behind her, Rokoa turned around to see Ekry, and two others dragging out the struggling prisoners. With a wave of her other hand, gallows appeared next to the platform she stood on. A large stage setting, with two nooses hanging down.

Vysha turned back to the crowd and looked for descension, waiting for any man, woman, or child to speak out against what was about to happen to their King. She didn't have to wait long.

"We will never bow to you, witch!" a pudgy, balding man shouted, much to the dismay of his wife who attempted to shush him with tears in her eyes.

With a nod of her head, two Drykuan's entered the crowd, slitting the throats of them both. There was no remorse in their eyes when they stepped back out of the crowd, but the tactic worked — no one else spoke out.

Ekry stepped up onto the gallows that Vysha had provided, followed by Privina, who was leading the Royal Advisor. It only took a second for the ropes to be put around their necks, but Vysha wasn't ready for them to die quite yet.

She stepped up onto the stage and stood in front of the King with a wicked grin. Her voice was low, so the crowd below wouldn't hear her, but having the enhanced hearing of a Drykuan, Rokoa heard every word.

"You may be wondering why your daughter doesn't stand next to you with a rope around her neck?" Vysha's voice tone was malicious and playful. "Well, you see, we're recreating a scene that Nikolai set five hundred years ago. Maybe you remember it?"

Terror filled Calyx's eyes and his mouth opened to speak, but no sound came out as the color drained from his face.

"I am disappointed your son wasn't here to take part in it, so Remus here will take his place," she explained, "but your daughter is going to be featured in the best part."

"No..." Calyx gasped out.

"Once she has watched you hang to death, I will lead this crowd down to the beach, where pretty little Adelaine will be burned at the stake."

"No!" the King shouted, regaining his voice, "She is innocent. Please! Put me in her place!"

"INNOCENT?" Vysha screamed, drawing the attention of every person in the crowd. "My Adric was innocent! He was only a baby and Nikolai watched from that damned balcony as the skin melted from his bones! You should be *thanking* me!" she insisted, before lowering her voice again, the crowd was left wondering, "At least you don't have to watch as she burns alive!"

Without another word, Vysha stepped over and pulled the lever, dropping the platform beneath both of the men. The sickening crack of their necks told Rokoa it had been a quick death for both of them. They were lucky.

As Vysha turned to the crowd, explaining their next destination, Rokoa forced the emotions raging within him down. He had mastered them before, why was it so hard now? Why couldn't he go back to the emotionless shell he'd been for the last millennia?

An image of Raelia smiling in the center of the forest clearing where they trained flashed in his mind. He shoved it away as Vysha came to him with a smug grin. She was loving every second of this. It was disgusting.

"I would like you to stay behind and tend to that Ayla girl. Give her more of the tonic. I can't have her waking until after I've dealt with Raelia."

Rokoa nodded, grateful he didn't have to witness the next step in the woman's revenge. He turned to walk away. However, Vysha placed a hand on his arm, stopping him.

"Nazario will be with her. Tell them nothing of Raelia's whereabouts."

Silently, he nodded once more, turned around and headed into the castle.

"Where *is* she?!" Nazario demanded when they saw Rokoa walk through the door. "And don't tell me she died in battle, because I know she was with Ekry on those stairs when Vysha declared the victory!"

That took him by surprise. "Who said she was dead?"

"Ekry."

That explained it. Ekry hated Raelia since day one. Of course she'd say that.

"She's alive."

"Then why-"

"Listen. There isn't much time," Rokoa held up the small vial of the tonic. "Vysha sent me to give this to Ayla."

"It looks like the same stuff Ekry gave her last night."

"It's keeping her from waking up."

"No... What?" Naz's confusion was clear, but even more than that, betrayal raged in their eyes. "Why would Ekry do that?"

"Because Vysha doesn't want Ayla to be able to communicate with Raelia."

Their eyes widened. "I don't-"

"Have you ever heard of the *Veleshein Tiago*?"

Terror drained the color from their cheeks as they asked, "Why would Vysha need to do that?! She's already got Dandelion powers..."

"I don't have time to explain, but I will not let Raelia be hurt. I want you to prepare to run at the drop of a-"

"But Ayla! I can't leave her here! Raelia wouldn't leave her here!"

"Ayla will be going too. If I don't give this to her now, she should wake by tomorrow," Rokoa explained. "It is *imperative* she doesn't communicate with Raelia though, so I'm leaving you in charge of making sure she doesn't."

Nazario nodded their understanding, and Rokoa tucked the tonic back in his pocket before striding back out the door.

⁂

The following morning, just after sunrise, Ekry came to collect him. She didn't tell him where they were headed, but it became obvious as they continued down flight after flight of stone steps.

"Who are we bringing up from the dungeon?" Rokoa asked, afraid he already knew the answer.

"Who do you think?" Ekry scoffed. "You really need to get your head in the right place. I'm not the only one that sees your weak spot for the girl and when Vysha lifts the curse and Yizark and Dhovina get here, you're going to pay for it."

He remained silent and kept his eyes looking straight ahead. Choosing not to deny or admit to the accusation.

She eyed him suspiciously, but didn't say anything else as they stopped in front of a cell. Rokoa peeked in, blocking all but a sliver of light that lit up a tuft of short red hair.

Eloi looked worse than he had only a few days ago. Tears had tracked lines in the dirt on his face, leaving his cheeks streaked and giving him an even more disheveled appearance.

"What are we doing here?" he asked, looking at Ekry.

She jerked her head and continued to walk down the long corridor of cell doors. As they turned a corner into another stretch of the dungeon's hall, she replied, "Vysha wanted you to know where he was. I think she intends for you to execute him once Raelia is out of the way."

His eyes widened. "I thought she was going to let him go?"

Ekry just laughed, as if that was the dumbest thing he'd ever said, and, if he was honest with himself, it probably was.

They turned one more corner, this time stopping in front of the first door they came to. She held out a key, which he took and shoved in the lock.

When he opened the door, it took effort to force the rusty lock to finally squeal open.

Raelia was filthy, covered in grime and dried blood. Her green eyes were darker than he'd ever seen them before. She looked surprised to see him, and she waited for him to speak.

"We've been ordered to bring you to Vysha," he told her, forcing all emotion from his tone.

The confusion was clear on her face, but disappeared quickly and a few moments later, they were walking through the maze of tunnels to get out of the dungeon, the Drykuan's on either side of the prisoner.

"Wh-where are we going?" Raelia's voice sounded rough, as if it was painful to speak.

Rokoa kept his gaze straight ahead, knowing his resolve wasn't strong enough to chance a glance at her.

"Vysha wants to see you."

She fell silent for a few moments and he could feel her eyes on him, burning every inch they raked over.

"Rokoa? Was any of it real?"

He wanted to shout to her that of course it was real! Of course he was her friend and if he was honest, he wanted far more than friendship! If he knew it wouldn't doom them both, he would have knocked Ekry unconscious and ran with Raelia right then and there!

If only he could tell her everything... He wished so desperately he could, but he knew silence was the only way to truly save her.

A sudden thought presented itself, and before he could stop, his free hand shot to Raelia's hip. Slipping two fingers into the waistband of her pants, he gripped the strap of the satchel he'd given her. Silently, he begged her to remember that it was still there. That he had given it to her. That he gave her something more precious to him than anything else he'd ever owned. In his mind, he begged her to understand it was real and the satchel she still wore at her hip proved it.

They turned one last corner, and then dumped Raelia in some lavishly decorated room. Ekry slammed the door behind herself, but stood in front of it. She had obviously been told to guard it until Vysha arrived.

A few minutes later, the door squeaked and bumped into Ekry. He heard her mutter a vague threat to Raelia, but didn't pay attention to what she said. His mind was too focused on getting Raelia to understand the gravity of her situation. He had to make her see it. How though?

He leaned against the wall, mind completely lost in thought. He could hear Raelia moving things around in the room and pacing back and forth. He knew she must be looking for a way out, but he also knew she wouldn't find one. He hoped she didn't use the weapons in the satchel to force her way through them. She'd never make it, and then his plan would all be for naught.

Ekry watched him carefully, as if trying to read what was going on in his mind. It wasn't until Raelia stopped shuffling around in the room that Rokoa even noticed the other Drykuan was looking at him.

When his gaze connected with hers, she opened her mouth to speak, but closed it. Only a moment later however, her voice rang out, "Life is about to get so much easier once this is all over with! That girl has been more trouble than she's ever been worth! "

"You may be right," he allowed, nodding.

Rokoa heard Raelia's shuffling feet and realized she was listening at the door. He realized this was the solution to his problem. This is how he made Raelia understand.

"I don't understand why she doesn't just kill the petulant brat! She has no use for her!" Ekry continued, a look of irritation taking over her features.

"Vysha wants her power," Rokoa reminded her, making sure his voice was loud enough for Raelia to hear on the other side of the thick wood. "She has to be alive for the *Veleshein Tiago*."

"But she *is* a Dandelion, so why does she need this little girl's power? There's no-"

"Every Dandelion manifests differently," he interrupted. "She wants the extra gifts Raelia possesses. I think she also believes her to have an elemental Mark. Besides, it's not our duty to ask questions."

"But she *eats* their *skin*!"

He feigned a look of panic as he shushed Ekry. "She eats their *Marks*. That's where the magic lies, so as unfortunate as it is, she has to for the *Veleshein Tiago* to work properly."

"Do you think each of them has a different flavor?" Ekry laughed. "I bet that Galys guy tasted like a book or paper or even ink!"

Rokoa couldn't help the grimace of disgust, and was thankful Ekry thought he was agreeing with her.

"I wonder what Raelia would taste like?" she continued. Her eyes narrowed at him. "I bet you'd know better than anyone else," she laughed.

Once again, choosing not to respond, he leaned back against his place on the wall. Thankfully, before Ekry pushed him for a response, Vysha appeared in front of them.

"Is she in there?"

They both nodded in response.

"Excellent," Vysha's answering smile was wicked, and she looked at him expectantly.

He forced a matching grin. "You have her in a corner. She'll do whatever you say now."

The woman nodded excitedly before shifting past Ekry and opening the door. They both followed her in, and waited.

It was hard for Rokoa to keep quiet during the short exchange between Raelia and Vysha, and even more difficult to keep a passive expression. Somehow he managed, however, and soon, Raelia did as told.

Vysha stepped forward when the girl's eyes stopped blinking and peered down at her face. "She's out. We'll begin the ritual at sunset."

Relief washed over him at her words, but Rokoa kept his face emotionless.

"Ekry, I want you to keep watch at the door. Make sure no one enters this room before sunset."

Ekry nodded, and left the room as Vysha turned to him.

"Did she show you where the father is being held?"

Rokoa nodded.

"Good. I want you to bring him to me when we begin the ritual. I will use his blood to bind hers to mine when you execute him."

Rokoa nodded once more.

"Until then, I want you to check on the other Mark Bearers. Make sure they believe Raelia is dead," she continued. "Let me know if anyone is doubting it."

"Consider it done."

Without another word, Vysha hurried out the door, shutting it behind herself. Rokoa looked at Raelia's sleeping form wistfully for a moment before following her. He said nothing to Ekry as he passed. He had limited time, and he wouldn't waste it.

The first stop he made was to Ayla's bedside. Nazario still sat with her and their eyes were accusing when Rokoa walked in.

"You said she'd wake up!" they accused.

"She will!" he promised. "In a couple hours, at most. When she does, get her food and drink. Be in the stables at high noon and bring anything you want to take with you. You won't be returning."

After leaving Nazario, Rokoa hurried to the room he claimed for himself. It was a large space, with an enormous tapestry hanging from the wall. The picture it depicted was one of the Red Lady of legend. It looked down at the murderous light on a beach surrounded by bodies.

He moved to it quickly, ducking behind and opening the door it hid from view. Inside, a young man sat on a cot, head in his hands as his silky, dark blonde curls fell over his fingertips, hiding his face.

As he entered, the man's soft brown eyes found Rokoa's silver. The sadness and grief he saw there pulled more emotion from him than he wanted to admit.

"You're leaving today," he told the young man. "Is there anything you want me to get for you?"

"Oh, *now* you want to help me?" The Prince asked with a dark venom. "Now that my father and sister are dead? You told me you'd help me to free them!"

Rokoa sighed. "I'm sorry. I... I wasn't expecting it so soon."

Alton turned his head, and Rokoa could hear a small sniffle. "I can't believe they're gone..."

The rage in the Prince's tone seemed to have vanished, leaving only sorrow. Rokoa couldn't understand why he'd had let his anger go so quickly, but he was thankful for it. They didn't have time to argue.

"Do you remember the ritual I told you about when I found you before the battle?"

"Of course. You said you needed my help to prevent it," Alton answered, confused. "You told me it's the only reason you were letting me live, how could I forget?"

"Vysha started the process. Raelia has consumed the elixir to prepare her body."

"WHAT?!" Alton jumped up, his eyes narrowing. "What are we going to do?!"

"This was the plan from the beginning! Calm down!" Rokoa bellowed. "I brought Raelia's horse from Paodra with the Drykuan steeds. He's in the stables. Is her other horse here?"

Alton nodded.

"Good. At high noon, you and a few others will be leaving with her and you're going to go south."

"South?"

"To the Taevidian Empire."

"Do you really think I'm going to leave my Kingdom to that woman?! You can't be serious!"

"Will you shut up and *listen* to me?!" Rokoa demanded. "It's temporary. Raelia will wake in a day or two, and when that happens, Jamina will begin tracking her!"

"Tracking?"

"Nazario will explain on the ride. We don't have time. When she wakes, tell her she has to learn about Vysha's past. It's the only way to defeat her! Remind her of the conversation she listened to between Ekry and I. She needs to remember it. She needs to remember the name of the ritual. Do you understand?"

Alton nodded hesitantly.

"Protect her. She's the only one that can fix this," Rokoa's voice cracked and he mentally cursed himself for letting his emotions get the better of him. He cleared his throat before continuing. "Keep her safe."

Preparing the horses and carts for the journey was easy, especially when the stable boy saw Alton. At the Prince's direction, the boy followed every instruction to the letter, and Rokoa had no doubt he would keep their secret if asked.

When he and Alton began discussing the next steps, Nazario showed up with a groggy Ayla in tow.

"I know you said noon, but I couldn't handle waiting," they explained.

"No. This is good," Rokoa explained. "I could use your help."

"What do you need?"

The Drykuan grabbed them, leaving Alton and Ayla behind as they darted across the field toward the castle entrance. "All I need you to do," he explained to them as they hurried toward the corridor where Raelia slept, "is create an illusion for Ekry. Once I'm in, keep the illusion going as you make your way down the stairs. I'll meet you at the door."

Naz nodded his understanding, and when they reached the top of the stairs, closed their eyes.

"She's in," they said. "Hurry."

Even knowing she was in a false reality, it seemed strange to see Ekry's eyes unfocused as she stepped forward, reaching for something that Nazario showed her. Rokoa slipped easily past and shut the door behind himself.

Without a moment of hesitation, he walked to the window, placing his hand on it gently before closing his eyes in concentration. A second later, the glass vanished, and he turned to Raelia. He froze mid step when he saw the kyloxis perched on top of her sleeping form.

The beast's narrowed eyes gave no doubt to the danger it threatened if Rokoa came any closer to his precious bonded partner.

Rokoa held up his hands. "I'm not here to hurt her," he insisted, stepping closer slowly. "I'm taking her to her father. To her friends. They're going to take her away from here."

Zayric looked down at Raelia's face and then back at Rokoa before gently stepping off of her chest, as if giving permission for him to proceed.

Rokoa quickly scooped her into his arms, but before turning to the window, jerked his head to the beast. "Hop on. They're going to need any protection they can get."

As if understanding every word, the fox leapt onto Rokoa's shoulder. He laid around the back of his neck and dug his claws in to hold on.

The ground was further down than he'd expected, but the jump was easy for a being with unparalleled balance, strength, and speed. He held on to Raelia tightly, refusing to let any harm come to her as he dropped from the window.

Without a moment's hesitation, he made his way to the door where Nazario waited.

"Can you carry her?"

They nodded.

"Keep Ekry in her illusion. Take Raelia to the stables. Stay out of sight. Get everyone loaded up and be ready to go on my say. Don't release Ekry's mind until I tell you to. I have one more stop to make."

After he safely tucked Raelia in Naz's arms, Rokoa hurried around the side. Alton told him of the secret entrance into the dungeon's and checking to make sure he wasn't being watched, he ducked into the small wooden door.

Getting Eloi was simpler than it should have been, and only minutes later, Rokoa made his way back toward the stables with his arm around the other man's waist.

A shout echoed across the grounds, but Rokoa ignored it. He couldn't stop. Not until Eloi was safe with his daughter.

Another shout. His name this time.

Vysha's voice sent chills down his spine.

"STOP!" she screamed from behind them.

He continued running until finally the stables came into view once more.

That's when he heard it. The whistling of an arrow on the wind. He turned too slowly, and Eloi screamed in agony as the arrow buried itself into his back.

"We're almost there!" Rokoa shouted. "We have to get you to-"

Eloi stumbled, falling face first into the grassy earth. His breath ragged. When Rokoa turned him over and looked into the man's brown eyes, he knew he couldn't go on. "Leave me," Eloi gasped. "Save my daughter. Please..."

"GO!" Rokoa shouted. "GO NOW!" His face was contorted with emotion as his eyes connected with Nazario's through the open stable door.

"Go to them..." Eloi continued, his breath rattling in his chest. "Save her..." His eyes rolled back into his head, and his body went still as a tuft of his auburn red hair blew in the invisible breeze.

Rokoa didn't move as heavy footfall came his way. He focused his hearing, listening as the cart rolled out of the barn on the opposite side. He couldn't see them, but as he was grabbed by Vysha's Drykuan soldiers, he could hear the crunch of leaves as the cart rolled into the forest.

He didn't fight as they dragged him away from Eloi's body. His eyes closed. Even knowing that he was probably being taken to his execution, Rokoa couldn't help but sigh in relief as he pictured Raelia's face. His heart ached, wishing he could have stayed with her — missing her already, but even knowing he would likely not live to see her again, he couldn't bring himself to regret the decision to send her away.

Dirythian Dandelion Spotify Playlist

Music has been a hyper obsession my whole life. Every book, movie, and big life moment always has the perfect song to go with it.

The Dirythian Dandelion series is no different! If you scan the QR code below, it'll take you to music that inspired Mark of the Indicative.

Brixxi's Shrimp Curry Recipe

Ingredients

– 3/4 to 1lb medium shrimp thawed, peeled

– 1/2 tablespoon olive oil

– 1/2 medium onion, chopped

– 4 cloves garlic, minced

– 3 heaping tablespoons Thai red curry paste

– 1 cup chicken broth

 – 1/2 tablespoon fish sauce– 1 can coconut milk (13.5 ounces, full fat)

– 1/4 red bell pepper, chopped

– 1/4 yellow bell pepper, chopped

– 2 tablespoons fresh basil, chopped

– Scallions, chopped, to taste

– Optional

* Lime juice, to taste

* Sprigs of cilantro chopped, to taste

* Salt and pepper, to taste

Instructions

1. Brixxi likes to serve this over rice! If you want rice, start cooking it now

2. Add oil and onion to stewpot over medium-high heat. Sauté onion for 5 minutes.

3. Stir in garlic and curry paste. Cook for 30 seconds.

4. Add the chicken broth and fish sauce. Let it come to a boil and cook for a couple of minutes.

5. Reduce the heat and stir in coconut milk.

6. Add shrimp and bell peppers. Let simmer gently (don't let it reach boiling) for 5 minutes or until the shrimp are cooked through.

7. Add lime juice to taste (Brixxi likes to use 1/2 a lime) and salt & pepper as needed.

8. Add basil, scallions, and cilantro (optional) prior to serving. Serve over your favorite rice (Brixxi's choice is Jasmine rice)

Notes

- Shrimp can be cooked without tails, if preferred
- Add less chicken broth if you want a thicker broth

About the Author

Karlene is originally from Snohomish, Washington. They now live in Tucson, Arizona with their partner, three kids, three dogs and three ferrets. Oddly enough, they hate the number three. They are an AuDHD gremlin, a member of the LGBTQIA+ community and prefers they/them pronouns, but is okay with she/her as well. When they are not homeschooling their children or writing their books, Karlene enjoys singing karaoke, hiking, and traveling to any corner of the world they haven't explored before.

www.ingramcontent.com/pod-product-compliance
Lightning Source LLC
Chambersburg PA
CBHW010731310726

48971CB00010B/2801